PRAISE FOR
INTERSTELLAR MEGACHEF

'A stunning achievement, and an absolute
feast for your brain, your heart and your soul.
Devour it at once—it'll leave you sated
and hungry for more.'

Samit Basu,
author of *The City Inside*

'This book is a goddamn delight.
Absolutely bursting with flavor and
thrumming with possibility—
this is science fiction at its best.'

Tashan Mehta,
author of *Mad Sisters of Esi*

'If *The Great British Baking Show* and
The Hitchhiker's Guide to the Galaxy had a
child, it would be *Interstellar MegaChef*.'

S. B. Divya,
Nebula and Hugo nominated author of *Meru*

'A densely multilayered narrative confection
that's a funny, smart, and entertaining dive into
how much food habits can tell about people
and cultures across the world(s).'

Indrapramit Das,
author of *The Devourers*

T0282009

PRAISE FOR
LAVANYA LAKSHMINARAYAN

'Smart, vivid, engaging.'
The Guardian

'Impressive.'
SFX

'Exciting, imaginative, provocative.'
Locus Magazine

'Bold and creative.'
Starburst Magazine

'Stunning and thought-provoking.'
The British Fantasy Society

'Breathes new life into dystopia.'
The Washington Post

'Innovative.'
Strange Horizons

'A new masterpiece.'
SciFiNow

'Vivid and engaging.'
The Times of India

'Immersive and skilfully wrought.'
Stark Holborn

INTERSTELLAR MEGACHEF

Also by Lavanya Lakshminarayan

The Ten Percent Thief

INTERSTELLAR MEGACHEF

FLAVOUR HACKER BOOK ONE

LAVANYA LAKSHMINARAYAN

SOLARIS

First published 2024 by Solaris
an imprint of Rebellion Publishing Ltd,
Riverside House, Osney Mead,
Oxford, OX2 0ES, UK

www.solarisbooks.com

ISBN: 978-1-83786-233-7

Copyright © 2024 Lavanya Lakshminarayan

The right of the author to be identified as the author of
this work has been asserted in accordance with the
Copyright, Designs and Patents Act 1988.

All rights reserved. No part of this publication may be
reproduced, stored in a retrieval system, or transmitted, in any form
or by any means, electronic, mechanical, photocopying, recording
or otherwise, without the prior permission of the copyright owners.

This book is a work of fiction. Names, characters, places
and incidents are products of the author's imagination
or are used fictitiously.

10 9 8 7 6 5 4 3 2 1

A CIP catalogue record for this book is available
from the British Library.

Designed & typeset by Rebellion Publishing

Printed in Denmark

MIX
Paper | Supporting
responsible forestry
FSC® C104608

For Shiv, my compass on
this journey across the universe,
and for Scamper and Tugger,
who light the way.

A Brief History of the Nakshatrans

2301 CE 1 Anno Earth	Nationhood collapses on Earth, giving rise to a new, united human civilisation that calls itself One Nation Earth.
2325 CE 25 Anno Earth	The Nakshatran Programme is founded on Earth. Its intent: to reinvent human culture across the universe.
2350 CE 50 Anno Earth	The Nakshatran Charter is drafted and made public at the First Nakshatran Conference. It envisions a new era of peace and cooperation, as human beings dream of new futures amidst the stars.
2361 CE 61 Anno Earth	The first Nakshatran spaceflight is launched, seeking a new planet for humans to call home.
2375 CE 75 Anno Earth	*Nakshatran One* lands on Primus. It is Year One of the Interstellar Era.

...as we venture beyond the borders of the Solar system, we will do so with courage and good cheer in reckoning with the unknowable; with boundless optimism for what we will discover; with grace for the hardships we will endure; with curiosity and not conquest as our guide, dreaming of serenity and harmony across the universe; in honour of those pioneers, our ancestors, who first set out to explore the stars.

—Preamble to the *Nakshatran Charter*
2350 CE | 50 Anno Earth
(Pre-Interstellar Era)

Lucky bastards who get to escape the star-fucked Earth.

—Askari Menon, citizen of OneNation Earth,
upon viewing the first Nakshatran spaceflight
2361 CE | 61 Anno Earth
(Pre-Interstellar Era)

The stars stretched out, ripples
of time growing ever larger in the void.
The people of the Earth chose to look
beyond their fractal self-absorption, their
trite squabbles and imagined borders;
They turned their gaze upward to contemplate the
endless river.
We arrived
from that time, children of a new age of wonder,
the Nakshatrans.

—The *Nakshatranāma*,
translated from proto-Nakshatran
to Ur-speak by Honour Gabriel,
400 Anno Earth | 325 Interstellar Era

ONE

PRIMUS WORE ITS atmosphere like a sheen of condensation
dewing upon a spun-sugar confection. Its star Suriya
was a blazing disk, off to the east, and its moon Ibnis
was a crescent-shaped sliver hovering over a smudge of
marshmallow clouds, against a bruising pink sky.

The shuttle portscreen displayed a tumble of radiant
purple sheaf-grass, emerald green spindle-trees and turquoise
waters racing past in a blur of candied colour. The planet
rushed up to greet me, inviting me in from the cold, dark
silence of space into the warm embrace of its gravity.

I was a long way from home. And I was happy.

I was raised to dream big, to fulfil magnificent purpose.
I was going to do exactly that, even if they were going to
hate me for doing it my way. Ever since I was capable of
imagination, I'd nursed the near impossible and entirely
top secret, wholly-disapproved-of-if-they'd-ever-caught-

a-whiff-of-it ambition to escape the planet Earth and win *Interstellar MegaChef*.

I'd never had the courage—or the desperation—to leave until a few māsas ago. Until...

I pushed the ugly memory from my mind.

The shuttle docked and I slipped sideways, grabbing the harness that strapped me into my jumpseat. The muscles in my calves cramped and my neck throbbed gently as I felt the tension from this last leg of the journey slip away. It had taken an entire nava getting from space station Allegro to Primus, the last hop in three māsas of interstellar travel. I chose the long-haul route through freight jumpgates instead of flying first class on a warpship to throw them off my trail, and my Refugee Rehabilitation Vehicle was exactly as promised in those stacks of holoscrolls bleeding fine print they made me sign when I applied for amnesty: a no-bells-and-whistles, zero-creature-comforts escape route, shitty hot chocolate by the cup chargeable extra. It got me off my home world, though. Highly recommended for anyone with interstellar ambition on a tight budget, fleeing from their past!

The shuttle's flight systems began to disengage with a succession of beeps and alerts on my portscreen. The planet I'd longed for all my life lay beneath me. My heart pounded in great big dollops of anticipation with a dash of paranoia. They might yet be waiting for me at the Refugee Centre in Ursridge.

Oh, wait.

No-one I knew on Earth, or anywhere else in the universe, would expect me to be insane enough to emigrate on a refugee visa. Nobody would ever imagine I'd make a beeline for the heart of the United Human Cooperative, because they couldn't imagine doing it themselves.

I could.

If hundreds of Ur-dramas where immigrants wound up in Uru, Primus's megacity, flat broke but chasing their hearts' desires against all odds, surviving in shackpods and hex-housing until they built a community of friends, caught a big break and skyrocketed to stardom—all illegal lack of scrollwork forgiven—said it was possible, then I could do it, too.

The vacuum seals around the ports depressurised. The strap-in sign blinked off, and I got to my feet shakily to gather my belongings. I wanted to get a move on to avoid the inevitable crush of Immigration.

Don't get me wrong. I wasn't born yesterday. Ur-dramas are not reality and that's a well-documented fact if you've watched a newscast even once in your entire lifetime. And at thirty years of age, I'd done my fair share of news-gazing, like any vaguely law-abiding citizen of a Fringe planet devoted to war, the destruction of its own climate, and profiteering in the face of serving the greater good. A Fringe planet like the Earth, say.

So I was all set with my very legal scrollwork, for a start. And an unshakable belief in the capacity of the universe to be a beautiful place, and in my ability to make the most of every chance I got. Any work of art peddling pipe dreams has the power to change the galaxy, because if someone's imagined it, it can be done.

The tech-tamper switched off with a deep, echoing *woof-woof-woof*, and I was assaulted by a small, bright green sphere flecked with red and chrome. It whirred into me, pummelling from all sides and I began to laugh.

'Kili! Kili, stop! That tickles!'

Saras! Kanno! Anbe!

Switch language to Vox, please. Or Ur-speak. We're off-world, need to get used to it.

Kadavule!

Kili. Speak Vox. Or Ur-speak. Thank you.

I said this sternly, but the sound of Daxina, my South-Earth language, filled me with the warmth of familiarity. Despite my excitement that I was no longer on a planet doomed to self-destruction, I felt a twinge of guilt at having to distance myself from all sense of belonging so rapidly. Kili tended to nativise when excited, but planetary vernaculars were looked down upon on Primus. Or so I'd heard on my way here.

Kili emitted a string of whoops and dove into me, stilling his motorised wings in an instant and nuzzling against my cheek. It was like being kissed by warm sand on a beach. His comms channel slid snugly into an empty space in my mind, a place on my Loop I hadn't realised was super quiet until just this moment, when Kili's chip synced with my implant.

How long was I out? Where are me? I mean I. Where am I?

I rubbed the little machine along a curve.

We're on the planet of Primus. Shuttle docking station. Somewhere in the Arc, I think.

You're kidding me. We made it off Earth alive? We're not in heaven?

I thought we agreed that heaven was an Earth-myth. I sighed.

No time for theological debate! Kili whirred into the air and spun and shimmered. _News. Big news!_

Have you been scanning my comms? Again?

Yes, and sorry, and you'll forgive me. You'll see.

He holorayed an ornate scroll in the air. It unfurled and revealed a gold-embellished script against a backdrop of fireworks.

From:
Grace Aurelle,
Chief Chef,
Interstellar MegaChef Studios

To:
Saraswati Kaveri

You've Earned A Spot On *Interstellar MegaChef*!

Dear Saraswati Kaveri,
    Looking for your one shot to rise to the top of the pots
in the cutthroat, competitive, cultured world of interstellar
cuisine? Look no further. After carefully reviewing your
holoray application and your against-all-odds audition
holovid, we think you might have what it takes to be an
Interstellar MegaChef!

'Oh, my goodness! Kili, it worked! I told you it was worth
it!' I bounced up and down on the balls of my feet, all
thought of Immigration queues extinguished.

_Yes, it was totally worth risking your life to shoot that
audition holovid while rebel forces threatened to take over
the city and your kitchen crumbled all around you. In fact,
as a high value target—_

'Don't say that out loud!' I snapped, shushing him.

Relax.

We need to be careful, Kili.

Sorry.

'Accepted,' I said easily. 'Now let me read!'

Bring your best recipes and make us your signature dish!
Here's everything you need to know...

A *boom* knocked me backward onto my cot before I
could finish reading. The holoscroll winked out.

'Wait, no!' I yelled, right as Kili's wings locked up. He
froze in midair for a terrifying second before plummeting
to the floor. I stumbled off my cot, landing hard on my
knees, and rolled, my hand outstretched. He smacked into
my palm before bouncing off and rolling away under the
jumpseat.

'No, *no!*' I scrambled after him. He was my only friend

on this sur-fucked planet. I'd never seen him drop... not *dead*, he couldn't be dead.

A loud ping indicated an announcement on the shuttle's comm-system.

'*Welcome to Primus, seekers of asylum! A bright new life filled with hope and adventure lies ahead of you!*' said a cheerful AI voice.

'*But first, we've got to get through some procedures and protocols.*'

My portscreen view of the planet below was replaced by a human figure. They had long brown hair pinned up in a tight braid, a heart-shaped face, and wore a dazzling smile.

'*Following the recent violent events on several Fringe planets in the United Human Cooperative—planets from which some of you have migrated—the Secretariat of Primus has seen fit to upgrade our security measures.*'

The vacuum-sealed door to my pod popped open.

'Don't move!' A human shouted in Vox, clad in a blue and green bio-lock suit.

I raised my hands in the air. The human held some kind of scanning device, which beeped away in a frenzy.

'*Our A-Star Security service are probably knocking on your pod-doors right now, with a smile to welcome you to our glorious planet, and to carry out a block of brisk and effective checks for your own safety,*' the voice chimed.

'Where's your off-world tech?' the guard barked at me.

'Under the jumpseat.' I kept my voice calm and used perfect Ur-speak, despite my racing heart. I pointed for good measure, in case my accent was hard to follow. 'What's wrong with him?'

'Temporarily disabled. If it's well-designed, it wouldn't have hurt,' the guard responded.

'Oh, thank goodness.' I let go of the breath caught in my throat.

'Earthlings shouldn't sun-fuck our language,' a second figure muttered, wandering into the room and picking Kili up. They casually tossed him from one hand to the other, examining him. 'Seems harmless enough.'

'Miss, can I see your scrollwork?' the first guard said to me in Vox. 'All your tech will be impounded for a nava and scanned. Any mods? Auxes?'

'No,' I said. 'My scrollwork's on my Winger.'

'Your what?'

I pointed at Kili.

'Primitive,' the second guard smirked, dropping Kili into a myco-fabric bag.

Panic surged through me, but I kept my tone even. 'Please don't hurt him.'

'It's a dated piece of metal and circuitry,' the second guard said. 'It won't feel a thing.'

'Don't you have any other copies of your scrollwork?' the first guard asked, while the second muttered something under their breath.

'Oh, yes. Wait.' I fished around in my bag, hunting for a papyroscoll copy, while the guards exchanged a look. The second one sniggered as I handed over my physical identification.

'Sara—Sarasti?' The first guard struggled to read my name off the scroll. 'Pronouns?'

'Sah-rah-sua-thee,' I clarified, suddenly embarrassed by my multisyllabic nightmare of a name as I broke it down for them. 'She/Her.'

'Right. Sara-saute. I'm Harmony Jos,' the first guard said. 'They/Them. Follow me; it's decontamination, bio-scans and inoculation for you.'

I balked.

'Surely you're joking,' I began. 'Do you know wh—?'

'Yes?' Harmony Jos cut me off.

And then I stopped myself. It didn't matter who I was—

or had been—back on Earth. Here, I was a nobody on a refugee visa. I took a deep breath. 'Do you know where the bathroom is?' I asked meekly.

I followed them out the door and into the beginning of my life on Primus.

EVERY NIGHT FOR a nava, Primus's clear, smog-free skies revealed a swathe of universe spiralling into infinity beyond its atmosphere. Left alone to my thoughts, with nothing for entertainment but a well-thumbed papyroscroll copy of *A Beginner's Guide to Primus*, I had an endless glimpse into the unknown, in what felt like a tacky Ur-drama metaphor about the uncertainty of my future.

Sometimes it was like looking into the void. A bleak and impassively infinite expanse that would swallow me whole.

At other times, starlight glittered in its depths, calling to me, telling me to reach out and grasp it.

Most nights, I felt the universe pressed against the insides of my skull like the inside-out squeeze of transitioning through a jumpgate, blended with the hangover from one toddy punch too many—nauseating and all too real, forcing me to drag myself back indoors into the welcome comfort of sleep.

I wasn't homesick. The furthest thing from it, in fact. The gentle caress of the wind was a thrill I'd never experienced, coming from the arid Earth. The refugee camp was on the Ursridge cliffs, right at the edge of the supercontinent Prima—the biggest landmass on this planet—and from high up on its ledge, I watched soft white sand spill down to the clear turquoise waters of the Sagarra Sea, rolling in and arcing out in mesmerising rhythms. Unfortunately, the cliffs were patrolled by sting-drones, which dive-bombed me each time I stepped across the invisible line that seemed to mark the boundaries of my access to this world.

Once I'd read *A Beginner's Guide to Primus* twice over, I took to lolling about the camp's lilac meadows of sheaf-grass, waiting for Suriya to set and Ibnis to rise, its Lost Moon trailing it like chocolate chips through the night sky, stars swirling out of the darkness and looping my thoughts back to my many anxieties that weren't homesickness. The first of which was, when the sur-fuck were my *Interstellar MegaChef* dates?

They'd taken Kili before I could read that vital bit of information, and I had no access to my personal comms. I'd accosted every official-looking person I could see to try and wheedle five minutes of using the Loop off whatever peripheral they might have to offer. Turned out one nava—nine days, each of which, incidentally, lasts twenty-fucking-eight hours here—was a non-negotiable quarantine.

I tried to help out in the kitchen to stay in touch with my knife skills, but I was still being bio-scanned, and the chefs insisted I wouldn't know how to cook what they were serving. And they were right. A sodden mass of gloopy, berry-flavoured spheres and some kind of vat-grown fowl turned up on my plate on good days. On bad days, it was an indescribable terrine or a pâté, marbled in Primian fashion.

I was midway through scooping my lunch into my mouth—Primians ate with bare hands—and swallowing it unenthusiastically, when a drone whirred into the air above me. I fell over in surprise, dropping the remains of my lunch, then staggered up to my elbows in the little hollow I'd made in the sheaf-grass.

A message scrolled in the air in front of me.

Refugee #EA989170081 SARASWATI KAVERI:
QUARANTINED PERSONAL TECH APPROVED
Please head to the Ursridge Impound Bay to retrieve your artefacts.
Have a nice day!

I jumped up and raced across the sheaf-grass, which drew its purple fronds delicately away from my treading feet, shrinking into itself in a wave that rippled to the horizon. If the Primian officials cleared Kili, I'd have my MegaChef details with me. More importantly, I'd have my friend back.

Lungs screaming, I reached the impound bay, wholly expecting to confront a wild mass of people pressing against its flowmetal windows, forming a queue that was anything but, Earthling-style. I tucked in my elbows—primed for shoving people out of my way.

My shoulders relaxed when I realised the only person ahead of me was a deep orange E'nemon. Their elaborate tentacle array was drying out in the chill, but they still swirled a pair of fronds together in a wordless greeting. I brought my forearms together, twisting left arm over right, bringing my palms together in a human approximation of the gesture. The E'nemon's tentacles turned bright yellow, bobbing up and down.

I assumed they were laughing at me, and grinned apologetically in return. I hadn't been able to verbally communicate with many people—all my translation tech lived in Kili. More importantly for the E'nemon, their biosuits, which harvested moisture from the atmosphere, seemed to have been impounded, making it a struggle to breathe despite the saline hydration facilities at the Centre.

A human behind the flowmetal window handed the E'nemon a large package, which sprung apart when they touched it. They placed a tentacle upon their biosuit and it immediately wrapped around their person, a transparent sheath. Their tentacles pulsed yellow and pink with delight as they sashayed away. The human at the window beckoned me forwards, a name-tag scrolling across the glass—*Honour Al'ya, She/Her*.

'Name, please,' she said, sounding desperately bored.

'Saraswati Kaveri.' I smiled brightly, attempting to be friendly in the face of indifference.

'Planet of origin.'

'Earth.'

'Huh.' She looked up at me, leaned forwards, scanned my face. I took an involuntary step backward, then stood my ground.

'Well, it checks out with the Loop records.' She tapped her temple beside her right eye. Her pupils flickered back and forth, reading information only she had access to. 'Don't get many of you through here. Applications from *your* lot are almost never processed.'

My smile froze upon my face, and my cheeks began to ache.

'Still, you've been cleared. And there are no issues with your tech.' She handed me a small box. 'Harmony and serenity be upon you,' she concluded in Vox.

I returned the formal words of parting in perfect Ur-speak and relished her look of confusion. I slowed my movements to a crawl, and grasped the box, pulling it through the window and doing my best to appear non-threatening.

I walked away at a steady pace, counting my breaths, trying not to display any emotion. Not excitement at being able to see Kili again. Not simmering anger at... I couldn't quite place it, but it had something to do with how tightly I was holding myself, as if desperate to be invisible. I felt myself grow smaller. *Nothing to look at here, look away, look away.*

'You look like you've got something to hide.' An electronically simulated voice crackled to life beside me.

I spun on my heel and nearly dropped the box and its precious contents, only deflating when I saw the E'nemon from earlier, swaying my way. Their tentacles thrummed a sympathetic purple.

'Try being from a species that started an intergalactic war,' they chortled. Their vox-box rendered their laughter *shi-shiri-ri.*

I laughed. 'That's ancient history, though.'

'The universe's memory runs long, shi-shiri-ri.' Ripples of bright yellow light spread out through their fronds. The intricate woven texture of the E'nemon's biosuit glimmered amidst the sea of fronds, and I was pleased they had proper access to hydration again.

'Thanks for the reassurance.' I smiled. 'I'm glad you've got your suit back.'

'So am I! Of course, nothing compares to the waters of E'ne'enmo'oqe'— My eyes widened at the unfamiliar words. The E'nemon stopped abruptly at my confusion. 'Samudra, as our home worlds are called in Vox.'

'Ah! I'm sorry,' I stuttered.

'Not at all, En is a challenging language. The Vox translation of my name is Starlight Fantastic. It's lovely to make your acquaintance.'

'Saraswati Kaveri, it's lovely to meet you.' I repeated the gesture of twisting my forearms together, which was made somewhat more complicated by the box I was carrying.

'Shi-shiri-ri-shiri-ri, oh, thank you for making such an effort!' Starlight Fantastic cried, their tentacles spinning together in delight, a rainbow of colours radiating through them. The movement ebbed, the light dimming to a dull blue. 'You're from Earth? I couldn't help but overhear.'

'That's right.' My shoulders tensed automatically, waiting for some kind of judgment.

'I hope it wasn't too hard for you, escaping the troubles on your home world,' they said.

'I'm glad I escaped with my life,' I lied. It felt awful, but I couldn't take any chances. I grew up in a place where walls had ears.

'I'm sorry. I was in the Fringes—I'm a trader—and my ship was attacked by pirates, which is how I wound up here. I'm heading into Uru by star-rise, in case you'd like transport.'

It felt even worse to have lied after that offer, especially when I found my pulse racing at the thought of having a ride off Ursridge already. 'I—I might just take you up on that, thank you!'

'Meet me by the Transport Pods if you'd like to tag along. I've got flight clearance on this world.' Starlight Fantastic's tentacles bobbed up and down. 'And don't worry. These central planets are all the same when it comes to outsiders. And you humans are still a fairly young people. Harmony and serenity be upon you.'

I repeated the formal farewell and headed to a towering spindle-tree that bloomed neon blue flowers, its soft spiny leaves blanketing the ground around it. I'd come to think of it as my own in the span of the nava, which was a silly thought for a runaway with no claim to anything, really, whose entire life now fit into a box. I pressed my palm to a scanner on the box, and the flowmetal sprung apart. Kili whirred out in a burst of energy.

Saras! Kanno! Anbe!

I sighed.

Switch language to Vox, please. Or Ur-speak. We're off-world, need to get used to it.

Kadavule!

Kili. Speak Vox. Or Ur-speak. Thank you.

How long was I out? Whoa, there are real plants here!

Kili burbled, then took to the skies in glee. He darted and spun around, zooming around the spindle-trees and dive-bombing the sheaf-grass until it retracted in terror.

These plants respond to us. Look at me, Saras!

Kili, the MegaChef invite, please.

Whee!

Kili.

All right, already, he sulked, bobbing back towards me. _Here you go._

The same scroll unfurled, and my eyes raced over its contents until I got to the most important bit.

Bring your best recipes and make us your signature dish!
Date: 14 Axta, 9:30 a.m.
 Good luck, and may the best chef win!
 Heartily,
 Grace Aurelle

Note: Interstellar MegaChef Studios is committed to
promoting a competition filled with healthy intercultural
and inter-being representation, cultural diversity and
morphological positivity. We have a zero-tolerance
policy for slurs, violence and shaming. Any participants
demonstrating unacceptable behaviour, in the eyes of the
Studio, will be immediately removed from the competition.

I screamed. A bundle of metal thwacked me in the stomach.

Gosh, Saras. Are you okay? Are the plants attacking? I have an entire database on carnivorous planets, are we on one of those? No we're not, you said Primus—

Kili. The audition date. 14 Axta.

Yeah?

That's... um... tomorrow.

What?

A fist seized my heart, closing around it and choking the breath out of me. The sheaf-grass fluttered like the landscape of an underwater world, one bereft of oxygen, with the weight of the sky pressing down so hard it was going to shatter me.

'Starlight Fantastic!' I gasped.

What?

Starlight Fantastic! They're an E'nemon, they asked us to meet them at the Transport Pods if we needed a lift.

_We do._

We definitely do.

Let's go!

Kili raced ahead, bobbing on the low breeze and drifting from side to side along gentle currents. I followed close behind all the way to my homepod, cramming the remainder of my personal belongings into my travel case in a hurry.

Perhaps I permitted myself a moment of pause, reflecting upon the hours of thankless apprenticeships at snooty restaurants back on Earth, the life I'd escaped, the twenty-one kinds of nausea I'd experienced at the jumpgates, and the hope that I was finally free to chase down my dreams.

I flung my arms out wide. _It's destiny._

Kili spun midair and bobbled before me, laughing. _It's egomania._

Neither of us was wrong, but neither of us was entirely right.

Tread lightly.

–Principle 1, The Nakshatran Charter
50 Anno Earth | Pre-Interstellar Era

TWO

ANY BEING ON Primus who wasn't a scientist or an isle-dweller lived on the supercontinent Prima. Near the centre of the giant landmass—on the Exian plateau—sprawled the megacity Uru, the widely-accepted cultural capital of the United Human Cooperative, and home to more than half the Primian population. It was ringed by the Urswood, the rivers Serenity and Unity wending their way through its heart. Sweeping away from its borders and into the wilderness beyond was the Arc, a vast, untouched haven, intentionally left to its own devices, thriving with the planet's natural ecosystems all the way to the Eastern Outpost and the Western Shore on either side. The only humans who made their way across this land were the Wanderers, who were tasked with ensuring that it remain unspoiled.

Sur, Sand and Shore was a caravan that plied its trade in the Arc, a large sphere of flowmetal that opened outward like a kamalam, blossoming in a twinkling of lights that glittered off bottles filled with every bottom-shelf alcohol and potent elixir known to Primian-kind. It was most popular along a strip of beach called the Ur-Sands, where it was looked down upon by the Uru elite but all the rage with the Arcsiders for its Ibnis-viewing parties. And yet, despite being half a nava away from the next big rave, the traveling pub had never been as packed as it was today. Word had spread down the Wanderers' Path that an Ur-sider had seemingly cracked and was buying everyone drinks.

28

Serenity Ko felt alive. She shimmied and popped up on the drink-smeared bar with a dance partner whose name she'd already forgotten. Smooth-synth flowed through the bar's speakers, a mellosax rising over a glissando of keys, a shimmering rhythm section underscoring it all. Tomorrow she'd be back at work and all over the Loop, but today was all hers.

As the song ended with a sparkling flourish of keys, her partner helped her hop off the bar to wild cheering and applause from everyone—human and alt-being alike. Everyone except the person she'd arrived with, that is. He was sulking somewhere in the shadows. Serenity Ko was content to avoid him.

The bartender—a cute caravaner with a lip piercing, whose holo-tag on the Loop read *Harmony Viana, They/Them*— handed her a shot of something clear and frothy. 'House special!' they yelled over the din, 'We call it the Sandstrike.'

Serenity Ko leaned in with her best approximation of a seductive smile. 'Why don't you pour yourself one, too?'

'If you're around when this party wraps up,' Harmony Viana said with a grin.

Serenity Ko knocked back her shot. It was smoky with a sharp burn, and she smacked her lips. 'Oh, this party won't stop until I leave.'

'How about we get back to Uru before star-rise?' Someone grabbed her elbow.

Serenity Ko spun, and was momentarily dizzy. Her smile slid off her face when confronted with Honour Aki, a frown notched deep into his forehead. He put his arm around her to steady her, and she shrugged him off.

'Why don't *you* leave?' she said rudely. 'I'll make it back on my own. This is *my* party, and it's just begun.'

'Ko. We've been here six hours. Day-drinking. We've got work tomorrow.'

'Aki. I'll handle it,' she snapped. 'I don't need a babysitter.'

'*You* invited *me*, remember?' Honour Aki said, crossing his arms over his chest. His biceps rippled attractively, but then Serenity Ko caught a glimpse of his expression—worried, somewhat annoyed—and the flutterwings in her stomach vanished with a poof. She scowled.

'Yes. *I* invited *you* to celebrate *me* and *my success*,' Serenity Ko said, drawing the sentence out, insultingly slow. 'Instead, here you are, bossing me around and trying to kill *my* party.'

She waved at Harmony Viana behind the bar, and they promptly laid down another shot—this one was electric purple with an incandescent orange layer on top. She had no idea what was in it, but she downed it anyway.

Honour Aki threw a hand up in exasperation. '*This* is why I can't leave you alone. You're going to do something reckless. And… and I care about you. In the time we've been together—'

Serenity Ko sputtered and nearly spat out her drink. 'Don't be ridiculous, Aki. We've barely been together two māsas. And—' She raised her voice for the benefit of Harmony Viana, who was eyeing them closely from behind the bar. 'And we've been *non-exclusive the whole time*.'

Honour Aki's lips turned down in a sulk. With his square jaw, and his auburn hair flopping over his left eye, he was annoyingly kissable. '*You've* been non-exclusive, you mean. *I've* been true to you.'

And there they disappeared again, those damned flutterwings. Serenity Ko rolled her eyes. 'That's on you.'

'I… I was hoping you'd come around and love me. The way I love you,' Honour Aki said hopelessly.

'Wait, what? Did you just use the L-word?' Serenity Ko felt on the verge of throwing up. It could have been from the alcohol. It was definitely from Honour Aki's announcement.

'Yes. So?' Honour Aki reached out and held her by the elbows. He gazed deep into her eyes. 'Ko, I—'

Serenity Ko stepped back, eyes wide in horror. 'Aki, what part of "I'm not looking for a relationship and I don't want a relationship" have you not understood in the last two māsas?' she yelled, right into a pocket of booming silence as the music died abruptly.

'Sorry, sorry,' Harmony Viana called from behind the bar. 'Power surge, let me just restart our drive…'

Serenity Ko registered a sea of faces, all staring at her. She glanced at Honour Aki, who was on the verge of tears. 'Well. Star-fuck me. This is awkward.'

'I don't care. I need you, Ko. *I love you, Ko.* I promise I'll take care of you.'

Serenity Ko was horribly aware of their audience, watching with bated breath, clinging to every word like they were a live re-enactment of a sordid Ur-drama, wondering what she was going to say next. 'More shots on me?' she said, laughing too loud. The drive whirred back into life and smooth-synth filled the afternoon air. Whoops and cheers went up, and they were no longer the most interesting thing on offer.

'*That's* your reaction to my declaration of undying love? *That's it?*' Honour Aki rounded on her.

'Aki, I don't think this is working for me,' Serenity Ko said coldly.

'What?'

'It's over.' She turned her back on him. 'Go find someone else who can give you a happy ending. It isn't me you're looking for.'

'Can't we… can't we discuss this? I'll back off, give you space—'

'Nope.' Serenity Ko shrugged. 'It was fun while it lasted. I'll Loop you the cash for your ride out.'

The seconds slid past and Serenity Ko's entire being tensed. She sensed his presence leave her side and counted all the way to ten before turning around. He was gone. Her shoulders sagged and she leaned against the bar.

'Are you this shitty to everyone?' Harmony Viana asked.

'Only the needy ones,' Serenity Ko smirked.

'On the house,' Harmony Viana said, putting another shot down.

Serenity Ko downed it without thinking twice. 'Talk about ruining my celebration.'

'What're you celebrating, anyway? Anything I can help with?' Harmony Viana winked.

'Well,' Serenity Ko said, leaning forwards. 'I'm—'

'Harmony Viana, as I live and breathe!' A tall human brushed past Serenity Ko and the caravaner squealed, hopping halfway over the bar. They pulled the stranger into a tight squeeze. *Courage Anto, He/Him* flashed across Serenity Ko's HUD.

'What're you even doing here?' Harmony Viana's cheeks flushed.

'Checking in on my favourite caravaner! The Loop told me you were in the area, but I was on the Path back in the Urswood, and I was convinced I'd miss the ferry to the Sands. It is *so* good to see you!'

Serenity Ko scowled at the interloper's back. The man dropped onto the barstool beside her. He was dark-skinned, clothed in dull green but for the beads woven through his high top-knot. Gemstones coruscated on all his fingers. A Wanderer Savant. She'd heard of their existence, but she'd never seen one in real life. Her fascination was peppered with annoyance. He was an attractive, if unwelcome, interruption.

She ordered another drink, and Harmony Viana served it up while barely registering her existence. Serenity Ko sipped on a neon blue nīlatini, complete with moss-berries on a stick, while the caravaner and the Wanderer caught up in a rush of conversation.

She glanced around Sur, Sand and Shore and saw a happy couple kissing, a group of friends playing a wild game of bira-pong, a pair of strangers who'd clearly just met and were *very* into each other; and she felt unutterably, miserably alone. She slid into the Loop and escaped into its comforting Immersive Reality, the HUD blurring the world around her. She didn't need the company of these nobodies, even though—and she cringed as the thought struck her—even though she'd tried to buy it and evidently failed.

Serenity Ko slipped into XPerience Inc.'s most exclusive offering, the one she'd designed from inception to launch, the one that was going to make her famous and get her promoted to Evocateur Extraordinaire. SoundSpace bubbled over her visual in pop-art letters, an effervescence of ossiowave rising to flood her eardrums. She scanned her options.

Playlist | Favourites | Library
SURPRISE ME!

She blinked twice to choose, and waited for her surprise to kick in. In under a second, XP Inc.'s bio-circuits scanned her heart-rate, hormones and breathing, triangulated her location in the entire known universe, and delivered a smash hit upper of a song to raise her flagging spirits. 'Deep Pink Day' by SurGazer flooded straight into her brain, high-fidelity ossiowave drowning out the din of the Caravan. She swiped her right thumb over the tips of her fingers to raise the volume. Right as the song began, her surroundings blurred, fading into the background as visions flooded her mind, a blend of personal memory and XP Inc.'s carefully curated databases.

Suriya rises over the Sagarra Sea with the shimmering ride of a drum intro. A wave crashes into her and she squeals with delight. Her mother holds her hand as chimes begin to sparkle.

There are so many shells on the beach, and they bob towards each other on the waves, stringing together in time to a cyclical melody played on keys. The pink swirly one at the centre begins to spiral, radiating flecks of copper and rose until it rises to fill the entire sky. Behold, it is a new Suriya, and a rising glockenspiel-synth syncopates in time to its streaming rays.

She flies towards it, the ground falling away beneath her feet in a crescendo of crashing waves and sonorous synth-harp...

A slow trickle of endorphins dripped into Serenity Ko's system, and she smiled as the SoundSpace sim ended.

I built this.

Sure, a team of one hundred and fifty helped prototype, write the code, put the experience databases together and test it, but it was *all her vision*, and nobody was going to take the achievement away from her. Not today, not ever.

She slipped out of the Loop with renewed vigour— the afternoon was still young—and caught a glimmer of gemstones on a hand waving in front of her face. '—lost to the world, aren't they?'

She pushed it away. '*Excuse me,* I'm right here.'

The Wanderer Savant seated beside her laughed. 'Well, you weren't for an entire three minutes. Typical Ur-sider.'

'How can you tell?' Serenity Ko shot back.

'It's in your clothes, your hair, your accent, the fact that you're paying for everyone's drinks tonight. And it's a dead giveaway when you lose yourself in pointless simulations.'

'I *built* the fucking simulation I was lost in,' Serenity Ko said coolly, taking a sip of her nīlatini.

'We're in the presence of royalty, then.' The Wanderer Savant hopped off his stool and made an exaggerated bow. 'Courage Anto. And you are? Other than being a cog in the wheel at XPerience Inc., that is?'

'Serenity Ko,' she eyed him warily, then felt a surge of anger. Who was this rural bumpkin to pronounce judgment upon her, anyway? It took *years* to get Immersive Reality right, to nausea-proof it, disorient-detect danger...

'One of few words, rooted far outside reality,' the man teased with a lopsided smile.

'Listen. I'm just minding my own business and having a good time,' Serenity Ko snapped. 'And I'll have you know that I just designed the raddest, most badass, most sur-fucking incredible Immersive Reality experience ever created.'

'Holy sur-fucking wow,' Harmony Viana chimed in from behind the bar. 'We don't like your type out here.'

'So I've heard,' Serenity Ko said casually.

'No, most folks here *really* don't like you,' the Wanderer Savant—Courage Anto—lowered his voice, all trace of humour gone from his expression. 'It's not personal. It's just...' He waved his glittering hand vaguely.

Serenity Ko drummed her fingers on the bar. 'Huh?' This was all getting very confusing for her. All she wanted was another drink and someone to shag for the evening— preferably someone who wouldn't want to cuddle and exchange Loop-comms afterward—and she was in the company of two very attractive strangers who were both talking at her in riddles. Everything about this day was going horribly wrong.

'Do you ever holoscroll the news, Serenity Ko?' Courage Anto murmured.

Her mind was a spinning maze from the thought of her upcoming promotion and a heady brew of alcohol. The scowl that creased the Wanderer's deep brown skin was killing her vibe, and as a dizzying mellosax solo curled out from the speakers, she felt a headache coming on. 'I really don't care,' she said callously. 'It's boring.'

The Wanderer Savant flinched as if she'd slapped him. 'Your "boring" is our reality. There have been protests across the Arc,' he said coldly. 'Nearly two thousand years of human settlement on Primus, sixteen hundred years since first contact with intelligent alt-beings in the galaxy, and the Nakshatran principles that have kept us thriving—treading lightly, being one with the wider world—are slipping from our grasp. Nobody cares to go Wandering anymore; it isn't comfortable enough, it doesn't *pay* enough to generate off-world travels, or fancy experiences... And it's because of Ur-siders like you, who create realities that are bigger than our own, dreams to disappear into instead of caring for the world we inhabit. The *real world*. Our numbers keep dwindling because fantasies are more appealing than reality.'

'Employment is a *choice* on Primus. Nobody conscripts you to the Arc.' Serenity Ko rubbed her temples as her headache intensified. Why the sur-fuck was she debating philosophy with this beaded weirdo? 'And nobody can force anyone to head out into the wilderness if they don't want to. You want humanity to be stuck in the present; people like me want to help humans realise their dreams.'

'I like you less with each passing moment.' Harmony Viana rolled their eyes.

Something snapped deep within Serenity Ko. 'I don't need *you* to like me. But the rest of them?' She jabbed her thumb at the crowd behind her. 'They're going to *love* me.'

Every Primian citizen was awarded a given-name upon their coming of age at seventeen. It was carefully chosen by their personal mentor and their families, from one of the nine virtues encompassing the spirit of space exploration in the Nakshatran Charter. It was a parting wish, a dream for the future.

In the eleven years since Komala Siriharan had dropped her birth name in favour of Serenity Ko, she had seldom embodied serenity. True to form, she grabbed a fork and a glass from the bar, hopped up on her barstool, and struck her glass repeatedly until the conversation died down to a murmur.

'What're you doing?' Harmony Viana hissed.

Serenity Ko ignored them. She swayed up on her perch and peered around the Caravan. Fairy lights adorned its curved roof. A light sea breeze blew in from her left, and beyond the open flowmetal frame, white sand led all the way down to the crashing waves and a resplendent heliotrope sky at the horizon. Tables were scattered with bottles and glasses in varying states of half-emptiness. A sea of faces—mostly human, some not—looked at her expectantly.

Serenity Ko faltered momentarily, her spiralling mind wondering if this was sensible. Then she caught sight of Honour Aki at full attention, straight-backed and staring at her in stark contrast to what the fluffy floor cushions around him were begging of him, a pipe in his hands sending MellO vapours into the air unnoticed.

He mouthed something at her. Serenity Ko imagined it was some kind of warning. *Don't do it*.

She did it. She beamed at her audience. 'My friends in Ur-Sands,' she began. 'Arcsiders of Primus, children of the Nakshatrans. I'm Serenity Ko, and I'm an Evocateur Elite at XP Inc.'

A loud, deep voice began to boo her, and a chorus picked up around it.

'No need for all that. I'm your benefactor for the evening, drinks on me, you're welcome!' she said cheerily and loudly over the hissing and catcalls. 'I'm giving away free subscriptions—for an entire year—to our latest offering, SoundSpace: the most immersive musical journey in the universe!'

She threw her hands out and paused, her temples throbbing, her knees wobbly, and waited for the inevitable applause.

The first thing Serenity Ko attempted to dodge was a wedge of everberry pâté. Her timing failed her, and it caught her in the neck. She slid off her barstool, and it came crashing down beneath her, along with the remains of her drink, as she tried to grab the bar to steady herself. A weather-worn boot caught her in the shin. A pomme-fruit pastry spattered across the front of her clothes. A saucer missed her nose by inches and struck the bar behind her.

'Told you we didn't like your lot,' Harmony Viana said smugly from somewhere above her.

'Vi, we need to get her out. This is bad for all of us.' Courage Anto grabbed Serenity Ko under her armpits and hauled her up, his Savant's rings digging into her flesh.

There was a tinkling sound like a million shiny metal tokens cascading out of a slot machine in one of Joy Street's gaming dens. Glasses shattered, a spray of shards filling the air like crystal confetti. The Wanderer Savant dragged Serenity Ko behind the bar and pushed her head down, ducking with her. 'That was most unwise.'

'What the sur-fuck?' she swore. 'I just offered them a ton of free stuff. At my personal expense!'

'I warned you,' Courage Anto said firmly. 'Do you know how meaningless your nanopills are when you've got the stars for a roof and sheaf-grass for a bed?'

'What's that got to do with anything?' Serenity Ko was dizzy. She was going to throw up.

'Your subscriptions, your nanopill upgrades, your entire head-in-the-clouds simulation show—it doesn't matter to anyone here, Serenity Ko. It's so low down on their list of priorities it might as well not exist. Stop asking stupid questions now, and let's get you to safety.'

Serenity Ko retched and heaved, clutching her stomach.

'Throw up later, run now.' Courage Anto grabbed her arm and dragged her out into the crowd.

'Honour Aki!' she shouted. 'Aki!'

She dug her nails into the Wanderer Savant's arm. 'My friend. We need to find him.'

'I'll get you out first and come back for him.'

They ducked and weaved through insanity. People were yanking beads and baubles out of each other's hair. Luminoweave tunics were ripped apart, shreds of fabric hanging limply on their frames, their prismatic effect fading into bleak grey as the loom's connections desperately searched for a way to close their circuits. Mods and stimulo-suit shreds trailed across the ground in heaps of ports and wires.

'Call your crazies off!' Serenity Ko screamed at him. 'I didn't mean to do this. I was only trying to have a good time!'

Courage Anto gritted his teeth as he shoved his way past a large human trying to overturn a table. Serenity Ko felt naked and defenceless in the midst of the mob. She put her hands in her pockets, hopelessly raking around for a weapon. All she had were the starshot XP nanopills.

She had XP nanopills.

'I've got nanopills,' she yelled. 'Free nanopills!'

The crowd stilled. She withdrew her hands from her pockets, her fists clenched around dozens of little cartridges. She held them up for all to see.

'*Free!*' she announced again. She flung them in a long arc, watching as they curved through the air, spilling down upon the crowd and sprinkling the ground in a starburst of insanely expensive tech rain. The crowd surged towards her, completely ignoring her offering.

'What in all the Nine Virtues did you do that for?' Courage Anto dragged her towards the open beach outside. 'Run. Call a flowcab. *Now.*'

Serenity Ko ran. She ran until she was right at the edge of the surf, then fell to her knees and heaved, gasping for breath and fighting nausea. She managed to slip into the Loop and send out an SOS. She then doubled over and threw up all over the pristine white sand. 'Oh, no. No, no. What the fuck is wrong with these savages?' she moaned.

'Nine Virtues, thank the sur-fucking cosmos you're okay,' a deep voice said over her. She squinted up through what was now a blistering headache.

'Aki. Why the fuck didn't you leave, you clingy sad sack?'

'Nice to see you too, Ko,' Honour Aki said wryly. 'Some people don't abandon their friends.'

Honour Aki held a bottle of water to her lips and she sipped on it, her throat parched. A low rumble filled the air and a sleek flowmetal hull the colour of the sky descended gently to the sand, its molecular doorways shimmering.

'Let's get out of here,' Serenity Ko slurred, stumbling to her feet.

Honour Aki caught her as she fell. 'Told you I'd take care of you,' he muttered.

Serenity Ko threw up again and closed her eyes. Honour Aki picked her up in his arms, trying to avoid the spatter of sick on her shirt, and carried her onto the flowship, a thoroughly unwanted knight in alcohol-stained armour.

'Uru, please,' he said to the E'nemon at the controls.

What do you call intelligent life on Earth?

A Primian tourist.

[audience laughs out loud]

What do you call an Earthling tourist on Primus?

You don't. You run for the hills.

[audience continues to laugh]

You... you, sir! Hey you, with the mods. [addressing
    audience member]

Are you an Earthling?

[audience member replies, indicating their mods: "No.
    I'm Primian, a chlorosapient."]

Nine Virtues, that's even worse!

[audience laughs weakly, the chlorosapient looks
    uncomfortable for a moment, then joins in]

No, I'm kidding. Of course I'm kidding! Chlorosapients
    are wonderful plants... I mean people. We really value
    them, don't we? Let's cheer for the chlorosapients!

[audience cheers]

Just taking a moment to be serious, folks. Xenophobia
    is a hate crime. Let's all remember that. Xenophobia
    is a hate crime. [pauses]

And we all know that crime belongs to the Earthlings...

[audience laughs hysterically, cheers and wolf whistles
    echo through the room]

—Curiosity Shai, on the Titters and Giggles Tour
2073 Anno Earth | 1998 Interstellar Era

THREE

I RUSHED TO the unconscious human's side, Kili whirring
and burbling beside me. I checked for a pulse and helped
their companion ease them into a seat, where they promptly

flopped over sideways.

'I'm Starlight Fantastic and this is Saraswati Kaveri. We picked up your distress broadcast,' Starlight Fantastic said, accompanying their introduction with many subtle twists and gestures of their tentacles, ribboned with blue for concern. 'Are you okay?'

'Get the fuck off me,' the human slurred, shoving me hard in the chest as I leaned over them.

'Rude,' I said.

'I'm sorry for Ko's behaviour,' their companion said, brushing a long strand of hair out of their eyes. 'She's had a little too much to drink. I'm Honour Aki, He/Him.'

'Nice to meet you,' I held my palms together in traditional Earth-greeting. 'Saraswati Kaveri. She/Her.'

He frowned and extended his hand. 'Not from here, are you?'

Fuck. I'd completely forgotten that handshakes were a post-plague trust gesture between human planets. I reached for his hand, my palm clammy. Score zero for diplomacy.

'Not to break up this grand United Human Cooperative-style peace talk,' Starlight Fantastic said, 'but could you strap in, please?'

The woman named Ko leaned back in her seat, fumbling with her harness. Her cheek pressed against the window as she stared groggily outside. '*Savages,*' she murmured.

I followed her gaze. On the beach beyond, some kind of large metal shack was being rapidly dismantled by a mob gone wild. A couple of humans caught sight of our ship and pointed at it. They tore away from the pack and raced across the sands towards us.

'I'm going vertical in a hurry. Please make it quick,' Starlight Fantastic insisted calmly, though their tentacles twitched, an uncertain shade of grey.

'Hang on.' The woman named Ko fumbled with her straps.

'Here, I'll help.' I quickly pulled the harness across her

chest and arms, and buckled it tight at the waist. 'I'm sorry you got in trouble, Ko. I'm Saras—'

'That's *Serenity* Ko,' she said, glaring at me icily through red-rimmed eyes.

'Right, sorry.' I wilted under her gaze.

Rude, Kili streamed sourly.

Very, I agreed.

Her companion appeared to want to put as much distance between them as possible, strapping in across the aisle and leaving me to take the seat beside her. I buckled in. 'All good, Starlight Fantastic.'

The engines swivelled downward and a deafening roar filled my ears as the vertical thrusters kicked in. We climbed away in a hurry, sand swirling around our craft, waves rippling in our wake.

'Good riddance,' Serenity Ko said.

'*You* started this,' Honour Aki snapped. 'Honestly, Ko, I'm amazed even *you* would do something this stupid.'

I tried not to pay attention to their conversation, distracting myself with the view as our craft zoomed over the Sagarra Sea, but we were in a rather cramped flight-pod and the passengers we'd picked up weren't exactly keeping their voices down, seated facing each other across the narrow central aisle.

'They talk a big game about Nakshatran values,' Serenity Ko sulked, 'and then they start a riot.'

'They over-reacted,' Honour Aki agreed. 'But—'

'But *what*? The use of violence was justified, all because I tried to give them free stuff?'

'I don't think free stuff was the problem,' Honour Aki said quietly.

'Go on, then.'

'You came across a little...'

'Yes?' Serenity Ko hissed dangerously.

'Overbearing.'

'Overbearing,' Serenity Ko repeated.

'Overbearing,' Honour Aki confirmed.

'Overbearing. Like throwing the *L-word* at someone out of the blue, when they have no interest in a relationship whatsoever? That kind of overbearing?'

Kili was nested on my lap, doing his best not to burble with laughter.

You want to ask, he pinged me.

It's killing me not to, I admitted.

Then ask.

None of my business. Or yours.

The former couple seemed to want to make it our business, though.

'We'd have avoided *all* of this if you hadn't broken up with me,' Honour Aki whined.

'What part of "We were never in a relationship" did you miss?' Serenity Ko thumped her head back against her neck rest.

At this point, I dropped all pretence of not caring. This was Ur-drama stuff. Their terse exchange smacked of unresolved issues meeting reckless behaviour resulting in bad consequences. I glanced at Starlight Fantastic and caught their gaze reflected in the ship's glossy displays. I raised my eyebrows and their tentacle tips flashed pink and curled up—they were uncomfortable witnessing this display of dirty laundry.

We were spared further embarrassment when Honour Aki looked away, eyes glazing over as he entered some kind of IR sim. Serenity Ko, meanwhile, exhaled loudly, slumped down in her chair and closed her eyes. A silence as frosty as the inside of a meat freezer sparkled in the air.

I took the opportunity to casually study the woman. She was tall and curvy with smooth, deep brown skin. Her dark hair fell in a long, elaborate braid which began high on the crown of her head, decorated by luminous stones. Her moon-shaped face was considerably pretty, but for the sheen of alcoholic sweat beading upon the bridge of her long, angular nose. I could place a mixture of aris-seed vodka and tinglebrew wafting off her; unmistakable, because they were rare top-shelf liquor back on Earth, though clearly not here on their home world.

Are you checking her out? Kili popped into my comms. _She seems like bad news._

Merely observing. I dropped my gaze and blushed.

Liar.

Twenty-one jumpgates. It's been a while, I said, annoyed.

The man shifted in the seat across from me, his slack face returning to some form of attention. 'Ko, I'm sorry,' Honour Aki said. 'I shouldn't have pushed you about our relationship. That was selfish of me. Just take me back and I'll give you all the spa—'

Serenity Ko's eyes snapped open. 'A different galaxy wouldn't be enough space from you.'

It appeared the Ur-drama had resumed.

Definitely bad news, Kili said again, as if I couldn't put this together myself.

I'm not doing anything, am I?

But you're about to.

He was right.

'You're bleeding.' I pointed at Serenity Ko's lemon-yellow sleeve, smeared with crimson.

She looked down, somewhat relaxing. 'Oh. So I am.'

'Starlight Fantastic, where's your first-aid kit?'

'Back of the ship, last shelf.'

I unstrapped myself and wobbled the short distance to the end of the ship. On Earth, we were still used to ground transportation, so I was still finding my sky-legs. I tapped on the green quinta-helix, the standard symbol for first aid all over the universe. A drawer popped out and I grabbed some fix-it tape.

The ship swerved.

'Crazy tourists!' Starlight Fantastic swore.

I tipped sideways.

'Oof!' Serenity Ko grunted as I landed in her lap, my elbow catching her smack in the stomach.

I looked up into deep brown eyes flecked with gold, staring at me in disbelief and derision. 'I'm so sorry!' I sputtered. 'Tape?' I held up the roll in my hands like a peace offering.

'Um, please get the fuck off me first?'

'All okay back there?' Starlight Fantastic asked. 'Sorry about that; tourists on a bubble-bike swerving all over the place. No sense of sky-lanes...'

'All good,' I said, scrabbling back from Serenity Ko and getting to my feet. I handed her the fix-it tape. She peeled a couple of strips off and stuck them on a large gash in her forearm. The smell of burnt clove and cinnamon filled the air as the antiseptic worked its way into the wound. She was grinding her teeth so hard I could hear them from half a metre away.

'What happened back there, anyway?' I asked, trying to distract her.

'Riot.' Serenity Ko said with disdain. 'Arcsiders being hostile, because *apparently* I'm a city snob and they can't stand the likes of me.'

Honour Aki cleared his throat and began to say something, but Serenity Ko stared him down and he mumbled inaudibly before shutting up.

I tried to pat her on the arm, and it came out awkward. 'There, there. I'm sorry. It must have been a shock.'

'Your accent is funny,' she said bluntly. 'What part of the great and glorious star-fucked universe are you from?'

'Earth.'

'Delightful,' Serenity Ko muttered, lying back on the cushions. She appeared to take comfort from the way they moulded around her. 'An *Earthling*, just when I thought this day couldn't get any better.'

A whirring ball of green and red streaked out at her. Serenity Ko shrieked. 'What the—?'

'Kili, *behave*,' I hissed, not wanting to start an international incident on my first day of refugee clearance. 'I'm sure she didn't mean to be obnoxious. After all, xenophobia is very anti-Nakshatran, as I'm sure Serenity Ko is aware.'

Across the aisle from me, Honour Aki snorted, then developed a sudden, hacking cough.

'Yes, harmony and serenity be upon you, et cetera.' Serenity Ko rolled her eyes. 'Sorry, never met your kind, only heard the worst of you, I'm sure you're none of those stereotypes, welcome to Primus, we hope you enjoy your stay here, don't forget to catch the sights in Uru.'

Kili's rotors spun double-time and he chirruped angrily. She frowned at him. 'What *is* this thing?'

'My Winger. A Sentient Intelligence from Earth. His name's Kili.'

'Now *this* is fascinating,' Serenity Ko said, leaning forwards to peer at him. Kili whirred out of her reach. 'He's touchy, isn't he? Backward, and ancient as sun-fucking Earth, but fascinating.' She turned to regard me. 'If you're planning to be here for a while, you'll want Loop access as soon as possible, though.'

'I have Loop access,' I said irritably, and jabbed my thumb at Kili. 'Him.'

'Doesn't the lag drive you nuts?' Serenity Ko asked. 'I don't know about Earth, but here we've got these nanopills...'

'Got them on Earth, too, thanks,' I said. 'But all that intel buzzing around in my head? I'd rather not. I like to have a very distinct sense of self, thank you.'

'Do you *never* want to experience Immersive Reality?' Serenity Ko asked, jaw dropping. 'You're kidding. Here, look. Is your wingy-thingy equipped with a mindstream channel? I can try and send you a lo-fi version of this IR experience I just designed. I'm an Evocateur Elite at XP Inc.—'

'Ko, stop trying to sell her a subscription,' Honour Aki said.

'Nobody asked you,' Serenity Ko snapped.

Both of them stared at me expectantly, and I felt trapped like a rat in a very narrow maze. 'Er...' I hesitated. The silence continued. 'I don't want to put you to any trouble, so it's all right—um—no, thank you.'

She leaned forwards, gazing into my eyes as if I were a newly discovered species. '*Fascinating*,' she said again, much to my annoyance. 'How quaint and Earth-primitive.'

My ears turned hot and I looked away. She appeared to lose all interest in me, and slouched down into her seat. Honour Aki's fingers twitched in a sequence and I watched him recede from reality and into another simulated daydream.

I craned my neck to peer through the viewport.

'Let me make this easier,' Starlight Fantastic said, tentacle tips glowing yellow and orange in delight. They tapped one of their displays, and the flowmetal ship glimmered around them for a moment, before its walls, floor and ceiling turned clear as glass. 'Don't worry, it's one-way,' they said.

My breath rushed out of me in a *whoosh*. Rising starlight danced its way into the violet sky. After an entire nava spent stargazing at the refugee camp, I'd thought I'd be over the planetside view. I wasn't. To think that life on this planet can look up every evening and behold the edge of the universe calling them onward... it was something I never experienced back on Earth; the city I came from was wreathed in clouds and smog.

The rolling rills and humps of Ursridge were falling away now, tussocks of sheaf-grass bobbing in the wind, great golden ori-birds swooping down to roost in the spindle-trees. Other craft wound their way alongside us, following invisible lines in the air only their pilots could see.

'How are you navigating?' I asked.

'Sky-lanes are satellite designated, fed directly to each registered, licensed ship,' Starlight Fantastic explained. They paused, as if hesitant, then turned all the way around, seemed to register the steady rise and fall of Serenity Ko's chest—now in deep sleep—and lowered their voice. 'You really should consider getting a Loop subscription—the nanopill kind. You just need to pop these pills every month. They link to your neurons and create bio-circuits that are uplinked to the Loop. Instant access to a cosmos of information.'

'I know how they work,' I said, a little defensively. 'But I have Kili—'

'You can pair it with your Winger, I'm sure. Everyone on Primus has one.'

'Do you?' I asked.

'I do,' Starlight Fantastic replied. 'Even though the E'nemon is a collective consciousness, and all experiences, memories and information are shared by all of us. Helps me stay in touch with other peoples.'

I tried to wrap my head around this. 'So... you're a self-contained Loop? But that sounds like there's no privacy!'

'Humans have a very different notion of what that means,' they said gnomically.

'Does that mean anyone can access your memories? So everyone in the E'nemon will know we've met and you're giving me a ride?'

'Does that concern you?' Starlight Fantastic's tentacles twisted together into knots, pulsing deep grey with worry.

'Only when it comes to the humans back on Earth,' I laughed casually, but my heart pounded in my chest. *It's too early to be discovered.*

'Oh! We don't have a language understandable to humans, visually or verbally.' Starlight Fantastic's tendrils brightened and fell slack.

'Running away from something?' Serenity Ko mumbled, blinking awake and regarding her surroundings with reddened eyes. 'Great place to disappear to, Uru.'

My breath caught in my throat as we banked left.

In the distance glimmered Uru, first and greatest of all the megacities in the United Human Cooperative. Splendid, strange, serene, a rippling, radiant wave of abstraction, evading my attempts to hold it in place and define it, to colour and contour it with my limited Earth-understanding of the shape of a city.

It cascaded like water, billowing like a yawning tide. It towered crystalline and amorphous all at once, none of its spirals fixed points in the sky as they folded and poured into each other, flowmetal evolving and shifting in an unending wave. It was like a great living creature lying fitfully at rest, its heartbeat pounding mystic rhythms to which its being breathed.

'Close your eyes,' Starlight Fantastic cautioned. 'Then look again. Best to take it in in bits.'

I followed their instructions, counted to ten, and opened my eyes again. The abstract ever-shifting form of the city was less dizzying as we drew closer, but every bit as mesmerising.

The flowmetal continued its hypnotic dance, shimmering and reorienting its facades as the mysterious brain that controlled it commanded. Twinkling lights were now visible pulsing across the city's concentric spirals, flowing outwards from no point of origin with no end in sight, glowing like star clusters upon the ground. I kept searching for a beginning, a centre to focus my attention on, but every time I followed a pattern down its pathway, it branched off again and again until I was back to closing my eyes. My head spun.

I blinked rapidly and looked out again. The flowmetal morphed and mirrored, counterpointed and contrasted as it sought out the most intelligent design for optimal function. Flowmetal is a bit of a misnomer; everyone knows this. It's a bio-tech compound that integrates with its natural surroundings, using bio-circuitry and quantum computing to take intelligent, sustainable, eco-conscious decisions, while leaving the lightest footprint possible on the world. Traditionalist lobbies on Earth had ensured it was never produced or adopted there, despite my failing home planet's desperate need for sustainable city solutions. I'd read about the tech, seen holoscrolls with pics and vids of Uru—sur-fucking hell, I was literally riding on a ship built from it—but it was surreal to behold an entire city harmonise to its intelligence in the fading dusk.

As if in a symphony, each neighbourhood appeared to follow its own score, its buildings—were they even called buildings here?—swivelling and tilting, pulsing and mushrooming, undulating into a greater wave of expression, a collective whole. There appeared to be no centre.

'What controls this thing? I can't find a core,' I said weakly.

Serenity Ko laughed harshly beside me. 'What a dated ideology! A point of control, an origin of power. So *Earth-typical*. The city is a cohesive, balanced system with a decentralised brain, or *brains*, as it were, all working together based on local information and conditions to optimise the experience for those who live on it. Its design was inspired by mycelia networks; don't tell me you don't go to university on Earth?'

I ignored the condescension in favour of losing myself in the view. We were right over the city now, slowly descending. Narrow streets wended their way between the seemingly living buildings, with only pedestrian traffic on them. The roofs around us spread wide as they reached into the sky, their mushroom-capped peaks unfurling each time a flowship landed, closing like an umbrella slowly snapping shut each time a ship took off. The city flickered and morphed more slowly up close—or perhaps I was just getting used to the sight.

Each neighbourhood was clustered around a large reservoir of water that reflected the sky in all its star-blossomed glory. Buildings swirled up into the clouds and shrank, widened and flattened to the dictates of the mysterious many-faceted brain communicating with them. Their luminous multi-hued shimmer was resplendent up close, like a mirage on a tarry Earth highway.

'Doesn't it get disorienting when you're indoors?' I asked without thinking, then braced myself for the inevitable scorn.

'The insides have grav-management,' Serenity Ko said. 'You're a long way from your steel and concrete planet—' She paused, then frowned. 'What's your name again?'

'Saraswati Kaveri.'

'Right, Sara. Like I was saying—'

'It's Saraswati. I prefer it that way,' I interrupted. 'Or Saras, if you're a friend. And it's too early to tell if you are, isn't it?'

'Oh, I'm definitely not,' Serenity Ko said with a sniff. 'Starlight Fantastic, this is my stop up ahead.'

'Right. Commencing descent.'

The flowship slowed, then hovered, gently setting down on an unfurling mushroom cap that rose up to greet it.

Serenity Ko unbuckled her harness like she couldn't wait to get out of the vehicle. 'Thanks for the ride!' she said brightly to Starlight Fantastic, then turned to me. 'And, um, I don't suppose I'll be seeing you again. So good luck and harmony and serenity and stuff, yeah?'

'Harmony and serenity be—' I began, but before I could finish the sentence, she was out the ramp and on her way.

'Sorry about her,' Honour Aki said, not meeting my eye on his way out. 'Thank you, really, for your patience.'

The air in the flowship seemed lighter in their absence. I took a deep breath, like I did every time I saw a cake rising in the oven, my chest swelling with hope.

'Where to, Saraswati?' Starlight Fantastic's tendrils curled outward with curiosity, a teal blue.

'Um,' I hesitated. I hadn't considered that at all. 'Uh, where do people live around here?'

'I got you,' the E'nemon said.

My heart pounded as the city dropped away beneath us. My destiny was right around the corner, on the streets below, waiting for me to reach out and grab it. As our ship rose, I caught sight of a space-flare display, high in the stratosphere above us, and tasted the promise of the stars.

We name this planet Primus: the first, but by no means
the last human settlement in the far reaches of space.
And here, in our new home, we shall build the world
the Earth was meant to be. We shall chart the future
of humanity...

—Pioneer Nadira D'Cruz
Nakshatran Dispatch from Primus
75 Anno Earth | 1 Interstellar Era

FOUR

ALL HISTORIC MOMENTS of diplomacy are marked by
promises of equality and performances of goodwill,
carefully woven together to cloak their true purpose: the
establishment of power.

Under the guise of a celebratory cultural exchange with
the alt-beings who called themselves the K'artri-tva, the
banquet was a demonstration of the might of the United
Human Cooperative. First contact had been established
with intelligent life from the K'arta System a few sur-
decades ago, and after tentative initial forays in which both
sides committed to being their peace-loving, non-violent
best selves, an agreement had been reached to allow for free
travel and trade between the inhabited planets of the K'arta
System and those within the UHC.

The celebrations surrounding the signing of this treaty
had been orchestrated to impress upon those in attendance
the pristine superiority of post-Earth, neo-human culture.
Members of the human delegation also included those from
the more unsavoury corners of human occupied space, as
it was meant to be a grand show of human unity, but the
UHC had entrusted the event to the representatives from

Primus, and Optimism Mahd'vi, despite all her reservations about this new species of alt-being, had made sure not a table setting was out of place. She'd flown in a team of the best Primian chefs Uru had to offer, set the ambient lighting to an appropriately calm luminescence, and decorated the warpcraft hosting the event with art and cultural artefacts from the Museum of Primian History. Relics included a wing fragment from the first shuttle to land on Primus, the tablet recording Nakshatran Pioneer Nadira D'Cruz's observations from her first nava planetside, and a holoscroll print of the Nakshatran Charter.

The Grand Monarch of the K'artri-tva stared at these artefacts with their deep, soulful eyes. They chittered their appreciation of human history in a high-pitched voice, their vox-box translating from their language into Vox. They possessed a smooth carapace in radiant hues of blue, and jagged crystals grew like rough, uneven scales along a single line down their back. Tucked away were two pairs of wings, glittering like quartz crystals. Their body elongated and narrowed towards a head with a bird-like beak. Their Consort wept at the beauty of the words on the Charter, lifting a luminous purple claw to wipe their tears away.

Optimism Mahd'vi watched this display of deference with skepticism. She was nothing if not a realist, and bore her given-name without a shred of irony. She was nervous about the influence of this strange new species of alt-being—yet another in a long history of alien intelligences—upon her domain. As the Primian Secretary for Culture and Heritage, she was responsible for the preservation, evolution and propagation of the Primian way of life, and that effectively amounted to *human* culture, since the rest of humanity's philosophical leanings were decidedly infra.

The space-flare ballet, choreographed and orchestrated by the best artistic minds on Primus, danced about in the stratosphere below, visible through the transparent flowmetal of the warpcraft's floor. Perfectly synchronised sinfonia streamed through the ship's dinner hall.

As the representatives at the banquet studied their gilded holoscroll menus, Optimism Mahd'vi's thoughtstream beamed reports from around United Human space to her, and they were both distasteful and concerning. Humans around the cosmos were throwing K'artri-tva parties, bobbing to the strange rhythmic beats of K'artri-pop, custom-building decorative stalacto-mods...

There was nothing the UHC wanted less than accusations of xenophobia, not when there were far more advanced beings out there with warfaring histories and well-trained armies. And yet, Optimism Mahd'vi's job was to ensure Primian culture—thereby, human culture—clung to its roots and continued to thrive. It was always a painful process to be open to a new set of customs, to include other influences in festivities and entertainment, and be seen to embrace them in the public eye, while limiting their practical reach to ensure they did not become a threat.

She brought her thumb and forefinger together to watch a video of two humans in the Urswood, stalacto-mods twinkling under the light of Ibnis, swaying to a K'artri-pop song, then sighed and slid out of the Loop. She would have work to do to publicly encourage/privately suppress these new trends, and Optimism Mahd'vi wasn't looking forward to it one bit.

She glanced at the seating arrangement around her, and exhaled in relief. At least she'd minimised the risks of a diplomatic incident during this gathering.

Delegates from the civilised worlds Chomo and Sagaricus in the Paloma System, Unity in the Kepler system, and Primus's neighbour Harid in the Suriyan System had been obvious invites, and were seated near the head of the table with the First Secretary of the UHC and their honoured alt-being guests. The ambassador of Mars had been invited because despite being Solar, the planet hadn't declared war on the rest of the universe, yet, and personally, Optimism Mahd'vi liked his wry humour.

Representatives from various space stations, including Allegro, Orbius, Titan, Ceres and Luna—the latter standing in firm opposition to the politics of the planet it revolved around—had made the long journey to the off-world feast. Even the Fringe planets, the troublemakers of the UHC, had been asked to send envoys, and excited at the prospect of inclusion, they had all made an appearance.

Optimism Mahd'vi eyed the barbarians from Amicus, Nova Terra, Davidia and Enceladus with distrust, and the primitive from Earth, seated at her right hand, with utter disapproval. He was some provincial princeling from their Daxina Protectorate, an ornate bejewelled head-dress and long robes made of natural silk glittering upon his person. It was typical of Earthlings to be flashy, and because they needed to be watched carefully, she'd opted to sit at the foot of the table, right beside him, where she could steer conversation towards inoffensive grounds and prevent his indelicate utterances from sparking a war.

Optimism Mahd'vi smiled to herself. Perhaps that was an exaggeration. But under the circumstances, a brawl would be bad enough. *And do they still duel on Earth? Barbaric planet.*

Of course, all humans in the cosmos owed their origins to the planet Earth, and there were entire customs observed to honour their ancestors during Nakshatra Nava, but in the nearly two thousand sur-years that had elapsed since Primus was first settled, those left behind on Earth had done little to restore their planet to even a shadow of its former natural splendour.

While the Nakshatran settlers chose to tread lightly, choosing planets free of indigenous civs to populate with human life, not terraforming their new home worlds unless absolutely required—either to compensate for the absence of life-nurturing resources, or in times of crisis; while they chose to negotiate conflicts through dialogue and not war machines, the Earthlings had, well… "devolved" was putting it mildly, to Optimism Mahd'vi's mind.

Uru was raised from flowmetal, a carbon composite with quantum nanocomputing that integrated itself into the world around it, the city breathing as one with the planet. On Primus, possessions were assigned and shared towards what served the ideals of serenity and harmony best. On Primus, it was compulsory to walk the Wanderers' Paths in service to the monitoring and maintenance of the natural world beyond the borders of Uru.

On Earth… Well, the gold and jewels gleaming at the princeling's throat said everything Optimism Mahd'vi needed to know.

A host of servers, immaculately dressed in unobtrusive grey, placed down the first course of their dinner. It was, naturally, Primian food, and in typical Primian fashion, it had been carefully assembled into a mirror of Primian philosophy.

A nest of circles lay intertwined upon the plate, made from a golden jus. Spheres of various colours dotted their points of intersection, and a slightly larger, deep blue sphere occupied a space off-centre.

'Nakshatran Flight,' announced a chef from the foot of the table. 'Each of the spheres is made from a fruit belonging to one of the planets in the UHC—the sour bite of n'artanga from Chomo, the deep woodiness of the mud-apple from Mars, the bright notes of the mamba-zham from Primus, and more. The jus that binds them together is made from an assortment of spices, and the deep blue sphere is made of ice-fruit, in honour of the K'artri-tva world. We welcome you to be a part of our story.'

There was polite applause and the chef bowed and took their leave. Across the room, the conversation dropped to a low murmur as the delegates reached for the first course with enthusiasm. Optimism Mahd'vi picked a sphere up in her bare hands and popped it into her mouth. She was somewhat aghast when the Earthling beside her requested a fork and knife. It was nothing short of savage to saw at and stab food—it was a primitive kind of violence. Even the K'artri-tva were making a conscious effort to eat with their claws retracted.

'Ugh, cold,' were the Earthling's first words. His Vox accent was appalling.

'Excuse me?' Optimism Mahd'vi couldn't help herself.

'Cold and practically flavourless. I miss home world food already.' In contradiction of his own words, he speared sphere after sphere on the end of his fork, and popped them into his mouth while chewing. 'I'm Jog Tunga. Earth.'

Optimism Mahd'vi fought the frown that was threatening to take over, and smiled at him frostily. 'I'm sure it was a long and arduous journey here. We're glad you could be present.'

Jog Tunga waved his hand noncommittally. 'Wouldn't miss it for anything in the cosmos. It's rare for your kind to invite us to these fancy dos.'

He swallowed, and his voice rose, unnecessarily loud. 'It's a shame there's no Earth fruit represented on this plate, though.'

Several other delegates stopped eating and looked up. Optimism Mahd'vi stifled a groan and resisted the urge to kick the young princeling under the table. She glanced at the head of the table and her heart sank—the Grand Monarch of the K'artri-tva appeared to have heard, and now turned their great head towards where Jog Tunga stabbed at his plate.

'No Earth fruit?' their vox-box translated while they chittered in confusion.

'Nope, none, your Grand Monarchy-ness.' Jog Tunga shrugged, and Optimism Mahd'vi winced. 'Disappointing, but you get used to this kind of thing in the UHC.'

'Are you not united?' their Consort asked. 'Is not human civilization one?'

Everyone had stopped eating and was watching the scene unfold with bated breath. The K'artvi-tva operated in perfect synchronicity, and unity and conformity were extremely important to them. Optimism Mahd'vi's brain raced to find a way to circumvent disaster. The First Secretary of the UHC had a grin plastered across his face, and she wanted to crawl under the table and disappear when she saw the bottle of Shimmer Soma in front of him, half empty. He drained his glass and poured himself another, seeming to achieve greater buoyancy. Optimism Mahd'vi resisted the urge to throw a dinner plate at him.

The silence was deafening. Jog Tunga chewed thoughtfully and swallowed, draining his glass before continuing, all eyes upon him. 'Well, we're united so long as we all play second fiddle to the great Primus. The dish we just ate is Primian cuisine, the entertainment you'll witness later will be some kind of Primian culture-fuck.'

A collective gasp went up from the dignitaries assembled at the table.

'Is this true?' the Consort interjected, addressing everyone present. 'We're interested in trading with the humans to learn how to appreciate differences and diversity. Following a dominant leader isn't weakness; it's a sign of wisdom and acceptance on my home world. But we believe we need to learn to do more to aid our co-existence in such a populated universe. And you do it so well—your inability to conquer a single other intelligent being is proof enough.'

'Oh, empire is dead here,' Jog Tunga said casually. 'On paper, at least. Instead, we have some cultures whose ideas are popular, and... some who are relegated. Forgotten. Who don't even get token tasteless fruit-spheres in their honour.' He grimaced theatrically.

A few of the delegates at the table laughed, and the tension cracked. The Grand Monarch and their Consort joined in.

At that moment, one of the chefs—the one who'd announced the dish—rushed in, wringing their hands together. 'There's salt!' they cried. 'There's salt in the spice jus.'

'Ah, salt.' Jog Tunga said dismissively. 'Wars have been started over less.'

Optimism Mahd'vi finally found her wits. 'The spice jus is what binds us all!' she said, raising her glass and rising to her feet. 'After all, all our stories lead back to Earth and are connected to it.'

'Hear, hear.' The Martian ambassador winked at her, and joined her in her toast.

The representative from Luna seemed unhappy at this statement, but one by one, everyone rose to their feet and toasted the Earth as their home of origin. Jog Tunga sat smugly in his chair, and Optimism Mahd'vi dearly wanted to wipe the grin off his face.

'Thank you for your kind words,' he said insincerely.

'I would love to hear all about your culture,' the Consort said. 'Perhaps we could establish a conclave?'

'That would be lovely.' Jog Tunga bowed his head. 'I thank you for your interest.'

And with that, the hideous incident was defused. Optimism Mahd'vi glanced at Jog Tunga, who was humming a barbaric tune to himself, his legs crossed at the knee, one foot tapping to the beat. She slid into the Loop and scanned him, and proceeded to download all the information she could dig up on him.

Everywhere she looked, there were threats to Primian culture circling her beautiful home world, and she was going to have to do something about it. It would have to be something big, an unmistakable assertion that Primus was the unshakeable soul of the cultured universe.

Optimism Mahd'vi had *thoughts*.

Primian cuisine can be summarised in a single word: ras.

—Optimism Wight,
the Wight School of Culinary Tradition,
from (NOT) Everyone Can Cook
1845 Anno Earth | 1771 Interstellar Era

FIVE

ENTERING ITS TWENTY-FIFTH year and stronger than ever, *Interstellar MegaChef* was the most widely-watched programme in the history of Loop programming. The culinary contest was a gladiatorial gastronomical challenge, not for the faint of heart (or nuclear-powered core), that pitted dozens of the greatest chefs from across the known universe—people from all species included—against each other to crown a champion each year.

Its judges comprised the most discerning food critics and creators on Primus, those who'd risen through the ranks and fought bitter plated duels for their place among the who's who of culinary culture. Occasionally, a judge would retire to do greater things on the interstellar world stage, and a spot would open up. In recent years, under growing pressure from an increasingly inclusive universe, the judging panel had expanded to feature non-humans on special episodes, and even the occasional non-Primian upstart.

It was a well-known fact that Primian cuisine was *the* most elevated, *the* most delightful, *the* most creative and tasteful of all the food arts anywhere in the cosmos. It did not come easy to everyone, and rightly so, for its emphasis on ras—or essence—was innate to Primian culture. "Tread lightly," as the old and ever-relevant adage went.

So it was much to the establishment's chagrin when the producers revealed that joining the judges this year, for the *entire season*, were Pavi and Amol Khurshid. Unknown to either of these young chefs, and entirely behind closed doors, protests had been staged, the current judges had threatened to quit, special perks were offered per episode, and the issue had come to a temporary, if uneasy, settlement. It was widely agreed that Pavi and Amol Khurshid were pretenders of the most deplorable kind: Earthling immigrants who dared to aspire to Primian cuisine, and worse still, successfully so. Their restaurant, Nonpareil, was booked out a year in advance, their faces were on every culinary holoscroll out there, and they were frequently and grudgingly invited to the most exclusive degustations. It was sickening, the other judges wholly agreed, but they resolved to smile and wave for the cameras, and hope this new fad would soon pass.

Pavi and Amol weren't entirely unaware of the tension in the Judges' Lounge that evening. It preceded them like a cloud, announcing their arrival at every room they stepped into. It had been this way ever since they first arrived on Primus. It was impossible to tell which smiles were false and which genuine, but in Pavi's estimation, all of them seemed brittle.

'Such a delight to have you, and welcome to our humble lair,' Grace Aurelle, the head judge—or "Chief Chef"— said in a low raspy voice. She ran her finger around the rim of a cocktail glass in her hands, and licked the salt off it, gazing at them with cool blue eyes. 'What do I call you? *Pavi* and *Amol* seem so naked, so lacking in... *social standing*, without given-names, don't they?'

Pavi's temper rose, but she smoothed it over with an easy smile. 'Unfortunately, we aren't eligible for given-names since we aren't Primian citizens. So naked and lacking in social standing we will have to be.'

Grace Aurelle tilted her head back and laughed, her

thick, long, braided grey hair whipping to the side like a scorpion's tail. 'I like you already,' she said.

Pavi exchanged a look with Amol. It was a certainty she didn't.

Grace Aurelle continued. 'Let me introduce you to the rest—though, really, they need no introduction. Courage Ab'dal, They/Them, owner of Leaf and Bone; Harmony Rhea, She/Her, author of a dozen award-winning cook-scrolls; and, well, me. My pronouns are She/Her.'

Pavi resisted the urge to lower her tall, slender figure into a curtsy—a vulgar Earth habit that would drop her in their estimation quicker than you could say *Earthling*. The judging panel was intimidatingly star-studded; no party or restaurant opening she'd ever been to had hosted the like of the culinary wizards before her in this room.

Her twin, seeming to read her mind, stepped in to smooth things over in his calm, predictable fashion. Amol, portly and amicable, smiled at the imperious gazes upon him, eyes twinkling. 'We're honoured to be here!' he said in that bright, enthusiastic tone Primians expected from off-worlders of any sort. His Ur-speak was impeccable, his accent more polished than his sister's.

'You must have had a great Ur-speak tutor,' Courage Ab'dal remarked. 'We were expecting both of you to speak Vox.'

'Or worse, one of the regional vernaculars from Earth,' Harmony Rhea tittered.

Amol laughed brightly, and caught Pavi's eyes flashing in anger. 'We're as far from the barbarians as we might be, seeing as we attended boarding school here.'

'Huh. I read about that in your interview in *The Consummate Cuisineologist*,' said Grace Aurelle. 'But let's talk later, after we're done with official business. We're reviewing audition videos from our contenders to see what we might expect tomorrow.' She gestured at the lavish flowmetal bar behind her. 'Pour yourselves a drink and join us, will you?'

Pavi was aware of the eyes boring into her back as she and Amol walked towards the bar. This was a test of elegance and skill. Every single thing about the cocktail she created would be scrutinised—the ingredients she chose and their symbolic value in Primian culture, the techniques she decided to display, and her performance in assembling them. All this would speak volumes about her, and she must not forget to add a personal touch, something to indicate her roots or her personality, as part of the greater whole.

A line of top-shelf spirits and liqueurs crowned the bar— cloudy blue Saxeny, bubbling pink Rosestahl and crystal clear Minerali among them. To use one of these would be a sign of hubris, symbolising that she had achieved the pinnacle of Primian culture already; and so she demurely settled on a green bottle twisted like coiling vines. Verdatis would do nicely—it symbolised growth. Beside her, Amol made a similar choice, picking a robust, ochre Sherberry, which hinted at being grounded yet radiant.

The manner of the making was as important as the end result, which isn't to say it was done with flourish: quite the opposite. All Primian cuisine was made with elegance, a minimalism of movement that underscored precision, getting to the essence of flavour. Pavi poured out a shot of Verdatis, immaculately measured to a precise 45 ml. She created a familiar blend of speckled white mento-leaves and neon yellow citrine-fruit, using a syringe to extract their ras from the solitary specimens lying on the table, adding a spot of concentrator.

She injected her ingredients into a mid-sized edible sphere, a staple in any Primian kitchen, taking care to ensure the speckled white and neon yellow marbled its surface as they spread across it. It was vulgar to use whole natural ingredients in one's food—it hinted at excess, at indiscriminately taking from the land. She popped the sphere into the cocktail glass, then added a dash of hot chilli ras, a direct infusion into the cocktail. The cocktail turned effervescent with a delightful popping, and she raised it in a toast to the other judges, who politely applauded.

'Clever,' Grace Aurelle smiled approvingly. 'Mento-leaves for calmness and citrine-fruit for playfulness—a classic Primian pairing, I'll say—with a personal touch of chilli for your fiery ambition.'

Pavi smiled and took a sip of her cocktail. 'My spin on the greenwood pop.'

Beside her, Amol raised his Sherberry with honey caviar, and carefully crafted cocogel flowers.

'Cheerful disposition and charm. Cocogel for eccentricity, and the floral shapes for harmony with the earth.' Grace Aurelle raised an eyebrow. 'My, what an interesting pair of siblings you are.' She indicated two wingback armchairs on either side of her. 'And now, to review this year's worthy hopefuls.'

Pavi settled in at one end of the judging table, Amol across from her at the other.

Harmony Rhea tapped her thumb and index finger together, sliding into the Loop. She flicked her wrist out, as if dealing cards. The visio-nodes embedded in the table caught something and flared blue, and a holostream appeared.

'Behold the luminous final twenty-four,' Grace Aurelle said with condescension.

'I can't wait to watch them fail all through this season.' Courage Ab'dal cracked their knuckles.

The first chef auditioning prepared a meen crudo, knife slicing through vat-grown meen-fish in a blur.

Harmony Rhea pretended to yawn. 'Another flashy demonstration of knife skills a la the Ninno School.'

'We get one of these every year,' Courage Ab'dal said, for Pavi and Amol's benefit. 'Can slice through any kind of meat or vegetable, but ask them to use a syringe and they're all ham-fisted.'

'This one isn't very good,' said Grace Aurelle. 'Look at the edges of the meen-fish? They're fraying. Consistent, yes, but fraying. This is a chef who's going to rail against tradition for whimsy.'

And sure enough, the traditional meen crudo, meant to symbolise being one with the waves of the ocean, took an unexpected turn when the chef in question added a citrine-fruit infusion.

Pavi tutted, and her ears grew hot when everyone turned to regard her. 'Unconventional. All flavour is supposed to be derived from ocean ingredients in this dish.'

'Exactly!' crowed Grace Aurelle. 'I have a feeling we might just get along, despite our.... *differences*.'

A succession of chefs displayed their best work in the kitchen, each with techniques hailing back to one of the great schools of interstellar cuisine. It was breathtaking to watch them work, but most of them, being human, would eventually slip up; and then the judging panel would crow, looking forward to weaknesses they could exploit over the next two months' filming.

One chef from the Serenius College of Sweet Treats stood out for their remarkable piping techniques.

'Flawless!' gasped Harmony Rhea. It was the only nice thing she'd said in their entire discussion.

Another chef used micro-pâté to great effect in a futuristic dish created from hundreds of little layers, evoking Ancestor Rock, where the first settlers of Primus left their handprints in the moss.

'Ingenious,' gushed Courage Ab'dal.

A B'naar cook impressed them all with xir delicate use of xir mechatronic limbs to create petalescence.

'That's your dark horse for the season,' Grace Aurelle said.

There were also an E'nemon and an Askalion chef among this year's contenders.

'This is the politically correct faction,' explained Courage Ab'dal. 'They don't last very long, but there are mandatory spots reserved for them by the Culture and Heritage office. Part of our PR as an inclusive planet.'

At the end of the twenty-four videos, during which Pavi and Amol had chimed in with the occasional observation laced with snark, Grace Aurelle half-rose, stretching her long arms luxuriantly over her head.

Harmony Rhea frowned. 'Hang on. There's one more.'

Courage Ab'dal shook their leg restlessly. 'Aren't we done with twenty-four? I've got all my notes.'

'This is a "wild card," apparently,' Harmony Rhea explained. 'The producers think views of our first episode will skyrocket, thanks to her.'

'Oh! I think I signed her invite,' Grace Aurelle said. 'Let's get this over with?'

A short, curvy woman smiled brightly at the camera. Her face was oval-shaped and dimpled, her skin golden brown and heavily freckled. Her hair was pulled back in—

'A ponytail?' asked Grace Aurelle in shock. 'Did she just get out of bed?'

The chef in question proceeded to cut a slab of meat on the counter in front of her, explaining the dish she was making.

'Her Ur-speak is deplorable,' Harmony Rhea said, giggling.

Pavi exchanged a look with Amol as her heart sank. She recognised that accent all too well.

Courage Ab'dal gasped. '*Is that an open flame?*'

The woman on the video tossed something onto a metal pan and held it over a fire.

'Barbarian!' Grace Aurelle said in shock.

Suddenly, the woman glanced behind her and a large spot of plaster dropped from the ceiling into the kitchen. She looked hurriedly back at the camera, keeping her smile in place with a visible effort.

'What is going on?' Courage Ab'dal frowned, leaning forwards.

The walls of the kitchen in which the woman stood began to shake, and pots and pans fell off them with loud metallic chiming, a discordant symphony to accompany the unnerving sizzling of fat on the fire. A large hole appeared in the back wall, and smoke whooshed through it.

'Is her city collapsing?' Harmony Rhea asked, aghast.

Undaunted, the woman on the video began to throw *whole vegetables* into the pot, stirring it with a hastened violence, shredding herbs and tossing them in after.

'Nine Virtues, she's savage!' Grace Aurelle whispered.

As she began to pour her concoction into a large earthenware bowl, the video blurred out of focus and the screen went black.

'What the star-fucking hell is this?' Courage Ab'dal asked, clearly shaken.

Pavi's insides were cold, and her hands trembled as she tried to sip her cocktail. She knew exactly where this video was from, and while she didn't know the cook in it, she knew the opinions she was going to be expected to express come judging the next day.

'Huh. Her name is Sara-southey Karri,' said Harmony Rhea, reading off something only she could see. 'Ran some big shot restaurant called Elé Oota on… *No way!*'

She slid out of the Loop, eyes as big as saucers, and looked from Pavi to Amol, back to Pavi. 'She's from *Earth*.'

Civilisation is not determined by the majesty of history, art and architecture alone. It is most keenly observable in the manner of a people; living, breathing beings who share a culture and a philosophy and strive to embody it, evolving to incorporate external influences but retaining an internal compass.

—Serenity Medi,
Primus: A New Hope for Humanity, Seventh Edition
2051 Anno Earth | 1976 Interstellar Era

SIX

THERE ARE DOORS to the future, and then there are *doors* to *the future*. I stood before the latter, flowmetal frame looming high over me, trailing vines from a pair of trellises. As soon as we started filming, the doors would open inward, and I would step through them into the kitchen. The producers of *Interstellar MegaChef* seemed to have taken great pride in making their set in the studio grandiose, intimidating and impersonal. And it was having its intended effect on everyone around me.

My hands were trembling—terrible for any knife work. I wish I'd been able to walk off the nerves, but Starlight Fantastic had insisted on dropping me at the studio in Collective Two. My allocated living space wasn't in walking distance, being forty-one minutes away by public transport, and Starlight Fantastic said it took a while to master the flowtram routes. I'd left Kili with them since I wasn't allowed any external tech, and they'd promised to pick me up after catching the show at home, since there hadn't been a spot for them in the live audience. I wound up being over an hour early and had the chance to observe my competition as they walked in.

First, a pair of identical twins with deep brown hair and tattooed sleeves took one look at me, glanced at each other, wordlessly decided to pretend I didn't exist, and settled themselves in a corner, muttering to each other. A tall, slender woman with several piercings smiled at me tersely, her gaze passing right through me. As the room began to fill, there were a few handshakes of familiarity, coupled with the inevitable ill-concealed sneers that clearly marked chefdom across the universe. It was evident that a lot of these chefs had grown up around each other, or knew each other's work through the culinary network on Primus. An E'nemon swayed in to impassive stares, and I looped my hands together in greeting, which they returned weakly before wilting against the wall, the tips of their fronds a delicate shade of green.

The tension in the room was so thick you could throw it in a pan and fry it. It was basted in bravado, sliced by stray chuckles, simmering in its own juices. A ravenous hunger underscored it all—to win at all costs—and the longer I breathed it in, the more it got to me.

I took a deep breath to try and still my shaking hands. Nothing that happened here could be worse than everything I'd left behind, including everything I'd endured while staging for some of the best chefs on Earth. Cesare Caesar had never let me do anything other than grate parmesan for the six months I'd spent at La Luna. Ahana Shah had stood at my shoulder muttering a constant stream of obscenities at me every time I plated for her at the pass at Nizami, which was every night for a year.

An intern of some sort—discernible by their starstruck expression, their scrabble to be as invisible as possible, and the way the chefs around them obligingly ignored them—walked through the crowd, handing out chef's jackets. They were emblazoned with the *Interstellar MegaChef* logo, a fiery C ending in a swoosh like a comet's tail.

'Thank you!' I said, smiling at them. They were so shocked they dropped my jacket and stepped backward stammering, stumbling into one of my competitors, and tripping over their own sneakers. The chef whirled around and caught the intern, who squeaked, horribly embarrassed, muttered their thanks, and made a run for it.

The chef stepped forwards and extended their hand with a smile; the first I'd received in that room. 'Curiosity Olea, He/Him. Wight School of Culinary Tradition. Staged with everyone here in Uru, and I tell you, they're all beastly pricks. Did you ever work with Boundless Min'ma? Worst of the lot.'

'Saraswati Kaveri, She/Her. Aren't chefs the same everywhere in the galaxy?' I shook his hand, grateful to have found a friendly face at last. He had a long blond braid and deep brown skin, his eyes crinkling at the corners as he smiled. And then his forehead creased as soon as he heard my name, the smile fading.

'Oh, wait. I thought you were from the Am-Am School—didn't I once beat you at an Inter-School Cook Off?' He looked me up and down. 'But no, your Ur-speak's strange.' He slowed his speech down dramatically. 'Is Vox better? You don't seem like you're from here.'

A little bubble of annoyance rose in me, but I smiled more broadly and responded in Ur-speak. 'I'm from Earth.'

'Earth? For real?' Curiosity Olea's eyes widened, and he switched to Vox immediately. 'How'd you even get in the door?'

My gut dropped like a stone. Something sharp and hot twisted inside me, worming its way through my veins. My jaw ached from smiling. 'Being a professional chef has nothing to do with your address,' I said politely, carrying on in Ur-speak.

'*Everything* in Uru depends on your address. There's Uru, and there's not,' he said, shaking his head in disbelief before turning away. I saw him join the twins who'd walked in right after me, and all three of them threw a sidelong glance my way, no doubt gossiping about my home planet. If the tech-dampers hadn't been in place to prevent cheating, I'd bet my life savings they'd be looking me up on the Loop.

And sur-fucking hell, I wish they would.

Except they wouldn't find me if they searched for Saraswati Kaveri. *I should have name-dropped my restaurant and risked blowing my cover.*

My restaurant, Elé Oota, had been one of the most sought after culinary destinations back on Earth, booked out months in advance in the Daxina Protectorate. I'd staged for, worked with, and learnt from the best chefs on Earth, and I'd carved a name for myself in the ten short years since I'd graduated culinary school as one of the most promising talents in the world.

And then everything I thought I'd known about my career as a chef had been wrested away from me. The conspiracy ran so deep I hadn't seen the knife coming, but come it had. I needed to get even with them, to show them I could do this without them.

A wave of nausea engulfed me, and I tried to shove the memory of everything they'd said and done deep down.

Not now. I am worth it. I'm going to win.

My fists clenched involuntarily as my father's words rang out in my ears again: *"Do you think any of your success would be possible without who you are? Without who we are?"*

Not. Now.

'Untrue, father,' I muttered. 'Un-fucking true. Just you wait.'

My sister's hysterical giggles wrapped around my skull, refusing to let go. Sweat dripped down my nose and I fought the urge to sink to my knees and hug myself.

They'll think they're getting to you. Chin up, Saras. You got this.

I fought the cramps that had started to knot my shoulders and blinked rapidly. The lights were brighter than before. An AI voice chimed through a speaker set into the wall.

'*Two minutes to go. Remember, chefs: head to your assigned stations as soon as the doors open. Best to smile and wave at the cam-drones. Look cheerful and happy to be here. And may the best chef win!*'

I was going to destroy them all.

I'd been through this hundreds of times, every single night Elé Oota opened for service. No matter what challenge they threw my way, whether they restricted my ingredients or seized my kitchen equipment, I'd come up with delicious food as I'd always done. I'd staked everything I had to be here, and it was going to be worth it.

The second hand ticked down. A bell chimed. The doors slid open.

An array of lights and colour flooded my retinas. Heart hammering, I strode through the doors, waving blindly and smiling even though I couldn't see what I was grinning at. It took several seconds for my eyes to adjust as I walked to my cook station, and I spotted three cam-drones the size of sunbirds flitting about. I mustered some flair and tossed each one a kiss. I'd done this on Earth before. *Why should this be any different?*

A cam-drone settled upon my shoulder for a first-person perspective, another on the counter for a hands-eye view of my skills. The third hovered in front of me, beaming my likeness across space. There were about a dozen larger wall-mounted cameras and mics hanging unobtrusively from the ceiling, and there were flashing spinning lights everywhere.

I couldn't hear anything other than the deafening roar of applause from the live audience, somewhere beyond the cloud of illumination. The show's host, Boundless Eli, spoke into a microphone, and I didn't catch a word. I forced my shoulders back and my centre of gravity downward, feeling the weight of my sneakers on the floor, drawing into myself.

It's just like service at Elé Oota. Sure, there were cameras. And an interstellar audience. And it was broadcast live because, you know, it's always more fun to watch chefs fuck up in real time. Live on Primus, at least; given inter-system lag, by the time the Earth got this broadcast it'd be a *nava* old, even with jump node comms.

Sun-fuckers, I hope you're all watching.

Stray words in Vox made their way to me from the host. He was introducing the judges.

'Are you okay?' A tinny electronic crackle sparked at my elbow, accompanied by soft whistling sounds.

To my right, the B'naar contestant glowed and dimmed as xe whistled beneath a glass dome, xir featureless spherical form enclosed in a humanoid mecha body. Xir vox-box translated xir language of clicks and whistles, and xe reached out a mechanical limb to touch my arm. 'Are you okay?' xe repeated. 'It'll be okay.'

Xir mechanical limb was surprisingly warm on my arm, and slightly spongy. It felt like sunlight was streaming into my body from the point of contact. I tossed xir a thumbs up. 'All okay,' I said.

'All okay,' xe whistled, bobbing up and down on xir mechanical struts as xe moved back to xir station, several metres to my right. 'Good luck. Happy cooking.'

'You too!' I called after xir. *Happy cooking.* That's exactly what I was going to do.

The roar of the crowd finally died down. Chief Chef Grace Aurelle's voice rose to fill the silence. 'Twenty-five of the best chefs from across the galaxy stand before you. But only one will win the title of Interstellar MegaChef!'

I am here for a purpose.

I scanned my cook station. It was traditionally Primian. A flat, featureless flowmetal counter lay before me with a holo-display to its right. There was a set of knives, a collection of syringes in a range of thicknesses, and some glass pipes and beakers. There was no other equipment on the surface. A sleek oven rested below the counter, and it was unlike anything I'd ever used in all the kitchens I'd worked in. My fingers began to twitch as panic rose within me again.

Where's the stovetop?

I knew Primian techniques weren't big on open flames, but Earthling food was all about fire. I could probably make the Primian stuff, but that wasn't what I'd come here to do. I was here to make my mark on my own terms, with food I'd served to patrons from all over the galaxy back on my home world.

'You have one hour to bring us your signature dish,' Grace Aurelle announced. 'No restrictions on any ingredients in the pantry, or on cooking techniques. We want to see *you* on a plate.' Small and diminutive but commanding, she stood at the centre of the circle of cook stations, flanked by the other judges. She paused dramatically. 'Your time... starts... *now!*'

I needed to act fast. All the other chefs rushed to the pantry, but contrary to the din I'd expected—sneakers pounding across the floor, pots and pans clanging together and ingredients being thrown into baskets pell-mell—they did so in a terrifyingly efficient silence. I craned my neck and saw them operating with an energy that was more coordinated than chaotic, their movements swift and dance-like, twirling around each other and reaching past one another like the Primian ballet.

Fuck. Focus.

I needed to check if I could access a stovetop before choosing my ingredients and implements, and I needed to find out if I could have one *now*. I tapped on the holo-display before me, and exhaled with relief when I saw that

I could customise my cooking surfaces. My flowmetal counter was easily manipulable, into everything from a sous-vide machine to a water bath, a stovetop or a pressure cooker, and many of them all at once. Without a second's thought, I hit the stovetop option.

A section off to the right moulded itself into a four-burner that lighted itself immediately, right as the display turned red and blared: *WARNING: FIRE ACTIVATED!* Sirens screeched through every speaker in the studio.

'What? Stop. *Stop!*' I yelled, hopping up and down and dropping my towel. I whirled around, desperate for assistance.

The chefs behind me dropped their kitchen equipment—silently—and stared at me in shock and confusion. Three producers, a medic, and the intern from before, bearing a fire extinguisher, raced towards my station as a set of overhead sprinklers turned on immediately, dousing the entire set. And me, of course, standing mouth agape and aghast at the commotion I'd inadvertently caused.

'Are you out of your sun-baked mind?' Chief Chef Grace Aurelle hissed, before realising her mic was switched on, only to then accost the nearest technician with a murderous glare. A pair of hands dragged me away from my station. The intern with the extinguisher doused the already sputtering fire in an unnecessary spray of foam. A producer snapped at me in rapid Ur-speak.

'What are you trying to do? Burn down the set?'

'I'm trying to cook!' I yelled. 'What the fuck is wrong with your set?'

'Cook? *Cook?* You lit a fire!'

'I was going to cook with it!'

'Nobody cooks with fire!'

'On Earth, *everyone* cooks with fire!'

The producer fell silent. The others around me stilled. The only sound was the gushing sprinkler system and an argument between Grace Aurelle and another producer off in a corner, only a few words of which were audible.

'—*can't say* sun-baked, *it's a slur*—'

'*Was it broadcast live?*'

'*We killed the stream when the fire started.*'

'*I'll apologise.*'

The producer in front of me smiled. 'Harmony Davi, He/Him.' He stuck out his hand, clearly trying to divert my attention. 'I'm sorry about the misunderstanding. Are you okay? In all the years this show has been broadcast, we've never had anyone use fire.' It wasn't lost on me that he'd switched to Vox.

'You're kidding right?' I said, the bitter taste of panic still at the back of my mouth. 'I thought there were no restrictions on cooking technique and equipment.'

'Even so...' The producer shrugged. 'You're an Earthling, right? We've never had one of your kind in our kitchen. We were somewhat... *unprepared*. And so was our tech. We're sorry.'

Right as I was about to retaliate with how utterly unfair this was, how culture-assumptive and outright xenophobic, my head spinning from experiencing the paranoid over-reaction from everyone and everything—including their flowmetal tech—to cooking with fire (*for fuck's sake*), Grace Aurelle's heels clacked on the wooden floor and she stopped beside me, her eyes wide with concern. 'I'm so sorry about the little mix-up, Chef. It should never have happened.'

She placed her hand gently on my sleeve. I felt her fingers tense, shuddering slightly at the dampness of my chef's jacket, soaked through from the sprinklers, but she left them where they lay and squeezed my arm. She lowered her voice. 'I do hope you'll forgive us all, especially my indiscreet use of language. I didn't mean to cause any offence; it was in the heat of the moment...' She laughed weakly. 'No pun intended, of course. A spontaneous outburst, much like your decision to use fire, hmm?'

She smiled at me, and at the small cluster of people around us, squeezing my arm tighter. The competition was still giving us a wide berth, though a quick glance revealed the likes of Curiosity Olea casually leaning against the nearest cook station, no doubt trying to catch snippets of our conversation.

Grace Aurelle spun me around to face the live audience. 'Fire,' she said, throwing her arms out wide. 'We haven't used fire in decades in professional kitchens across Primus, have we? Such a fascinating, *quaint* cooking technique! Always good for a spot of entertainment.'

Everyone around us, who'd been hanging onto every word and gesture involved in our exchange, laughed, in a sudden sea of sycophancy. The live audience joined in right on cue. Under the uproar, Grace Aurelle dropped her voice and muttered in my ear, still smiling, 'Just remember this, Chef: if you want a career here in Uru, you'd best not create a scene out of this unfortunate incident.'

I smiled back, equally falsely, utterly trapped. 'Heard and understood, Chef.'

My insides burned with shame and anger as the producers decided to restart their broadcast in twenty-five minutes. Backstage, I was handed towels to wipe myself dry. A man from makeup blow-dried my ragged curls, which stuck out every which way despite copious quantities of product, and I was handed a new chef's jacket. The security team temporarily disabled its alarms to be indifferent to my stovetop preferences. I was asked to provide a list of all the appliances I'd need to make my "off-world native food," and they were all pre-approved.

The good news was, this meant I wouldn't set off any more automated sprinklers.

The bad news was, it limited all my contingency plans to

using the appliances I'd asked for. If anything went wrong while I was following my traditional Earth recipe, I'd be left out to dry with limited options for improvisation.

I pointed this out to the producer from before—Harmony Davi—and he just patted me on the back. 'You're an interstellar contestant on the most prestigious cooking show in history. You'll make it work.'

Unconvinced and somewhat miserable, I walked back towards the holding room with the other contestants, my sneakers squelching.

'You wouldn't happen to have a solution for damp socks, would you?' I asked the intern as I passed them by.

The intern made an indiscernible sound and fled out the nearest exit.

'Well done,' Curiosity Olea said with a smirk as I stepped back out. I ignored him and heard him chuckle as I closed my eyes and tried to regain my composure. My heart was pounding, my head had started to hurt, and all I wanted to do was go home and sob into my pillow while sipping on hot, spiced kashāyam in anticipation of the clogged sinuses all my weeping would bring on.

But I'd left any semblance of home twenty-one jumpgates behind me. If I had any shot at dignity left, I had to go back on set and cook the best meal I'd ever made in my life. And more importantly, I *needed* this—this stage, the validation from total strangers in no way beholden to my family. I couldn't go anywhere near Elé Oota any time soon, not until I regained my shattered self-worth.

I grabbed the insides of my jacket cuffs and squeezed until I could barely feel my hands. And then I let go and opened my eyes. One more minute to go. One more shot. I was *not* going to throw this away.

Uru, heart of the planet Primus, soul of the United
Human Cooperative, has given the universe new
meaning through its art; look no further than the
holoreels of Serenity A'ina, arguably the greatest
director of all time; the scroll-murals of the anonymous
artist, Boundless Vision; the Seventh Sinfoni of
Courage Metta; or the great Primian novels *Black Hole
Sur* by Good Cheer Sol'dad and *One Hundred Years
of Wandering* by Honour Xi'na. The realm of pop
culture is similarly never wanting, with Ur-dramas by
the dozen, the dawn of smooth-synth and smash, the
endless possibilities of Immersive Reality sims...

−Courage Medi,
A Beginner's Guide to Primus, Seventh Edition
2068 Anno Earth | 1993 Interstellar Era

SEVEN

SERENITY KO BELONGED to a small handful of those
cultivated in immaculate taste, capable of translating
it into experiences to meet the ever-evolving needs of an
interstellar audience. Straight out of university, she'd
passed a slate of extremely tricky recruitment challenges set
by XPerience Inc., and they'd immediately filed paperwork
with the Employment Council to requisition her. It wasn't
how things normally worked in Uru, but the Council
subjected her to another series of tests, and classified her
a Techno-Aesthete *Savant*. As a result, she skipped straight
past the apprenticeship she'd been intended for, evaded
mandatory Wanderers service, and found that the reward
for genius was a full-time job where the stakes were always
high, and the pressure never let up.

In downtown Uru, Serenity Ko passed through a tunnel of swirling light and colour. The words *Experience Your Best Life!* pulsed across its walls, rendering differently to each viewer depending upon their sim preferences. Serenity Ko had designed most of the sims herself. She tapped her fingers together to bring them up on her HUD, and they overlaid upon her vision, dimming the flashing lights of reality beyond them. She slid into the Loop and a flip book of options fanned out before her. She waved her forefinger in the air, skimming past her favourite Groove Along, Bubbletown and Electric FloraLand sims all the way to SoundSpace—her latest, and proudest creation.

Her tech scanned the code embedded in the tunnel's walls and pushed a few Loop circuits, with which it was synchronised. Less than a second passed. A sonorous, magnificent theremin flooded Serenity Ko's ossiowave channel, tending towards but never reaching resolution, interspersed with the sparkle of chimes. The tunnel's holographic visuals shimmered and reconfigured to a carefully curated audiovisual experience that celebrated the recent success of XP Inc.

A twenty-something Grace Kube, clean-shaven with long, swept back hair, gives an acceptance speech at the Aesthete Guild; his first demonstration of XP Inc.'s proof of concept.

Serenity Ko grinned at the sight of Kube. He'd been a mentor to her, if a brutally honest one, and she'd done her best to do him proud. She couldn't wait to hear what he had to say to her today. The tunnel walls slid past her as the walkway propelled her forwards, and she heard his raspy voice say '… serenity and harmony…' before the vision changed.

Courage Na'vil wins the United Human Cooperative Award for Outstanding Achievement in Neuropsychology.

Optimism Sah'r peers through a nanoscope, visuals of her slides swirling around her in lo-fi holograms.

Serenity Ko tracked obstacles and people in the tunnel using her HUD. On the map on the bottom right, she caught sight of a small blip, labelled *Curiosity Nenna, She/ Her*, who was gaining ground on her fast. She sighed, and dismissed the SoundScape, right as Nenna appeared at her elbow, brimming with enthusiasm.

'Serenity Ko! How was your nava-end? I had a great time going over the new prototype for OutdoorMax+, and ooh, it's beautiful, but also, I had so many ideas for how we could make it *better*. I was hoping I could run some of them past you this morning!'

'Nenna, you do know you aren't supposed to work over the nava-end, don't you?' Serenity Ko said, frowning.

'Oh, yeah, no, don't worry. I did this in my free time. I mean, my free time away from my free time; that is to say, when I wasn't at the Insomnia Theatre, which I highly recommend... but no, I don't suppose you want *my* pop culture recs—you really are the expert—still, if you were considering an immersive live performance with adaptive sim environments—'

Serenity Ko winced at their newest intern's extraordinary ability to ramble. She'd popped three cleanse compounds an hour ago to counter a terrible hangover, and they were still taking effect, so the hint of a headache lingered at the centre of her forehead.

'—seriously, I followed this one narrative thread into an ancient Earth sim, like pre-war climate catastrophe lush green fields stuff, and I thought, what if we could integrate inter-being histories into our experiences? Imagine—'

'I can see it already!' Serenity Ko said hurriedly, then smiled as Curiosity Nenna's eyes widened in hurt. 'Why don't you draft a holoscroll proposal? We can look at it together, as a design team, and run a brainstorm later this nava.'

Curiosity Nenna beamed, bobbing up and down on the balls of her feet. 'I knew it! Nine Virtues, you're going to love it! I mean, unless you hate it, and I'm totally up for criticism—'

'I love it already. You'll need to convince the others. I know you'll nail it and we'll have a great brainstorm.' Serenity Ko beamed, wondering how to add this sur-fucked meeting to a schedule where she was already double-booked every day of the nava. The tunnel down into XP Inc.'s offices ended at a long, curved flowmetal doorway.

Welcome, Serenity Ko, Techno-Aesthete Savant, Evocateur Elite!

As the doors parted, the office's AI popped her personal goal up on her HUD: *Design the Future of Reality!*

It was coined by Grace Kube as part of his onc-time initiative to inspire his team to grand visions. He'd once proposed that the team spend the work-nava living together in one of the office's commune-pods to bond better. It fell apart faster than it could be implemented when Optimism Terra and Boundless Pico went to war over the former's inability to do their own dishes, aided by Grace Kube's insistence that he alone was exempt from the experiment— their Director of Design had dropped his dream upon his then-enthusiastic but rapidly exhausted second-in-command. Serenity Ko had called it off after three days of failure, and personally delivered the bad news to Kube, who shrugged indifferently and, much to her delight, proceeded to bitch the entire team out to her over cocktails at the Lounge.

Almost in response to this thought, Serenity Ko's stream exploded with messages from her team.

Ko! Where in all the star-fucked galaxy are you? said Courage Praia. *_Help.* The neuros are pummelling the Inner Peace design mod._

A visual of a downward spiral in shades of black and grey under a rain of fireballs filled Serenity Ko's consciousness.

She sighed. Courage Praia might be her best friend in

the office, but they were prone to being too soft-spoken, a natural target for Courage Na'vil and his department.

A stream from Courage Na'vil popped up, right on cue. _Serenity Komala Siriharan, please respond._

Serenity Ko rolled her eyes at this. Nobody, *nobody* on Uru used their given-names and their birth-names together like this after they came of age. Her own *grandmother* didn't call her by her birth-name, and she'd *chosen* it. Courage Na'vil might be a genius, but his second-generation immigrant tendencies shone through every single time. Where was he from? Ko tried to remember. Was it space station Allegro? Or one of those ghastly Fringe worlds? He wasn't Earthling, she recalled. Enceladus? It didn't really matter; he needed to work on it if he wanted to fit in.

Courage Na'vil continued. _Serenity Komala Siriharan, your presence is immediately requested on the sixty-first whorl to arbitrate a dispute between the statistical recommendations of the Neuropsych and Neurophys team and the somewhat ill-informed and intuitive early design of the Inner Peace mod by your own team. Dash informs me that you have been in office for thirty seconds, therefore I assume that you will be able to make it to the Astronomical Club conference room in another four and a half minutes. I look forward to a fruitful and exciting discussion with you._

A field of radiant purple streaked with gold arose to surround the comm.

She ignored the stream from the man she'd titled their Nutter In Chief and walked past the enormous ground floor cafeteria. Visio-nodes across the walls were being used by groups of employees experiencing sims in cliques.

The adreno-bros, their shorts and flip-flops encased in a slim haptic sheet, ran around on a bright green tactile mat, waving their hands in the air and making complex gestures—their haptic implants taking care of in-sim controls—and swearing at each other.

'You sur-fucked savage, cover me! You're supposed to be on my team.'

'It *burns!* It's all over me!'

'I got you.'

Her irises flicked across their visio-node, scanning the shared-stream. It swept across her vision.

The adreno-bros were in a high-intensity collaborative game of *OutCooked 5: Outwit, Outlast, Outcook!* A warpcraft swerved through an asteroid cluster while they struggled to assemble Primian delicacies at their cook station. Serenity Ko stifled a laugh as the swearing escalated.

She flipped through the other entertainment on offer. The suits—in their suits—titillated their limited imaginations by watching graph after graph update from some anecdocumentary on XP Inc.'s competitors. The sub-cults were surprisingly sharing the same space, breathing the same air, and had appeared to put aside their differences on the strongest organic warpcraft transformer in the BioMexx League fandom to watch the latest episode together.

Serenity Ko loved studying people's entertainment choices—they helped inform how she approached designing them. XP Inc. built sims, offering them for subscriptions, bolted onto the Loop. When space exploration had first begun, humans had required external peripherals to access the Loop across star systems, but had then adapted their tech to take the form of bite-sized packets of nanotech. Ingested, it was absorbed into the bloodstream, its synthesised organelles making their way to targeted synapses, bio-circuitry meeting tech wizardry to expand consciousness and processing power. The ancient Earth-civ's semiconductor was a piece of DNA. The last step involved training fingertips to issue haptic commands, carried out in a device that resembled the lovechild of a fingerprint scanner and a nail dryer. It was completely painless. Only tech-backward outer worlds and Fringe planets still used the old tech.

At first, XP Inc.'s offerings had focused on health monitoring and weather warning systems. One thousand years later, they were the gateway to Immersive Reality, where Serenity Ko made dreams come almost-true.

She tutted as an official comm popped up on her HUD.

San*AI: Greetings Ko! This is a reminder to fill out your quarterly evaluation form. This is a great opportunity to reflect upon your contributions to our org's growing success, assess what could have gone better, and inform your goals as we move into the next quarter. Your form is due one nava from now, and we trust you will send it in on time!

Have a great day, from everyone at BR.

A field of buttercups and other flowers blossomed in shades of bright yellow.

Ko dismissed the thoughtstream—Being Resources was the most annoying department in the entire org—and pressed her pinkies together twice to disable all incoming communication.

Her attempt was interrupted. The *one* message she'd been waiting for all morning swooshed in.

Kaapi and a chat in ten? Ideatheque.

She dashed an acceptance back to Grace Kube right away. Here it was, at last: the promotion she'd worked herself near to death for. She took a deep breath, then stepped back into the tunnel and dropped a pin on the Ideatheque whorl. She turned the ossiowave feed up, rubbing her thumb over the tips of all her fingers.

The gentle strains of a key melody streamed across her tympani, drowning out the murmur of tunnel conversation. She smiled and nodded politely at the other people stepping onto it with her, and pointed to her ears to indicate she was occupied. She then leaned against the railing of the walkway, watching faces alight and disembark until she found herself alone, riding all the way to the eighty-seventh whorl.

The XP Inc. offices were designed like a vast flower, rising into a ziggurat as one spiralled inward. It stood out from the tilting, undulating city around it in its gentle rise, but still synchronised with all its decentralised programming to be an optimised part of the greater whole. On some days, the top of the ziggurat was a depression, like a great caldera; on others, it soared into the sky like a spindle. None of this disrupted the inhabitants of the space much, thanks to advanced grav-management systems. Serenity Ko had no way to tell how the building had morphed today.

She stepped off the walkway and took an exit through a doorway shrouded in old-fashioned lightbulbs. Tall potted plants flanked it on either side. She pushed through the flowmetal entrance and into a cool green space trailing decorative plants from the ceiling. Tinted glass windows radiated filtered light. At the centre of the atrium stood a large flowmetal table styled to mimic wood, surrounded by a chaotic assortment of comfortable-looking armchairs.

The Ideatheque.

'I've never been happier to see the inside of this office in my life,' Serenity Ko said, announcing her presence. 'I had *such* a nava-end out on the Ur-sands.'

'Here, have a kaapi and take a seat, Ko.'

Grace Kube, the Director of Design of XP Inc. and the leader of Serenity Ko's team of designers, stepped out from behind a large colaculus plant, blossoming deep scarlet flowers. His skin was sun-kissed and deep brown, the envy of any Primian, though his head was shaved bald and bore the scars of several implants from his younger days as a modder, on the hunt for the most immersive technology available, legal or otherwise.

He held a bright purple mug decorated with sur-flowers. His clothes hung ragged on his lean frame, as if he'd had a violent encounter with a bougainea creeper.

'You look terrible,' Serenity Ko remarked. She tamped down her rising excitement. She could almost *taste* what was about to happen, but she wanted to play it cool, give nothing away.

She accepted the kaapi and placed herself on a squashy blue-patterned wing-chair.

'You look worse,' Grace Kube said, smirking.

Serenity Ko considered bragging about the riot she'd started in the Arc—after all, she'd heard tons of stories from Grace Kube's wild youth, including one in which he'd nearly been abducted by a B'naar gang after first contact, when tensions between humans and the alt-beings were still running high.

'You're thinking of telling me about the riot you started.' Grace Kube took a sip of his coffee, from a black crystal mug. 'We already got a full report and paid for the damage—you're welcome, but of course, I'm sure your version of events will be far more charming. Save it for drinks this evening?'

Serenity Ko kept the muscles in her face calm, but her heart hammered away, parsing every word, twisting it and examining it from every possible angle to try and see what he was hinting at. Drinks in the evening meant the promotion was imminent, surely?

'I wasn't aware we were having a party today,' she said demurely.

'Hmm. *A party* is one way of putting it. I'm sure you know why we're meeting first thing today.'

'Early data is in from the SoundSpace sim,' Serenity Ko said brusquely, trying to fight a smile. 'It's doing really, *really* well. This is our most successful launch yet.'

'It is, isn't it?' Grace Kube said noncommittally, tilting his head to the side and studying his fingers. An awkward silence hung in the air, and Serenity Ko rushed to fill it.

'Well, don't keep me in suspense,' she said. 'Why am I here? Are we discussing next steps? I have a holoscroll proposal for an eighteen-month roadmap. The Evocateurs are already working on Phase Two.'

'Yes, they are,' Grace Kube said. 'So tell me Ko, how do you think you did on this project?'

This was it.

Obviously, her promotion had already been discussed and signed off on by the three heads of XP Inc.—the Triumvirate, as she called them. But Kube wanted to make her work for it, to feel out her capacity for self-assessment, soften any criticism and heap praise upon her successes. It was a classic format for delivering good news—withhold it to retain power, and only deliver congratulations when the person on the other side is reduced to grasping for words. So Serenity Ko performed her end of the dance.

'Right from its conception as an idea, I took charge of the prototype and delivered it in record time, working round the clock with my neurodev team and sim artists. I handpicked the Evocateurs who worked with me once we were greenlit— nobody with less than two years' experience, given the ambitious adoption targets for SoundSpace. We sampled music from across the cosmos, live-gigged it, listened to ancient Earth archives, sampled billions of holos, worked with the musicians at the Sinfonia and the Archivists on Music Theory, and I was there *in every meeting*, making sure I weighed in on *every decision*.' Serenity Ko allowed herself a little self-satisfaction. 'Were there things I could have done better? Yes. I could have been nicer to the team. Maybe I could have given them more time off...'

Her voice trailed off as she registered the absence of any kind of enthusiasm in Grace Kube's expression.

'What is it?' she asked nervously, genuinely anxious, then laughed. 'Did I break the bar on all performance calibrations?'

Grace Kube took a sip of his kaapi and studied her. 'Well...'

'Well?'

'You certainly worked very hard.'

'Uh-huh.'

'But did you work *smart*, Serenity Ko?'

'What?'

Serenity Ko nearly dropped her kaapi mug, and the microcrystalline foam sloshed over her hands. 'You mean, did I deliver only the most successful piece of Immersive Reality that XP Inc. has ever created?'

Grace Kube sighed. 'Is it a stellar success? Yes. Is it all because of you? Nope. In fact, I'd venture to go so far as to say it's successful *in spite* of you.'

Hot tears of rage simmered at the edges of Serenity Ko's eyes and she blinked them back. Grace Kube didn't notice, but ploughed on. 'You want to be an Evocateur Extraordinaire, yes? You came in here fully expecting to be promoted, and why wouldn't you be? Impeccable track record, obsessive work on SoundSpace, et cetera. An Evocateur Extraordinaire is a leader, a visionary, a dreamer who doesn't try and do everything on their own, who recognises that Primian culture is about harmony, not power. The position demands teamwork, delegation, give and take...'

'So you're telling me that my commitment, dedication and passion were *bad things?*' Serenity Ko's vision swum.

'You need to know when to let go. It's not the end that counts, but the means by which it's achieved.'

'You're going to go all cosmic guru on me? Really?' Rage pulsed against the insides of her skull. Serenity Ko tasted salt at the back of her throat.

She placed the coffee mug on the table and rose to her feet. 'This is bullshit and you know it. Nine Virtues, what is it? Are we facing cost-cutting? Well, haha, I just delivered a great top-line solution with SoundSpace. Is it Honour Aki? Did he bitch me out?'

A look of confusion crossed Grace Kube's face, and Serenity Ko hurried to cover it up. 'Is it the fact that I'm only the best damned Evocateur Elite ever to work here, Techno-Aesthete *Savant* I'll remind you, and it makes you insecure that I'll have *your* sur-fucked job in the next year if I keep going the way I am?'

Grace Kube didn't flinch. He managed to look *bored*.

Serenity Ko wiped the tears from her cheeks in embarrassment.

'Anyway, Ko,' Grace Kube carried on after a moment. 'I'm putting you on mandatory leave for two navas so you can calm down and gather your thoughts. Reframe your perspective on your role at XP Inc. Think about your personal goal, long and hard. Come back refreshed.'

'You're... you're *firing* me?' Serenity Ko sputtered.

'It's not garden leave. It's a sabbatical.'

'This is outrageous!' Serenity Ko snapped.

'I'm sorry you feel that way.'

'This is an affront to everything I've done for this org!'

'It's constructive feedback.'

'I can't believe you'd stab me in the back like this, Kube,' Serenity Ko said coldly.

'There, there. Let me buy you a drink this evening to commiserate.'

'No, thanks.'

Serenity Ko turned to leave.

'Offer stands until the end of the workday. Have a great vacation!' she heard him call from behind her.

Serenity Ko slammed the door to the atrium shut behind her and kicked the potted plant at the entrance. It hurt.

Fire is the favoured recourse of barbarians.

—Grace Menmo,
from the sim *At Home in the Kitchen*
2065 Anno Earth | 1990 Interstellar Era

EIGHT

MY HANDS WORKED on autopilot as I set up my mise en place. The contestants around me faded to a blur in my peripheral vision, though years of working in professional kitchens made it impossible to tune them out completely. I was hyperaware of the clockwork rhythms of each knife snicking into its cutting board, a syncopated drumbeat punctuated by the occasional scrape and crack. I spotted seven different kinds of vat-grown protein and over a dozen sources of vegetable and fruit ras, every flowmetal counter morphing into a different appliance even as my entire being zoned into a dish that was my origin story as a chef.

Now look, if I *really* wanted to guarantee my acceptance on this show, I'd have chosen to make something Primian. I'd studied their techniques, and even though I'd never had the chance to use them in the kitchen, I was fairly confident in my ability to create something respectable. A safer bet would have been to create something that bridged the gap between our culinary worlds—an Earth-origin dish "elevated" by Primian technique. But I found that surfucking pretentious, and that wasn't why I was here in the first place.

I was here to win with the food I'd been making for decades, that had earned me a spot on Earth's culinary scene.

Also the food that shattered your self-esteem—don't forget how it all ended.

I shoved the dark thought away, organising my space and going over the recipe in my head.

I'd spent the first seven minutes after the restart configuring my cook station, not just to make sure I'd have access to all the tools I needed, but also to double-check that I wouldn't set off any more alarms.

I grabbed my ingredients from the pantry, earning a few curious stares as I tossed whole onions, tomatoes, inji, garlic and other vegetables into my basket.

'*Savage,*' someone muttered. Primians prided themselves on their restraint, picking *one* of each kind and distilling its flavour, infusing it in some sort of inevitable pâté or terrine. *Sorry folks, on Earth we like our flavours bold and our ingredients chunky.*

I ignored the other contestants, grabbing a bundle of cilantro and four entire banana leaves. I was delighted to discover the latter; I'd resigned myself to substituting it with some kind of metallic foil. Earth vegetation was notoriously controlled on this planet, from everything I knew, and aluminium had long since been banned. Even better, I found actual whole spices. I'm sure there were Primian protocols for how to use them, but I picked entire jars of them from the shelves. None of their names was familiar, so I had to sniff, taste and take my chances on what I thought would work best together.

There was no karimeen to be had on Primus—to be fair, it was scarcely found in the wild on Earth—so I chose a similarly textured vat-grown fish from the freshwater display.

The cam-drones around me flew in close as I ground local drylands chilli and black peprino-corns together using a mortar and pestle. I brought the spices together in a large glass bowl, blending quantities intuitively without measures, sprinkling cilantrina powder in, with pinches of turmeric and salt, tasting—always tasting—to make sure the different kinds of heat were all balanced. I ground inji and garlic into a paste and added it to the bowl.

I'd learned to think of the optimal flavour for this marinade as a mouth-watering sucker punch to the senses. That wasn't an original thought I could take credit for; Kanakamma, our family cook while I was growing up, had said as much the first time I'd traipsed down to the kitchen, all of eleven years old, to learn what this extraordinary fish, served at our dinner table wrapped in a banana leaf, had been. My parents and my sister had treated it like every other meal we'd ever had, choosing to spend the meal discussing a strategic alliance with the Tunga family, but I hadn't heard a word, consumed entirely with the fiery feast on my plate.

Kanakamma had been my first teacher in the kitchen. It was *her* knife technique—not something I'd learnt at my fancy culinary school back on Earth—that I used now, as I carefully cleaned, de-finned and deboned the fish. I was going to present the fish whole, to whip up a spot of shock and awe in the judges.

This recipe was my making and my undoing. It had inspired me to sneak down to the kitchens every chance I got, to tinker with food and experiment with flavour, when ideally—according to my parents, at least—I should have been studying the geopolitical history of Daxina and its role on One Nation Earth, and learning how to bedeck myself with gemstones to impress state dignitaries.

I salted and laid the fish to rest a while, before marinading it, and had moved on to dicing vegetables when I heard a voice say: 'Interesting technique, Chef. Whole vegetables. Are you sure that's not excessive?'

I glanced up to see Harmony Rhea hovering by my cook station. One of the cam-drones focused on her, while another continued to film my hands in action.

'I'm from Earth, where traditional cooking uses whole vegetables, unlike on Primus.' I smiled.

'I'd have thought you'd come here to make Primian food, like all the rest,' she said, throwing her hand out to indicate the other contestants. 'After all, it's the only way to find a place in any kitchen in Uru.'

'I'm here to represent my culture,' I part-lied. 'Uru's kitchens and their opinions of me are a secondary consideration.'

'Bold.' Harmony Rhea's lips curved in a supercilious smile. 'Coming from a planet steeped in antiquity, I look forward to encountering the... *culture* you're so keen to demonstrate.'

She strutted away, and I kept my smile plastered to my face as a cam-drone lingered on me for a reaction.

I placed my prepped fish in a bowl, and spooned marinade on top of it.

I was here to represent my culture, that much was true. But if I was being really honest, I was here to represent *me*. Sure, I was a product of that culture, and I'd mastered it and thrived. And then there'd been the unpleasant incident, when my accomplishments were diminished, and my credibility questioned...

Don't go there, idiot. Focus.

Right, I wasn't going there, not now. There were real reasons I'd shut down Elé Oota after an unprecedented run of success, paid my carefully curated team of chefs six months' severance, used the rest of my savings to fake my documents so I could apply for a refugee visa, falsified my last name, shorn my hair off and had nanobleach therapy to lighten my skin unrecognisably, and taken a freighter through twenty-one jumpgates to get here.

My stovetop ignited with a *whoosh*. I threw a pan on and dropped some thenganut oil in, followed by my whole fish. As it sizzled, I became aware of a loud silence around me.

I looked up.

Every single chef had stopped work at their stations, and

they were all gazing at me open-mouthed (except for the E'nemon and the B'naar chefs, who didn't have hominid facial features).

I flashed them a thumbs up.

'My, my, *fire!* Our Earthling chef's gone ahead with it, after all!' Grace Aurelle announced loudly for the benefit of the cam-drones flocking around her.

The other chefs continued to stare. To my left, the heavily-pierced chef who'd looked through me at the start began to cough, and glared at me as she resumed whatever she was doing with a syringe and some kind of sous-vide machine.

I worked the intensity of the flame as the oil sputtered and the pungent aroma of frying fish filled the air. Perhaps I'd watched one Ur-drama too many, maybe I was just an egomaniac on a mission, but when I won this show, I intended to reveal my true identity, to precisely zero shock and awe here on Primus—because Earth-politics were a distant not-problem to them—but to considerable dramatic effect back on my home planet.

That'll show them. That'll teach them they can't destroy me with words, that I don't need them.

I pulled the fish out and laid it to rest on the side, putting my arasi accompaniment in a pressure cooker to steam, before moving onto my chunky tomato curry.

I stir-fried onions, heaped in finely chopped tomatoes and began humming to myself. I stirred in some locally grown substitute for curry leaves, poured in a paste made from puli and water, and let the vegetables simmer and reduce. I grated and sprinkled thenganut generously onto it, adding cilantrina, doing everything on instinct just as Kanakamma had taught me.

She'd been fired when they discovered I was learning how to cook from her instead of going to my after-school private tutoring—that bastard Chicko had ratted me out. All my tantrums had come to nothing. And when I opened

Elé Oota and tried to locate her to hire her, there'd been no trace of her in all of Daxina.

I tasted, made some adjustments, then added my fish to the chunky sauce, coating it and basting it.

With family like mine, who needs enemies?

I glanced up at the clock. Twenty minutes to go.

I prepped my banana leaves, heating them one at a time over a low flame, then removing their central rib to make them more pliable.

I garnished a banana leaf with oil and condiments, heaped sauce on it, followed by the fish, now coated and fragrant as a summer's day by a placid sea—at least, according to the history holoscrolls; we didn't have placid seas on Earth any more. I wrapped it all up, tying it with twine and placing it in another pan, lined with oil.

The scent that filled the air took me right back to my home kitchen as child, to Elé Oota where we'd prepped and served this dish hundreds of times, to a whole career that had risen like a star and then fallen like a meteorite.

I'm going to take it all back.

I covered the pan with a lid, lowered the flame, and stepped back, eyeing my handiwork with pride. I released the pressure from the cooker and retrieved my steamed arasi, placing it in a small bowl. I then turned the banana-leaf-encased fish over, letting the other side cook. Five minutes to go.

I began plating, my hands steady as I composed my dish. I had no idea how they'd react to it on Primus, but it was all me. And I dared them to say anything negative about the flavours, or its authenticity as Earth food.

The judges began their countdown. I held my hands up to signal I was done, and my flowmetal counter encapsulated my dish in a transparent heatsheet that would hold it at its current temperature.

'Three... two... one!'

A loud ding sounded around the kitchen. Someone

groaned off to my left. To my right, I heard a string of cusswords, and saw one of the identical twins kick their station and wince—they'd left an elaborate layered gelée marbled with rainbow colours off their plate.

'Well done, chefs!' Grace Aurelle proclaimed, bringing her hands together in applause. 'We're really excited to be tasting your signature dishes, and will be summoning you one at a time to present them to us.'

The first chef summoned was the one to my left. Her name, it turned out, was Optimism Chloe, and she presented an elaborate braised meat dish, featuring a vat-grown protein heavily infused with an assortment of vegetable ras. She explained how it symbolised her personality and her relationship to food—a common Primian practice I found particularly dull, unimaginative and facile, if anyone cared to ask for my opinion.

'I admire your restraint. Your presentation evokes the minimalist tradition of the Nakshatrans,' Harmony Rhea trilled.

'Flavours are balanced, delicate,' muttered Courage Ab'dal. She was sent back with applause, and the next chef was called forwards. I zoned out as polite comments, rave reviews and blistering critiques made their dutiful way out of the judges' mouths. Most curious were Pavi and Amol Khurshid—two chefs whose names I was most familiar with, owing to their Earth-origins—who offered scathing criticisms of everything that passed their palates. The B'naar contestant to my right was given encouragement, though advised to work on xir kneading technique for the dough xe'd used in xir mayberry tartlets.

I didn't register them calling my name until all eyes turned to look at me.

'Our own fire-starter from Earth.' Grace Aurelle smiled, though it didn't reach her eyes. 'Please step forwards and let us taste the delectable fare you have to offer.'

I stumbled towards my dish, a bead of sweat trickling down my brow. I scooped it up in my hands and walked towards the judges' table, at the centre of the circle, with all the confidence I could muster. Cam-drones flitted around me.

'And what have we here?' Grace Aurelle asked, raising an eyebrow as I placed my plate on the table for all to see. The cam-drones zoomed in, their wings a blur as they attempted to cover my dish from every possible angle.

'Meen pollichathu,' I said coolly, ignoring my thudding heart. 'A traditional dish from the coast of the Daxina Protectorate on One Nation Earth.'

'Could we have that in Vox, please?' Pavi Khurshid asked coldly, to much snickering around her.

'Er, right…' I cleared my throat. *Keep calm. This isn't any worse than Ahana Shah at Nizami.* 'It's spiced fish fried in a banana leaf, served with a side of steamed grain.'

'How… *humble.*' Courage Ab'dal wrinkled their nose, poking at the banana leaf with a finger.

'Presentation lacking,' Harmony Rhea crowed. 'How is this supposed to represent you? Or is this supposed to indicate you're a mess, just like your home planet?'

The words hit me like a slap across the face. That was positively xenophobic. I might have been imagining it, but Harmony Rhea cast a sidelong glance at the Khurshid siblings.

I stood my ground. 'This is how it's traditionally presented. It's an ancient dish, dating all the way back to pre-One Nation days—'

'Fascinating,' Grace Aurelle said, cutting me off. 'But how does it represent *you*? What makes it your signature?'

This was not how I'd envisioned this going down at all. I knew I'd taken a risk by not creating something Primian, but this hostility was unexpected, especially before they'd even taken a bite. I'd watched fifteen seasons of this show and it never went this way.

'It's the dish that made me fall in love with food. It's the reason I decided I wanted to cook for the rest of my life.'

'Cute,' Harmony Rhea rolled her eyes. 'It certainly *looks* amateur.'

There was tittering from all round us.

'I haven't delved into the symbolism of all the ingredients I've used,' I said, drawing on my strength. 'I believe that food possesses a history that goes beyond its creator, encompasses the world that produces it, and is forgotten the moment someone else savours it, drawing it into their own story and breathing a second life into it. I know that's not how it's done on Primus—every ingredient here has its own meaning. But this is my personal philosophy.'

'Lofty.' Courage Ab'dal smirked.

'The proof's in the eating,' Grace Aurelle chimed in. 'Alas, there's only one enormous banana-leaf wrapped package on the plate.'

'I'll go first,' Harmony Rhea said. She picked it up and her perfectly painted lips parted to bite into it.

'No!' I said.

'Stop!' Amol cried.

'Don't do it!' Pavi shrieked.

The other judges stared at the only Earthlings in the room in some confusion.

'You've got to unwrap it,' I explained, heat rising to my cheeks.

'Quaint,' muttered Harmony Rhea.

'Inconvenient,' said Courage Ab'dal.

Grace Aurelle said nothing, only eyed the Khurshid siblings for a long, cool second. 'I believe we should let our *Earth-origin* judges taste this,' she said slyly. 'After all, none of the rest of us has any experience with *Earth* cuisine, so we'd best leave it to the experts, hmm?'

I glanced at Pavi and Amol, who regarded me indifferently. A little pinprick of hope welled up within me. They were

Earthling immigrants, familiar with these flavours from their past, even if they'd left them behind and reinvented themselves on Primus. Surely anything they said couldn't be as cruel as the other judges' opinions so far.

Amol unwrapped the banana leaf, and prodded the fish with his fingers.

'I'll tell you what I see,' he said quietly. 'I see hubris. I see wastefulness. I see all of Earth's baggage and philosophy wrapped up in this singular dish.'

'Whole vegetables, diced and liberally used,' Pavi said with disapproval. '*Barbaric.*'

'Cooked over an open flame,' Amol said. 'Such a violent act of transformation.'

'*Archaic,*' Pavi pronounced.

My knees buckled. *I must have misheard.*

'Let's taste?' Amol turned to his sister. He scooped a piece of fish off and mixed it into the rice, popping it into his mouth. His face contorted, his eyes closing as he drew deep breaths and swallowed. He ran his tongue over his lips before his mouth settled into a grim line.

Pavi followed. Her eyes widened as she chewed, sweat breaking out on her brow. When she swallowed, her shoulders relaxed for a moment and then she snapped to attention.

They were unreadable.

'Well?' Grace Aurelle prompted.

The entire set was silent. All the cam-drones hovered in on us, and I felt sweat trickling into the small of my back.

The sibling celebrity chefs exchanged a glance.

'Overspiced. Zero subtlety,' Amol said.

'Texturally vulgar,' Pavi added.

'You've made it a long way to demonstrate to the entire universe that you can't cook.' Amol looked me in the eyes as he said this, his gaze unwavering. He knocked on my dish twice and shook his head in disapproval.

Pavi turned and walked away, reaching for a napkin and wiping her hands. 'You'll never make it as a chef.'

I blinked back hot tears of rage. *This isn't happening. This can't be happening.*

Grace Aurelle waved her hand towards the dish in dismissal. I picked it up and returned to my station, trembling all over.

I should say something. I should tell them who I am. I can't; it'll make no difference to them.

My thoughts were a ragged tumble of contradictions.

I ran fucking Elé Oota. They're privileged I'm cooking for them at all. I don't need their validation.

A small voice piped up in the back of my head. *Well, if you don't need their validation, why are you here?*

I blanked out while the rest of the contestants' plates were offered up for judgment. I'd come here to win. I'd been prepared to lose, but I hadn't expected to be *disgraced*.

Time crawled like an insect down my spine as the chefs made their way through the last few contestants' food. I awaited the inevitable relegation. It arrived interminable hours later. The bottom three were called to the centre of the floor. I pressed my hand down onto the counter to steady myself, and closed my eyes, counting to ten, acutely aware of the cam-drones still on me. I reopened them, head spinning, and walked to my spot.

The twin who'd left a critical component off their dish was with me, and so was another chef whose appraisal I hadn't bothered paying attention to.

'The judges have made their decision,' Grace Aurelle announced. 'Saraswati Kaveri, please hand in your chef's jacket.'

Hands trembling, I unbuttoned it, stepped forwards and placed it in her hands. Her eyes twinkled in amusement. I shook hands with each judge, muttering something noncommittal about being grateful for the opportunity.

Amol Khurshid grasped my hand and shook it firmly. I felt something pass from his to mine.

I stepped away, out of the glare of the spotlights, beyond the reach of the cam-drones and back through the trellis-styled flowmetal doors that I'd been certain had opened onto the pathway to my dreams. They slammed shut behind me.

I stopped, my chest heaving, my breathing ragged. I looked around me. The room was empty. I ran.

In the bathrooms, I bolted myself into a stall and doubled over, hyperventilating. I dropped something in my hand and looked down. It was a physical card, an old-fashioned thing crafted from papyro-scroll.

Amol Khurshid
Head Chef & Owner
Nonpareil
Collective Four, Uru

Amol had scrawled a note beneath it.

Call me if you ever need a job

I picked it up and stared. I flipped it over. Stared at it again.

What the actual fuck?

And then the tears came.

Shaking, doubled over, ugly crying my little heart out, I part-laughed, mostly-sobbed at the absurdity of it all.

Courage Meri: I need a holiday!

Tera Berra: Ugh. So do I. I can't wait for our term exams to be done. I hear there are mine trams in the Osmos Girdle, an entire underwater city on Sagaricus. The Suriyan flares are gorgeous where I live on Harid.

[Courage Meri sighs]

Tera Berra: Ooh! Meri! Come home with me for winter break!

Courage Meri: I could...

Tera Berra: You could, but...

Courage Meri: I need a holiday at home. Back on Primus. I miss my family...

—from *Teen Trouble*, Season 3, Episode 9
2058 Anno Earth | 1983 Interstellar Era

NINE

Serenity Ko squinted into the brightness of reality. Her preferred optics had glitched when her pod entered the flowtram tunnel. XP Inc. was supposed to have seamless Loop transmission, and that something as simple as a wall of natural rock had caused it to disconnect for a few seconds was annoying. The bright lights of the pod around her did nothing for her headache; perhaps she shouldn't have spent the evening out with Courage Praia plotting Grace Kube's demise over shots of FireSpirit. She definitely shouldn't have hooked up with Honour Aki right afterward, but she'd been wasted and he'd thoughtstreamed, and now she had nothing but regrets and fifteen pings from him that morning already, all of which she was avoiding as she made her way to her parents' space in the Nineteenth Collective.

Uru curled on itself like a nautilus shell, divided into forty-two Collectives and currently growing ever so slowly into its forty-third. Heart Station connected them all via flowtram, right at the centre of the city in Collective One. Along its curvature, forming the borders of each Collective, swathes of woodland grew where it had always grown, forming public gardens—some manicured, some grown wild—all the way to the Urswood region of the Arc, surrounding the city on all sides.

Flowtram pods travelled overland, underground, and occasionally overhead on maglev tracks above the groves and gardens, marketplaces and monuments; efficient and scenic all at once. As her pod resurfaced, Serenity Ko was entirely indifferent to the looping, physics-defying Unity River monument, while a pair of off-world tourists seated across from her pulled out physical memcorders and took a flurry of holosnaps. The commemorative water feature at the heart of the Fifteenth Collective celebrated humanity's first contact with intelligent life, and as the vehicle stopped at Unity Station, half its passengers stepped off it.

Serenity Ko's fingers tapped against each other as she flicked through the visio-filters in her library, trying to find the right one to let just the right amount of sunlight filter through. She hated last-minute travel plans, and being outdoors and on the move was the worst—especially since the route from her living space in the Ninth Collective often coincided with the tourist trail of Uru—but her sibling had streamed her late the previous night.

Family dinner tomorrow, big news! he'd said.

Serenity Ko was looking forward to nothing less than having to admit to her family that she hadn't landed the promotion for the sim that she'd dodged calls, missed festivals, and skipped about forty-one family dinners for. The thought of having no big news to compete with her sibling's own—and really, what on earth could it be?—was galling.

The fingers of her right hand twitched like those of a Rumian monk counting energy beads, and she breathed a sigh of relief as her favourite cloudy filter triggered her bio-circuitry, limiting the light levels her eyes were processing. Then she scowled. She'd had to manually reset her reality filters. Terrible user experience. She'd have to address the issue at the earliest meeting, brainstorm a solution with the neurodevs, and have it prioritised on their Optics roadmap.

She tapped her thumb and forefinger together. The XP Inc. dash rolled across her field of vision. Her comms inbox had eighty unread messages from the last hour. She was tagged on sixty-five messages.

She streamed a meeting invite.

Fixes to Optical Reality Filters

Optic Filters reset with real-world interference, need manual reset

P0: Solve for UX

Brainstorm: 19:00 hours UT

A notif popped up.

XP Inc. comms temporarily disabled! See you in two nava, and happy holidays!

'Kube, you star-fucker!' Serenity Ko swore, earning herself a filthy look from a tourist who'd just boarded the pod, two kids in tow, one of whom dropped their sorbetto cone and burst into tears.

She stared out the window. The flowtram zoomed over the heavy flowstone mantapas of the Vyāsr faith at the edge of the Nineteenth Collective. Serenity Ko shut her eyes, refusing to look down through the transparent undercarriage. She hated it when she hit the maglev section of this route home. The craft descended rapidly, swaying all the way down. It touched solid ground with a gentle bump, and the core purred softly. Flowmetal rippled as the doorways pulled apart, and Serenity Ko stepped from one of the craft's many exits, her knees wobbling.

The station was an immense maze that lay open to the sky, arranged in concentric whorls like the petals of a rosa-bud. Flowtram platforms and lines were laid out on parallel tracks all along ground level. On the upper stories, set back from the centre of the station, sub-orbital ships of various shapes and sizes, alloys and technologies docked in neat lines on landing pads for as far as the eye could see. Ko spotted a vintage N-71 from the earliest settler days, and marvelled that it was still in running condition. Lights flashed from the ceilings, highlighting their path into the crowded pedestrian corridors on either side.

Muted conversations reached her as she strode through the ever-shifting whorls towards the exit.

'I wonder what traffic is like at noon.'

'In the city, you can bet it's a disaster—'

Serenity Ko directed a quick glance at the speaker. They had greendust jewellery woven into their hair, and they wore large feathered earrings that fell all the way to their navel. Dream-priests from the Urwoods monastery always bemoaned life in the city. Serenity Ko was tempted to point out that this was how the *real world* worked, but thought better of it.

She quickened her pace through the maze of bridges and corridors until she reached the exit. Her eyes scanned the crowd at the terminus, in search of a familiar face.

She grinned and waved. 'Amma!'

She ran up to her mother and gave her a tight hug.

'You've lost weight!' her mother said. The corners of her eyes crinkled.

'This already? Give me a break. You have no idea what I've just been through—'

'It's a compliment!'

'No, it isn't. You're *constantly* assessing me—'

'Okay, I'm sorry for saying nice things. How was your ride here?'

'Eh, the usual commuter boredom,' Serenity Ko said. 'You didn't have to pick me up.'

Her mother eyed her appraisingly. 'The last time you announced you were coming home mid-nava and staying for a while, a girl named Harmony Tara had just broken your heart.'

'Unfair,' Serenity Ko sulked. 'I'm only here because Rihan said he had big news.'

'In the middle of the morning?' Her mother's nostrils flared. 'C'mon, kiddo. Everyone knows you're a workaholic.'

'Can we talk about this later?' Serenity Ko's hands twitched. 'At least this time I'm not wasted and weeping, and it isn't the middle of the night.'

They passed through the Circle, the station's carefully designed outdoor shopping area. Restaurant fronts offered seating; knick-knacks and baubles glittered at every gift shop and tourist trap. A group of Wanderers were silently protesting in its central atrium, carrying signs that read *Fix Anti-Nakshatran Consumerism*, *Escapism is Indifference*, and *Sims are Not Reality*, among other equally un-catchy slogans. The human in greendust jewellery from the tunnel stood at a counter where pedestrians could volunteer to be Wanderers. Serenity Ko rolled her eyes.

'Are you hungry?' her mother asked.

'Nope, I had quite a big breakfast,' she lied, stomach rumbling as she sped up and desperately tried to distract her mother as they passed the greenhouse.

'Ooh! Look, they have such lovely astrianas!'

'Can't we just go home?' Serenity Ko whined.

Her mother drew to an abrupt halt, admiring the potted plants on display. Astranias grew in concentric rings, seven slender tubular petals at a time, each a different colour. 'You know, I think we may be able to squeeze a couple into our garden. We have some wiggle-room for non-essential plants, especially after we installed the hydroponics section.'

'Don't you want to save it for some more patchy plants that look like they have a disease?' Serenity Ko giggled when her mother rose to the bait.

'Coleus is marvellous!' Her mother's eyes glinted dangerously, daring her daughter to argue. 'It was brought here all the way from the Earth, with the first settlers. And your Ammamma will really appreciate some…'

Serenity Ko let out an exasperated sigh. Her mother had won. If there was anyone she had a soft spot for—and was equally terrified by—it was her grandmother.

The man at the storefront abruptly appeared by her mother's side, as if sensing the cracks in their collective resolve. Serenity Ko leaned back and watched her mother step through the intricate turns of haggling over the price. Her face was animated, frizzy hair blowing in the wind, a wide open smile giving way to a slight frown, her eyes sharp and focused one moment, and then friendly, conspiratorial, as the conversation intensified. The shopkeeper suddenly acquiesced, shaking his head with a wry smile.

Her mother then spent the better part of ten minutes picking six perfect potted astrianas. Serenity Ko was only half-listening as she explained why she'd chosen each one. Fatigue washed over her, mixed with undertones of warmth and contentment.

A dronelift carried the plants, following them down the pathway to their vehicle.

'I talked him down to four thousand creds for six,' her mother beamed. 'Three for me, three for your grandmother.'

'You live in the same house,' Serenity Ko huffed.

'Yes, but we cannot agree on what makes the perfect garden, and you know this.'

'Kaapi?' Serenity Ko suggested weakly.

'Good idea. Go pick some up.'

Serenity Ko staggered over to the Kaapinated stall and ordered two organic, low-chicory kaapis with extra cream. She wanted nothing more than to fall asleep in her own bed, and it conflicted with her growing need to respond to her comms. Her fingers twitched like those of a sim addict with Haptic Shock Syndrome.

This was beginning to feel like every other vacation she'd never been on ever since she'd started work at XP Inc. All she wanted was to be back in the office, to prove that star-fucked dictator Grace Kube wrong. She fought her jittery fingers, desperate to get back into the fray. She pulled up her dash, and took a look at her to-do list. There were over a dozen meetings listed for the nava—she'd internally categorised all of them as high priority, and she was now unable to attend any of them because Grace Kube had locked her out. Her last comm was from Courage Na'vil, who'd sent her a strongly-worded note about her unavailability at such a "critical juncture," as he'd put it.

I'd have expected a tad more professionalism from you, but perhaps maturity is a skill that you are yet to learn on the job, so I shall suffer your irresponsibility in patience. I am revising the meeting invite to...

Serenity Ko resisted the urge to publicise her thoughtstream, which was currently filled with colourful expletives. She was hot all over, pins and needles creeping through her fingertips. A trickle of sweat ran down her nose and she scowled at the abrupt change in temperature.

'Ko, you're looking a bit peaky.' Her mother appeared at her side.

'It's nothing, work stuff...'

'Are you all right?' Her mother pressed the back of her hand to Serenity Ko's forehead, irises flickering across what must have been a temperature read on her dash. 'You're burning up!'

'Allergies?' Serenity Ko suggested vaguely. Her head was

a bit foggy. Maybe she just needed to lie down. It had been an absurd two days. One riot, one non-promotion, more alcoholic beverages than she could count...

She lost track of what her mother said next and stumbled over her own feet. Her knees were weak, incapable of holding the rest of her up. Someone grabbed her and propped her up.

'Amma?' she said uncertainly.

The world was far too bright; in fact, it was pockmarked with craters of light. Where were her visio-filters when she needed them? She tapped her thumb and forefinger together to pull them up and a warning flashed across her dash. She tried to read it but the letters were blurry. A voice spoke out—or was it in her mind?

Energy to bio-circuitry low, currently offline. Full body scan reveals temperature is far above normal, rerouting circuitry to investigate and take homeostatic measures...

Serenity Ko swayed.

She stood at the foot of a steep staircase. It coiled around another tall stairway, a double helix spiral leading up and up and up to somewhere she didn't know. It was a climb she knew she had to make, and she placed a foot tentatively upon the first stair. Her footstep sounded like a chime, ringing clear and high into the darkness around her. The stairway glowed with a light of its own.

Serenity Ko stepped forwards, and a new note echoed around the mysterious chamber she was in. A sense of urgency filled her; she had to get to the top. She took the stairs two at a time. A chorus of chimes filled the air, a harmony so strange it should not have existed.

Is this a SoundSpace sim? She needed to find this band.

She sped on into the darkness, her excitement growing with every turn of the stairway, her foot never missing a step, her hand sliding along the banister. She heard voices calling her name.

Something crunched. She looked down. There was a crack on the stair beneath her bare foot. It spread outward. The next stair she stepped on shattered the spell of the melody, replaced by a rising dissonance. She held her breath as pieces of stairway slid into the deep darkness below. The twin stairway coiled, twisting and spinning as if it were a writhing beast stirring into life. It leaned dangerously inward. It mirrored, replicated, cracking and splintering. More crashes and clangs with every step, a cascade of discord swirling around her. Serenity Ko looked up, her breath coming in heavy gasps. It was unravelling from the top, unwinding. She closed her eyes and braced herself for the inevitable impact. It spun faster than thought, flinging her out into the endless dark.

Serenity Ko got to her feet shakily and found herself on stage. She was naked. All the lights were on her. And everyone she had ever known was in the audience: her parents, her grandmother, her brother, all her colleagues at XP Inc., ex-lovers, former friends...

'Does anyone have a t-shirt I can borrow? A robe?' she called, horribly embarrassed.

Their faces regarded her in stony silence.

She fled, or tried to. She was rooted to the spot, unable to move, the lights growing ever brighter. One by one, everyone in the audience left, until it was just her family. They rose as one, as if they were attached to each other in their vegetative wordlessness, and shuffled away.

'Amma?' she asked, her voice plaintive. Her mother didn't look back.

Serenity Ko was alone.

The ground caved beneath her. She fell into thin air, floating down with impossible velocity into what seemed to be a warm bed. She couldn't move. She was trapped in it, held firmly in place by heaped blankets. Her eyes ached.

She summoned all her energy and rolled, and the world

tilted so she was standing on a wall-that-was-now-floor, the bedroom furniture suspended at shoulder-height on one side, light fixtures blazing radiant on the other like a million little stars all defying gravity. Ko fell to her knees and crawled down the wall-that-was-now-floor towards the window. It was sealed shut.

'Help!' Serenity Ko cried. 'Let me out!'

'Ko,' a voice soothed.

'Amma?'

'Ko. Come, get back into bed.'

A pair of arms wrapped around her, helping her up and guiding her back to a soft mattress, a pile of pillows and blankets, and into the comfort of a hug.

'Don't leave me,' Serenity Ko moaned.

'Of course I won't,' her mother said.

'Nobody loves me.'

'Silly girl,' her mother stroked her hair. 'We all love you to bits.'

Serenity Ko's eyes flew open. 'Where am I?'

'Home.'

'RASAM GRAIN-PULP.'

'I have no appetite, Ammamma,' Serenity Ko said slowly, the words thick and heavy on her tongue. She was propped up in bed, leaning against the pillows and generally feeling like she'd like nothing more than to bellyflop all over them and return to unconsciousness.

Her grandmother tutted, and stirred a spoon into the steaming hot broth she held in a bowl on her lap. The pungency of tamarind-ras rose into the air, mildly infused with peprino-corns and cilantrina. She filled a spoon and held it out to Serenity Ko, ancient hands trembling.

'Eat,' she insisted. 'I even mixed in extra ghee, just the way you like it.'

Serenity Ko scowled, parted her lips with reluctance, and obeyed.

The heat spread through the insides of her mouth, searing her upper palate and awakening her dulled sinuses. 'Ammamma, your rasam grain-pulp remains the best ever, even after—'

Her grandmother cut her short with another spoonful of flavour. 'What's stressing you out so badly, hmm?' she asked sternly.

Serenity Ko fell silent.

'You're dehydrated. We had to use saline-bots to feed you these last two days,' her grandmother said. 'You've been delirious. Not another heartbreak?'

Serenity Ko sulked. 'No.'

'You're here for a while, your mother says. So a work thing?'

Serenity Ko exploded. She threw her hands up and buried her head in them. 'I didn't get the promotion, all right? I'm a failure. There! Will everyone leave me alone now?'

Her grandmother frowned in puzzlement. 'Who said you're a failure?'

'Everyone. Kube froze me out with some obscure excuses and put me on two navas' leave. The star-fucker.'

'Don't swear,' her grandmother hissed. She shoved another spoonful of broth down Serenity Ko's throat. 'Did he call you a failure?'

'No, but… I was *supposed* to be promoted!' Serenity Ko spluttered.

'Don't talk with your mouth full.' Her grandmother's face registered disdain. 'Doesn't make you a failure, though. Who needs external approval? Work stuff is different from life stuff, and success and failure are relative…'

Serenity Ko laughed bitterly. 'Ah, yes, life stuff. There was a riot. Then that idiot Honour Aki mooning over me—he said he *loved* me, can you believe it? And then Kube said I didn't deserve the promotion and—'

'Wait, what riot? And who loves you?' her grandmother asked innocently, but Serenity Ko saw her lips twitch up in a look she knew well. Ammamma was fishing for matchmaking gossip.

'Forget I said anything,' she mumbled.

'I make you rasam grain-pulp, hand feed it to you, and this is how you repay me?' Her grandmother tutted. 'I was the first person to give you a bath! I held you while they pierced your ears as a baby, did you know? And *this* is the gratitude I receive?'

'Ammamma, spare me the histrionics.'

The old lady smiled wickedly. 'It was worth a shot. Keep your secrets.' She rose to leave. 'But when I come back, you'd better have finished that bowl completely.'

Serenity Ko shovelled spoonful after spoonful of rasam grain-pulp into her mouth with earnest displeasure. It was delicious, but she was cranky. It was all well and good for Ammamma to say she wasn't a failure, but she hadn't lived the last three days of her life with her. And she was *supposed* to love her anyway, on account of her being the youngest and most adorable grandchild.

Dad popped in while she was chewing. 'Doing all right?'

Serenity Ko made a face. Appa appeared at Dad's side, and turned to his partner. 'She's as happy to see us as ever, don't you think?'

'Don't be mean,' Serenity Ko whined.

'Sorry, we've been worried about you, Ko...' Dad began.

'We'll lecture her later.' Appa laid a gentle hand on his shoulder.

'You're right, shouldn't leave her mother out of that.' Dad grinned. 'Do you want company? We can chat about the latest episode of—'

'Very tired,' Serenity Ko lied.

'We'll be back later, then. We're glad to see you awake.'

Serenity Ko felt bad about lying to them, especially since

a warm, bubbly feeling was spreading through her. It was so good to see both her fathers; she didn't know how long it had been since the last time she was home. Several māsas, she supposed, but she needed to check in on work. She brought her thumb and forefinger together to draw up her dash but it was blank, except for information monitoring her current state of wellbeing. She was not being very well at all, from the looks of things.

'Fuck *me*.'

Did nobody understand how hard it was to stay at the top of her game?

She thoughtstreamed Courage Praia on their personal comms channel, and when her dash told her she wasn't allowed to slide into the Loop just yet, she began to feel terribly tired and sleepy. She spooned more broth into her mouth and began to drift on its wave of flavour.

She is six years old. Ammamma is teaching her how to play the chordophone, but her fingers keep slipping on the four primary strings and are unable to reach the three secondary ones that are supposed to accent rhythm. Her fists clench in frustration. Her grandmother leaves for the garden and returns with a bundle of freshly washed herbs. She hands them to Ko, and as Ko shreds the cilantrina, eager for a distraction to mask her failure, they leave a sharp scent in the air. Ammamma takes the instrument from her and places it across her lap. She strums, and notes spring into the air like liquid glass, molten and forming a greater symphony of belonging.

The vision spun away. Serenity Ko started. A stray thought drifted into her through the weave of the memory. She ate another spoonful of her rasam grain-pulp and closed her eyes, letting her mind wander, imagining herself floating down a river made of tastes, scents, and sounds. A blurry figure appeared, and she chased it...

She chases Rihan through their garden. The thistlebobs

and fresh tomato vines blur; she's intently focused on her target. There are large flowers—arrioses—blossoming in the sun. Rihan says he's leading her to a candy tree, and she doesn't want to lose his trail. They stop before a towering bush, bursting with bright red fruit.

'Candy,' Rihan says, pointing. 'Try it!'

She rips one off its stem and takes a big bite. Tears spring to her eyes and the inside of her mouth is on fire. Rihan flops over onto the grass giggling, then sits up when she doesn't scream for their mother.

'Doesn't it hurt?' he asks, confused.

She grins through the pain. She's never felt more alive. Rihan is terrified, sobs a confession to their mother, is grounded for two navas.

Time shifted and warped, reeling her in. Her mind was on fire. She soothed it, herding it back into that magical, logic-defying liminal space between wakefulness and exhaustion. She ate another spoonful from the bowl in her hands, stepped into the secret rooms it held in wait for her.

It's her first day at school; the building is enormous, sweeping arcs and domed roofs leading to the horizon. She brings home her very first algorithmic equation and her mother pins it to the refrigerator, beaming with pride. The smell of a simmering broth made from tamarind and tomatoes fills the air...

A web of memories half-forgotten enveloped her, leaping over each other and spinning into her mind in a cascade. She swallowed more rasam grain-pulp, greedy for its nourishment, its wholesomeness, its unlocking of doorways into other times, other spaces filled with hope and love.

Her first kiss—his name is Boundless Peri, and he tastes sweet. Graduation day, and there's salt on the rim of her peprino-tini glass. Her first ever day at XP Inc. and the herbaceous smell of fresh tomato vines growing in the pantry.

Something shattered.

Serenity Ko jerked upright.

An empty bowl lay in slivers on the ground. She clasped her hands over her mouth in shock, her mind a morass of fear and inspiration.

What the sur-fuck had just happened? She hadn't remembered Boundless Peri in a decade. She'd *never even known* she'd once tried to learn the chordophone from Ammamma—had that been real?

Does it matter if it's real? A thought bubbled up in her. *Or is it enough if it's joyous, sensory, evocative, an escape?*

She looked down at the shards of the bowl, looked around her childhood bedroom, really *seeing* it for the first time in years. It was as if a stone had been rolled away from the corridors of her heart, memories tumbling out of their caves to flood her senses.

Holographic posters of Legends of the Future still adorned the walls. They were from her first concert; her parents had chaperoned her and Boundless Peri because they were afraid she'd get crushed in the crowd. Her comforter was the same deep purple, patterned with swirls of nebulas and stars, a souvenir from her first trip to the Cosmic Fantasies Theme Park. Her augmented reality toys from her favourite adventure-sim, *Teen Trouble*, occupied the shelves along the walls, along with a number of keepsakes—shells and rocks from the Ur-sands, a luminous stone from a family vacation in the Osmos Girdle, a pressed flower collection from the Urswood...

She stopped the journey abruptly, and cycled back to what had started it all. *A humble bowl of rasam grain-pulp, frequently made in her family's home, eaten one spoonful at a time, each mouthful of heat a memory of discoveries, familiar faces, love...*

The thought she'd been following down the river revealed itself, rising to the surface of her mind from its churning currents. The waters stilled, and the spoon, still in her hands, dropped with a clatter.

This is it.

If SoundSpace hadn't been enough for Grace Kube, well, she was going to hit him with a sim that was even more revolutionary, possibly insane, probably both.

What if every bite you eat could simulate dreams, make you relive your happiest memories?

Evocateur Extraordinaire was small-time ambition.

What if food could be a journey, transporting you to other times and places, inventing new realities, evoking old ones?

If she could find a way to build this... well, *fuck.*

What if I hold the future of food in my hands?

This could change the entire known universe.

'MellO is a recreational drug on Primus. It is completely legal, comes in different forms and grades, and everyone on the planet is encouraged to experiment with it in their pursuit of serenity and harmony.'

—Courage Medi,
A Beginner's Guide to Primus, Seventh Edition
2068 Anno Earth, 1993 Interstellar Era

TEN

SERENITY KO SLUMPED back against her pillows surrounded by papyro-scrolls and ink, flipping through her notes and reviewing them. She'd been unable to slide into the Loop. Each time she tried, her dash popped up an error about conserving her energy until her biorhythms returned to normal. The only upside was that the Loop was probably blocking Honour Aki's attempts to reach her on her behalf, which was a relief, but as her brain raced on ahead into uncharted territory, examining her universe-altering idea from every possible perspective, it turned frustrating to be unable to document her thought trail. She'd stumbled out of bed and found the archaic tech reserve stashed at the bottom of a drawer.

Papyro-scroll originated on Earth, notoriously resource-heavy to produce and fallible in its physicality. It was only used in early school, and Serenity Ko grimaced as her Ur-speak letters came out jagged and unreadable—she hadn't used a stylus in two decades.

Technically, this was meant to be used in emergencies only, as a last resort in case there was a catastrophic tech fadeout that left everyone off the Loop. But surely working out a universe-changing idea on the scale of what Serenity Ko was designing counted as an emergency.

Nobody, not ever, never in the history of time had thought of creating Immersive Reality food.

Until now, she thought with a grin.

Primian food was all about presenting symbolic flavours on a plate, which lent itself well to sim design. Serenity Ko wasn't sure exactly how it worked; she tended to zone out whenever chefs at fancy restaurants started going on about how their dishes were an homage to an obscure Nakshatran philosophy or whatever, which had been boring enough when she'd had to endure it in university.

What is Primian food all about, anyway?

She'd jotted this down as an open question to outsource to one of her interns, perhaps Curiosity Nenna.

She was far more excited by the rest of the pieces of the puzzle now falling into place. It was simple enough. The Loop was the interstellar link between civilisations; an archive of history, science, philosophy, self-expression, art, and creation that bound all humanity—and many other species—together with a shared understanding of the universe they inhabited. Anyone who wanted in could swallow a nanopill, and it integrated with the self on a cellular level, spawning a network of bio-circuits that ran in parallel with the body's manifold systems.

XP Inc. had plugged into it, beginning with humble offerings that could enhance and manipulate personal experiences before seamlessly transitioning to designing sim-worlds for people to escape into. They'd refined this tech over decades to develop Immersive Reality, where someone could create meaning for themselves, becoming part of a shared world and yet inhabiting it uniquely, within and without.

To make her Immersive Reality food proposal work, all Serenity Ko would have to do was figure out exactly how her fever dream of memories, brought on by her Ammamma's rasam grain-pulp, had worked on a neurological level—and she'd listed out numerous hypotheses already. She'd done it once with SoundSpace; she could do it again.

Then it was a simple matter of understanding food and flavour—a month's research would do; building an XP Inc. database of audiovisual accompaniments to different flavour cues—her team would need this dumbed down for them, if SoundSpace had been anything to go by; and then figuring out how to make this work predictably and consistently—really, that was user testing's problem, but she'd monitor it closely.

Popping it onto various subscriptions programmes would be the easiest bit, once she got the company to buy into the idea. And for that, she'd need Grace Kube onside.

She began to draft her strategy to win him over. He probably wouldn't resent her for the tantrum she'd thrown when they'd last met, but she wanted to make sure there was no room for error.

There came a knock at her door.

'*Sur-fucking hell and fuck the Nine Virtues sideways,*' she swore.

'Nice to see you, too.' The flowmetal door slid open.

'Rihan!'

'Ko!'

Serenity Ko shoved her scroll-work aside and threw herself at her brother, pulling him into a fierce hug. She wobbled on her unsteady feet and he gently pushed her back down on the bed.

'I love that you're taking your downtime so seriously.'

'Oh, this,' Serenity Ko laughed weakly, waving her hand over the notes scattered around her. 'Just a little thought experiment.'

'Right, definitely an emergency worthy of papyro-scroll hell.' Her brother frowned. 'Definitely a higher priority than recovering from *passing out* from *dehydration* and what is, no doubt, a cocktail of stress, drugs and whatever else you've been up to in the three navas since you stopped returning my comms.'

Serenity Ko crossed her arms over her chest. 'I've been busy.'

She was suddenly hideously embarrassed by the state of her room. Four different types of dated sim-tech lay on her desk in a tangle of wires, a stack of neatly ironed laundry sat on her armchair, waiting for her to put it away, and the floor was a mess of Bloxxos from various unfinished building projects, the kind she started each time she visited and ultimately never got round to finishing because her XP Inc. comms were always firing.

'Pardon me for the outrageous guesswork, but the fact that you're here at all has nothing to do with my message, does it? About having big news?' Her brother leaned against a wall.

'Of course it does—'

He held up a hand to stop her mid-sentence. 'I'm guessing a shit day or nava at work—something didn't work the way you wanted it to—and maybe... a heartbreak? No.' He paused when Serenity Ko rolled her eyes. 'Some kind of clingy stalker sitch with whoever your flavour of the nava is.'

'He said he *loved* me! Who the fuck does that?'

Optimism Rihan grinned. 'I knew it!'

'I mean, *really*...'

'You should be resting, though.' He frowned at her papyro-scroll pile again. 'Has nobody told the XP Inc. folks?'

'I'm on garden leave,' Serenity Ko's voice came out small.

'You've been fired?' Optimism Rihan's jaw dropped. 'I'm

so sorry, Ko. I had no idea…'

'No, not fired, I'm feeling dramatic,' Serenity Ko sighed. 'I didn't get my promotion, Kube told me I'm some kind of dictator, enforced two navas off so I can gain perspective, blah blah.'

'Is that why you're working overtime?' Optimism Rihan asked. 'Because that's a rubbish reason. You don't need promotions to know your work is good.'

Her brother tucked a stray strand of hair back into his braid, and Serenity Ko eyed him with a mixture of admiration and resentment. His short, petite frame was outlined by his high-collared luminoweave jacket, and his thick, unruly hair was woven into a side-braid. His smile was so genuine, his confidence in her worth so high, she wanted to smack him—all content and self-assured, calm in the face of any circumstance, with his deep brown skin, glossy in the dim light, a nose-pin glittering on his perfect…

A nose-pin?

'Are you getting married?' she blurted out.

'Hah! You noticed at last!'

'OhmyfuckingNineVirtues you star-fucker!' She tumbled out of bed and dragged him into another hug, stepping on a Bloxxo brick and swearing, hopping away from him and clutching her bare foot.

'Are you okay?'

'Fuck me, you beast, you never told me!'

'Right, it's my fault you never respond to comms.'

She punched him, then hugged him again. 'Is Eria here?'

'Downstairs with the fam. Are you coming, or is work more important?'

'Fuck off.'

He grabbed her arms and held her by the elbows, at arm's length, looking her over and pausing to stare intently into her eyes. 'Seriously. Are you feeling up to joining us?'

'I wouldn't miss this for anything!'

'Finally, my sister reveals she has a soul lurking under that chronic workaholic demeanour.' He smiled.

Serenity Ko took a step back, fingers twitching. 'I've a bit of a favour to ask, though.'

'Go on.'

'You wouldn't happen to have any MellO on you, would you?' She smiled innocently.

'You're kidding,' Optimism Rihan said. 'You're just fucking out-of-your-mind kidding.'

'No, I'm serious. I'm so on edge, Rio,' she wheedled. 'And I have to unpack and find my stash…'

'Ko, recreational drugs and recovering from a blackout never pair well,' Optimism Rihan said, shaking his head. 'Unbelievable.'

'Stick-in-the-mud.'

'Degenerate.'

'Be down in ten?'

'See you.'

If Serenity Ko had cared to look, she'd have seen him stop at the door and turn to regard her, his brow furrowed with concern, but instead, she turned her attention to trying to access the Loop again, and when that failed, set about stacking her papyro-scrolls as neatly as she could, which effectively translated to choosing the best half of the bed on which to pile them.

She pulled a small cube out of her flowmetal backpack and shook it. It molecularly decompressed, expanding out into a travelling case packed with everything she'd remembered to throw in when she'd left for her parents' home, stumbling about in the half-light while trying not to wake Aki up in the fear that he'd insist on dropping her off at the flowtrams.

Little sachets of premium MellO littered what appeared to be a rat's nest of clothes, shoes, perfume and hair accessories, and she grabbed one, dissolving it in a cup of water and knocking it back. The intense buzzing in her ears began to dim, and the fidgeting that had preoccupied her tech-strapped hands eased. A sense of bliss enraptured her, as her hyper-focus on her predicament at work dissipated, and she stepped out her door and practically sailed down the stairs, eager—even excited—to be a part of the celebration.

Unlike on other worlds, housing on Primus wasn't determined on the basis of the highest bidder. Primian citizens couldn't just waltz into the Collective Allocation Council offices, set their sights on a swanky space of their choosing, and purchase it with their earnings. Nobody *owned* property on Primus—it was against Primian law to hoard resources, including land. Primians viewed themselves as guests on the planet, and so spaces were allocated based on the size of the family, the composition of each hex, and the requirements of the Collective around them.

Her parents' home was a standard space on Uru. Its upper floor was occupied by bedrooms, and a common staircase led down to the lower floor. Family holosnaps twinkled down the stairway, which was lined by a neat row of indoor plants—this was her Ammamma's doing; she believed in curated garden spaces. The stairway led into the living room, with a dining room off to one side beside the kitchen. Sure enough, Serenity Ko found Appa tinkering with seasonings for their dinner. He pressed a syringe into a cilantrina leaf and extracted its ras, slipping another one into a chilifruit and distilling its potent heat.

'You look much better,' her father said. 'The rest are out in the garden.'

Serenity Ko gave him a swift peck on the cheek. 'I thought I'd say hello to you first, Appa.'

'And me?'

'Argh no!' Serenity Ko fought off her other father, who'd crept up on her and announced his arrival by poking her in the ribs. 'Dad, that tickles... Come on!'

She whirled around and scowled at him, and he grinned in return. 'Nice to see you up and about, kiddo. You gave us quite the scare.'

'So I've heard.' Serenity Ko rolled her eyes.

'Here.' He pressed a glass of water into her hands. 'Hydrate.'

Serenity Ko took a sip of the least alcoholic beverage she'd consumed in days and made a face.

Her fathers exchanged a glance. 'You know, if you're having a hard time...' Appa began.

'You could always talk to us,' Dad finished his sentence.

'Instead of going on a bender,' Appa added.

'Every. Single. Time,' Dad said.

Serenity Ko had the decency to blush with embarrassment, and a stab of guilt twisted in her gut. 'I'm sorry.'

'Have you seen your therapist lately?' Appa frowned in concern, infusing a delicious mix of steamed grains with a spice blend that filled the air with its aroma.

'I've been really busy...' Serenity Ko dithered. The guilt worming its way through her turned into stabbing knives.

'Nothing's more important than your health, kiddo,' Dad chided. 'Listen, I know you didn't land the promotion you wanted...'

'Ugh, did Ammamma tell *everyone?*'

'...but you're bigger than your accomplishments, remember?'

Serenity Ko looked from one father to the next, and their contentment was utterly frustrating. She didn't begrudge them their happiness, not in the least. It was their unconditional love that got to her; the zero expectations they'd always had of her while spoiling her silly right from her earliest memories.

Dad was a career go-getter, just like Amma, while Appa was a stay-at-home spouse and a wizard at all things domestic. Why was it such a problem if she held herself to the same standard, at least on one front?

'Ko?' she heard someone call from the garden.

'Gotta go,' she mumbled, pushing through the kitchen door.

Each room in a space opened into one of three courtyards, shared by a block of six spaces, arranged around them like a hexagon. The shared garden was where families tended the produce they used to cook with. Much to her Ammamma's disapproval, it turned out that everyone in their hex liked their gardens grown wild.

Serenity Ko stepped outside and waved at a couple of the neighbours, who were tending to their plants, then found her family off to the right—Good Cheer Eria catching the fading rays of setting Suriya, her brother's arms wrapped around her—while Ko's mother and grandmother argued in hushed whispers over the new astrianas.

'Eria!' Serenity Ko exclaimed. 'Congratulations! Let me see!'

Tall and slender, her skin streaked with delicate green makeup, Good Cheer Eria disentangled herself and leaned down, letting Ko examine her engagement nose-pin. It sparkled in the sur-light.

'Gorgeous!' Serenity Ko gushed. 'I am so happy for both of you!'

She meant it, too. Optimism Rihan wrapped his arm around his fiancée and kissed her, and Serenity Ko was simultaneously moved to near-tears and nausea at how beautiful they were together.

When her brother had first announced he was seeing Eria, and brought her home to meet the family, she'd been surprised—and a bit concerned, if she were being honest—to discover her brother's girlfriend was a chlorosapient. She'd always thought of them as cultists, their beliefs going far beyond the Nakshatran maxim to "Tread lightly," with their chlorophyll mods to derive sustenance from the light of the stars and their archaic plant-worshipping rituals. But

Good Cheer Eria had been lovable from the start, and had opened Serenity Ko's eyes to the idea that it was possible to have other points of view and still get along just fine.

'Are you feeling better? You know what you need?' Good Cheer Eria said, the words racing out of her in a rush of enthusiasm. 'Sur-light. Lots of it. Why don't you spend a nava-end away at one of our retreats? The Urswoods are lovely this time of year.'

'Work,' Serenity Ko said, shuddering inwardly at the thought of direct sunlight. 'You know how it is.'

'Heh,' her Ammamma chuckled from where she was pruning the nearest astriana. 'Liar.'

'Ma!' Her mother knocked the shears from her hands, pointedly changing the subject. 'Leave *my* astrianas alone.'

'Just a little trim,' her grandmother said, puffing up angrily. 'They're all so unwieldy.'

'They're wild.' Her mother beamed proudly.

'Savage,' Ammamma hissed.

'Pure,' her mother countered.

'Dinner is served!' Dad struck a spatula against the back of a plate.

'And just in the nick of time, it appears,' Appa said, appearing at his shoulder.

Her fathers had laid out all the good plates and glasses. An aged bottle of OakBrew was passed around, though her mother poured Serenity Ko an inordinately small portion with a warning look, refilling her water glass, and placing the good liquor far out of her reach.

The table was laid with steamed grain, fragrant rogan josh—the vat-grown meat served on the bone—slivered pearlfish, and especially for Eria, an edibite terrine infused with herb ras, so as not to offend her chlorosapient beliefs. Chlorosapient mods didn't produce enough energy to fuel the human body, but they did their best not to eat foods that involved the use of actual produce. Edibite was a chlorosapient-produced nutritive substrate. Ras infusions were entirely acceptable.

'To Rihan and Eria, congratulations!' Ammamma said from the head of the table, raising her glass to the happy couple. 'We're so happy you're sharing this moment with us, and we wish you a lifetime of happiness.'

She took a sip of her drink and passed it to Dad, who was seated on her right. As was custom, everyone sipped from their glass and then passed it to their neighbour. Dad launched into his toast, and Serenity Ko zoned out, her mind now foggy with tiredness and far more agreeable than usual, thanks to the MellO and alcohol. She looked around at her family, beaming with love as they toasted her older brother, and her insides almost melted with a sudden sense of contentment at belonging at this table.

Almost.

Her comms beeped. She was back on the Loop. A flood of notifications popped up on her dash as she slid in, her fingers twitching.

Thirty-one unread thoughtstreams from Honour Aki. She smirked and ignored them.

She passed another drink to the right after a sip, staring vaguely into the middle distance, seeing her family around her but not quite with them. They were all so perfect. Optimism Rihan was *so* adult, all of a sudden—a completely functional grown-up. Her fathers and her mother had never once let her down. Her grandmother had been prodigious in her day—people still begged her to teach them how to cook.

And what was she? What had she ever done to deserve being here, other than being born to these people?

She took another sip, passed to the right, dashed off a thoughtstream to Courage Praia, ignoring half a dozen messages from her friend expressing concern.

'Ko, are you in there?' Her brother waved his palm before her face.

Serenity Ko snapped out of the Loop. 'Sorry, so tired,' she lied.

Her brother gazed at her coolly, evidently seeing right through her. 'Your turn to say nice things about us,' he quipped, though his smile didn't quite reach his eyes.

'Right.' Serenity Ko cleared her throat. 'To my brother and the most beautiful woman I've ever met—'

Words tumbled out of her on autopilot, and she only half paid heed to them. Her family dulled to a haze as her mind sped through her Immersive Reality food project—or as she'd taken to thinking of it, Feast Inc. She barely paid attention to a word through the rest of dinner, and when her grandmother presented a multi-layered spun sugar confection for dessert, the lights in her brain went off all at once.

People still beg her to teach them how to cook.

Everything she needed to begin was right in front of her, in the shape of one little old lady. She reached for a layer of the sweet thing and crammed it in her mouth.

'Delicious!' she said from around it as it crumbled on her tongue.

Ammamma smacked her arm. 'Don't talk with your mouth full.'

This was going to be a piece of cake.

'The Nakshatran Programme seeks to establish seven unique cultures on seven different planets. After having observed the seven Stations here on Earth, I can confirm that the project is going well. The children are left to their own devices, to peruse immense archives of books and videologs. They are encouraged to form independent opinions, to debate with each other and their human facilitators. Bias inevitably creeps in, but the facilitators do their best to encourage alternative thinking, freeing their wards from the trappings of life on Earth, permitting them to explore their visions and formulate new structures of civilisation. In four years, young representatives of each Station will meet for the first time, to determine the path ahead for humanity...'

—Rahim al-Asaad, 'Hope in the Stars',
reporting for *New Frontiers Magazine*
46 Anno Earth, Pre-Interstellar Era

'After a week of healthy debate and free exchange of perspectives, we give to you, the people of One Nation Earth, the Nakshatran Charter. We hope this will lay the foundation for a human cooperative society in space, as each of our missions takes to the stars. We seek to unite and work together across the galaxy, ushering in a new era...'

—Nadira D'Cruz,
Representative of the Nakshatran Council
50 Anno Earth, Pre-Interstellar Era

ELEVEN

IT WAS NECESSARY to remind the universe that Primus was at its very centre.

Astrocartographers would argue differently, but they weren't running the whole damned show. To be fair, nobody was. The United Human Cooperative was a society that sought a free and equal galaxy for all humanity, and governance was decentralised, left in the hands of each planetary authority. Interplanetary trade was probably the greatest power there was; worlds that misbehaved suffered sanctions to bring them in line, and planets that didn't have plenty were offered free aid by those that did. It was a perfect system of harmony and equality, ruined only by the Secretary for Trade strutting about the Secretariat as if he owned the place, which drove Optimism Mahd'vi quite up the wall.

She sat in her chambers, her fingers templed under her chin, an impassive expression on her face.

The Secretary for Trade was already seven minutes late for their meeting. Her cam-drones, which had been following him around the corridors of the building, made it evident to her that this was some kind of power play. He was currently laughing with the extremely young, extremely gorgeous, and extremely capable Secretary for Technology Harmony Utra, no doubt both flirting with her and consolidating their next play to assert Primian technology in the wider galaxy. *If they were less self-absorbed, they'd notice that almost all tech across human space relies on Primian development,* Optimism Mahd'vi thought. *They'd use the platform they've built to try and consolidate Primian culture, too.*

And then she scowled in realisation. They were waiting for her to *ask*. So they could ask for something bigger in return.

It took less than seven minutes to cross the Secretariat from end to end, and Courage Ilio was in a corridor less than three minutes away.

The Secretariat sprawled like a many-tentacled squid, occupying the heart of Collective One. It housed the governing body of the same name, and was charged with governing Primus, comprising representatives of the Technix, the Cultura, the Naturo, the Moneto, and the Astro. The Nakshatran settlers had identified these guilds as the five pillars of their government.

The Technix were primarily responsible for advancements in science and technology, making the planet more habitable, preserving human lives, and enabling communication with outer worlds. The Cultura preserved their history, established traditions and practices, and concerned themselves with the arts and self-expression. The Naturo ensured the planet remained pristine, and were frequently at loggerheads with the Technix. The Moneto, natural allies to the Technix, were concerned with trade, while the Astro looked outward, towards exploration and relationships beyond the planet's atmosphere.

Every decision that concerned the wellbeing of the planet and its people was made only when representatives from each guild were present in the room. There were multiple overlaps between these wings of government, so when each individual on Primus graduated university, and sought employment, they were assessed by the Employment Council—an offshoot of the Cultura wing—and assigned a major trait and a minor trait, based on their personalities and capabilities.

Optimism Mahd'vi had been evaluated as a Culturo-Astra Expert right out of university, and while most individuals experienced shifts as their personalities developed in different directions, the assessment had stuck over the course of her career. She was primarily concerned with the history and heritage of Primus, as evidenced by her study of Nakshatran culture in school, but she was also outward looking enough to care about events in the wider universe. Interstellar diplomacy that dealt with Primian culture had been a natural fit for her.

She'd started her career as an intern to Good Cheer Kaza, then been assistant to Curiosity Shera, and had finally found her way to the top, as Secretary for Culture and Heritage, where she was determined to use her power to reinforce the worth and continued relevance of Primian culture. It was an endeavour at which her predecessors had failed, at least in her opinion, leaving her to clean up the debris of their legacies.

She exhaled slowly as Courage Ilio *finally* made his way down the hallway and to her chambers. She rearranged the neutral mask that passed for her face at these meetings.

'Maddie!' Courage Ilio beamed, knocking twice on her door as he entered.

She smiled politely. She hated that nickname; he persisted in using it. 'Courage Ilio,' she said properly. 'How delightful that you could make our meeting.'

'You know how it is, Mads, there's always someone who needs a favour from us tradies.' Courage Ilio winked. 'Not unlike being in your shoes, I'd imagine. What was that petition from the public we heard last week? "Bring back epic-poetry slams"?'

'That's correct.'

'Nowhere near as impactful as exporting our sucre-spheres to the space stations, of course. But it'll keep the homeland happy.' He stroked his beard absentmindedly. 'You've seen the scrollwork, I hope? And I can count on your vote next nava?'

'Of course,' Optimism Mahd'vi said. 'It's part of our food-tech that stems from our culture.'

'Great—'

'I see you're bringing in a ban on the import of cricket

chips,' Optimism Mahd'vi said, cutting her contemporary off before he could shift the discussion entirely to suit his needs. 'Why?'

'Too many anatomical similarities to the K'artri-tva,' Courage Ilio said. 'They're kind of… *insectoid*—is that the right word? And as our newest allies, I don't want to send them the wrong message.'

'Cricket chips are Earth's biggest interstellar export,' Optimism Mahd'vi said drily. 'This will hit them badly.'

Courage Ilio beamed. 'I was hoping you'd bring that up! I heard all about that savage at the banquet—it'll serve them right for disrupting proceedings, don't you think? I wonder why they sent him, too. Absolutely vulgar. They usually send that other Daxina chap, Godfrey…'

'*Godavari.*'

'All the same. I think it was an intentional insult,' Courage Ilio said conspiratorially.

'And you think retaliation is the right response?'

'Come on, Maddie. It's just temporary. Let things solidify with the K'artri-tva and we'll make amends.'

Optimism Mahd'vi laughed. 'You don't know the Earthlings like I do, Ilio. They don't believe in forgiveness, and they're at the heart of an entire star system that believes in their war-faring ways.'

'Our spies on Luna will tell us if they attempt anything,' Courage Ilio said dismissively. 'Mars has always been neutral. Enceladus, Ceres and Titan are politically insignificant…'

Optimism Mahd'vi cut him off. 'Everyone has a price. And Earthlings are feral; good at sniffing these things out. Besides, that clown Jog Tunga has been cosying up to minor K'artri-tva royals, hosting them on his craft and surfing solar flares in our very own backyard.'

'You're paranoid, Mads.'

'I'm experienced,' Optimism Mahd'vi said pointedly.

Courage Ilio's eyes filled with genuine sadness. 'Mads, I

know you were chased off the Earth during a time of civil unrest...'

'You mean you know my family was slaughtered, all for bearing the name Kaveri, which was apparently a crime because we were one-time rivals to the overlords of an insignificant Protectorate—the same one our barbarian who's schmoozing with the K'artri-tva is from, I must add, and that I escaped as a refugee with my brother.' Optimism Mahd'vi's eyes flashed a warning. She paused. 'I know how these Earth-rats work, Ilio. Something's brewing.'

'What do you want me to do?' Courage Ilio raised his palms helplessly. 'Bring back *cricket chips?*'

'The K'artri-tva are a monarchy. Their culture is spreading rampantly across the planet—kids are listening to K'artri-pop all over the place, techno-hobbyists are designing non-essential mods mimicking their crystal wings... In no time at all, their dramas and reels will be all the rage; it's starting already. I want to make this difficult to access. The same goes for Earth, and anything Solar.'

'But... *how?*' Courage Ilio sputtered. 'I don't own the Loop; everyone has free access. I don't—'

'Harmony Utra. Bring her in on this.'

'We can't do magic.'

'You can make other pop-culture extremely expensive to access, though,' Optimism Mahd'vi said. 'I don't need it all gone. I just need it to be painful to participate in.'

'We've never done this before. It's censorship,' Courage Ilio said, growing red-faced. 'It's... it's *anti-Nakshatran.*'

'It's self-defence. It's been hundreds of years since we were at war, and I anticipate a threat.'

'Because of *one Earthling* at *one multicultural banquet?*'

'Yes.' Optimism Mahd'vi leaned forwards. 'You've met Earthlings before, haven't you?'

Courage Ilio nodded.

'They're usually pathetic, needy, insecure little creatures

who quail when their betters—us, most humans; Nine Virtues, most *alt-beings,* really—surround them. They're usually so grateful to be in the room where anything's happening at all that they're on their best behaviour, at least by their standards.' Optimism Mahd'vi's nostrils flared in indignation. 'This Earthling was arrogant, antagonistic, and *intentionally* so.'

'He can't have known he'd be served that dish. He just made the most of the opportunity.'

'He might have had spies.'

'Maddie!' Courage Ilio flung his hands in the air in despair. 'Listen to yourself. You're about to start a cold war.'

'I'm about to prevent a war of any kind. You haven't heard the rest of my requirements yet.'

'There's more?' Courage Ilio's shoulders slumped.

'I want to remind the universe of the supremacy of Primian culture,' Optimism Mahd'vi said, getting straight to the point. 'I want you to propose a drop in exchange rates for our cultural artefacts, whatever they are. Holoscrolls, Ur-dramas, epic poetry reels, sinfonia recordings, sims—widely accessible, free to participate in wherever possible.'

Courage Ilio's face paled. 'You're asking me to devalue our creators and artists.'

'I'm asking you to promote them widely, no matter the cost.'

'I can't pass this law unilaterally.'

'But you can propose it, and I can get you votes from all the rest.'

'Why would I do that?'

'To save the universe.'

'You're asking me to break every single Nakshatran ideal this Secretariat was founded on.'

'Yes.'

'I can't.'

'You must.'

'No, listen to me, Mahd'vi. I *cannot*.' Courage Ilio rose to his feet and slammed his fist down upon her table. The scroll-slab on it rattled. 'I *will not*. I wasn't raised to believe in censorship, or xenophobia, or cultural hegemony. I was raised to believe that the best ideas live on, catch fire, inspire the universe, and make it a better place. I will not impede the free and fair exchange of ideas, no matter the alleged threat, of which, by the way, you have absolutely zero proof.'

Courage Ilio took a deep breath. Optimism Mahd'vi sat in stunned silence, as if she'd been struck.

'If you want me to participate in the promotion of Primian culture—which I do every opportunity I get, I'll remind you, or have you forgotten that our Loop nanotech goes out with at least two dozen Primian sims pre-loaded?' Courage Ilio studied her face. 'If you want me to push our culture even more strongly, then find me something revolutionary. Something the universe has never seen before. Not the same self-congratulatory Ur-dramas and epic poems about our past. Find me something that looks to the future, and to the world that could be.'

Optimism Mahd'vi's heart juddered. She wiped her sweaty palms on her thighs, waiting for him to run out of steam.

He lowered his voice. 'If you ever ask me to do something so blatantly anti-Nakshatran again, I'll report you and have you debarred.'

He whirled around and stormed through the door.

Optimism Mahd'vi's hands shook. She clenched them into fists, clutching the fabric of her trousers until they stilled. Her thoughts chased each other in circles. She hadn't anticipated so much resistance. She would find a way to work around it, and if she didn't, she'd tear it down.

Before the Earthlings arrived on their doorstep and it was too late for them all.

'Come, Earthling. Come, Amican. Come, Cerean. Let us forget our petty differences and forge a path ahead together in the spirit of the Nakshatrans, here on Uru. Never before has humanity had greater hope for unity, and I swear this to you, I will lay down my life for you all, if only you will join me in the spirit of harmony and serenity.'

—Optimism Enva,
from *Uru: Origins*, Season 7 Episode 6
2060 Anno Earth | 1985 Interstellar Era

TWELVE

THE GOVERNMENT OF Primus was not an empire, brandishing archaically vulgar totalitarianism and oppression. It was *civilised*, a reflection of neo-humanity, and was chartered to encourage all cultures to thrive and celebrate their differences. This isn't to say that it didn't consider itself vastly superior to the rest of the cosmos, and that it wasn't deeply concerned with the pursuit of power, because like all governments in the known universe, power was its primary concern. It was the *means* through which power was sought, consolidated and perpetuated that really differentiated it from all the rest—those barbaric Fringe planets, the alt-beings with their tedious war-torn pasts… Really, the greatest power of the Primian government lay in its subtlety.

Or so Optimism Mahd'vi had concluded after yesterday's falling out with Courage Ilio. She smiled for the cam-drones at the unveiling of a new holostatue dedicated to human unity. She tugged at the luminoweave ribbon in her hands with care, choosing to knot it in a ceremonial polyphony braid. Wild applause burst forth from the crowd gathered in front of her, while a flurry of cosmic heart emotes streamed across her optics on the Loop.

On Primus, the Secretariat pursued power with the utmost discretion, in broad daylight, preferably before large audiences much like the one that filled Heart Square today.

She finished the braid in an eight-way knot and stepped back. The statue glowed and shimmered, bearing a dark-skinned round face, its head shorn in the style of the Amicans, its dress the flowing, many-layered seerai characteristic of Harid, featuring a metal cummerbund from the space station Titan. And then it shape-shifted in segments, animated, alive. It now wore a skintight exosuit from the watery planet Sagaricus, everfeather ornaments from Allegro... It morphed again, its hair growing out into a long Primian braid, extending halfway down its back.

Optimism Mahd'vi waved at the crowds while her team of four personal assistants—all AI—responded to the outpouring of love and support on the Loop from viewers around the galaxy. She forced an even brighter smile as the statue sprouted an ornate headpiece, heavily embellished and wrought in gold, symbolic of the Earth. She wasn't superstitious, but the Earth had been popping into prominence ever since the banquet.

And then there'd been the Annual Report on Culture earlier that morning. Zero good news for Primus, paired with Courage Ilio's self-righteousness about freedom... It was glitches all the way down, prompting a last-minute lunch meeting with the head of MegaDrama Studios, who'd streamed to say they were late, as usual.

So Optimism Mahd'vi let herself be ushered by her bodyguards off to a corner of Central Square. The droids formed a phalanx around her as she seated herself on a flowmetal bench and immersed herself in the Loop, where she had multiple infostreams running in parallel. Most of the streams followed various persons of interest she'd begun to track ever since the banquet, bolstered by data from the Annual Report, and whittled down from over a hundred candidates by her AI. An E'nemon and a human on Harid were co-writing an indie comicscroll expressing dangerous ideas about the importance of local vernacular languages, and it had usurped the epic poem the *Nakshatranāma* as the most popular scroll purchase that year. A K'artra-pop band had surged to the top of the charts.

A single stream—perhaps the most significant—tracked the history and whereabouts of Jog Tunga, the savage Earthling. He was still vacationing in the Suriyan system, riding solar-flares from rock to rock. Optimism Mahd'vi had personally reviewed every scrap of data that had turned up, and had discovered that the princeling from Daxina happened to be allied with the Godavaris. This was of particular interest to her.

The Godavaris controlled Daxina, while persistently making bids for greater planet-wide power, and while Optimism Mahd'vi cared not a whit for their present-day political outlook and policies, the family's past was inseparable from her own. They had hunted her entire family across the Daxina peninsula, murdering them in cold blood, leaving her an orphan. She didn't remember her parents' faces or names; there was no record of them she could access. All she knew was that she'd escaped to Primus with her brother and their nursemaid when she was a toddler.

Jog Tunga's smug face grinned out at her from a pic at a hot spring on the asteroid Cynos, where he was surrounded by a bevy of men and women in various states of undress. What was he after? Considering he'd thrown in his lot with the homicidal Godavaris, it would not end well.

Beyond her optics feed, the phalanx of drones parted to permit Curiosity Ariam an entrance. Optimism Mahd'vi dismissed her stream, refocused her thoughts on the meeting agenda, and regarded the producer in front of her. They appeared dishevelled as ever; their high braid was wispy, their high-collared sweater untucked, intentional ladders running up their leggings. They calmly took a drag from their MellO vape, radiating the kind of nonchalant shabby chic aura only those who believed their positions in the world were irreplaceable could possess.

'Your Excellency.' Curiosity Ariam blew a smoke ring, then dove in for a handshake and a customary air kiss. 'I'm sorry I'm late—you won't believe how *diva* the latest crop of Ur-drama starlets is. I was with Boundless Nnika—you remember her, won a Drammy for her performance in *Stars Unfiltered*? Well anyway, she had a little problem with one of the men in her polycule running rogue—jealous sort, knew he'd be no good when she first introduced him to me, tried to break up the happy family, whatever. Well naturally, I was all yeah I-told-you-so, and she did *not* take well to that.' Curiosity Ariam paused briefly to suck on their vape. 'So ever since, she's been upsetting our schedule on *Stars Unrivalled*, didn't bother showing up all through the last nava, totally MIA. Turns out she started a second polycule on Allegro, one of our interns spotted a pic on one of *their* private streams, and I had to fly out to that sur-forsaken space station last night and drag her back by threatening to cancel her contract. The tantrum, *fuck the stars and me sideways!* She refused to leave without her new fam, so we had to arrange a bigger transport last-minute, bloody extortionist, and now she demands another nava off because the two 'cules have met and are trying to work out how they'll co-exist, and I'm poly myself, but I'll be fucked if I let this stuff get in the way of my professional commitments, you know what I mean?'

Optimism Mahd'vi nodded noncommittally, letting Curiosity Ariam run out of steam. She rose to her feet. 'Phalanx, sound-bubble please.'

What she had to say didn't need to be overheard by any casual bystanders.

'What about lunch? I'm starving.' Curiosity Ariam took another hit of MellO.

'In a moment; I need to show you something,' Optimism Mahd'vi said. She led them to the holostatue.

'New?' Curiosity Ariam tilted their head to regard it. It shape-shifted; face tattoos native to Ceres, hair slicked back in a tight bun from Mars, Primian luminoweave tunic, sheath-dress from Davidia, waist-high grav-boots from Luna, spiderweave head-dress from Unity.

They took a step back, their lips twisting into a smile. 'Freaky. I kinda dig it.'

'Do you?' Optimism Mahd'vi asked idly, leading the producer down the street as its flowmetal warped and shifted all around them. She stepped through the back entrance of Leaf and Bone and the droid phalanx dissipated, flanking them instead, their sound-bubble still enveloping them in a glimmering haze. She nodded at Courage Ab'dal, the Executive Chef, who was midway through shattering an imperfect plate of food served up by one of their line cooks, and strode towards the chef's table, where she was a frequent guest.

She gestured to the empty chair across from her, and Curiosity Ariam flopped into it, tucking their long legs off to one side. 'So how can I help, your Excellency? You never get in touch until you need something.'

'Look around you,' Optimism Mahd'vi said.

Curiosity Ariam looked. The disgraced chef had been dismissed, like crumbs being flicked off a placemat. The remaining small assemblage of chefs moved with perfect precision, slicing vat-meat, extracting ras, assembling gels and infusions in near-perfect silence, working to a music only they could hear in rhythms that echoed and complemented each other.

'Serenity and harmony,' she added, 'embodied in every aspect of their aesthetic.'

A server wordlessly filled two angular glasses with starfruit wine.

'Do you know the significance of this drink?'

Curiosity Ariam sniffed. 'What am I, an off-worlder? It was brewed after the first Nakshatran harvest, and served at the Founders' Feast.'

'And when's the last time you tasted it?'

Curiosity Ariam frowned. 'It's been a while… It's ridiculously expensive, and hard to source. And most people at the studio prefer cocktails…'

'A bastardisation of good brews, yes. A culinary tradition that originated on Earth.'

'I'm sorry, where are you going with this?' Curiosity Ariam's frown deepened.

Optimism Mahd'vi raised her glass and looked Curiosity Ariam in the eye. 'To revelations,' she said dramatically, taking a sip. Curiosity Ariam followed her lead.

'That statue you "dug" in Heart Square is everything this wine is not,' Optimism Mahd'vi continued. 'A patchwork mess, an unfiltered ocean of self-expression from across the universe, all blending together to form a single amorphous, unidentifiable, ultimately mediocre muddle that is supposed to reflect humanity at its most united, if least pristine.'

She paused. Curiosity Ariam shrugged. 'It's good PR, though, isn't it? All the inclusivity-diversity stuff—we're up to our necks in it with our programming. And it's working, too. We had this Earthling on *MegaChef* a few days ago—record-breaking views for the first episode. Predictably, she fucked up good—cooked over an open flame. *An open flame!* Shame, really, because the novelty of having a barbarian on your show can really boost ratings in the long-run—interplanetary for the inclusivity, at home for the spectacle, but judges have the last word. I know Davi

146

tried to talk them out of it, but it was a no-go, something about professional pride—*divas*, all, I tell you. And the contestant was some bigshot chef back on Earth, too, ran a major restaurant. Sarah-something Kaveri. We're thinking of bringing her back in some kind of second-chances episode...'

Optimism Mahd'vi, who'd stifled three yawns while Curiosity Ariam prattled on, was jolted out of her stupor. 'What was her name again?'

'Sarah—stati? Saras-southey? Something Kaveri. Primitively unpronounceable.' They paused, then leaned forwards slyly. 'Not a person of interest, is she?'

Optimism Mahd'vi smoothed the barest hint of stray emotion out of her face in a well-practised breath.

Kaveri.

Surely there hadn't been another survivor? *And on Earth, too.*

She was aware that Curiosity Ariam hadn't said a word in many seconds—a personal record, going by their decade-long work relationship. She smiled politely, ignoring her juddering heart.

'Person of interest?' Optimism Mahd'vi scoffed. 'Hardly. I want to watch the footage, without having to get through the entire episode. Nothing quite like watching an Earthling fail. Comes as easy to them as breathing.'

Curiosity Ariam laughed. 'I'll Loop it to you. It's spectacular.'

'Indeed.'

Optimism Mahd'vi instructed her AI assistants to scour the Loop for any records on a "Sarah—something" Kaveri. This was personal business; she could look into it on her own time. She buried her excitement at the development, and brought the conversation back into focus. 'You're right about the diversity play; it's excellent PR, so long as it makes people feel good without destabilising *us* as the centre of the multi-cultural universe. Unfortunately, it doesn't always go according to plan.'

'Uh-oh. Why do I sense bad news?'

'Because it's incoming. We had the Annual Report on Culture this morning.'

Curiosity Ariam tilted their head back and exhaled slowly. 'It's *really* bad news, isn't it?'

'*Uru: Origins* is spiralling,' Optimism Mahd'vi said bluntly, cutting right to the chase. 'It's your longest running show, the most popular Ur-drama out there, second in ratings only to *Interstellar MegaChef*. And it's dying.'

Their server placed two perfectly plated portions of food in front of them, and refilled their glasses with starfruit wine. Curiosity Ariam knocked their drink back in a single swallow, and the server refilled it again. Optimism Mahd'vi raised an eyebrow.

'If you're going to fire me, I'm going to make the most of this very expensive lunch,' Curiosity Ariam said stiffly.

'Stop being dramatic,' Optimism Mahd'vi retorted. 'I'm here to talk solutions with you.'

'Oh. I'll revert to being civil then.' They relaxed visibly, leaning back into the cushioned chair.

'Always a good idea.'

'What's going on out there in the galaxy, then?'

Optimism Mahd'vi laid it all out before them. Kartri-dramas were all the rage, but that was a phase, thanks to the recent cultural exchange. Far more troubling was the upswing of entertainment being produced by the rest of human-occupied space, being swallowed whole across the galaxy. 'Comicscrolls have replaced our epic poetry; there are indie dramas from backward rocks in the far-flung galaxy—you've heard of *Empire Quest*, the low-budget, high-stakes show about political intrigue and violence from Earth?'

Curiosity Ariam nodded slowly.

'Can you imagine that kind of tripe usurping the philosophy of serenity and harmony that we carry in all our programming? Do you know what repercussions that could have on all humanity if it occupies people's minds as a dominant philosophy? And fuck me, its biggest audience is right here, under our very noses, in Uru.'

'Yeah, we've been disturbed by this, too,' Curiosity Ariam said. 'But we've got our hands tied as the universe expands, and the spaces between our worlds shrinks. We can't prevent the inflow of free entertainment.'

'It's impossible to contain,' Optimism Mahd'vi agreed. 'And it's closing in on us. Everywhere. Look at us, in one of the last holdouts of *proper* Primian cuisine. Even our food culture is being diluted—there are upstarts everywhere with their experimental restaurants. And fucking *cocktails*.' She laughed and drained her glass.

'It feels like you're getting at something, but I'm not sure exactly what it is.'

Optimism Mahd'vi leaned forwards and dropped her voice, despite the sound-bubble that encapsulated them. 'What I'm about to say... You can appreciate the *delicate nature* of the whole thing?'

'My lips are zipped, not a word leaves this table.'

Optimism Mahd'vi nodded. 'We're losing the culture war to the rest of the universe. For nearly two thousand years, we've established ourselves as the pinnacle of human expression, and now it's slipping away to lesser cultures. What do we blame? Interplanetary immigration, a cooperative vision for society instead of imperialism, no censorship of self-expression... it's all tangled up together. And of course, I *believe* in all those ideals, but I fear the change that is coming. We are the very embodiment of what the Nakshatrans envisioned for a better future for humanity. We carry their philosophies in our every manner of being. We've propagated them to the rest of the universe, and except for a few revolutions, humanity has co-existed peacefully despite all its cultural differences. *It's all thanks to us.* And we're losing our grip.'

Curiosity Ariam nodded, leaning forwards to mirror Optimism Mahd'vi.

'We need to find a way to re-establish our dominance, and do so subtly. Let me repeat that: *subtlety is key*,' Optimism Mahd'vi whispered urgently. 'We must appear to be inclusive at all points. We must not discriminate, or reveal that a threat exists at all. But we *must* reclaim our position as keepers of human culture.'

'What can I do?' Curiosity Ariam asked.

'We're on the verge of marking two millennia of Primian culture. The first Nakshatrans landed here one thousand, nine hundred and ninety-nine years ago. A celebration is in order.' Optimism Mahd'vi smiled. 'And you have the biggest broadcasting platform in all the galaxy.'

'Propaganda?' Curiosity Ariam gasped.

'Such a *vulgar* word.' Optimism Mahd'vi scowled. 'I prefer to think of it as programming that reminds the universe of our unshakeable place in it.'

The civilised way to assert power was to present one's citizens with choices in which the superior one was clearly visible.

'I'm open to any ideas you might have that could help us realise this. I'm calling it the Millennium Festival.'

'I like it.'

'I'm glad you do.' Optimism Mahd'vi smiled. 'After all, you're going to need something new to replace *Uru: Origins*, now that this is its final season.'

'What?'

'Come on, Ariam. Twenty-one seasons long and spiralling. It's over.'

Curiosity Ariam sighed. 'The Millennium Festival it is, then.' They scooped a delicately layered petalescence cup off their plate, filled with three different gel spheres in marbled earth-tones. They popped it into their mouth and stifled a moan. 'This stuff is good, I hope we get to brainstorm more often.'

'Something tells me we will.' Optimism Mahd'vi smiled.

Mission accomplished, she thought. *And now for the latest Earthling.*

'It's promising, because it's better than most of the slop that passes for fine dining out there. But...'

'But?'

'It's not quite there yet, if you know what I mean. Give her another decade, though. I'm optimistic.'

—Ahana Shah, Executive Chef of Nizami,
on the opening of the new restaurant Elé Oota,
in an exclusive interview with the *Earthling Epicurean*
2069 Anno Earth | 1994 Interstellar Era

THIRTEEN

KILI WAS MY only friend on this sur-fucked planet, and I was beginning to question how long our relationship would last. All I wanted to do was curl up in my blankets and disappear from the face of the cosmos. Instead, natural light streamed into my space through the windows that had, until this point, been dimmed to pitch black.

'Kili, stop.'

I prodded the display beside my bed. A deeply satisfying shadow fell across the room. Only to be replaced by sur-light. Again.

Saras, it's nearly noon.

I tapped on the display again. _It's the middle of the night somewhere in this galaxy._

You've had two entire days to sulk about *MegaChef*.

A warm natural glow filled the room. I promptly killed it. _I spent three māsas in spaceflight to get here. I'm allowed to mourn._ I groaned.

Why don't we mourn outdoors while soaking in popular and possibly underwhelming tourist experiences, like every other off-worlder who's ever visited Uru?

_No._

Just look at all this neat stuff!

Kili holorayed two dozen livestreams from across the city of Uru, featuring popular tourist destinations, prestigious *Interstellar Traveller*-starred restaurants, not-so-secret hiking trails and food marketplaces.

_ How about this? We step out for a couple of hours. If you hate it, we'll come straight back home and you can go back into hiding._

And so I found myself showered and smelling of citrine, in a fresh 3D-printed wrap dress with a heavily beaded Primian collar and a form-fitting waistline, sulking on the flowtram route to the Uru and Beyond Marketplace, touted as one of the most dazzling avenues in all the known universe. Kili nestled on my shoulder.

He burbled with excitement when we passed the Unity River monument. _Let's take a closer look?_

_No._

My bones ached with the weight of exhaustion and hopelessness. They'd hurt that night, too, all those māsas ago, for entirely different reasons: a blend of being hungover from the celebrations and a long cross-continental flight through heavy weather.

It's taken me twenty-one hours to fly back to Daxina after the Golden Knife Awards. Clutched in my hands is my very own Golden Knife for the most promising young chef anywhere on Earth. I still can't believe I've won, but the dizzying feeling of achievement recedes as I'm ushered through VIP portals, my luggage already collected for me by an unseen bodyguard. An electric limousine pulls up at my family's private exit from the airport.

Celebrating with my team at Elé Oota is evidently not an option, although this win is as much theirs as mine. My chauffeur steps out and holds open the door. I miss the feeling of Kili nestled on my shoulder—he's still deactivated in my backpack.

I slide into the car. A familiar smile greets me and I dislike it at first sight, even though it belongs to family. My sister looks me up and down and wrinkles her nose, as if I've arrived with a suitcase full of cow dung. 'The family needs to talk.'

'Nice to see you, too.'

'We both know that's a lie.'

My sister Narmada returns to perusing the content scrolling across her lenses. She ignores me for the rest of the car ride home, which suits me just fine. After all, she's the Priestess Immaculate of the Daxina Protectorate, betrothed to Jog Tunga, the heir to the Tunga clan fortune. She has better things to do than congratulate her only sibling for achieving the greatest culinary recognition on the planet.

I reach into my backpack and reactivate Kili. Something tells me I'm going to need all the moral support I can get. Kili flits out and immediately tucks himself into the crook of my neck. My sister tuts, and mutters something that sounds like "childish." She whirls towards me as the car draws up to the gates of our mansion. 'I wish you'd get rid of that Winger and upgrade to some real tech. It's just embarrassing to the family.'

Kili judders in response. I pat him reassuringly and look my sister in the eye. 'Nope.'

Kili, my only friend in the universe, chittered in delight on my shoulder, snapping me back to the present. The flowtram swooshed towards the north gate of the Cosmic Fantasies Theme Park. Enormous flowmetal gates glimmered translucent in shades of black, purple and neon pinks, holographic comets and spaceships streaking across their surface, supernovas exploding and nebulas coruscating. And this was just my basic view, without personalised sims beamed straight into my brain. A twinge of temptation tugged at my insides.

This has been on your bucket list for ages, Kili said innocently.

Everyone who walked in through those gates was beaming like a child about to unwrap their birthday presents. It was more happiness than my heart was ready to hold.

Not today.

Are you just going to spend all day on the train?

Maybe.

Kili flitted before my face, startling me.

Saras. His wings whirred gently. _I'm sorry they were such assholes, but you've been through stuff like this before. You'll bounce back. You always do._

It wasn't untrue. You had to have thick skin to be a chef. The professional kitchen was a lifetime of rejection and lurking in the darkness waiting on a kind word, or even a noncommittal one. More often than not, it involved keeping your head down in the face of the indefatigable hostility coming your way for no discernible reason whatsoever. My food and its creator—me—had been called "rubbish" an awful lot, especially through my early days in the industry, and still I'd persevered. All right, I'd shut down my restaurant and fled after that night.

Mani, the butler and my parents' most faithful sycophant, ushers my sister and me into the silence of tasteless opulence, the kind of hush that can only arise from glittering chandeliers on the ceilings and marble busts indiscriminately hoarded at auctions. My footsteps thump dully on elaborately woven carpets, blood-red skeins interwoven with so much gold, a single carpet could feed a village for a year. Tapestries hang from the ceilings—the family tree, the family crest, the family motto; portraits line the walls as I trudge through the East Wing, dragging my feet until my sister hisses and pinches my arm. 'Mama and Papa have been waiting hours for you. Give them the respect they're due.'

I grit my teeth and climb a flight of stairs—bannisters delicately carved with a hideous assemblage of tigers hunting, peacocks dancing and jasmine creepers creeping— leading to the War Room. The fact that we're meeting here sets my nerves on fire. I've never been invited in, but I've always noticed that right after there's a family meeting, the Protectorate is plunged into some form of turmoil: water crisis, bloodless coup in a faraway district, scandal in a neighbouring Protectorate, just about anything else you'd expect from the overlords pulling the strings behind a puppet government; a monarchy pretending to be something else.

The doors swing open for my sister, and she holds her hand up in a blessing of peace as my parents drop to their knees, prostrating themselves before her. Ordinarily, the custom would be performed the other way round, and she and I would fall to our knees as a sign of respect for the wisdom of our elders, but as Priestess Immaculate in a state run according to the River Creed, Narmada is a divine embodiment of water on Earth.

It hits me like a lightning bolt. That's why she's so mad at me—or one of the reasons, at least. She's been around me for hours and I haven't acknowledged her divinity yet. I laugh out loud before I can stop myself. Three heads turn towards me in unison, and my father's lips twist in a look of disapproval I've come to know well. It's the way he lets me know I exist.

'Ah. Saraswati.' He raises his hand for a blessing.

I stifle a sigh, step into the room and drop to my knees. I don't want blessings of any sort from these people, regardless that they happen to be my parents, but I've waited so long to tell them I don't believe in their faith that a little longer won't matter. Especially since I've been summoned to the War Room. This does not bode well in general, and I don't want to give them further reason to pick on me.

'How lovely of you to remember you have a family.' My

mother smiles falsely, and all I see are her canines. They cut through me even as she waves her hand towards a chair. 'Sit.'

I glared resentfully at a wide-eyed five-year-old child, her face turned upward in wonder as she stepped through the gates, their holographic visuals swirling open around her in a shimmer of silver and gold. On either side of her, her loving parents held her by the hand, and lifted her into the air with a whoop, laughing with delight as she skipped through the entrance, swallowed into the fantastic realms that lay beyond. So that was what a normal family looked like.

The flowtram lurched as we left the theme park's station.

I hope my parents have torn whatever's left of Elé Oota the fuck down, and built a finishing school for princesses in its place.

The thought came out so jagged it hurt.

Let's not go there, Kili warned.

'Why not?' I said out loud. 'It turns out my whole life was a lie.'

Nobody was lying about how good you are, Kili said loyally. _Because you're mega-fucking talented and brilliant and undeniably one of the best chefs in the galaxy._

'That's not how things ended on Earth.'

You didn't stick around long enough to see how they ended.

I'd always thought that night would turn out to be the killing blow to my reputation and career. But nope, I was wrong. When they immortalised me in my own biopic, *Interstellar MegaChef* would go down as the killing blow.

I never want to see the inside of a kitchen again.

You don't mean that.

I kinda do.

I don't believe you.

'You know what I mean, Kili,' I said impatiently. 'My restaurant was very convenient to my parents until it wasn't. They—'

Right. Your *parents*.

'Not *just my* parents. Every other food critic on that sodding planet was in on it.'

How do you know?

'I *don't* know. There's no way to tell.'

What if the people who lied to you are the ones who told you you aren't good enough? Kili asked. _Your parents, say._

'I considered it.' And I had. 'Until I got here.'

I scowled at the Harmony Knot as our train drew towards it. This is where we'd have to change lines to get to the Uru and Beyond Marketplace, and I did not want to step out into the world. Kili shot off my shoulder and hovered by the doorway, shimmering red, green and gold. I rose to my feet and shuffled over, nearly losing my balance as the flowtram descended.

It was one of Uru's most famous installations, a panoply of Earth-origin fauna intertwined with plants native to Primus: bougainvillea wrapping around rosinia creepers; beaumontia blossoms nestling petal to whorl beside astriana blooms; unending spirals of green tumbling into each other around the trunk of a magnificent tree, grafted together from saplings of oak, apple, spindle-wood and stonefruit; a breathing monument that connected the history of the Nakshatrans—with their origins on Earth—to modern day Primus.

I dragged myself off the train and stood in the shadow of its canopy. All around me, tourists human and otherwise flicked on unseen lenses and pulled out various kinds of recording instruments, posing for holosnaps, beaming livestreams, and calling loved ones across the galaxy. Even Kili flitted around me, trying his best to get me to smile. I scowled at the monument. It seemed to be mocking me after *MegaChef*, excruciatingly ironic; the gulf between Earth and Primus had never felt more immense. Much like the gulf between my own measure of my talent and reality—a glittering illusion echoing across the universe.

As if choreographed, a flight of many-hued flutterwings descended in hive-like synchronicity, alighting upon florets, whispering across my vision, brushing against my bare skin while sur-light peeked through gaps in the leaves.

Isn't this glorious? Kili trilled, spinning around me, his lenses flickering green as he recorded every moment of my discontent.

'Is it?' I muttered.

Kili paused midway through a figure-of-eight flight pattern and zoomed towards me. He bobbed up and down, making the Winger equivalent of eye contact, his display switching to a frowny emote. _We need to talk._

'We *need* to go back to sleep and never wake up.'

Kili holorayed a live map of the park surrounding the Harmony Knot. _There's a vacant bench about forty feet away. Why don't we go sit down?_

He bobbed away without waiting for a response, and I jogged to keep up with him before he could be flagged as unidentified tech. The bench was an extension of the Harmony Knot—half curious fuzzy vine, half jasmine creeper, threaded through a sinewy flowmetal structure. Warmth spread through me the minute I sat down, as some kind of inbuilt temperature control kicked in.

There. Doesn't that feel better? Kili hummed, dropping on to my shoulder. _ Look around at what a beautiful day it is._

I looked. It was. And I was feeling none of it.

The smiles on people's faces seemed to grow wider, the light streaming down upon me brighter, and I more nauseated with each passing second. I was a failure, on Earth, on Primus—everywhere in the known universe, really.

No, worse. I was an egomaniac, so convinced of my

abilities that I'd ignored everyone who'd ever said I'd amount to nothing. And they were right. My insides stung. I was a *stupid* egomaniac.

I take my chair in the War Room. I pointedly place my Golden Knife award—a big, shiny, golden trophy, impossible to miss—on the Strategy Table. It settles with a thunk *and glitters in the light of the chandeliers. My parents eye it like it's a turd. My sister smirks.*

'You know how we feel about foreign junk in this Protectorate,' *my mother says, sniffing.*

'It's an award,' *I say coldly.* 'International recognition for my restaurant. You'd know how good it was if you ever bothered to visit.'

My parents exchange a glance. My sister sniggers and doesn't bother to conceal it.

'Right. Your restaurant. I'm glad you brought it up,' *my father says.*

'We think your little hobby has gone on long enough,' *my mother says.*

'You've spent more than ten years messing around in the kitchen like some* servant, *disgracing our family and everything we've been building,' my father says.*

'What, a totalitarian regime? An institutionalised human rights violation thriving on wealth disparity, the hoarding of clean water and food, religious fundamentalism and thought policing?' *I ask casually.*

My father slams his hand down on the table, and I jump, heart hammering. 'Don't be flippant. If it wasn't us in charge, it would be someone else. At least you're on the safe side of history. For now.'

'Your ingratitude is unbecoming,' *my mother chimes in, tutting.*

'If you ask me, this is just another sign that we need to rein her in.' *My sister flips her hair and shoots me a nasty grin.*

'What's my restaurant got to do with anything?' I snap, sitting up straighter. I don't like the direction in which this conversation is heading.

'Its purpose has been served,' my father declares imperiously. 'It's time to move on.'

'The family needs you to do your duty,' my mother adds, holding up her hand as I open my mouth to argue. 'It's the least you could do to repay everything we've done to support you.'

'You've done nothing for me,' I say flatly. 'You've derided me in private, ignored me in public, refused to accept that I can come from this messed-up family and still chart my own path, and bring some good to the world in the process.'

My sister giggles, looking from my mother to my father. 'Oh!' She claps her hands. 'She really doesn't know?'

My parents join in, my dad's laughter booming from somewhere deep within him. 'Do you think any of your success would be possible without who you are? Without who we are?'

Kili is hot on my shoulder. I feel like I'm about to throw up. 'What do you mean?'

Saras. Reliving the past is getting you nowhere. Kili interrupted my thoughts.

'Trying to chart my own future has got me nowhere.'

Kili's wings spun erratically, all out of sync, causing him to bobble up and down. I'd learnt to recognise this as mounting exasperation.

If you *must* relive the past, then *this* is the version I insist upon. Kili righted his wings and whirred a metre away from me. His display glowed blue, and he holorayed a cluster of images, text scrolling beneath each one.

'Please don't do this,' I groaned.

A perfectly plated portion of pazham bajji, precisely hand-sliced in symmetric proportions, batter fried to golden goodness, ensconced in an edible nest made from honeycomb, a mango relish on the side, popped out of the slew of images. Beneath it was a glowing review:

> ...the flavours at Elé Oota are bold, a declaration of the glorious history of Daxina. The balance of its eleven-course tasting menu is symphonic, a blend of tradition and cutting-edge technique that resonates with mastery. Executive Chef Saraswati is a culinary star.

'Why are you showing me this?'

Another holorayed graphic zoomed into prominence. It cycled through a montage of seven of my most well-loved signature offerings at my erstwhile restaurant, from paati's pandi curry (glistening pork simmered in spices, served on a bed of rice) to deconstructed palkootu (chunks of pumpkin, lightly spiced, served with a pea and ragi couscous, a hearty coconut broth poured over it to bring it all together). Arya John, food critic and reviewer for *Earthling Epicurean*, popped up on video.

'*...in all my travels across the Daxina Protectorate, I never miss the opportunity to stop by Elé Oota. Chef Saraswati's extraordinary ability to puzzle, delight and push the palate to explore and embrace flavour is unsurpassed. Her food is clever, wholesome and elevated.*'

My heart skipped a beat at her words. I remembered the first time she'd dropped into the restaurant. I couldn't believe that such a senior reviewer was bothering to experience my food, and I was so nervous I botched plating not one, but *two* dishes intended for her table, and had to redo them, much to the chagrin—and later, amusement—of my other chefs. She'd given me a rave review, and had returned to the restaurant a dozen times since.

But that was in the before. None of that mattered anymore. Had any of it even been real?

'Why are we looking at this?' I buried my head in my hands as another graphic spun outwards towards me.

Because you need to be reminded of just how good you are.

I snorted. 'You mean I need to be reminded of just how far my parents' influence reaches.'

You know that's not true. Not everyone can be bought and sold.

'According to my parents, they can.'

Are you calling Arya John a sellout?

'Well, maybe not her specifically...'

What about José Rodrigues? Zorah Ali? Keerti Ramakumar?

Videos, articles, and pics, from food guides, newsreels and social streams, tumbled forth from the Loop as Kili surrounded me in a holorayed sphere, a pixel tent proclaiming all my talent, potential and hard-earned success at me while I sat in the middle of it, refusing to acknowledge it. I couldn't. Not after the way that conversation with my family had ended.

My father leans forwards. 'Do you really believe there's a place for fine-dining in this sun-fucked world?'

My sister grins with glee, and my mother gazes at me unwaveringly as my father draws up a map. It projects holographically up from the Strategy Table, a sphere expanding into the Earth, engulfing my Golden Knife award, so all I can see is the bleak reality of the planet I inhabit. Large black spots mark places that have been annihilated in war, red zones mark places that are being submerged by rising sea levels. Three green areas mark allies to the Protectorate I live in; the other dozen or so are zoned orange.

'Tell me, Saraswati, where did you go to culinary school?' my father asks, steepling his fingers.

'Protectorate Paradiso,' I say, utterly bewildered.

'*Right, and what is their relationship with the Daxina Protectorate?*'

'*Hostile,*' I reply. '*Sanctions against us for human rights violations.*'

'*Alleged human rights violations,*' my father says firmly, while my mother says, '*At least she's been paying attention to the news.*'

'*So who got you in, past the government stand on issuing zero travel visas to our people?*' my father asks.

'*My application.*'

'*Nope. Your parents. Us,*' he continues relentlessly. '*And where have you worked?*

My heartbeat is erratic. '*E-everywhere,*' I stammer. '*The Oceanius Protectorate, United North, the Spring Alliance...*'

'*Right, and are any of those states allies?*'

I shake my head, no.

'*So who got you those jobs? Who ensured safe passage?*'

'*My... my applications, my credentials, praise from my instructors at the Culinary Institute. Former employers and their recommendations...*'

My sister giggles again. Her face is really beginning to annoy me.

'*Your parents. Us. Diplomacy, coasting on our prestige and power,*' my mother drawls, almost bored.

'*And your little restaurant,*' my father says condescendingly. '*Where did you get the funds to start it?*'

'*I... I crowdfunded, found investors—no, come on, really I did!*' I slam my palm down on the table. '*Do you know the number of meetings I had? The pitches I put together? Tasting menus, vision boards...*'

'*Yes, Papa's employees really loved all the free food,*' my sister says, tittering.

'*Shell companies. To reinvest our money, the inconvenient kind nobody ought to know we have,*' my father says, evidently bored.

'You live in this house and think your dirty money's a secret?' I scoff.

'If you aren't sleeping with notes stuffed under your mattress—which I assure you, you aren't—it's because we rerouted it into our... investments,' my father says. 'Including your restaurant.'

I rise to my feet. 'I'm not falling for it.'

'And your run of success.' He raises his voice. 'Who bought off all those reviewers? Ensured people were eating at your restaurant? Kept you in business?'

'I won't listen to this!' My fists clench at my side. My head feels like it's being squeezed in a vice.

'Show her,' my mother yawns.

My father pulls up a list of financial transactions carefully curated for this presentation. Clearly, my parents have been sitting on this for a while. The list of prestigious food critics on it makes my head spin. I sink into my seat.

'Why?'

'While you were off playing cook over the last decade—a job we hire people to do for us, by the way, far beneath your station and your dignity—we fended off an enormous coup,' my father says calmly. 'We had to find a place to hide the money. So we laundered it through you.'

'But... my accounts, my savings, the funds and salaries and profits... they're all mine.'

'Who do you think owns the people who run your finances?' My sister rolls her eyes, then tilts her head in my father's direction.

'You're lying,' I say softly.

'Maybe we are.' My father shrugs. 'But we're the only reason you're a name at all. Every shred of success you've ever had belongs to us.'

'And now it's time for you to express your gratitude,' my mother says primly. 'We need you to help the family—not as a cook, but as a daughter of the House Godavari.'

And then I'd shut down the restaurant, filmed my audition vid, faked my scrollwork and run away, swearing revenge, while a rebel uprising raged on the streets of Daxina… only to find myself humiliated on *MegaChef*.

Kili was still prattling on about my successes. _The great Ben Macquarie begged you to teach him your coconut chutney recipe. The Spice Brothers were willing to help turn Elé Oota into an elite franchise. Even Ahana Shah turned up for dinner…_

'And she told me my pāyasam was heavy-handed on the saffron,' I moped.

She's a mean old crow, but she showed up. That must count for something.

Kili had a point. My former mentor had never had a kind word to say when I was in her kitchen, so the fact that she'd shown up in my restaurant, even if it was to criticise my dessert, surely showed she believed in me.

Saras, you built something good, and you earned every bit of recognition, no matter what your parents had to say about it.

'Could've told me this three māsas ago and saved me a spot of interstellar travel.'

I tried! Look at what you left behind when you didn't listen.

The visuals from the Loop shrank, replaced by pics and videos from my archives, bubbling up all around me. My former sous chef, Kartikeya, grinned at me from behind a monstrous sugary dessert that was melting into a puddle of goop, one of our many behind the scenes experiments gone wrong. Juno tossed me a thumbs up from beside the tandoor in my kitchen. I'd first spotted her on the streetside selling barbecued fish—her face small and pinched, the spiced aromas wafting off her improvised grill impossible to ignore. I'd barely taken a bite when the local police showed up to harass her for protection money. I name-dropped my parents and they scurried away like the rats they were, and I offered her a job on the spot, training her to run the enormous oven at Elé Oota. As a bonus, we had a constant supply of fresh, local fish from one of the few untainted streams in Daxina, which ran through the village where her parents lived. When I'd shut down the restaurant, she'd been heartbroken.

I'd lied to them all. None of them knew the real reason I'd left. I didn't want it to break them like it broke me.

The first menu I designed popped up on the holoray, surrounded by pen and pencil concept sketches for the plating. I'd saved the first invoice from my meat supplier, the first social streams post announcing our opening, pics of the resumes of the first chefs I'd hired…

It was all too much. I'd let them all down, all because of who I was.

It rushed back to me in splinters, fragments of conversations piercing my armour like shrapnel, coalescing into a crystal clear memory, jagged as it rose through my consciousness. The hurried farewells, the rushed escape, my desperate hope for a brighter future out in the stars.

I sat in silence, tears streaming down my cheeks. The stars had fucked me good.

A good chef meticulously prepares their ingredients, invites you to dinner, and dazzles your palate.

A great chef cooks for you at a moment's notice with whatever they have on hand, and seeks not to astound your intellect but to sate your senses.

—Grace Menmo, from the sim *At Home in the Kitchen*
2065 Anno Earth | 1990 Interstellar Era

FOURTEEN

'AMMAMMA!' SERENITY KO smiled brightly over her morning cup of kaapi.

Her grandmother eyed her suspiciously. 'You're never this happy in the morning.'

'I feel so well-rested now I'm back home, surrounded by the family I love.' Serenity Ko beamed. 'Anything I can help you with?'

'No.'

Ammamma returned to the meticulous task of preparing her super-secret spice blend. The molecular processor on the kitchen counter beeped and whirred while she sliced, spliced and fused the ras of her base spices together. She'd been making this family blend for decades, ever since she learnt it from her mother, but the mastery over science and artistry it took to get the flavour profiles of each individual spice just right, the proportions in which they were put together, and the eventual whole—always more profound and complex than the sum of its parts—still demanded complete attention. It also demanded complete silence.

Much to her annoyance, Serenity Ko carried on in that falsely chirpy tone she thought nobody could see through. 'I really needed those two days of rest, you know? And now

168

I'm all recharged and good to go.'

'Go already? You just got here,' Ammamma muttered, peering through the lens at a magnified, molecular view of a smudge of chili ras. 'Well, I guess that's typical Ko. I'll call you a flowcab.'

'No, no. I'm just good to... *hang out,* enjoy my downtime, I don't know—maybe learn something new?'

'Huh,' Ammamma said, wholly disinterested. Her granddaughter continued to make word-like sounds and she tuned them out as she tweaked capsaicin values, manipulating the chili ras to produce a faint hit of sweetness in the wake of its heat.

If Serenity Ko had ever bothered to pay attention to what her family were doing, especially in the kitchen, if she'd been a tad less indulged as a child, and a few more rules had been laid down, she'd have known that spice blend day was when everyone gave Ammamma a wide berth. She was aware of none of this.

'So I was hoping,' she announced loudly, 'that you'd be willing to teach me how to cook?'

Ammamma nearly dropped her scoopula—the tiny glass tool she was using to measure out chili ras, one portion at a time—and bumped her chin on the lens of the processor as she looked up in utter shock. She stared at her granddaughter, who stood across the kitchen island from her, radiating the kind of innocent goodness that meant she was up to something, and it was likely no good.

Serenity Ko tilted her head and let the stray lock at the centre of her forehead fall across her face, her lips pursed in a small smile, in her best impression of the baby holopics her mother frequently shared on the family comms stream—to which everyone replied with heart emotes. For good measure, she threw in a dollop of all the charm that inevitably worked for her with singles seated on barstools across the planet.

'It's not every day that I get two navas off to explore other pursuits, or develop new passions, or...'

'Finish *anything* you start, like all your Bloxxos?' Ammamma interrupted her skeptically.

'Well—'

'And your AtmosOne race-craft project?'

Serenity Ko turned red. It wasn't her fault her teammate, Courage Nuno, had fallen desperately in love with her while they designed their amateur racer for the popularly broadcast *AtmosOne: Formula Enthusiast* season, proclaiming his feelings and asking her to start a family with him in front of hundreds of cam-drones, right before the first race started, while she had a snoop-tool in her hands and was debugging their controls dashboard. She couldn't possibly be held accountable for sticking it through their windshield and storming off.

'That wasn't my fault, Ammamma.'

'What about your keys lessons?'

Serenity Ko sensed their conversation derailing, and swung it hard back on track. 'Right, but you know, I'm thinking I need to take more time off. Enjoy my life a little more,' she lied. She'd spent the last two days locked in her room under the pretext of recuperating, secretly giving Courage Praia a high-level view of Feast Inc. so they could float it about the office on the downlow, while also working out the next steps for this as-yet-unapproved project.

'That's an admirable thing to do,' Ammamma said. 'Now, please excuse me and get out of my kitchen. Spice blends are terribly complex, which you'd know if you'd ever bothered to make one yourself—'

'I'd love to help you right now,' Serenity Ko interrupted.

'No.' Ammamma dismissed her with a wave of her hand. 'Shoo. Get out. I'm sure you'll find some sims that can teach you what you want to know—maybe take up portraiture, or poetry.'

'I want you to teach me how to cook,' Serenity Ko insisted.

'No.'

'Please. Ammamma. Teach me about food. Everything there is to know.'

Serenity Ko quailed under her grandmother's scrutiny. She felt hideously, uncomfortably exposed, stripped bare of all deception, and wondered if she should have thought this through some more. While her grandmother was her sharp-tongued yet loving and loveable Ammamma to her, to the wider world she was Grace Menmo, formidable food critic, redoubtable culture commentator, successful restaurateur, relentless writer; the woman who'd given form and shape to what it meant to be Primian, one holoscroll volume at a time over the course of an entire career. Serenity Ko watched an entirely terrible transformation taking place right before her.

Ammamma—no, Grace Menmo—stepped back from her food machine. She stood up straighter, throwing off the hunch brought on by her advanced years, and brought her fingers together, clasping her hands as she laid them down on the counter. Her nails were perfectly manicured. She leaned forwards ever so slightly, seeming to draw the room in towards her, and tilted her head appraisingly. A smile curled up the side of her wrinkled face, and her eyes glittered like cold gemstones, betraying nothing of the grandmother within.

Grace Menmo, not Ammamma, gazed coldly at Serenity Ko.

'You want to learn about food,' she said flatly. '*You*.'

'I do.' Serenity Ko tried to meet her challenge head on. She dropped her silly charming granddaughter act and took a sip of her kaapi, her manner now all business.

'You've never spent a *day* in the kitchen.' Grace Menmo arched an eyebrow. 'You live off your loving neighbours in your hex, or the food here at home, or eat out.'

'I want to change that.'

'You don't know where to begin.'

'Isn't it enough that I *want* to begin?'

'Perhaps.' The old lady's nostrils flared, like they always did when she was amused. 'Why?'

'I want to expand my horizons—'

'Liar.'

'I want to be more self-sufficient—'

'Fraud.'

'I want to appreciate our culture—'

Grace Menmo studied her granddaughter. 'It's a new project, isn't it?' She half-smiled.

Serenity Ko beamed and swept in, her charm firing on all cylinders, meeting her business-proposal face to make the most of this crack in her grandmother's facade.

'It is,' she said, before launching into her sales pitch. She'd practised it in front of the mirror half a dozen times in hope that the conversation would get this far. 'I have a vision for a future in which food could spark memories and inspire dreams. Imagine the humble fish flatbread taking you back to your childhood, to the first time you held a net in your hands and scooped fish from a vat, marvelling at its glittering scales. Imagine beholding that in your mind's eye, exactly as you remember it, scents, subtle sounds and all.'

This bit was, admittedly, manipulative, because it was her grandmother's earliest memory of food, but Serenity Ko was going to press every advantage to bring this negotiation home. Grace Menmo looked at her, her expression unreadable.

'Imagine,' she continued, 'being able to taste an everberry pudding, that classic homage to our earliest Nakshatran settlers, and instead of simply acknowledging that your dessert is a tribute to them, being able to see the world through their eyes, via a sim that transports you to Nakshatran Rock, where everberry grew wild and many-hued on its towering, thorny bushes, the sweet scent of new beginnings in the air.'

Grace Menmo nodded her head ever so slightly, and Serenity Ko carried on. She broke down the tech, she explained how she was going to transform every culinary experience into an augmented reality festival of light and sound, colour and taste.

'Imagine how we could transform what food *means* to our culture—to every culture; to the universe itself. Help me make this dream come true.' She dropped her voice theatrically, holding her hand out, palm upward. 'All I ask is that you help me begin.'

'You want to begin? All right,' Grace Menmo said. She passed her hand over the micro-dishes of spice ras before her, freshly distilled earlier that morning from fruit, seed and leaf all growing in their garden. Peprino-corn, cumin, cilantrina, fennel, inji, chili, and half a dozen other ingredients filled the air with their heady, distinct aromas.

'I'm not a sadist, so I won't subject you to making your own spice blend right away,' she continued. 'But if you pass this very simple test, I'll consider helping you.'

Serenity Ko raised her chin. 'Whatever it is, I won't just pass. I'll do you proud.'

'Normally, I'd insist you were blindfolded, but that'd just be cruel.' Grace Menmo smirked.

Serenity Ko did not like the glint in the little old lady's eyes.

'Bring me a nanospoon.'

Serenity Ko's heart stuttered. What on earth was a nanospoon, and where could she find one in this dratted room? She rushed around the island and threw open every kitchen drawer in her path—swirly metal thing not spoon, weird pronged thing not spoon, plates, funny-looking tweezers, knives, *a plastic gun?*

'Beneath the flowmetal cook station,' the old lady said drily. 'It's the long empty counter with the display beside it.'

Serenity Ko yanked the drawer out. Spoons! So many shapes and sizes. Her heart sank. She grabbed one of each kind and plonked them all down on the island.

Grace Menmo surveyed them soundlessly, a cheek muscle twitching. 'Pick up the nanospoon, Ko.'

Serenity Ko pouted.

'Stop behaving like a five-year-old. It's the metal one with the really tiny scoop.'

Serenity Ko, still pouting, passed it to the old lady.

'Taste test,' Grace Menmo announced. 'With every ingredient completely visible. Identify any five spices correctly and I might just help you.'

'Bring it on,' Serenity Ko said boldly.

Grace Menmo scooped a near-invisible portion of black extract and placed it in her granddaughter's mouth. Serenity Ko waited for the flavour to hit her tastebuds. It didn't.

'Well, what is it?' the old lady said impatiently.

'I... can't taste anything,' Serenity Ko said, rolling her tongue around her empty mouth.

Grace Menmo exhaled loudly. 'I suppose your palate isn't sensitive enough to taste the proportions most competent home cooks are used to dealing in. We'll use a chai spoon.'

She picked up a small, but somewhat more familiar-looking spoon, and scooped up the black goop, shoving it into Serenity Ko's mouth.

Serenity Ko spluttered. Her mouth was on fire. She rushed to the kitchen sink and spat it out, tears streaming down her cheeks. 'Pep—' she gasped. 'Peprino-corn.'

'Beginner's luck. There's fresh tomato juice in the fridge. It'll help.'

Serenity Ko was two steps ahead of her, and she gulped the juice down, straight from the jug.

'Pour the rest into a glass?' the old lady suggested. 'Less savage.'

When Serenity Ko had recovered sensation in her tongue somewhat, she presented herself at her grandmother's—no, still Grace Menmo's—side again. It felt good to have guessed her first spice correctly. She should have a handle on the rest, easy. What the old lady didn't know was that Serenity Ko, while not a cook of any sort, was a connoisseur of flavour. Something brown-green was spooned into her mouth.

'Cumin.'

'Wrong.' Grace Menmo grinned triumphantly. 'Fennelo.'

'You win some, you lose some,' Serenity Ko countered.

'We'll see.'

A deep, earthy spice with a hint of sweetness came next, in the form of a brown ras. Serenity Ko could swear she'd tasted it in over a dozen cocktails. 'Cinnamon,' she proclaimed.

'Wrong,' Grace Menmo said remorselessly. 'Nutmeg.' For a brief moment, Ammamma reappeared behind that steely gaze, and added, 'You were close on flavour profile, though.'

She was far less kind when Serenity Ko decided rosinia tasted like clove, and stonespice tasted like bel-leaf.

It began to go downhill for Serenity Ko then, like a children's Ur-fable set in slow motion, a malevolent old lady spooning indistinguishable bits of sludge into her mouth, her wicked smile evolving into a nasty cackle with each subsequent failure to name the sometimes hot, sometimes sweet, sometimes unplaceable flavours as they rolled across her tongue. She *knew* what these things were—at least, she knew what kinds of foods she'd tasted them in before— but she had no idea what the plants they'd come from even looked like, or what they resembled, and how they tasted in their distilled form.

She guessed the sharp, acidic flavour cilantrina right, which was a brief highlight in what turned out to be an exercise in despair. Her frustration mounted as the number of untasted samples dwindled, until there was just one left, and she knew she'd failed the test.

The old lady spooned it into her mouth. The heat hit her with the full force of a spaceship seeking escape velocity, and memories flooded her as tears leaked down her face again. 'Chili,' she hissed. 'Unmistakably chili.'

She gulped the last of her tomato juice, then rushed to the fridge to search for grain-pulp, cramming it into her mouth with her bare hands until her tongue was no longer numb. She dabbed her eyes on her tunic sleeve, the tears coming partly from the spice, mostly from her frustration at having failed what should have been a simple enough test for anyone vaguely interested in food. If her grandmother was determined to be Grace Menmo, then Serenity Ko wouldn't show her a hint of weakness.

She turned around, and walked nonchalantly back to the site of her ordeal.

'You didn't pass,' Grace Menmo said.

'I know. But I got three right, and that's potential.'

'Three out of sixteen is failure.'

'Three out of sixteen is hope.'

A long pause ensued in which Grace Menmo's flinty demeanour softened, and Serenity Ko saw a shadow of her Ammamma behind it. She held her breath. Would it work?

'Fascinating,' Ammamma said. 'Your courage and optimism.'

Serenity Ko exhaled. Job done.

'But still failure.' Grace Menmo's mask was unreadable. 'Guess I won't be teaching you, after all.'

'Why not?' Serenity Ko asked, trying to keep her voice from getting high-pitched like it did every time a tantrum approached.

'Grace Menmo hasn't taken any professional requests since her retirement from the public eye thirty years ago,' she said flatly. 'I will not do so now, especially for someone who demonstrates such an abysmal absence of any skill whatsoever in the kitchen.'

'But…' Serenity Ko spluttered. 'But you're my *grandmother!* And you just sprung this stupid taste test on me!'

'You know me better than to play the grandmother card,' Grace Menmo said drily. 'Besides…'

'Besides what?' Serenity Ko said angrily.

'If you had an inkling of intuition for taste—even if you couldn't master how to cook—that'd be a place to start.'

'Then teach me!' Serenity Ko stamped her foot.

'Stop acting like a five-year-old.'

'Stop treating me like one.'

'Ko…' Grace Menmo melted back into her grandmother's stooped form, leaning against the kitchen island. 'You're missing the point completely. This test wasn't about putting you down. I did it to show you that there are some things you can't conquer just by brute force.'

'I don't want to *conquer* food, I want to *use* food…'

'I think it's a rubbish idea.'

'You *what?*'

'Not the concept. No, the concept is quite brilliant, really. It'll help Primian cuisine stay relevant despite ever-evolving tech leaps—and the everberry pudding is long overdue a reinvention or two, if you ask me—but it isn't about the concept at all, my dear granddaughter.'

'It isn't?'

'It's about you. It's about your reasons for wanting to do this.'

'Ammamma…' Serenity Ko hated how her voice came out a whine.

'Ko.' Her grandmother sighed. 'Food is about bringing people together, about creating memories and nurturing happiness. Food advances and reflects culture. It is *not* just another meaningless conquest in the relentless pursuit of ambition.'

'But you just said the concept was good.'

'The concept *is* good. Here's something you aren't going to agree with, or want to hear: I don't think you're ready to develop it.'

Serenity Ko slumped forwards over the counter. 'All I want to do is learn,' she whined.

'I'm not saying you can never build it, or that you're not the right person to develop this idea. You're my granddaughter, and I think you're brilliant,' Ammamma said gently. 'But you don't respect food the way you need to, or understand where it comes from, or care about the deep-rooted origins of our Primian culinary traditions. Forget the rest of the universe, you ambitious maniac.' She rubbed her back to soothe her. 'You need to feel broths and sauces bubbling up through your bones, dream of pillowy pastries and tart-shaped shells strewn across white sand beaches. Scents need to call to you and flavours sing to you, if you really want to do this right. And you're just not there.'

'I could get there if you helped me,' Serenity Ko sulked.

'It's not your how, it's your *why*,' Ammamma said. 'Come back when you want to do it to enrich your soul.'

'I won't give up so easily.'

'No, perhaps not.' Ammamma sighed. 'And maybe I've got a place for you to begin.'

Serenity Ko snapped upright, her eyes gleaming. 'Anything. I'll do anything.'

'You just ruined my spice blend proportions with this taste test.'

'*You* made me do it.'

'Don't talk back to your grandmother.' Ammamma scowled. 'All these spices need to be replaced, and you're going to do the replacing for me.'

'How?'

'Grab some syringes and harvest them from the garden.'

'And then you'll teach me how to cook?' Serenity Ko smiled brightly.

'Don't push your luck,' Ammamma warned, though her lips twitched into a ghost of a smile.

Serenity Ko rushed back to the kitchen drawers. She'd seen syringes in there somewhere.

'Third drawer to your left,' Ammamma said exasperatedly. 'I've sent you the right proportions on the Loop.'

Serenity Ko grabbed a handful of syringes. She rushed out the kitchen and into the courtyard with the shared garden space. This was easy—she had steady hands, all she needed was to extract ras from each plant and she'd be done in no time. She looked around the sea of colour—so many kinds of greens and browns and reds, purples and pinks and blues—and was filled with wonder. Until a hideous thought struck her.

She clenched her jaw and swore, before putting on a sickly sweet tone and heading back to the doorway. She hated asking for help.

'Ammamma,' she called. 'I don't know what any of these plants are.'

From within the kitchen, she heard her grandmother mutter, 'Idiot child.'

'Walk these streets that take you on a cultural journey
across the cosmos, all without ever having to leave the
planet!'

—Marketing slogan for the Uru and Beyond Marketplace

FIFTEEN

SOMETIMES, ALL IT takes is crying on a park bench on another
planet to raise your spirits. It helps when you have your oldest
friend around, even if they aren't human. It gets extra special
when your newest friend shows up and gives you an extra
warm hug, especially when they have nearly a dozen arms.

The tips of Starlight Fantastic's tentacles curled lilac with
concern, wilting as they stepped back from me.

'You look terrible,' they said. 'I'm sorry about *MegaChef*,
that was unacceptable and positively xenophobic
behaviour.' Starlight Fantastic rubbed my back with two
of their arms. 'You handled them with such courage and
grace. You were extraordinary. *Are* extraordinary.'

'Thanks.' I smiled. 'I'm just stuck. I have no idea what
I'm going to do next.'

'I'm sorry, it must be so difficult.' Starlight Fantastic's
fronds knotted together, turning blue. 'I can't even imagine
what it's like to have your home ripped away from you—
you've been through something so painful…'

You want to tell them the truth about leaving Earth?
Kili asked.

_Not yet. I don't know if I can trust them—or anyone on
this planet,_ I streamed, writhing with guilt.

'Just know that you can count on me to be in your corner,'
Starlight Fantastic added, their tentacles pulsing with little
flashes of yellow.

180

'Thank you again, really. I mean it.'

They turned up for you, I think they deserve to know...

Not yet, Kili. I sighed. _When the time is right, I will. I promise._

It was saddening that I'd been conditioned to be paranoid, even in the face of kindness.

The tips of Starlight Fantastic's fronds turned a delicate shade of pink, and they eyed me uncertainly. 'I don't know if it's too early for this, or if you'd even consider doing it, but I called in a favour with a friend.'

'What kind of favour?' My shoulders started to unknot, my curiosity piqued.

'They're named Moonage Daydream, and they cater private events. Nothing fancy. They do popups at the Uru and Beyond Marketplace, and they spoke to their head chef, and if you want to—I don't know if you do, or if it's too soon, but if you want to—they're doing a popup there today, and they'd love to work with you. They'll pay you, too, and I figured as a refugee—even though Primus takes care of all its people's basic needs—if you ever want to leave this planet, you could use the funds...' Their tentacles turned bright pink.

I flung my arms around Starlight Fantastic. 'You are amazing! I don't deserve this. You didn't need to go to all the trouble...'

They returned the hug with close to a dozen arms. 'I believe in you.'

Are you going to do it? Kili burbled with excitement.

I stepped back and choked down a sob. 'I don't deserve this,' I said again.

Are you going to do it? Kili spun circles in the air.

'You deserve more. This is just a tiny shot of encouragement. If you want it, that is.'

My head spun with indecision. My cheeks grew warm, and as much as I tried to fight it, a bubble of excitement welled up within me. 'Today, you say?'

'Ah, let me just check with Moonage Daydream,' Starlight Fantastic said, then went silent as the seconds ticked by.

Are you going to do it? Kili practically yelled into my mind. He stopped whizzing around and fixed his pixelated eyes upon me. _It'll be star-fucking amazing._

'So they've prepped for service. Moonage Daydream's sent me their recipes—they're all nouveau-Primian, I can send them to you on the Loop if you'd like. And they'd like to know if you want to be there today? They open in an hour.'

I looked from Kili, fixing me with an unblinking LED stare, to Starlight Fantastic, whose tentacles were now streaked silver with hope. I exhaled. 'I'm not sure if I'm ready, or how good I'll be... but I'll give it a shot.'

Kili whooped and began flying figure of eights in the air. Starlight Fantastic glimmered gold with satisfaction, and an incoming transmission popped up on my Loop.

'Let's catch the first tram there?' I asked.

'I've got my shuttle in the parking bay here,' Starlight Fantastic said. 'Follow me.'

You set this whole thing up, didn't you?

Who me? Kili hummed innocently. _Nope._

Right, Starlight Fantastic just happened to show up at the bench we were sobbing at all on their own. With a job offer in hand, too.

Bench *you* were sobbing at. *I* was being a supportive friend.

Thank you. I grinned as we reached Starlight Fantastic's craft. The flowmetal doors slid open and I strapped myself in.

'Did you get the recipes?' Starlight Fantastic asked as they performed pre-flight checks.

'Yes, thank you.'

'I'll leave you in silence to study, then. Ten minutes to Uru and Beyond Marketplace, tops.'

I can't believe I'm going to cook again. I shuddered as Kili holorayed the recipes for me.

I'm so excited you get to cook again!

Shush, studying.

I forced myself to ignore the stunning view of Uru rippling and flowing outside the craft's windows. The recipes were anything but straightforward, at least from an Earth chef's perspective. They all relied on combining various types of ras with concentrators, and infusing them into terrines, gels, spheres and liquids of different consistencies. Typical Primian stuff. I assumed the "nouveau" tag came from the occasional use of off-world flavours, so as not to upset any hardcore traditionalist palettes.

'Do you know what station I'm supposed to be at?' I asked Starlight Fantastic, mildly overwhelmed by the onslaught of information. Holovids of ideal consistencies, spice ratios in microgrammes and harvesting techniques for each type of ras spun before me.

'Moonage Daydream didn't quite say, but they're a really small team, so I guess everyone does a little bit of everything?'

'Oh. Great.'

'Is that a problem?'

'Not at all,' I lied, throwing myself back into my perusal of their recipes. There was no way I was going to remember them all; I'd just have to ask to be put on the simplest task of all, which at this point appeared to be preparing the ras infusions for each recipe. Not applying them, though— there were specific aesthetic requirements for each kind of combination.

'Touchdown in two minutes,' Starlight Fantastic announced.

'Already?' My voice came out in a squeak.

You'll nail this, Kili piped up reassuringly.

One of the landing pads burgeoned beneath our craft, and we descended smoothly onto it. I caught sight of a spiralling narrow-laned marketplace before our craft was swallowed up into its pod and we continued to descend.

'I'm so excited for you!' Starlight Fantastic said as the flowmetal doors slid open. We stepped out into light, crisp air carrying a thousand different elusive fragrances and sounds our way. The vision before me was a blur of light and colour, humans dressed in everything from everfeather and greendust ornaments, frostshine glistening off Pulu scales, chrome and neon B'naar mecha exosuits glinting in the sur-light, vendors all calling out from behind their displays, some at ground level, others hovering on anti-grav platforms. Every display beamed holographic signage, all overlapping in rainbows.

I walked past the stalls in a daze, taking in everything from home remedies for scalepox to potent ras-blend aphrodisiacs, warp drive enhancers, flowmetal manipulators and stencils for DIY flow-smiths, multi-utility robotic limbs with so many mods they made my head spin, hybrid plants and florals by the dozen that meshed native Primian flora with off-world species in bizarre geometries, all wafting powerful aromas I'd never smelled before. It was a surreal fusion of the traditional and organic with technologies I didn't even know existed, from cultures across the universe, all packed into a tightly-coiled spiral of streets, side by side with little-to-no elbow room, all flourishing, an intergalactic millefeuille.

I heard a polyphonic chiming of bells, which should have sounded atonal but somehow pealed together right at the edge of harmony, with some kind of woodwind instrument playing counterpoint. I looked up to see a wide circular tent hovering thirty feet in the air, like an acoustic stage, with a pair of Axians—one playing some kind of strange harp, and the other a woodwind that resembled four flutes assembled together at different lengths. Exotic-looking instruments surrounded them, all made to suit their incredible physiognomy, which included double-jointed opposable thumbs and wrists, and an impressive lung capacity. They were practically human in appearance, but human players of Axian instruments were rare because of all the mods they required to play melodically. The Axian with the harp caught my eye, winked at me, and flicked their harp pick down at me. Heat spread through my cheeks as I caught it, and I giggled.

Cute. Want me to broadcast your Loop deets to them? Kili said smugly.

Shut up. It seemed my day was looking up.

We turned right after following the narrow street for a while, and I was smacked in the face with the scents of food being prepared a hundred different ways. Stands filled with fresh produce of every conceivable kind were interspersed with serving counters displaying live food from the only semi-permanent structures I'd seen so far in the marketplace—their flowmetal bubbling into hemispherical stalls, windows wrapping around them for lighting, ventilation, and a view of the kitchens within. I couldn't help but notice that the vast majority of the stalls were Primian, but they were impressive nonetheless.

We walked past a harvest-station; a profusion of natural produce lay on display, with customers lining up to use syringes to distil their ras. A kitchen beside it offered Primian street food; it looked to me like flavoured sheets of flaky pastry. Another store sold vat-grown proteins, everything from venison to fish, and my stomach knotted as we passed their freshwater display, memories of my *MegaChef* debacle lurking too close to the surface. The kitchen beside them was serving up proteins with a strange type of marbling; they appeared to be cured in various kinds of infusions. I paused to watch one chef layer a vat-grown fillet of bison in a rich green and gold suspension, and they flashed me a smile, while my heart sank at how primitive my presentation on *MegaChef* must have seemed.

Move on, Kili said. _You're starting to spiral._

I did just that. It became apparent to me that there wasn't a single kitchen in the meandering marketplace that used an open flame to do its cooking. Other cultural offerings included powdered punchfruit from Pulu, Axian cheeses, and sorbettos styled after the frostfruit on Chomo. No sign of any Earth food, though.

'There's an Earthling stall right at the end,' Starlight Fantastic said, as if reading my mind. 'Maybe we can stop by there after your popup? Because we're here.'

They stopped at a nondescript flowmetal structure and twisted their tentacles in greeting. An E'nemon appeared behind a stall that didn't seem to have any pre-cooked foods on display. They reciprocated the gesture. 'Starlight Fantastic, you brought her!' They turned to me. 'Welcome, Saraswati. I'm Moonage Daydream, and it's such a pleasure to meet you.'

I did my best to emulate their greeting by twisting my arms together, and they laughed like Starlight Fantastic first had when I met them. '*Shi-shi-shiri*, oh, Starlight Fantastic wasn't lying about you. You're delightful!'

'It's such a pleasure to meet you,' I said. 'Thank you so much for this opportunity.'

'Come on in!'

The flowmetal of the stall swung forwards creating a doorway, and I stepped into a kitchen filled with alien scents, equipment and produce, Kili whirring behind me.

'This is my Winger, Kili.'

'Lovely to meet you! And here's Curiosity Zia. She curates our humble food experiences.'

A short, slight woman, her hair tied in a messy braid threaded with beaded jewels, stuck her hand out, and I took it. She had radiant neon face tattoos.

'Thank you for having me,' I said. 'I love your tats.'

'Thank you! And no problem! I know how hard it is to catch a break on the food scene here in Uru.' She grinned widely, and her smile reached her eyes. 'I've been fired from half a dozen restaurants for introducing unconventional flavours to Primian cuisine. Welcome to The New Palette, we're only open only once a week for lunch, because that's all we can afford.'

She jabbed her thumb at the stall beside the popup. 'We use most of their produce, and it changes nearly every week. They're former Wanderers, so their expertise is in foraging.'

'That explains all the shroomings and berries on the menu,' I said, nodding.

'I caught you on *MegaChef*,' Curiosity Zia said. 'I thought they were unnecessarily hard on you. We're happy to give you a shot.'

'Thanks! I don't know if I'm going to be much help, though. First time actually working with Primian flavours.'

'Don't worry about it. Say, you don't mind if I put a notif up on the Loop that you're our guest chef for this week, do you?'

'Um…'

_Do it,_ Kili said. _The people will love you in your element._

'Sure,' I said. 'Whatever helps the popup, I suppose.'

'Awesome. You're going to meet a ton of our regulars, they're great. Moonage Daydream will help set you up.'

Her eyes glazed over, and I figured she was updating the Loop.

Moonage Daydream introduced me to their third chef, a Primian named Courage Oslo. He walked me through their process: Curiosity Zia would handle the pass and plating, Moonage Daydream would take care of the cook station—fire free, I couldn't help but observe—and Courage Oslo would handle garnish.

'Do you think you can take care of our infusions? We do them live, so our ras has as much fresh flavour as possible.'

'Sure, can you show me how to harvest ras? Never done it before,' I said, putting on my apron and grabbing a towel.

'It's simple,' Courage Oslo said. 'Stick a syringe in and draw until you hit the right measure, hit the right combination for each order and pass them to me at one go. I'll handle the rest.'

He then proceeded to show me how and where to draw ras from different types of ingredients—caps for shroomings, flesh for root vegetables and berries, veins for leaves. I drew a deep breath; it was very precise, the complete opposite to my intuitive style in the kitchen.

'I usually do it all,' he added. 'And it gets crazy! So it's great to have your help on this today.'

'Looks like we've got a crowd gathered outside, folks!' Curiosity Zia called while we all added final touches to our mise en place. 'Opening in ten, that good?'

'Yes, chef!' I called, a burst of adrenalin flooding through me.

Isn't this exciting? Kili buzzed.

Terrifying.

You love it.

I love it.

Before I knew it, I was surrounded by syringes while Courage Oslo whispered urgent instructions to me. 'Two orders of root medley spheres; that's 25 µg wild carrot, 17 µg batatas, and 0.57 µg fennelo for each. Excellent. Thank you. A shrooming symphony; that's 51 µg of every single shrooming except the onaake—that's the feathered big one, overpowering flavour so just 0.30 µg of that, please. Great! You're doing so well. Berry-anna, lovely traditional Primian dessert, you ever tried it? No? On your list for after service, and I need 70 µg of fraiseberry, 28 µg of each kind of rubus—those are the small spherical berries, another 42 µg of everberry… you're a natural, way to go!'

Kili holorayed images of each ingredient as Courage Oslo called them out to me, which helped me keep track of what I was harvesting. My head spun, my hands working on autopilot, trembling at the precision of each measure, heart soaring each time I got them spot on.

'Oi, Saraswati,' Curiosity Zia announced. 'Meet Honour Kaya, they're one of our regulars.'

'Hello!' I said loudly. 'Lovely to meet you.'

Honour Kaya wore their hair buzzed on one side, and had piercings all the way up one ear. 'Great to meet you, Saraswati!' they yelled. 'I'd like my Berry-anna with extra sourness, yeah?'

'Got it,' I lied.

'Extra sourness,' Courage Oslo muttered to me. 'That means you extract 28 µg of each kind of rubus except the bright red ones. Get me 70 µg of those. Got it?'

'Yes, chef.'

'Great, next order: a leafy pastry, so that's 21 µg of the sourleaf and stoneleaf, 61 µg of palakki, 13.5 µg of mythi…'

The rest of Courage Oslo's words were drowned out by a loud whoop. 'There she is!'

A face appeared at the serving counter and pointed at me. A swarm of drones fluttered into the kitchen, as Curiosity Zia yelled, 'Stop!' Courage Oslo swore. I dropped the syringe in my hands and froze.

'How does it feel to be a failure, Saraswati Kaveri?' the face at the counter called. 'Harmony Selia, she/her, reporter for the *Gourmand Gossip*.'

'Um, what?' I said, still in shock.

'Get out of our restaurant,' Curiosity Zia snapped.

'Watch your tone, dearie. One bad review and you'll never cook again,' Harmony Selia said, tossing her braid over her shoulder. 'If you call this cooking, that is.' She wrinkled her nose up as Curiosity Zia served a many-layered gelee topped with some kind of spice grain. 'Really, blending Axian crumbspice with Primian root vegetables? Experimental even for this hole in the wall, no?'

'I'll handle this,' I said, stepping forwards and crossing my arms over my chest. It was a lot bolder than I felt, but I felt terrible for bringing this lady—whoever she was, she was trouble—to Curiosity Zia's doorstep.

Harmony Selia smirked and snapped her fingers. At least a dozen more drones flew in, and more faces appeared at the window. All of them started screaming questions at me, and the world around me began to blur.

'How does it feel to be a failure?'

Kili popped into my thoughts. _Saras, get out._

'Do you feel like a sellout, now that you're making Primian food? Especially after serving Earth slop to our judges on *MegaChef*?'

Saras, you don't need to answer that.

'Did you run away from the Earth because you were a failure there, too?'

Saras, let's go. You don't need to answer any of these questions.

Something in me snapped. 'I came here because from everything everyone on Primus claims, it's a land of equal opportunity for all, no matter where they come from or what species they are. It's the Nakshatran way. But people like you? You don't embody it one bit.' My voice came out a pitch higher than usual. 'Moonage Daydream, is there a rear exit?'

'No, just the one out front, I'm afraid.'

'Cool, thanks.'

Let's run for it.

I ran for it. Drones pelted after me, filming my escape. I heard new voices calling after me, dozens of them—hundreds?

'That's the fail Earthling from *MegaChef*!'

'Fuck, I'm never eating at The New Palette again! They hire trash like this?'

I knocked into someone, and wheeled away from them. 'Nine Virtues, mom!' I heard them say as I spun away.

'That's the Earthling loser from *MegaChef*. Should I have asked her to take a holopic with me?'

The marketplace was suddenly a labyrinth of terrors. My breathing was jagged, my heart pounded loud enough to overpower my thoughts, but not enough to drown out the foreignness everywhere I turned; the overpowering scents, even the music I'd found so resplendent earlier on crashed upon me in cacophony.

Are they still behind us?

Just a couple of drones. Look, I'm mapping this place; there's a little archway up ahead. Turn left when I say now.

I put on a reinvigorated burst of speed. We were so close to losing them.

Now.

I spun on my heel, banking left, and ducked under an awning into a dark archway. I bent over, my breath coming out in rasps. 'What... the fuck... just happened?'

'I don't know, Earth girl, but you seem to be in bad shape,' came a voice from the gloom. 'Fancy running into you here.'

Endless masquerading without a single stitch!
Send us your feedback on the latest protoype...

—Advert on the XP Inc. Internal Comms Dash

SIXTEEN

SERENITY KO WAS having the type of day she associated with regrets, and this time, she couldn't blame it on alcohol.

She wholly regretted attempting to talk her grandmother into teaching her about Primian cuisine; her grandmother—evidently discontent with the idyllic pastimes of retirement—had turned a basic request to walk her through life in the kitchen, preferably in twenty-eight hours or less, into a supermassive quest, complete with side missions. Serenity Ko suspected her Ammamma was more motivated by schadenfreude than setting her granddaughter up for success. Serenity Ko could have—*should* have—walked away, but as much as she hated to admit it, she needed Ammamma's help. And now that Ammamma had set this up as a challenge, she needed—and wanted—her approval.

That's how she found herself at the Uru and Beyond Marketplace. Ammamma had sent her off on a "tasting mission," which involved rendezvousing with three independent chefs, tasting their Berry-anna desserts, and compiling a report comparing their flavour profiles.

Should have just done my research on Outcooked 5, she thought again, not for the first or the last time.

And then came mistake the second. Serenity Ko had fucked her day sideways by publicly streaming about a new, top secret research project at Uru and Beyond. Honour Aki thoughtstreamed her immediately to say he was on his way to help. Now here she was, playing cat and mouse with him in this warren of market stalls after successfully managing to avoid him entirely for the better part of a nava.

Serenity Ko wanted to scream.

She'd spotted his distinctive auburn topknot and three-forked braid ahead of her on the street, and ducked into the nearest archway—dark, gloomy, wreathed in shadows—to evade him. Only to stumble upon the strange woman from Earth and her archaic whirring mechanical companion, doubled over in the darkness, choking on her own breath and threatening to sob.

Days like this made Serenity Ko wish she'd never left her space.

She slid out of the Loop, leaving only her dark-vision filter on, and approached the Earthling cautiously. 'Are you okay?' she asked, not really wanting an answer.

'No,' the Earthling wheezed.

Chased by cam-drones, the funny little machine beside her said.

'Whatever for?' Serenity Ko snorted. 'Are you famous?'

'More... like... infamous...' the Earthling gasped, raising her head to make eye contact. Her light brown eyes swam with tears, and one streaked down her cheek, which was starkly pale in the dimness. She brushed it away hurriedly, and another one followed. 'Sorry, need a moment,' she choked.

'Sure, take all the time you need,' Serenity Ko said gruffly.

The Earthling slid down the wall and sat on her haunches. Her short halo of curls fell back from her face, revealing a strong, square jaw clenched in a grimace. She almost looked beautiful—

No, her nose was turning red and blotchy. She was clearly devastated.

Devastatingly beautiful.

Serenity Ko buried the thought in a cold, dark place she hoped she'd never rediscover. *I should walk away.* She glanced back at the Earthling, who was wiping her face upon her sleeve. She was so pathetically broken and lonely that it felt cruel to leave her alone.

The AI machine thing was nuzzling up to her cheek now, and the Earthling stroked it absent-mindedly, her eyes gazing off into the middle distance, which was a wall six feet away. Serenity Ko tried to be sensitively silent and still, but as the moments slipped by in the gloom, her fingers twitched and she shuffled her feet. The Earthling's head snapped around.

'I'm okay,' she said unconvincingly.

'Sure,' Serenity Ko said skeptically.

'Really.'

'I believe you.'

'Thanks.'

'Need a hand?' Serenity Ko stepped forwards, and stuck her palm out. The Earthling grasped it, and she hauled her to her feet, ignoring the sharp buzz that shot through her senses when their hands clasped. It was just like that day on the ship, except worse, because this time she was sober. She hurried to push the thoughts away into more cold, dark places, and jabbed her hands in the pockets of her jacket.

'Thanks again. I'll just hide here until Suriya sets and they can't find me,' the Earthling said.

Serenity Ko didn't have the heart to tell her the cam-drones were now familiar with her heat signature, and would be able to lock onto her whenever she was in close proximity. So she deflected. 'Right. Because "infamous," you say?'

The Earthling exhaled slowly. 'I fucked up on a reality show a few days ago...'

'Oh, the *MegaChef* thing?' Serenity Ko scoffed.

'Seriously, does everyone on this sur-fucked planet watch it?' the Earthling moaned.

'My grandmother does, so yeah, I watched you stuff up pretty bad.' Serenity Ko shrugged. 'But don't worry, this is Uru, it'll all be forgotten a week from now.'

There were people on the street outside yelling awful things at her, the AI whirred.

'Sorry about that. But they're just idiots letting off steam.'

'Yes, discrimination is just idiocy.' The Earthling sounded annoyed.

'All I'm saying is, it's perfectly safe out there, and we can step out, go our separate ways, and have a perfectly delightful day,' Serenity Ko said, trying to hide her impatience.

'I'm not leaving,' the Earthling said firmly. 'You're free to go.'

'Uh-huh.'

'Really, you don't know me from a spindle-tree,' the Earthling said haughtily. 'You're not obliged to babysit me.'

Serenity Ko had to admit she had a point. And yet, now that the woman had stopped crying, she seemed even more pitiable than before. She slid into the Loop, and flipped through a batch of prototypes that flitted across her irises, each one a different holographic experience. 'Everything would be easier if you just had Loop access,' she muttered.

'I do,' the Earthling sighed, pointing at her machine companion.

'I mean if you were plugged in directly.'

'What?' the Earthling said stupidly.

'I've got a prototype here for... where is it? Right, so it's a silly Immersive Reality mod we're designing for masquerading—you know, costume stuff?'

'I know what a masquerade is,' the Earthling snapped.

'Yeah okay, it's just that your Ur-speak is accented. Wanna switch to Vox?'

'My Ur-speak is fine.'

'If you say so.'

The Earthling glowered at her.

'Sorry, didn't mean to offend. As I was saying, this mod could work as cloaking tech for you—you know, hide your identity behind a disguise, physically simulate another appearance to other people on the Loop,' Serenity Ko continued, flipping through the programme's settings. 'But it needs internal Loop circuits. You whirry metal bird won't do.'

'I understand nothing you're saying.'

'Look, will you just swallow a nanopill if I hand you one? I'll hook you up with a subscription. You'll have a disguise.' Serenity Ko spoke like she was talking to a five-year-old.

The Earthling laughed. Serenity Ko looked past her optics feed at her and scowled. 'What?'

'You're asking me to accept pills from a stranger I met in a dark tunnel on a foreign planet,' the Earthling said with another giggle.

'Or you could just hide here all day,' Serenity Ko said grouchily, now wishing she'd walked away when she'd had the chance. 'We can fix this identity thing in ten minutes, the nanocircuitry will degrade in a month and you can go back to your primitive Earth tech if you like. It should also integrate just fine with your whirry drone companion.'

'Winger. His name's Kili.'

'Right. Kili. So what do you say?'

'Should I be concerned about my privacy?' The Earthling frowned.

'Nope. You can customise all that once you mess around with it.'

The Earthling looked at her Winger and they seemed to be streaming a private conversation. Serenity Ko watched the seconds flit by on her optics feed, all the time wondering why she was going out of her way to help this woman. *Must be my good heart,* she thought, with a twinge of regret.

'Fine.' The Earthling's shoulders slumped in resignation. 'Let's do this.'

Serenity Ko fished around in her pocket—good thing she always kept a stash on her for promo opportunities—and pulled out a nanopill. The capsule glistened white in the gloom as she handed it over.

'I can't hook you up with haptic controls here—I don't have the machinery—so you'll need to use voice prompts,' she explained.

The Earthling nodded, then swallowed the pill, grimacing.

'Well done.' Serenity Ko slid back into the Loop. 'In a couple of minutes you'll have an optics feed. Don't panic, just follow the voice down the hallway, yeah?'

The Earthling gasped. 'What have you done to me?'

'Follow the voice down the hallway. It'll be okay.'

'Oh!' the Earthling gasped again, then exclaimed in genuine delight. 'This is gorgeous!'

'You're probably in the Receiving Hall. No haptics, so pick voice commands as your primary input function.'

The Earthling then began a very one-sided conversation with the AI within the setup module. The only good to come of it was that Serenity Ko finally picked up her name—Saraswati Kaveri—and filed it away so she wouldn't come across rude for the next fifteen minutes.

Just you and me, little guy, Serenity Ko broadcast to the Winger.

Great. The Winger's broadcast was accompanied by the image of a wall.

So tell me, Kili. Is Saraswati really a fucking terrible chef, after all?

No. She's absolutely fucking brilliant. Kili sent across a burst of imagery that resonated with shiny medals and trophies, accompanied by scrolls and vids of rave reviews.

Seriously?

So brilliant one of the sur-fucking judges on the show offered her a job after he trashed her food.

Which one?

One of the Earthling twins. Talk about two-faced: stabbing someone in the back in public one moment, and coming on like a saviour the next.

_Everyone on this planet is a star-fucker. He was probably

trying to get on the Chief Chef lady's good side,_ Serenity Ko said.

Saraswati muttered commands into thin air.

Serenity Ko fidgeted with the buttons on her jacket.

So is she taking the job?

_No,_ Kili said archly.

Why not?

Why would she?

Um, to get on the inside, win their trust and then take them down? Perfect revenge setup.

Huh.

You think about that now. Serenity Ko sent a barrage of imagery that included raging fireballs and winky emotes.

I like it, but you should tell her about it, Kili said.

Why me?

I can't. I'm programmed to not communicate acts of deception and subterfuge, though I can condone them if they're presented to me.

It must suck to be an AI.

'I'm done! Wow, that was a head rush,' Saraswati said, interrupting their conversation. 'Kili, are you feeling okay?'

The Winger chirruped and burbled, bobbing up and down as if examining a new outfit. _Yes. All integrated. I feel a bit lighter, you know? Zippier, even._ Kili whirred around the dark passageway, streaming light in rainbow colours.

'You're welcome,' Serenity Ko said. 'Now look, a few simple rules and we can get out of here.'

She slid her thumb and fingers together as if dealing cards, and transferred the sim prototype to Saraswati, who said, 'Accept.'

'Right, so pick a masquerade costume. Your optics will work fine—just say "Dismiss" if they ever get disorientating, but make sure you don't kill the holoray,' Serenity Ko explained. 'You won't feel a thing.'

'Aaah... got it!'

On Serenity Ko's visual, a shimmer surrounded Saraswati as she was engulfed in a sparkling cloud. It dissipated to reveal her in a tight green tunic, belted at the waist with beadwork, and black leggings tucked into boots. Greendust jewels were sprayed across her hair—now in a high braid—and her face was equal parts enhanced and disguised beneath flattering green holographic makeup. She was momentarily breathtaking.

'Didn't take you for a Chloriana fan,' Serenity Ko said, stifling a gasp.

'Maximum makeup,' Saraswati said. 'Also, I grew up a diehard fan of Legends of the Future, best smash band of all-time, if you ask me. And it was either her or Enigma, and they're just not my vibe.'

It dawned on Serenity Ko that Enigma was *exactly her vibe*, and would probably let her walk right past Honour Aki if he were still lurking around.

'Hang on, give me a mo,' she said, then caught herself. *Hang on for what?* It wasn't as if they were friends. 'I mean, you're free to leave now, serenity and harmony et cetera,' she said hastily. As the words left her mouth, her fingers tapped out an intricate pattern against each other as she customised the Enigma costume to her liking, then triggered it.

She refocused on reality and caught Saraswati staring at her, as if hypnotised. 'What?'

'That's stunning on you.'

Heat rose to Serenity Ko's cheeks. 'Thanks.'

A silence filled with awkwardness and unplaceable tension seemed to smother the cramped archway. Serenity Ko shattered it. 'So um, you know, good luck with everything.'

'I owe you,' Saraswati smiled.

'Nah, the first month of the subscription is a free trial. You'll be charged after that, so it's no big deal...' Serenity Ko realised she was rambling and quickly changed tack. 'Ready to see sur-light again?'

Serenity Ko led them out. She noticed how Saraswati's shoulders tensed, then eased once she realised that absolutely nobody on the street outside had given her a second glance.

She spotted the first destination on her quest from Ammamma—a food stand shaped like a sorbetto swirl with a holosign that read *Sweet Surshine*.

'Okay, that's me,' she said, pointing at it. 'Nice to see you again. Serenity and harmony be upon—'

'Can I at least buy you a kaapi to thank you?' Saraswati interrupted her.

'Actually...' Serenity Ko's brain ticked double-time as a sudden burst of inspiration found her. 'You can buy me that kaapi and do me a favour. We'll call things square then.'

'Okay...' Saraswati's brows knit together.

'It's food related, nothing shady.'

And maybe you can tell her about your epic revenge plan? Kili broadcast.

'What epic revenge plan?'

'Kaapi?' Serenity Ko nodded in the direction of the stand. She walked the Earthling through her Ammamma's challenge, and Saraswati burst out laughing, right as they reached the sidewalk seating at the food stall. Serenity Ko's brain raced to find ways to make her laugh again, and she squashed the thought firmly, resisting the sparkle lighting up Saraswati's eyes.

'You're using me to cheat!'

'The old lady has, like, a hundred years on me or something,' Serenity Ko said. 'Come on! It's an unfair advantage. I'm just rising to the challenge. You're a qualified chef—somewhere in this star-fucked universe, at least. How bad could you be?'

She ordered two cups of kaapi and two Berry-annas, and missed the grimace that crossed Saraswati's face.

That was rude, Kili broadcast.

'What? Come on, don't take it personally,' Serenity Ko

said defensively. 'I don't know you from a grape. All I know of you is from that *MegaChef* episode. I don't really remember the flowship ride,' she half-lied. 'And then you were panicking in a dark archway for the last ten minutes...'

Saraswati rose to her feet. 'This was a terrible idea.'

Serenity Ko panicked. 'No! I'm sorry, what I meant to say was I'm sorry.'

'Are you sure my primitive Earthling palate will be of any help?' Saraswati asked snidely, sitting back down.

Serenity Ko paused, taken aback. She considered the best way to respond politely. She wasn't sure, not really. Except it couldn't get worse than her own ability to taste things, could it?

'Great, silence. That's all I need to know, thanks.' Saraswati's shoulders stiffened, her face frosting over in an expressionless mask.

'Look, I don't know how Earthlings do food, yeah?' Serenity Ko said honestly. 'But you can't be worse than I am, I guess.'

'Your confidence is heartwarming,' Saraswati said coldly.

Serenity Ko stifled her frustration. She *needed* this Earthling's help, and she was fucking it all up.

'I'm sorry,' she said sincerely. 'My auto-mode is no filter, and that can sometimes sound mean.'

'Sometimes?'

'Hey, I helped you, right?' Serenity Ko hated how her voice came out, whiny and defensive. 'I can't be *all* bad.'

'No, you probably aren't. But you could work on the words that come out of your mouth. I hate being in debt, so I'm going to help you, too, and then we can never see each other again?'

Serenity Ko expected a sparkle of sarcasm to light Saraswati's eyes and found none. She leaned back in her chair. 'Fine.'

Their order arrived right on time to interrupt what might have turned into a drawn-out staring contest. Saraswati gasped in delight and leaned forwards to examine the sugary confection on her plate, the kaapi all but forgotten. 'This smells glorious.'

Serenity Ko slid into the Loop and drew up her dash. 'I'm going to take notes while you taste, yeah?'

Saraswati rolled her eyes, annoyed, as if Serenity Ko had committed a grave crime by interrupting her first contact with the food on her plate.

I usually leave her alone at tastings. Kili slid into her thoughtstream.

What is she, some kind of eccentric genius?

Yes.

Serenity Ko watched Saraswati delicately sniff, then try each individual component on the plate—all of which she was hoping Saraswati would name for her. She closed her eyes each time, covering her mouth delicately while she chewed and swirled them around her tongue. Then she dug in with her hands, scooped up a generous portion of the dessert, and popped it in her mouth. She tilted her head back and exhaled.

Saraswati swallowed, then looked straight into Serenity Ko's eyes. 'Delicious,' she said.

The breath caught in her throat, and Serenity Ko forced herself to make words. 'It's supposed to be.'

'You haven't touched yours.' Saraswati dove back in for more.

'Yeah, better get started,' Serenity Ko said, wishing there was more air in the outdoors. She hated—absolutely *hated*—how beautiful people, even Earthling weirdos, could set her hormones on fire.

She studied the Berry-anna before her: sheets of golden-brown pastry covered in frothy foam, topped with little gel spheres in an abundance of colour stared back at her. She broke a piece off and popped it into her mouth. 'Fuck. Delicious,' she mumbled while chewing.

'So what are the flavours telling you?' Saraswati asked.

'I don't know... yummy, sweet, fruity?' Serenity Ko offered.

Saraswati sighed. 'Okay, here's my dubiously expert take on it, just because you asked.'

'*I said I'm sorry.*'

'Right.' Saraswati raised her eyebrows skeptically. 'Take notes. You'll need them. The dessert is a play on texture first: crunchy pastry, airy and light foam, and each sphere has a different consistency. Or did you not notice that?'

'Sure, yeah, totally noticed.'

'Pastry's slightly salted, foam isn't sweetened, and it's a nutty liqueur, to offset the fresh sweetness of the berry spheres.'

'Right, right.' Serenity Ko watched with satisfaction as notes scrolled across her dash.

'Spheres are rubus, fraise, everberry... ' Saraswati ticked the ingredients off on her fingers. 'But everberry is dominant for its sweetness. Did you get all that?'

'Yes, thank you.' Serenity Ko took a sip of her kaapi and choked. It was disgustingly bitter.

Saraswati snorted with laughter. 'You really need help, don't you?' she said, calmly sipping on her own beverage. 'Bitter things taste *more* bitter after sugary dessert. Write that down, too, while you're at it.'

Serenity Ko scowled and downed the rest of her kaapi stoically, fighting the urge to gag. 'Let's get this done with quickly.'

'Lead the way,' Saraswati said with a shrug.

The next food stand—Arcside Artistry—featured a very different Berry-anna.

'It all smushes together, so it's a lot more decadent. They use a compote instead of a liqueur foam, much fruitier overall,' Saraswati said.

Serenity Ko took notes in relative silence, partly awestruck by Saraswati's depth of detail, mostly embarrassed by a newfound sharp awareness of her capacity to make an idiot of herself. 'The final one on my list is The New Palette,' she announced thickly, reading off her dash.

Saraswati froze with a handful of sugar and cream midway to her mouth.

'Something wrong?'

'I'm not going there, sorry. I've helped you with two out of three. You're on your own now,' she said abruptly, her face paling.

'What? You can't hang me out to dry now!'

'Sorry, no choice.' The Earthling's voice shook. 'Like you keep saying, we don't know each other, and I think it's time for us to go our separate ways.' Saraswati rose from her chair. 'Thanks again for helping me out today.'

Serenity Ko felt a dozen different kinds of confusion hit her at once. 'I don't understand,' she said stupidly.

'And we're not friends. I don't have to explain.'

'Yeah, okay. You're right.'

Tell her about your revenge plan, Kili broadcast again.

'Oh, yeah, you had a revenge plan?' Saraswati asked impatiently.

'Yeah, if I were you, I'd take that job with the douchebag chef from the show. Win their trust. Take them down from the inside,' Serenity Ko said.

'Great plan, thanks.' Saraswati met Serenity Ko's gaze, then took an uncertain step forwards. 'Listen, I'm sorry I'm leaving you in the lurch. I was at The New Palette when the cam-drones showed up. I can't go back.'

Serenity Ko was caught completely off-guard when the Earthling threw her arms around her in a quick hug. 'Thanks again for earlier. I don't know if I'll ever run into you again, and I hope I don't, because talking with you is like being stabbed with a billion needles all at once, but I won't forget your kindness. Serenity and harmony be upon you.'

'Well, talking with you is like...' Serenity Ko struggled to assemble the rest of her comeback, which had been veering dangerously towards ending with the words "licking sur-beams." Instead, she stared blankly at Saraswati.

'Yes?'

'Forget it.'

'Guess I'll never find out.' The Earthling smirked.

'Serenity and harmony and all that star-fucking rubbish,' Serenity Ko called, as she watched the weirdo Earthling and her whirry drone companion get swallowed up into the crowd.

'Ko, is that you?' she heard a man's voice say behind her. She whirled around in her chair and crammed the rest of her Berry-anna into her mouth to stop herself from swearing.

Honour Aki beamed at her. 'Nearly missed you in your Enigma outfit, but luckily, the prototype glitched right as I was walking past!'

Stupid prototype, Serenity Ko thought. This day was all regrets.

It takes nearly a Suriyan year to get a table at the unparalleled Nonpareil, a restaurant so aptly named and impeccably cultured in its twenty-three-course tasting menu that it leaves all of us at *The Consummate Cuisinologist* lost for words. Before I make known the skill and subtlety of the culinary experience that graced our dinner table, I must acknowledge the mastery over Primian cuisine demonstrated by its Earthling Executive Chefs. Yes, you read right! Earthlings, but not Earth-primitive. No vulgar flavours and rich comfort foods to be found on this menu. Instead, a sophisticated tapestry of taste...

—Courage Anderson,
Chief Critic at *The Consummate Cuisinologist*
2073 Anno Earth | 1999 Interstellar Era

SEVENTEEN

THEY WERE RAISED to be echoes. Capacious galleries of flesh and bone, exhibits curated to reflect philosophies not their own, in language not their own, belonging to a people they would never belong to but would slip amidst like eels blinded to their own origins in the endless sparkling sea of the universe.

It had been half their lifetime since they'd migrated from Earth's stratosphere, and Pavi and Amol could barely remember their home planet. They'd been raised on its ghost self, their proto-dialect no more than a translucent sheen resting upon them, only perceptible to those who studied Pavi's slight tendency to wavering vocalisations when stressed, words tumbling out in a hurry, intonation up-down-up-down. Or the roughness in Amol's vowels when he was asserting himself, most apparent while bossing their team of chefs around. Nobody in Uru hurried, certainly not through speech, *especially* not in Ur-speak; it was a measured, rounded thing, smooth as a pebble sanded down by one of its vast, slow rivers.

They kept themselves—their origin-selves—well-hidden, primitivity seldom slipping through the cracks. They slid into Uru's culture like they'd always belonged. Early-career apprenticeships at all its finest restaurants. Poetry salons for Pavi and the sinfonia for Amol. Art gallery memberships, a few romantic relationships with Primian humans, second-generation at least.

Sister and brother flourished. They started Nonpareil as its executive chefs, earned two Interstellar Stars in the restaurant's first few years. They were well-favoured by food critics for producing the finesse demanded by Primus's population of discerning tastebuds. They rubbed shoulders with Uru's culinary elite, each new circle of gastronomical friends opening the doors to an *inner* circle, each inner circle looping and crossing over the others until they were firmly enmeshed in the fabric of Primian culture—albeit warily embraced by their hosts, all too aware that their welcome was the temporary kind. One wrong word, one foot out of line and it would all come crashing down.

It was a good thing that Nonpareil ran like clockwork, a world unto itself, completely in their control.

'Knead it gently, XX-29. You're supposed to be making mistbread, not stonemeal,' The near permanent scowl on Good Cheer Chaangte's face deepened, her Primian name ironic in many ways that escaped her. Pavi scoured a grimfish, keeping a close eye on her sous-chef and their newest B'naar intern, XX-29.

XX-29 struggled to modulate the hydraulics in xir mechanised six-arm frame, and punched a hole straight through the gorse-dough. Projectiles shot across the kitchen, sticking to the ceiling and plastering Good Cheer Chaangte's spectacles. XX-29 sang a soft howl of apology, xir globular organic body turning a melancholy blue within xir carbon-fibre frame. The B'naar were adapted to tunneling wormholes through space, but XX-29 had served a delicately cooked Primo-pheasant foie gras with spirusnap caviar at xir interview. The plate was symbolic of sunny glades and whispering reeds at the edge of Harmony Lake, an ideal Primian expression of timelessness.

Good Cheer Chaangte had raised countless concerns about XX-29, as she did whenever they hired an off-worlder, but Pavi and Amol had shut them all down. XX-29 whirred as xe recalibrated xir mechanised frame.

'Stop!' Good Cheer Chaangte cried. 'I'll do it.'

'Chaangte, stop bullying the intern,' Amol said calmly. Dough dripped off the ceiling onto his chef's jacket as he prepped the foam for the beest carpaccio with brightroot lecithin. Layered with the phosphorescent brightroot-infused foam, the carpaccio was marbled like a rainbow. The plate would soon be served in darkness, glowing in neon purples and blues, evoking the Cornucopia Caves.

'Chef, I must respectfully complain that this is going to ruin all of our gorse-dough ahead of tonight's service,' Good Cheer Chaangte muttered. 'There will be no mistbread.'

'Come up with an alternative dish, then,' Pavi said. Good Cheer Chaangte groaned, but immediately rushed to the pantry.

Amol raised his head and met Pavi's gaze. 'Thank you,' he mouthed.

His sister scowled at him. Amol sighed. Tensions had been high between them since the first episode of *Interstellar MegaChef*. If he was being completely honest, they'd been high since he'd answered that comms request from Earth, the night before the judging.

'Don't answer that,' Pavi said. 'Earthlings are only good for one thing—freeloading.'

'Bit harsh, don't you think?' Amol raised an eyebrow skeptically. 'Considering...' He waved his hand at themselves.

'We're barely Earthling,' Pavi said pompously. 'Trust me, no good can come of that comms request.'

'What if it's a job offer, or a contract? You heard what happened at the banquet with the K'artri-tva.'

'All the more reason. They'll suspect us of betraying Primus to the Earth savages if we get anywhere near them...' Pavi took a sip of her White Dwarf whiskey on the rocks.

'Nonsense,' Amol said, tasting his star sherry. The comms transmission continued to beep across his optics. 'Let me just hear them out.'

It had not gone well. It wasn't a contract, at least not the kind Pavi and Amol were used to signing. Pavi had struggled to look Amol in the eye ever since.

Good Cheer Chaangte returned to the kitchen with a smug expression on her face, no doubt having worked out a Plan B for their bread baskets. Hiring her had been a calculated risk. She'd been expelled from culinary school for sabotaging other students, and no restaurant wanted to take her in— except for the fledgling Nonpareil, whose Earthling chefs were widely regarded with suspicion. Good Cheer Chaangte had attempted to boss them around at first, until she realised they knew exactly what they were doing, after which she'd resentfully toed the line. Her sullen presence had attracted other Primian chefs to work at the restaurant, but Amol continued to monitor her closely. If Good Cheer Chaangte's prodigious knife skills were anything to go by, he and his sister would never see her coming.

Pavi delegated the batch of grimfish in her hands to Curiosity Nuri, then strode over to where Amol was admiring the marbling of his carpaccio. 'Do you think this little inter-being conflict is going to blow up?'

'I know whose side I'm on,' Amol said quietly.

'Chaangte will take most of our Primian staff if she leaves.'

'We'll find other cooks. Off-worlders, if we need to.'

'Yes, you've already made contingency plans, haven't you?' His sister scrunched her nose up in disgust.

'We don't know if anything will come of that. I was just following instructions.'

'Yes, instructions you let yourself be blackmailed into following.'

'They'd have found us anyway.' Amol held his hands up defensively. 'And come on, our parents' wellbeing is at stake!'

'I *told* you. We should have moved them here *years ago!*'

'Right, because they hand out immigrant visas to every Earthling they meet.' Amol rolled his eyes.

'She'd better not join us,' Pavi snapped.

'She won't. Too much pride.'

'If Chaangte does what I think she's planning to do, we're looking at an exodus.' Pavi eyed the Primian chef, who was glowering at their B'naar intern. 'We'll lose our reputation if most of our kitchen isn't Primian.'

A battery of hard dough bullets sprayed through the kitchen. Amol sighed. 'Here, kid. Let me help you.'

Service that night was spectacular. XX-29's mistbread came together with Amol's help, and evoked memories of soft rain on High Street. XX-29 turned a delighted shade of pink, thrumming in excitable arpeggiated soundwaves. The Cornucopia Caves carpaccio debuted dramatically amidst a nightfall-themed set of courses. All that was left was to ensure the Relic of the Eternals dessert went off without a hitch.

'Rougeberry spheres?' Pavi called.

'Stonesmoke cubes!' Amol commanded.

Their team of chefs scurried to their assistance. In near-perfect silence, they executed the last of their three-plate dessert serving with the precision of the cosmic ballet. They were right at the end of the night's service.

There was a hammering on the back door of the kitchen. Pavi dropped her forceps with a clatter, and a rougeberry sphere pinged off the floor. The thudding recurred insistently. Pavi ignored it.

Amol leaned over the intricate geometry of cubes he was assembling on each plate. Pavi placed the spheres in place, infused with ras from fresh berries, symbolic of the first meal of the Nakshatrans against a rocky outcrop. Good Cheer Chaangte dipped fresh green whorlbuds in liquid nitrogen and smashed them over each delicately constructed edifice, a fine crumb of petalescence descending upon each plate in turn.

Pavi and Amol dipped their hands into a plate to taste. If this one was finely balanced, all the others would be, too. Their food was mathematical, its flavours sublime. The dessert melted across their tastebuds, rich floral notes from the rougeberry spheres, a slight crunch to the acidity of the whorlbuds, and the mellow calm of stonesmoke cubes evoking a sense of timelessness.

Their Eternal Dessert was crafted to evoke a bucolic tranquillity, lush in honouring native Primian ingredients, awe-inspiring with its homage to Primus's humble origins. It represented the Nakshatran Rock monolith, thousands of feet high, in the mountains of Ursridge, covered in the palm prints of the first settlers on the planet.

'Chefs,' Pavi announced. 'This is Primian cuisine as it's meant to be—flavours dancing on a knife's edge, evoking infinity through every fleeting bite, created to move the soul like an ever-shifting music upon the tongue. I know we're spending a lot of time at *MegaChef* over the next few months, but to me, every one of you is worthy of wearing that title.'

Their handpicked team members clapped politely. Good Cheer Chaangte rolled her eyes. The battering at the door returned. The flowmetal boomed against its frame, shattering the calm of the kitchen.

'Service!' Pavi cried, snapping out of the moment. Forty-two plates were whisked away to eager diners by the wait-staff.

'Someone get the thrice-damned door.' Amol picked up the tasting plate and closed his eyes as he scooped more of the sugary confection into his mouth.

Good Cheer Chaangte dusted her whorlbud-stained fingers and wiped them on her hand towel. She scowled at Optimism Jordan, who threw open the door, only to be thwacked in the stomach by an umbrella. He doubled over, grunting in pain.

A thunderstorm raged outside, the streetlights were a blur, and a ragged figure stood on the doorstep, dripping water like trails of molten sugar. The figure opened its mouth.

'Oh! I was beginning to think you'd never let me in, that I'd be out in the rain all night—not a problem really, but it is rather cold outside.' The words tumbled out of her in heavily accented Ur-speak.

Nonpareil's handpicked team of chefs stared in shock. Pavi cringed at the barbarian sound of her own origins, and fought back a wave of nausea at the sight of the woman she'd hoped she'd never have to encounter again.

The woman stepped inside, followed closely by a whirring mechanical drone that hovered near her shoulder.

Amol dropped his plate. It shattered, spattering everyone with powdered sugar.

'Well, fuck.'

The United Human Cooperative does not discriminate between its member planets. All humans are created equal. All species are equal. This is the Nakshatran way.

—Marika Khan,
First Representative of the United Human Cooperative,
548 Anno Earth | 474 Interstellar Era

EIGHTEEN

I SUPPOSE I made what could be labelled a dramatic entrance.

If I'd had any say in the matter, it wouldn't have been streaming sheets of rain on my walk from the flowtram station to Nonpareil, but then again, I'd also lived most of my life outside the script of an Ur-drama. Epic revenge plans were new for me, so I suppose the weather was a nice touch. Bonus points for not being acid rain, too.

I brought my palms together in a traditional Earth-greeting, extremely pre-trust, all bravado. The collective shock registering across everyone's faces grew, and I felt quite smug with a side of panic at the thought of sparking a diplomatic incident, before I realised my political family was nowhere in the Suriyan System.

'Namaskāram,' I said in Daxina, and paused for a full three seconds, gloating in the stunned silence around me, before switching to Ur-speak. 'Saraswati Kaveri, and this is my Winger, Kili.'

Kili whirred off my shoulder and flew in an intricate knot, trailing streams of light from his person. In the corner of my vision, a tall, lean chef with straight blonde hair and glasses took a step back, and knocked over a large stack of syringes. The Loop tagged them on my visual feed—a bizarre sensation that would take time getting used to—

213

and labelled them *Good Cheer Chaangte, She/Her*.

Good Cheer Chaangte scowled at the chef standing beside her, a short, heavily muscled man whose nametag read *Optimism Jordan, He/Him*. 'Clean that up,' she snapped, and he scurried to do her bidding. *Well, that's an interesting dynamic.*

 Nobody else moved a muscle.

I cleared my throat. 'Serenity and harmony upon you. I'm here to meet Amol Khurshid, whom I believe has a job offer for me.'

'I said "call me,"' Amol said with a strained smile.

'I thought this would be quicker.' I smiled back.

'Typical Earthling, barging your way into everything.' Pavi muttered.

My insides wilted a little, my carefully constructed swagger melting. A trickle of sweat dripped down my forehead. Pavi took a step forwards. 'If you were slightly less savage, you'd have looked us up on the Loop, sent in your CV, and waited twelve weeks to hear back from us, just like the rest of the people in this room did.' She spun her wrist in a short, shabby arc, indicating the line of chefs behind her.

Fair point, Kili said.

Agreed.

Should have thought this through some more.

Yes.

I'd probably fucked this up badly. It took everything I had to stand my ground and to remember that this had been a spur of the moment idea; there were no real consequences to not being employed at this restaurant. I'd just leave the building quietly, stick to my original plan, and go... go where? My stomach somersaulted at the thought. I hadn't the faintest idea what I was going to *do* on this sur-fucked planet.

Amol put his hand on his sister's shoulder and muttered something in her ear. Her eyes flashed, and she threw a quick glance back at the other chefs, before searing me with a glare. 'Lucky for you, *we* have civility, and we won't turn you back out into the rain,' she said. 'Chaangte, show her where the office is. She can wait for us there.'

The tall chef's lips twisted in disgust, and she flipped her pale blonde hair over her shoulder. 'Follow me,' she said.

Kili settled on my shoulder and I walked behind her, out the kitchen and into the back rooms. She passed her hand over a scanner, and a flowmetal door dissolved. She pointed through it, and I stepped into a minimally furnished space with a desk, a handful of extremely functional chairs, and a large reed carpet.

'Thank you,' I smiled.

'I don't know what you're doing here, *MegaChef* failure,' Good Cheer Chaangte said, her eyes narrowing as she studied me. 'But if they hire you, know that I will find out.'

She turned abruptly and stalked off, and the flowmetal reassembled itself behind her. I exhaled and slumped forwards, burying my head in my hands. My limbs shook. All that brash posturing had been most unlike me.

Poker face, Saras. They might have cams in here.

I straightened up immediately. _You're right._

Really pushed your "Earth savage" routine to the limit there, didn't you?

I thought they deserved it after *MegaChef*. And it was so much easier to be rude than to be... me.

And it had been. I'd felt in control of the entire absurd situation, barging up to the restaurant and banging on the back door to demand a job like it was some kind of blood price. When Serenity Ko dragged me across the Uru and Beyond Marketplace tasting Berry-annas, and made the obnoxious suggestion that I try and take Nonpareil down from the inside—Pavi and Amol Khurshid with it—I'd laughed it off at first. But the thought had wormed its way insidiously through my mind, until it was all I could imagine. Other than Serenity Ko's mouth when she smirked, her lips barely parted, the right side of her face dimpling... which was just plain embarrassing and unnecessary, because I'd probably never see her again, and most of me was glad for it.

Moonage Daydream had thoughtstreamed a number of apologies for the incident at their popup restaurant, and Starlight Fantastic had insisted on coming over with dinner later that evening. I'd pretended everything was fine—as one does when you don't want to admit how shaken you are by something, and are in the company of a friend who's doing their best to cheer you up with "the best noodle-crunch and shroom-broth on this side of town."

I'd thrown on my favourite Legends of the Future smash album, and having it stream directly into my mind as ossiowaves was a whole new experience. I suppose I owed Serenity Ko for it, if I ever saw her again—part of me hoped I never did, the rest of me was probably worth ignoring, as it was likely what was responsible for my being on this planet at all.

As the ethereal sound of the everglass guitars cascaded over a throbbing bol-bass, I curled up in bed, determined never to step out again. Until the album ended, and the thought of burning down Pavi and Amol Khurshid's careers slipped its way back in. As the evening wore on, it had become more and more appealing. There was also the reality that I'd come here to this planet, twenty-one jumpgates away, with no Plan B in case *MegaChef* failed. Going back was not an option. Even if I ultimately did zero damage to Pavi and Amol, which was likely to be the case, I'd at least gain some restaurant experience working with Primian food, and that couldn't be the worst thing, could it?

So as the better part of my reasoning—namely, Kili—told me to go to bed and revisit this thought the next day, I'd shrugged on my coat, 3D-printed an umbrella from a vending machine, and stepped out into the rain.

The flowmetal swirled open and I jumped to my feet.

Amol strode in first, smiling tersely. Pavi was a step behind at his shoulder, muttering agitatedly into his ear.

'So you decided to take me up on my offer,' Amol said, extending his hand. I clasped it and shook it as he gestured at the chair behind me. 'Please, sit.'

There was frisson in the air between the twins as I retook my seat, as palpable and pervasive as the smell of burnt toast.

'It would have been nice to know you'd made her an offer,' Pavi said to Amol coldly, looking me up and down like I was an entree made from rotting meat.

Ooh, Kili said. _Siblings keeping secrets._

Everything here is an Ur-drama.

Amol took one of the chairs behind the desk, leaned forwards to appraise me with slightly less loathing than his sister, and nodded at her. 'Pavi, you knew we couldn't leave her out to dry after that episode.'

'I thought we were going to set her up with, I don't know, one of our friends, maybe?' Pavi paced the small length of the office. 'There are those experimental food nutters at Gorge Us, those triplets who run that dessert chain, the Happy Forager folks...' She rattled off a bunch of names, punctuating each one with a stab of her hand. 'All far more suited to her barbarian food!'

'Thanks, the barbarian is right here,' I said. Kili whirred angrily on my shoulder.

She rounded on me. 'Oh, you know what I mean! You weren't born yesterday. You saw what people here are like on *MegaChef*—to have a place in Uru, you need to be Primian, and if you aren't, you need to prove that you're the best of the second-rate off-worlders out there, by being as Primian as you can be.'

'All I saw were the two of you discrediting my food, and you knew it was delicious.'

'It was foolhardy,' Pavi snapped.

'Pointless,' Amol echoed.

'A political statement in a place that has no need of them,'
Pavi continued. She sighed, rubbing her temples. 'We've
worked sur-fucking hard to gain our credibility, so if you
think you can just walk in here and fuck with us…'

'You offered me a job,' I said, staring directly at Amol.

'So I did,' he said, running a hand through his braided
hair and unsettling it.

'Why?'

'Unimportant,' Pavi said coldly. 'It's done. Welcome to
Nonpareil, thrilled to have you on board.'

'That's… *it?*' I asked. 'That's my interview?'

'We've already tasted your food,' Amol said. 'Decent
flavour profiles, totally bizarre cuisine and presentation.'

'And Amol already offered you the job,' Pavi snapped. 'So
I guess it doesn't matter what my opinion is.'

Wow, they're really going for it in public.

_Is *this* the Primian culture they're always going on
about?_

Kili burbled with laughter.

'Your machine is making funny noises.'

Shush, I chided him. I turned to Pavi. 'Old tech, you
know how janky it can be.'

Brutal, Kili grumbled.

'I hope you have Loop access?' she asked.

I nodded.

'I'll stream you our entire recipe book; learn it by tomorrow.
We're only open for dinner service, and we expect you here
by noon. Don't get any fancy ideas about reinventing cuisine
or culture or anything about this place. You might have run
your own little shack back on Earth, but over here, you'll be
lucky if we let you extract ras. You can bring your mechanical
toy if he shuts up and stays put through service. Dress code:
black Primian minimalist; look it up if you don't know what
it is because I'm not going to explain. We'll print your chef's
jacket, pay you by the week on the Loop.' Pavi turned to

Amol with an exaggerated sigh. 'I'm running out of breath here. Will you give her the rest of the speech?'

Amol put his feet up on the desk and leaned back in his chair. 'There's not much else you need to know,' he said. 'Except when it comes to your designation and payment. All Primians are assigned to a specific guild, based on their skills, and graded according to their level. Everyone at the same guild-skill level gets paid the same. As an off-worlder, you'll need to head to the employment office and get your assignment tomorrow. It's in the Second Collective.'

'Understood,' I said. 'Is there a test or something?'

'Yes, it'll probably be some basic Primian food. Nothing you can't handle.'

'Thanks for your time,' I said, rising to my feet. 'And for the job. I'll see you tomorrow.'

'Noon,' Pavi said sharply. 'Don't be late.'

I WAS RUNNING very late.

Kili and I had spent the entire morning at the Employment Council offices, and I'd failed the basic Primian food test miserably. They'd asked me to make something called a Nakshatran Gelato, which, as it turned out, was not a form of ice cream on this sur-fucked planet.

Instead, it was a savoury dessert laid out in gelée sheets, infused with ras from nine different ingredients, from rougeberry to fennelo, arranged in a specific configuration on the plate, intended to represent the Nine Virtues that everyone on this planet aspired to and was named after. It was also a recipe most Primians mastered as children, which was something my examiner was most excited to tell me, while assigning me to the Culture-Aesthete Guild, Enthusiast Level. The translation: off-world hobbyist seeking a job in any restaurant that will have them, will work for exposure, happy to be underpaid.

...absolutely fucking discriminatory and completely unfair! Kili was still riled up about it.

Yeah, I said, my insides hollow with disappointment. And dread. I'd have to go tell Pavi and Amol about my classification, and endure the fact that it was now public knowledge.

They should have let you have Loop access.

Yeah.

Kili ranted on my behalf all through the flowtram route to Collective Four. I hopped off the tram and towards Nonpareil, cursing the flowmetal city as it dipped and whirled its way around me. It was disorientating; it's bad enough finding a place on a static street, but when everything rearranges itself according to sur-light or whatever the fuck else, while you're still getting used to nonstop information from the Loop on your visual, when you're running late for your first day as a grunt at your new job, it's harrowing.

I passed my hand over the scanner at the door, and when it swirled open, I was relieved that I'd been granted clearance to the kitchen. Fourteen pairs of eyes—most human, some not—turned to look at me.

'Right, everyone. Family will be seventeen minutes late thanks to Saraswati, so your lunch break will be seventeen minutes shorter,' Pavi announced.

'Saraswati will be joining us. She's from Earth, and wants to learn Primian cuisine,' Amol said more cheerily.

'Has she been to culinary school? At least a basic degree?' Good Cheer Chaangte asked unnecessarily, fully aware of the answer.

'On Earth, yeah,' I said frostily.

'Delightful,' Good Cheer Chaangte announced. 'Another incompetent to join the intern army.' She shot a B'naar chef, who popped up as XX-29 on my visual, a filthy look. XX-29 quailed, xir amorphous form shrinking within xir mechatronic frame.

'No more of that,' Amol said curtly. 'Chaangte, take

Saraswati on the grand tour, please.'

'My lucky day,' Good Cheer Chaangte mumbled.

The other chefs returned to their prep; clearly I'd caught them in the middle of it. The dinner menu must have already been discussed and decided upon, and everyone knew exactly what they needed to do.

'Spirited, showing up late on the first day of work,' Good Cheer Chaangte said by way of greeting. 'Stations.' She waved in the general direction of the kitchen. 'The last chef who tried that was fired on the spot, so what are you blackmailing them with, huh?' She raised one of her fine eyebrows and regarded me in silence.

'Nothing.'

'Cool, I believe you.' She scanned her hand at a door and we passed through it. 'Front of house.'

I had a momentary glimpse of a minimalist dining area. Soft, sleek black chairs and marbled dinner tables. Abstract art in greens and blacks rising in a holoray up the walls all the way to the high domed ceiling, and across its hemisphere. I caught sight of visio-nodes, and couldn't help but wonder what they used the space for during service. Creepers and vines flowered and trailed down a row of trellises, and at the very centre of the space, was a weird and wondrous tree that grew in a similar way to the Harmony Knot.

'Are you going to stare at it all day?' Good Cheer Chaangte was tapping her foot.

'We just got here—'

'Uh-huh.' She stepped back through the door we came from. 'So if you're not blackmailing them, what is it? Are you some famous person's kid?' She stopped abruptly, and I walked into her. She spun around. 'Wait, are you one of *their* kids? No, you're too old.'

She led me through the kitchen and into the back rooms we'd been in last night. 'Bathroom at the far end. Restaurant pantry to the right.'

'Okay, thanks—'

'But seriously, there's got to be some reason they're keeping you.' She leaned forwards uncomfortably close and studied my face. Her eyes were magnified behind her glasses. I smelt the freshness of her breath—mint and basil. I pressed myself back against the wall.

'I'm a good cook.' I said firmly. 'And a professional chef.'

At that she laughed, a full, throaty sound, her cheeks drawing up and accentuating her pointed chin. 'Good one. From Earth. Sure. Love it, kid.' She smiled so wide it was practically a snarl. 'I watched *MegaChef*, you know,' she hissed. 'You're a talentless nothing, and if Primian cuisine doesn't destroy you, I will.'

That's hostile, Kili said.

No shit.

'Family on your left, through here,' Good Cheer Chaangte said as a flowmetal door pulled open. 'That's where you can make us lunch. You don't have much time. Normally I'd tell a scrub to impress us, but in your case... Try not to poison us, won't you?'

I stepped into the family kitchen and my heart sank. Its shelves were nearly bare.

'Oh, good luck,' she sniggered, waving her arm to indicate the minimally stocked shelves. She carried on chuckling to herself as she made her way back to the restaurant kitchen.

I stepped into the family kitchen and browsed the contents of its pantry. Modest was a generous description of the ingredients on offer. The only protein was some strange gamey vat-grown meat I'd never seen in my life, so I was forced to go vegetarian. There were very few whole ingredients, but an assortment of syringes containing different types of ras, all labelled. Grains and lentils, a handful of fresh vegetables, and a floor-to-ceiling rack of spices completed the offerings. My visual feed popped with information supplied by the Loop—I'd need to mess with the settings to stop this from happening all the time, but I hadn't had the time.

I couldn't tell if this sparseness was normal, or if they were intentionally making life difficult for me. *Surely a high-end restaurant doesn't starve its staff?*

Looks like someone's forcing you to play in hard mode, Kili said.

I wonder who? I rolled my eyes. I'd bet my refugee visa that Good Cheer Chaangte had had something to do with this.

Too bad for her, and for anyone else involved; wholesome, traditional Earth meals don't need very much sometimes. I started to pack my basket with lentils of every kind.

Are you going Earth again? Kili asked.

Yup.

Provoking them. I like it.

The family kitchen was much smaller than the restaurant's kitchen, with a large, circular dining table occupying most of its centre, and filled with many appliances I had no idea how to use. I prepped. I first chopped cilantrina and threw it into the blender with a selection of mixed lentils, grinding it down and adding some kind of chilli spice blend. I set this aside to rest—it was already a nearly complete chutney.

Luckily, there seemed to be one of those convertible countertops, and I swiped through its options, hunting for a traditional Earth-style stovetop and oven. It rose out of the flowmetal, and I heaved a sigh of relief when it auto-ignited and the sprinkler system didn't go off. I moved on to making sambar with what little ingredients I had. There was no tamarind, so I used an equivalent sour spice— harvested from a similar-looking fruit—that I'd discovered in the pantry. The Loop told me it would cook well, and I decided to trust it.

I started to stew another batch of lentils, then added a pungent root vegetable I'd encountered in the pantry; something named gayam, according to the Loop. By the time I was grinding more lentils—surprise!—to make a batter for the star of the show, blending in water and salt and bursts of whole peprino-corn, I was laughing out loud at how many ways I could make this lunch from so little.

I set a deep wok on the stove, filled it with oil, and waited for it to start bubbling. Then, using the little flick-of-the-wrist technique Kanakamma had taught me when I was fifteen-years-old, I started hand-rolling the batter into little doughnut shapes, before dropping them into the wok and letting them deep-fry. My thoughts shut down and I was one with the flow of the movement—grab a handful of batter, swirl it around in my hand into a little circle of goodness, poke a hole in the centre and drop it in. Every time from the right height, every time at the right density. I fried batch after batch of the little golden brown pieces of starlight, pulling them out the minute they were crisp and placing them on a perforated rack to let the excess oil drain away. I hummed to myself while I cooked, in my element at last.

When I had forty-five vadas—or about three apiece for everyone in the kitchen—I began to plate them and put them on the dinner table. Each received a side of cilantrina chutney, and a bowl of steaming mystery-root-vegetable named gayam sambar. I checked the time on the dash on my visual feed. I was ten minutes early.

I stuck my head into the main kitchen. 'Chefs, family!' I announced.

'Already?' Good Cheer Chaangte was at my side in an instant. Her expression conveyed so much shock that it immediately confirmed my suspicions about her role in stripping the pantry bare.

'Not bad,' Amol called. 'Good sense of time, chef.'

'Yes, chef.'

One by one, the assemblage trooped in and took their places. The Loop scanned them all, popping up their names and pronouns, and I was glad for it, for a change.

'Ugh, smells disgusting in here.' Good Cheer Chaangte wrinkled her nose.

'I smell hot oil,' Pavi echoed, walking in behind her. 'Did you use fire?'

'I did.'

'Savage,' Good Cheer Chaangte said.

'Hmph,' Pavi snorted, though she threw Good Cheer Chaangte a warning look. Good Cheer Chaangte smiled innocently in return.

'This is a traditional Earth dish, usually made for breakfast,' I said. 'It's vegetarian, and it's called vada sambar.'

Optimism Jordan bit into his vada and it crunched audibly, much to my delight. 'Ooh, that's delicious!' he said, diving into the rest of the meal. Happy crunching sounds filled the air, as Courage Malia, Boundless Baz, and all the rest dug in.

'This is so fucking good,' Boundless Baz said, licking sambar off his fingertips.

'Overspiced,' Pavi said, although her plate was empty.

'I need to know how to make this,' XX-29 said via xir Vox box, while xir being made content humming sounds.

'Great job, chef.' Amol drained the last of his sambar. 'I'm not a fan of Earth food at all, but I respect you for sharing your culture with us.'

'Huh.' Good Cheer Chaangte said loudly. Her plate was the only one that lay untouched.

'If you're not going to eat that…' Optimism Jordan began. 'All yours.'

'Excellent.' He proceeded to dig in, fending off attempts by Boundless Baz to steal another vada.

Good Cheer Chaangte rose from her seat and bumped into my shoulder on her way out. 'Primitive,' she said, loud enough for everyone to hear, before strutting away.

It was the beginning of a beautiful friendship.

Primian cuisine is performative, symbolic. It is a reminder of our heritage; a connection to the wider world. An Ancient Earth saying, when translated into Ur-speak, reads 'you become what you consume,' and so we exercise the greatest awareness in order to embody our ideals.

—Grace Menmo, from the sim *At Home in the Kitchen*
2065 Anno Earth | 1990 Interstellar Era

NINETEEN

MIDWAY THROUGH SERENITY KO's second nava of imposed exile, Courage Praia turned up at her doorstep, a big grin upon their face.

'Kube got fired for appropriating XP funds and developing illegal mods?' Serenity Ko asked hopefully.

'Nope.'

'Na'vil then. He's been developing mind control all this time.'

'Nope.' Courage Praia's grin widened.

'Tell me, already,' Serenity Ko demanded, still on the doorstep.

Courage Praia smiled even bigger, scrunching their eyes up into little half-moons. 'I got them to release our research budgets,' Courage Praia said. 'Yours and mine.'

Serenity Ko was a shade disappointed that the news wasn't more dramatic, but it was still very good. She couldn't help but grin back. 'Well done!'

'It was such a big win for me; you should've seen me negotiate with Kube...' They launched into an extensive description of how they'd surreptitiously pitched the biggest thing in all the universe, and Serenity Ko's hands twitched at her sides. She supposed she should be happy for her friend; after all, this was the first time they'd ever stood up to anyone at work. But honestly, other people's personal growth stories were boring.

'Why don't you come inside and tell me all about it?' Serenity Ko thumped her friend on the shoulder and gently steered them through the door.

'Oh, right, okay…'

Serenity Ko firmly guided them past the living area, where Appa and Ammamma were mulling over an assortment of variously shaped gelées and terrines, popping them out of their moulds while muttering to each other.

'Hi, Aunty and Uncle!' Courage Praia said brightly. Serenity Ko stifled a groan. Her most recent philosophy around her grandmother had been "don't engage unless you need to."

'Praia, how are you? So good to see you!'

'No time for niceties, Ammamma. Praia's on a tight schedule.'

'No, I'm not—' Courage Praia began, but Serenity Ko stepped on their foot pointedly, causing them to sputter.

'No worries, we'll see you later then,' Appa called as Serenity Ko dragged her up the stairs to her room.

'So politeness is a no, then?' Courage Praia said.

'I have more important things to show you! For real. We can always hang out with my family later.'

'Right, like I've done every other night for the last four years.'

'Ugh, Praia, don't be difficult.'

She pushed them through the door to her room without the slightest trace of embarrassment at the state of it. Sprawled across every flat surface were heaps of papyro-scrolls. Her laundry still lay neatly folded upon the chair it had been on when she'd awoken from her fever dream. A new pile of unfinished Bloxxos were scattered across the floor. And beamed across an entire wall was a holoray compilation of the endless notes her grandmother had supplied her with on Primian cuisine.

'Whoa! And I was just going to ask you what it's been like working with your grandmother,' Courage Praia said, spinning in a slow circle to take it all in.

'An absolute fucking nightmare,' Serenity Ko groused.

And it had been. Every morning, Ammamma—or Grace Menmo, Serenity Ko could no longer tell who appeared before her each day—lectured her on the finer points and principles of the Primian culinary tradition. According to Primian philosophy, it was vulgar to use whole ingredients in the post-Earth era, even though Primus had never experienced a food shortage.

'Why?' Serenity Ko had asked.

Grace Menmo had launched into a lecture on the Anthropocene Era, tracing its history all the way tens of thousands of Earth-years ago to the Agricultural Revolution. She hadn't been amused when Serenity Ko asked about weapons during the revolution; in fact, she'd launched into a secondary lecture on violent crimes on Earth, leading into the Third World War, the formation of One Nation Earth, and the origins of the Nakshatran Charter, all of which Serenity Ko had learnt in University and promptly forgotten after acing her examinations.

As a response to the violent history of humanity on Earth, Primian food was created from blending flavour profiles in a non-violent way, unlike the primitive methods on Earth that involved open flame as a cooking method.

'A new era of self-expression, a new culture for all of human-occupied space to follow,' Grace Menmo had said.

'But they don't *all* follow it, do they?' Serenity Ko had asked. She'd once tried the tasting menu at StarFlight, an experimental restaurant that claimed it did cuisine as many ways as humanity did.

'All the *civilised* ones do,' Grace Menmo had said sourly, before embarking upon a lecture about primitive cultures, and how it was their role, as Primians, to guide humanity to a better way of life.

'Sounds like an empire in the making,' Serenity Ko had mused out loud, fragments of human history spinning through her brain.

'It is *not*,' Grace Menmo had snapped. 'It's based on elevating others to our culture, not oppressing them.'

'Sounds ineffective.'

Grace Menmo had promptly assigned half a dozen history scrolls as recommended reading, the spiteful old thing.

It seemed to Serenity Ko that every principle guiding Primian cooking existed antithetically to the cooking traditions of ancient Earth. Flavour was harvested from ingredients in the form of ras, hyper-concentrated, and then infused into various layered concoctions. Micro-portions, hyper-concentration ratios, blend-wheels, texturiser tech, splice science, scoop calculus… words and images floated across Serenity Ko's vision each time she shut her eyes, thanks to all the Immersive Reality breakdowns of entire Primian cookbooks that her grandmother saw fit to send her, from *Epicurean After Earth* (widely regarded as the first definitive guide on their new culinary culture) to *Gastronomy Today* (a cutting-edge weekly sim that introduced the latest techniques for one's kitchen).

Serenity Ko had had every intention of palming all this source material off to Curiosity Nenna—channel the intern's boundless energy, let her prove her value to the team, et cetera—but that plan had gone sideways when the cruel old lady she currently lived with took to quizzing her each day.

And then, much to Serenity Ko's horror, she'd introduced lessons that involved going into the actual kitchen.

'You can't build food experiences if you don't know how to build food.'

'You do realise that the food experience is a *sim?* Someone else will be building the food,' Serenity Ko had whined.

'Is that really how you do a Daxi-Amade infusion?' Grace Menmo had squashed the sphere in her grand-daughter's hands. 'This is basic stuff. Do it again.'

In a word: nightmare.

'Are you sure we aren't signing up to fail?' Courage Praia whispered, their eyes wide in an expression that was part awe-struck, part horrified.

Serenity Ko snorted. '*This?* This is just my grandmother making my life complicated because she can. I suppose it's because she loves me. Now sit,' she said bossily.

When Courage Praia looked around uncertainly at the absence of flat surfaces to rest upon, she knocked her *Formula Enthusiast* racing helmet off her desk. Courage Praia wedged themself into the space it had previously occupied.

Serenity Ko slid into the Loop. She beamed the roadmap she had been working on over her bed. 'I have this all charted out for the next three years,' she announced. 'It'll take us about a month of research before we can start prototyping the thing. We'll use the existing tech from the SoundSpace mod, should be done in three months total, easy. I'm thinking we go Primus first, and only then localise to other off-world cuisines and cultures. Sound good?'

A whole five minutes passed as Courage Praia scanned the information. Serenity Ko tapped her foot anxiously, started assembling a Bloxxo spaceship then dropped it, and was midway through mixing two shots of MellO by the time they spoke.

'Ambitious,' they said.

'So?'

'I like it. I think we can sell Kube on it.'

For the second time in a nava and a half, Serenity Ko smiled, and it was genuine. The memory of the first bubbled up, but it involved the Earthling she was sure she'd never see again, so she shoved it back down where it belonged, which was nowhere. Instead, she handed Courage Praia a shot of MellO. 'Now, about that research budget.'

THE FOOD AND nightlife district was generally understood to be in Collective Four. Serenity Ko was intimately familiar with most of its bars, but had seldom stepped into its fancy restaurants because food was an unnecessary interruption to the finer things, specifically the nutrition that could be found at the bottom of a brightly coloured cocktail glass. It was also deathly dull to suffer eighteen-course meals in silence, occasionally interrupted by a snooty server attempting to explain each of the myriad ingredients—pardon, "ras infusions"—on each plate. And yet she'd managed to find her way to the chef's table at Transformateur, and now owed her grandmother a big favour.

She wrinkled her nose at the tiny porcelain soup spoon on the table in front of her, holding what appeared to be a transparent jelly-like sphere streaked with blue. 'Flight egg,' the server announced.

'Ooh, it looks delicious!' Courage Praia exclaimed.

'It looks small.'

They'd already endured seven courses of minuscule portions. This was supposed to be the main course. Holorayed around the dining pod in which they sat were visuals intended to coax them into a sense of experiential ecstasy or angst, depending on the plate before them. At this moment, an orbcraft looped its way around them, flying through Primian skies, skipping across the clouds. As it spun its way across the walls curving around them, it picked up speed, swirling faster and faster until it was just a blur. It began to crackle with electricity, shooting jets of lightning across the screens. There was a pop, when the visual seemed to hang in time for a moment, before beginning to spin again, gradually slowing down until what emerged from the blurriness was a small feathered bluebul, its wings spread out in joyous flight.

'This would be so much better if it were a sim,' Courage Praia whispered.

'Exactly.' Serenity Ko grinned smugly.

The visuals started again, playing on loop, and Serenity Ko supposed they'd only end once she ate the ridiculous morsel in front of her. She scooped it up and popped it into her mouth. Some kind of creamy, citric flavour burst across her palate, but before she could appreciate how delicious it was—and it *was* delicious—the insides of her mouth seemed under attack by a flurry of little explosions, shocks of tartness springing into her awareness. In the seconds it took for her to wrap her head around what was going on, she reached the chewy centre of the sphere, which tasted like a herb-infused egg yolk. She choked, spluttered, swallowed.

'Delicious, but what a rip off,' she muttered, smiling at the server who was walking towards them with their next course.

Serenity Ko had to admit that the food was flavourful, but she couldn't quite articulate why. The moment she thought she'd apprehended a flavour, it disappeared before she could pin it down. It was ephemeral, insubstantial. Was this the kind of food that her Ammamma had built a career out of? It tasted like nothing she'd ever eaten at home. If such a bizarre culinary experience could thrive, entirely removed as it was from everyday cooking, it was a clear indicator that idiots would pay through their noses for extravagant dining. And she held the power to deliver it to them right in their own living rooms—assuming Feast Inc. was funded and she built it before anybody else. She thoughtstreamed her experiences of every single dish, along with its audiovisual experiences, to Courage Praia, and they swapped notes through the rest of their meal, building an extensive library of food-related feelings that they could incorporate into their design.

By the time dessert rolled around—three oblongs, each no larger than a petal, on a bed of some kind of moss—Serenity Ko was actually in great spirits. She popped each grain into her mouth, letting the flavours of jaggery, zafran and cashews burst across her tongue, swallowing Transformateur's signature dish—rice pudding three ways—in a single go. And then she realised she was still hungry.

'Did you enjoy the eleven-course menu?' Boundless Evi, the restaurant's Executive Chef and three-time winner of the Primian Premier Award, appeared at their table.

'Incredible,' Courage Praia said.

'Delicious,' Serenity Ko added.

'I'm delighted. You know, I learned all my fundamentals from your grandmother's extraordinary sim series, *At Home in the Kitchen*! I wouldn't be here if it weren't for Grace Menmo…'

Serenity Ko zoned out as the celebrated chef heaped praise upon her grandmother for a full five minutes. She was uncomfortably aware of a growing rumbling in her tummy, and many hurried sips of her oak-sherry wine did nothing to fill the void where she'd expected her dinner to have been. She noticed that Boundless Evi was staring at her expectantly in silence, having run out of platitudes, and rushed to fill the space with the first thing that popped into her mind. 'You wouldn't happen to have any steak pâté, would you? Or something… equivalently large?'

Boundless Evi's jaw dropped, her pale skin flushing deep red. She muttered something about having to see to a few other customers and strode away.

'Ko, what have you done?' Courage Praia whispered.

'Not my fault I'm still hungry,' Serenity Ko scowled, and her stomach growled in agreement.

The next evening, she decided to prep beforehand, and ate an entire berry goulash straight out the refrigerator, ignoring her grandmother's disparaging glare. She was grateful for it when she and Courage Praia stepped through the doors of Fantasy Land, where everything was life-sized and edible. The restaurant was only open once a nava, because it took their chefs that long to create and structurally assemble their edible restaurant. It was rumoured that Executive Chef Optimism Gon employed nearly three hundred chefs: a third conducted experimentation and research, a third did all the cooking, and the remainder were certified structural engineers.

This nava's theme was "Shrooms for Rooms," and the restaurant featured bioluminescent shrooms in dark crystal caverns, red-capped toad shrooms with little white spots in a woodland, and a flowing river with translucent rainbow-coloured shrooms growing along its banks. Everything looked like it was made of candy. It was not.

Serenity Ko winced as she bit into a piece of bark she'd sworn had to be either chocolate or a vat-grown protein. Instead, an earthy bitterness flooded her palate, and she choked it down to stop herself from throwing up on the edible floor. Her "guide"—that's what they called servers here—enthusiastically told her that it was intended to simulate the taste of bitternut bark, which grew wild across the Arc. 'Feel free to combine the weird and wondrous flavours of the wood!' her guide cooed. 'And don't forget to taste the shrooms!'

Serenity Ko scooped up an entire red-capped toad shroom, wrapped it in a handful of leaves, scraped some soil on to it, and reluctantly popped it into her mouth. She waited for her gag reflex to kick in, and was genuinely surprised when she found herself enjoying it.

'The toad shroom is made from vat-grown beest, cured in a ras infusion of leek-leaf, cilantrina...' her guide began, and because it was a one-on-one conversation, Serenity Ko was forced to pay attention, and the rest of her meal started to go downhill while her guide listed all the Nakshatran values that mirrored the woodland she was being encouraged to eat.

She glanced over her shoulder to where Courage Praia seemed to be similarly trapped and spoken at, while being encouraged to lick shrooms off the walls of the cave. Serenity Ko hoped they tasted like candy, and wondered who sanitised the entire space while she was at it. That caused her to immediately lose her appetite. Sure, they'd had bio-cleanses before stepping into the edible restaurant, but it was suddenly far less appealing to eat the place to the ground. She made a hasty exit, and forgot to stop by Optimism Gon's offices to invite him to tea on her grandmother's behalf, which made Grace Menmo very annoyed indeed.

It was with great reluctance that she then got her granddaughter onto the guest list at the Festive Forager. Serenity Ko and Courage Praia stepped into a large, domed building, just like any other lining the streets of the Fourth Collective, and were immediately transported to the heart of the Arc. The smell of wet mud and damp vegetation filled the air. Dim floodlights lit the space like so many golden moons.

Serenity Ko immediately received a thoughtstream on the Loop. It appeared to be a playing card with an elaborate image of the Harmony Knot on it, divided into ten segments. She was asked to focus on the different segments of the Knot's structure, and as each one spun into focus, an ingredient popped up. Once she had scrolled through them all, a message appeared:

Gather all your ingredients and help us make a communal meal!

'Fuck me,' Serenity Ko swore, as further instructions reeled across her vision. It turned out that she and all the other diners would need to go on a scavenger hunt for ingredients before Executive Chef Curiosity Kai would prepare their dinner for them live, while talking them through the process.

'Fun, isn't it?' Courage Praia beamed in the semi-darkness.

'Show me your list,' Serenity Ko demanded. Courage Praia streamed it to her. All their ingredients were different.

Serenity Ko hastily grabbed a set of syringes offered by one of the servers. She raced across the mulchy simulated-forest floor, hunting for the first plant on her display. Much to her chagrin, none of the ingredients were the kind she'd grown accustomed to harvesting ras from in her grandmother's garden; all of them were wild ones from the Arc. She supposed this was some kind of commentary on the lives of Wanderers, except offered at a price point that would lead real Wanderers to revolt. She hunted for a bush with spiny purple leaves and bright green flowers; her ingredients card called it a "caculent," and said she needed to harvest 25 μg of ras from its veins. The minutes passed by and sweat beaded on her brow until she spotted it, nestled in the roots of a spindle-tree. She knelt in the mud before it, regretting the fact that she'd chosen to wear a skirt this evening, and harvested it as best she could, just like her grandmother had taught her. She checked the time on her visual—ten whole minutes had passed! At this rate, it would take two hours before their chef could even begin assembling their meal. Serenity Ko needed a drink.

She grabbed a mug of bark-bira from a passing server and looked at her surroundings. Over a dozen diners ran skidding through the mud, dove into bushes, and scrambled up miniature trees conveniently pruned to facilitate climbing. They laughed and screamed with glee, seemingly discovering some kind of second childhood.

This was bullshit.

Serenity Ko refused to participate. Worst case, she'd turn up at the dinner table without her ingredients, the chef would nod sympathetically, the other diners would smile indulgently, and the dish would be prepared from a secret stock they had on hand for incompetent foragers just like her. She grabbed another mug of bark-bira, and waited for the better part of an hour to slip by. When most of the diners had made their way to the large circular table at the far end of the room, she sauntered over.

Chef Curiosity Kai stood in a hollowed-out space at the centre of the table. Before him was some kind of cooking counter. As each of the diners handed over their foraged ras, Curiosity Kai smiled graciously and thanked them for contributing to their recreation of the Harmony Knot, one of Uru's most central symbols of Nakshatran philosophy. Serenity Ko noticed that Courage Praia had managed to gather all *their* ingredients. *People pleaser*, she thought with a snigger.

Curiosity Kai held his hand out for Serenity Ko's syringes, and Serenity Ko smiled. 'I didn't quite manage to get them all,' she said, feigning embarrassment.

'Let's see what you've got,' he said in a low, gravelly voice.

Serenity Ko handed over a single syringe, and faked a sheepish grin.

'That's it?' he asked with genuine surprise.

'Afraid so.'

'I'm afraid it won't do.'

'Won't do for what?'

'To get you a seat at this table.'

'You're kidding.'

Curiosity Kai launched into a polite lecture about how the rules of the restaurant—made emphatically clear at the time of the reservation—stated that each diner would have to forage at least fifty percent of their own ingredients to partake in a meal.

'So you can go collect the rest and come back,' he said gently.

'I don't think so.' Serenity Ko smiled her most charming smile. 'Why don't we send one of the servers instead?'

'In that case, I'm going to have to ask you to leave.'

'With pleasure,' Serenity Ko snapped.

'Ko, what the fuck are you doing?' Courage Praia hissed.

'Exactly what I was asked to.'

The other diners tutted, and a couple of them gave Serenity Ko death glares as she stomped away. Their own dinners had been delayed, since someone else had to go forage her ingredients for her. Serenity Ko contented herself by storming into the neighbouring bar, The Twisted Flute, and ordering herself a slew of nanotinis. This went well until her grandmother's name sprawled across her visual repeatedly. She finally answered her comms.

'What?'

'I can't *believe* the disrespect you've shown to all my culinary friends.' Grace Menmo's voice was dangerously quiet, her face pinched in disgust. 'Each of them has earned their place in the world of Primian cuisine.'

'Sure.' Serenity Ko rolled her eyes. 'All arrogant, high-concept clowns in the kitchen.'

'Every single one of them is more qualified to design your food project than you are. I should never have taken you on as a student.'

Serenity Ko's heart skipped a beat. 'No, Ammamma, that's not true. See how hard I've worked, all the studying I've done, all the experiences I'm being open to...'

'And yet this is how you behave. I'm not going to help you anymore.'

Serenity Ko sat up ramrod straight. She dropped all pretence of dignity and began to beg. She didn't even take another sip of her nanotini as mer mouth ran dry and the words continued to tumble out.

Grace Menmo cut her off. 'You need to learn the meaning of respect.'

'I'll learn,' Serenity Ko whined. 'Just give me another chance.'

'Fine. One last chance,' Grace Menmo said.

Serenity Ko closed her eyes and sighed in relief, and in doing so, she missed the wicked glint that slipped into her grandmother's eyes.

These off-world blues
Are melting away
I'm at the very heart of it,
I'll be a part of it,
It's just the start of it,
I'm here on Primus to stay...

—Boundless Fran & the Ur-Siders, from 'Primus, Primus'
2043 Anno Earth | 1968 Interstellar Era

TWENTY

Two THINGS BECAME immediately apparent from my first five days at Nonpareil: I had no idea what I was doing in a Primian kitchen, and Good Cheer Chaangte delighted in my ignorance.

Each morning, I found myself scrubbing down countertops, a glorified intern. Every afternoon, I was assigned family, which I didn't mind since I got to mess around in the kitchen and actually cook. It helped that the pantry wasn't as depressingly empty as it had been my first day on the job. I turned out beest fry and shellfish curry, pepper rasam, bagara baingan, and an entire menu of Daxina foods presented as humbly—to Primians, entirely savagely—as possible. I dropped my fancy, pretty plating from the Elé Oota days and served things home-style, often in sharing portions.

Boundless Baz found his way to the family kitchen each day, dropping in for at least ten minutes to watch me work. 'I'm a second-generation Primian, but a quarter Earthling on my dad's side,' he'd confided the first time. 'I don't say it out loud, but I love this food. Reminds me of my grandparents.'

I always made it a point to give him an extra helping for his kindness.

Good Cheer Chaangte was not a fan, and managed to take more than ten minutes each day to stop by and tell me so. 'You know, I'm from the Wight School,' she began this afternoon. 'We're known for our infusions and marbling techniques. It takes precision, finesse, artistry and a steady hand. It's *true* skill.' She sniffed at the gayam I was chopping—with great precision into perfectly even long slices, for the record. 'We don't use brute force. We use seduction.'

I rolled my eyes and ignored her, but she carried on. 'Have you ever made a Saens flavour motif? Or a regression reduction glaze?'

She paused and looked at me pointedly for a response. I let the silence stretch out, yawning and void-like, watching her watching me out of the corner of my eye. She grimaced in frustration, and Kili sniggered on my shoulder.

'Of course you haven't,' she answered herself. 'Stuff teenagers do on this planet when they want a snack. Probably different where you're from—running around with knives and stealing food off each other, I'll bet. Explains the violent cooking technique.'

My knife *snick-snick-snicked* through the gayam, and I had to resist the urge to let it thwack into the chopping board as I finished the last slice. My palms were sweaty, and anger bubbled up within me, but I decided to ignore her bullying and focus on the consistency of the batter I was making.

She wasn't entirely wrong—as a scion of the Godavari clan, I'd been far removed from the realities on the Earth-streets, but it was a bit obnoxious of her to assume the same kind of savagery of all Earthlings. Most of the violence in Daxina was carried out by the foot soldiers of warring clans like mine—one of the many reasons I'd been desperate to escape them. Regular people just went about their business hoping not to be caught in the crossfire. And sure, food might have been scarce when the Nakshatrans left, but Earth had learnt *some* lessons in the devastation that followed. Most regions had vertical farmlands, there were crickets and vat-grown proteins for most people (of course, the über rich had access to natural meats), and there were even communal food banks for people below the poverty line.

Good Cheer Chaangte sneered, and I realised I was scowling.

'Do you know why Primian food doesn't use whole ingredients, unlike more primitive cultures?' She sauntered along the counter to stand right next to me. She gently flicked the chopping board, disrupting my neat little rows of chopped gayam, and smirked. '*Barbaric.*'

'Chaangte, enough. Aren't you supposed to be keeping an eye on XX 29's soufflé prep?'

I wheeled around and caught sight of Amol at the door. Good Cheer Chaangte strutted off, but not before throwing me a quick glance laced with distaste.

'I apologise for Chaangte's behaviour, but it's a relevant question, you know,' Amol said, stepping into the kitchen and sniffing the air. 'More fire cooking?'

I shrugged. 'Everyone likes the food I'm making.'

'Yes, it's definitely novel,' Amol said cautiously. 'But you can't use whole ingredients every day; you'll rack up an enormous bill, and then the Secretariat will raise our taxes, and the Culture and Heritage office will be all over us. We need to carefully estimate our consumption rates, and account for them, so we don't give in to excess.'

I wiped my hands on my towel, replacing it on my shoulder. 'Why?'

'Because it isn't Primian culture.'

'Of course it isn't,' I sighed. 'But I thought this place was inclusive.'

'So long as you follow Primian rules,' Amol explained. He then pulled up a chair, its legs scraping across the floor, and sat on it, regarding me with an expression that looked like sadness mingled with pity. 'Look, why don't I loan you some equipment? Take it back to your space and start messing with Primian techniques.'

'I don't—'

He held up his hand. 'You're working for us, and we don't need a chef on the team whose only job is to make family. Especially with such wasteful cooking techniques.'

My stomach knotted, my cheeks burning with indignation and shame.

He has a point, Kili said gently.

I know. I don't like it.

'Do you have Loop access?' Amol asked.

'Yes,' I answered, trying not to grit my teeth. *Why does everyone assume Earthlings are so backward here?*

'I'm sending you the most definitive introduction to Primian cooking, *At Home in the Kitchen* by Grace Menmo. It's a sim—you know what those are?'

'Yes,' I lied.

'Right, so take the rest of the day off and go to the research kitchen in the next room. I'll finish up here. Start studying, and make me a Primian dish tomorrow.'

'What?' My heart raced. That was too soon.

'Something basic. It doesn't need to be exquisite. Everything in the family pantry is yours. Feel free to take it home.'

What if I don't want to? I left the words unspoken as I washed my hands and left the kitchen. *What if all I really want is to be back at Elé Oota?*

Every time I cooked on this planet, I found myself steeped in nostalgia, loss slipping into my soul. There was a yearning for the kitchen I'd left behind, and I was beginning to realise that it had never been about our success. It was

243

our shared love for food, our love for—dare I think it—each other. The notion ripped me apart even as it brought me bittersweet joy, each time I cooked the food that connected me to the closest family I'd ever had. A proper, real family, twenty-one jumpgates away.

My sous chef Kartikeya's triumphant smile—her two front teeth larger than the rest, her hair in disarray—popped into my head, hovering over the perfect pot of mutton dalcha as it simmered over an open flame. Juno's perfectly slow-roasted grilled fish glistening, skewer after perfect skewer brought up to the pass, while she danced with the fires of a tandoor. Saina's impeccable pastries, especially the enormous chai croquembouche she'd assemble for private banquets, the cream in those puff pastries made from buffalo milk and seasoned with cardamom. She claimed she'd been inspired by the perfect cup of irani chai, an ancient tea recipe handed down through the ages in her family... I missed them, I missed them all, and the freedom of creating food that spoke to my soul.

It's too soon. You can't give up already. You didn't travel halfway across the galaxy only to throw in the towel at the first sign of hostility.

No, I hadn't. But I also hadn't expected so much resistance to culinary experimentation and cultural expression. And over what? Primus was more abundant than the Earth in its fresh, vibrant produce. Its population was less than a third of my home world's. There was literally *no reason* to obsess over ingredients and limit their usage to microgrammes, not when half of UHC space didn't—unless they did, and fuck the stars, I'd never been to any other worlds, so how would I know?

Saras, if you don't want to do this, you can just stop now, Kili said. _We'll find something else._

I don't want to do it, I streamed. _But I don't want them to think they scared me off because I wasn't good enough._

Who cares what they think? You have nothing to prove to them.

Why does it feel like I do?

You're projecting, Kili murmured. _But these people aren't your parents._

When I want the brutal truth, I'll ask, I snapped.

Kili whirred off my shoulder in a huff, his lights flashing red with anger. He settled on a tall shelf in a small ruffled ball, his screens emoting X-es for eyes. My comms were assaulted by visuals of fireballs and explosions.

I'm sorry, I said.

I need time, he sulked.

Fair enough.

I gave him time. I slid into the Loop and it grew to fill my visual feed. I had to manually select its intensity, choosing between Augmented Reality and Immersive Reality. Augmented Reality would let me access my surroundings, while visions from the Loop played out as an overlay, reality still visible in the background. Or so I'd learned. This was my usual setting—it was distracting, but at least I could still see the world around me. I'd never checked out Immersive Reality; it sounded like living in an else-world, and that scared me. But the minute my eyes focused on Amol's comms, and the sim he'd sent me, and I said 'Open' out loud, the Loop rushed in to fill all my senses. It was like being swallowed by a decadent chocolate ganache filling, the equivalent of a multi-sensory headache.

'When the Nakshatrans took to the stars,' a soft mellifluous voice began as I was transported into the darkness of space, 'they escaped the devastation of the Earth. A chosen few spacefarers, representative of different races, religions, sexes, genders, and ethnicities, were raised in isolation from contemporary events, encouraged to collaborate and develop alternate lifestyles, free from the wars that were tearing apart the world they inhabited.

Seven different Nakshatran Stations—seven different ways of being human—emerged, sheltered from the way of the people of Earth.'

A glittering path through the stars lit up. 'Walk,' I commanded, following the verbal prompts on my visual.

The sensation of floating through space tugged at my navel, as I was pulled along the pathway. After a while, branches began to appear, inviting me to drop into different periods of human history leading up to the formation of the Nakshatran Project. I knew all this from university, and so I said, 'Speed up.'

The sim worked faster. Ethereal music evoking the mysteries of the universe beamed into my mind.

'Would you like to visit the Earth-homes of the Nakshatrans?' The sim's voice asked.

'No, thank you,' I said. I'd read a ton of holoscrolls about them through my education; communal farms and kitchens, fair division of labour, libraries of holoscrolls to peruse so each Station could develop a manifesto for their own philosophy... each Nakshatran Station had four hundred humans chosen at random from the Earth's population of thousands of children. They were intended to take human civilization into space. Primus had been the first planet they were meant to set foot on; it hadn't been the last.

The sim sped past more branching paths, each leading off to a painstaking reconstruction of the Stations they'd inhabited on Earth, visible in my peripheral vision. Perhaps I'd save them for another day; right now, I needed to get to all the bits about Primian food and master them.

'Are you in a hurry to get to the sections on Primian food?' the sim's voice asked me.

It was unreal. We had AI back on Earth, and Kili was a Sentient Intelligence—an underappreciated tech evolution— but having my mind read by a piece of software was uncanny. Goosebumps formed on my arms.

'I can guess your thoughts thanks to the bio-circuits,' the sim's voice said. 'The nanopills that give you Loop access mesh with your neural networks. Would you like a detailed explanation?'

I shuddered. I definitely would, but not right at this moment. 'Later?' I suggested weakly. 'Right now, I just want to understand Primian food.'

'There's a spaceship up ahead,' the sim's voice said. 'Shall I speed us towards it? That'll take you to Primus, your destination, and you'll be able to step into my kitchens.'

A light went on in my head. The sim's speaker was Grace Menmo, famous food critic, restaurateur and authority on Primian culture. I'd heard of her all the way back on Earth—she was considered formidable across the food universe.

'Yes, I'm Grace Menmo,' sim-Grace Menmo said.

'Lovely to meet you,' I replied meekly, suddenly intimidated even though I knew I was speaking to a sim character and not the real human being she was modelled on. 'I'd love to get to your kitchens asap.'

'Board the spaceship,' sim-Grace Menmo said. I realised that we were suddenly standing in front of a large, long craft. 'This is a section of the *Nakshatra-I*, the craft that bore all Primian ancestors to this planet.'

I navigated into it using my... mind? I still had no idea what I was doing to control the sim, but decided to go with the flow.

'Before we get to Primus, there are some things about the origins of Primian food you need to understand, and they all begin on this spaceship,' Grace Menmo said. 'So look around.'

I stifled my impatience and studied the insides of the craft. Long metal surfaces ran along each wall, and digital displays streaming information I didn't comprehend were interspersed with viewports. The holo-projectors sat here and there on the counters, each one beaming something different: I spotted a three-dimensional star map, a holosnap of a group of humans—presumably fellow Nakshatrans—and some kind of ancient Earth film reel playing. In a little glass tray were various small rocks, perhaps mementos from Earth. A large chair was bolted onto the floor, off to one side. A glass comms tablet rested on the counter. And in a small alcove on the right was a bed; the shelves around it were covered in books, ancient Earth-tech for reading.

'This is the Nakshatran I trace my ancestry back to, according to all my scrollwork,' sim-Grace Menmo said, and I caught a trace of pride in her voice. 'Sarojini Ratna. She was a biologist on board the *Nakshatra-I.*

'If you head over to the second shelf to your left and pop it open, you'll find an entire selection of food that Sarojini survived on, on the long journey here.'

I followed sim-Grace Menmo's instructions. The shelf popped open with a voice command, and a drawer slid out. Small vacuum-sealed boxes floated out in what was presumably anti-gravity.

'Direct them to the counter.'

The boxes came to rest on the metal surface at my command. I studied the labels. Dal rice, steak and potatoes, chicken pot pie, mushroom and leek stir-fry, udon noodles with pork, cricket chips, and a host of other familiar names from Earth's culinary history, all neatly written in English.

'Why don't you open each one?' sim-Grace Menmo suggested.

The box of dal rice popped open, but inside, all I saw was a cream-coloured gelatinous substance on one side, with a yellow and green marbled gel on the other. I opened the steak and potatoes, and found a reddish brown gel-like terrine. Each of the boxes was similarly unremarkable, and filled with budget-traveller space-food, the kind I'd had on my refugee freighter.

'This is typical low-budget space food,' I said, shrugging in real life.

'It is,' Grace Menmo said. 'The Nakshatrans travelled in a time before jumpgates, in cryo-sleep for long periods of time, staying awake in shifts. For the better part of fifteen years, this is the only food they had access to while they were awake.'

'Okay...' I said slowly.

'No big deal, you're thinking. They land on a planet and the struggle to find food is over, right?' sim-Grace Menmo said. 'Except, no. The first Nakshatran Principle is "tread lightly." And that's what the earliest settlers did.'

The craft I was on descended through purple-pink clouds like marshmallows, towards a field of sheaf-grass and purple flutter heads. Towering in the distance were enormous granite cliffs and boulders, and I thought I spied what was now known as Nakshatran Rock. The ship landed gently, and it shimmered around me before transitioning into some kind of large tent.

'For decades, the Nakshatrans lived in tents much like this one. This was before flowmetal was developed, so they were limited compared with modern spaces. Nevertheless, they persevered,' sim-Grace Menmo explained. 'Look around at all the shelves. Each shelf contains frozen seedlings from Earth, but only a small handful that were compatible with Primus's existing ecosystem were ever transplanted. Determining this took years of research. And in all that time, our ancestors survived on space food—molecularly infused with flavour, constituted in some kind of gel, packed with nutrition. Step out onto Primian soil?'

I stepped out into wilderness; a forest teeming with life. I stood in a glade of sheaf-grass, tall trees growing around it, laden with exotic fruits of every colour, none of which I recognised. Fungi with intricate patterns grew wild, nestled where the tree roots stretched out into the leafy undergrowth. Birds twittered in the trees, a wild hare-like creature hopped through the grass.

'Once natural flora and fauna were discovered, our ancestors decided not to repeat the mistakes of the people of the Earth,' sim-Grace Menmo said. 'Instead of hunting, they set up Earth-tech to grow protein in vats. They *chose* to harvest only what was absolutely essential. This was the beginnings of ras. And as their tech grew more sophisticated, they realised they needed less to achieve flavour, a long way from what humanity has always believed on the Earth.

'This is the root of our culinary tradition on Primus.'

She paused, and let her words sink in. My head spun with questions. I'm not sure what I'd expected as a history lesson on the Nakshatrans—none of this was new information, but seeing their philosophy through the lens of food, and the food experiences they'd had on the long journey here, lent their molecular-level cooking techniques more meaning.

At the same time, it was odd that nearly two millennia had passed from that time of scarcity and uncertainty, and they'd only seemed to grow more rigid in the preservation of their tradition. From everything I'd experienced in my limited time on the planet, it felt as if to question, to innovate, or to explore different cultures was a threat to Primian identity—one they took extremely seriously. It was as if their outlook had never grown, or evolved, or assimilated the hundreds of different cultures—human and otherwise—that had found their way to Primus since. And I couldn't help but wonder what they were so afraid of. Nobody in the UHC had more authority on culture than Primus; even all the way on Earth, I'd grown up on a steady diet of Primian pop culture, all the way from *Uru: Origins* to the galaxy-shattering sound of smash.

'Do you see that stream?' sim-Grace Menmo asked, interrupting my thoughts.

'Yes.'

'Follow it.'

I did. I walked—or rather, the sim environment zoomed towards me, simulating movement—for a few hundred metres, until I spied a small cottage nestled between three trees with luminous silver trunks, their low boughs casting a net of shade over the ground. Peculiar little blossoms lined the forest floor. I walked up to the cottage—it was made from some kind of flowmetal, judging from the way it bobbed up and down, perhaps harvesting electricity from the light breeze I couldn't feel, but that whispered its way through the leaves.

I did the only thing I could. I raised my fist and knocked gently on the door. It swung open.

A tall, curvy woman, her straight, dark hair streaked with grey, opened the door. Her spectacles slipped down her nose when she smiled. 'Are you ready to try your hand at Primian cuisine?'

'Y-yes,' I said, my mouth dry.

'Welcome to my kitchen,' sim-Grace Menmo said.

The key to power lies in finding the right balance between hushed whispers and open declarations.

The B'naar Uprising of 1868 IE was quelled by dialogue, through offering well-placed incentives to the rebel forces, including early, if limited, access to developing Primian technologies. In exchange, it was revealed that Honour Sands ceded United Human Cooperative secrets to the rebels via a series of encrypted holoscroll messages, the contents of which are enclosed herewith. Much like the rest of this report, sensitive details are redacted for all those without appropriate Loop clearance...

—Curiosity Zaros,
Mission Commander, Operation Raspberry Boogie
Classified File GHC/PRI/ZI09981200000876265
1973 Anno Earth | 1898 Interstellar Era

TWENTY-ONE

THE MILLENNIUM FESTIVAL Planning Committee met every day under the aegis of Optimism Mahd'vi, who made it a point to cancel at least three hours' worth of *other* meetings each nava in order to review its progress. She'd personally chosen her fourteen-member team after assessing their pliancy and ambition, in addition to their core competencies. True to the way matters were conducted on Primus, admission was invitation-only, while the meetings occurred in broad sur-light in the Central Courtyard of the Secretariat.

The atrium had been suitably enhanced to convey a carnival atmosphere. The floor-to-ceiling windows were flung wide open, and pennants in all the colours of the Nine Virtues fluttered gaily in the breeze. At the centre of the courtyard sat a large, circular table, enclosed by a sound bubble to ensure the privacy of the super-secret conversations underway. All along the periphery, flowmetal booths invited passers-by to engage in popular games like blather 'n' bluff and crypticards, sample bite-sized Primian delicacies, engage in livestreamed poetry jams and sinfonia slams, all while encouraging them to sign up as volunteers for the Festival. This resulted in considerable excitement, and was met with unbridled enthusiasm by everyone in the Secretariat, even though it caused significant interruptions to the well-oiled daily functioning of its machinery.

A holographic diorama of Nakshatran Rock popped up after the first nava, and people were encouraged to press their palms into its lambent virtual moss to sign up for the latest updates from the Festival. Visio-nodes beamed historic films and performances from the Loop, with exclusive footage and behind-the-scenes interviews. Members of the Secretariat were encouraged to bring guests, admitted in ones and twos, to marvel at the unfolding celebration that promised a spectacle to come.

All the while, Optimism Mahd'vi ran her meetings like a tight ship, one eye on the expressions of delight and awe on every face that walked by, her mind entirely focused on setting gears in place for a cultural conquest the likes of which the universe had never encountered before.

Almost entirely.

Part of her mind remained preoccupied with Jog Tunga, whose movements her AI assistants continued to monitor, whenever he appeared in the public eye. He'd been frequently spotted in the company of various A-list Primian celebrities, and Optimism Mahd'vi had dug into their backgrounds for the slightest hint that they might be Earth-sympathisers. She was constrained by the very real law declaring surveillance illegal on Primus (and most civilised UHC planets), and had to make do with scraps and inferences.

She'd been even more preoccupied with the question of the other Earthling interloper—*the Kaveri girl*, as she'd taken to thinking of her. She'd viewed the *MegaChef* footage Curiosity Ariam had sent her at least a half-dozen times. There was no denying the young woman's Earthling origins; absolutely no other culture would encourage the kind of brazenness it took to cook over an open flame on Primus. And on a show as big as *Interstellar MegaChef,* too, where the outcome could make all the difference between a burgeoning career in cuisine and being relegated to the dustbins of culinary history. It was particularly strange behaviour for a Kaveri to take such an enormous risk, ignoring the manifold rewards that could be open to her if she just toed the line.

Perhaps things have changed on Earth, Optimism Mahd'vi mused. *Perhaps they're no longer hunting Kaveris like they're vermin.*

She caught herself—when did she start thinking of the Kaveris as "them" and not "us"? It was unsettling, something to be looked into at a later point, at her next session with her therapist, maybe.

It's the Kaveri girl, dredging up these unasked-for navel-gazing indulgences.

Optimism Mahd'vi *had* to know her story. She'd tried to look up her past on the Loop—Curiosity Ariam had mentioned she was a big deal back on Earth—but she couldn't find any information about a professional chef by the name Saraswati Kaveri. It was all very mysterious.

She was jolted from her thoughts when someone slammed their palm down on the flowmetal table.

'Well, *I* think a broadcast of the *Nakshatranāma,* featuring all the Poet Premiers still living, could really move the needle on epic poetry slams!' Boundless Tai said emphatically.

'I don't disagree!' Curiosity Ariam exclaimed. 'All *I'm* saying is that we shift the focus to a new generation. Find the most exciting amateur slam poets out there, get *them* to perform!' They met Optimism Mahd'vi's eyes. 'You're with me on this, aren't you, Mads?'

Optimism Mahd'vi stifled her annoyance. The nickname had been thrown around casually ever since Courage Ilio had attended their inaugural meeting.

'Come on, think about it—how are a bunch of half-dead poets, already famous and galactically-renowned, going to be fresh and exciting? Do you know how hard we've worked to streamline our programming to meet the ever-shifting demands of a more culturally curious audience? We need to find young, relatable people, not stuck-up performance snobs with degrees from the Primian Palace of Performing Arts. Let me tell you about Boundless Nnika—huge youth influencer, won a Drammy for *Stars Unrivalled*? You won't believe how we cast her—where we found her, that is. I remember our casting director and I—we must have been in our twenties back then—we were hooking up behind the lot, at this makeshift dive called The Twisted Screw, what an appropriate name, *I know*.' Curiosity Ariam laughed at their own joke, and then dove headlong into a rambling story. Optimism Mahd'vi took the opportunity to return to the problem of the Earthling.

There was a far more aggravating possibility as far as the Kaveri girl and Jog Tunga went. *Two* Earthlings hanging around Primus, *both* with links to the Godavari clan—while the rest of the Earth's population barely received travel visas to the planet—couldn't be a coincidence. *Could it?* What if they were in on something together, circling her precious planet, scheming acts of violence and rebellion?

'—fresh and exciting, looks to the future of Primian culture, engages the youth.' Curiosity Ariam jabbed their index finger at a hovering holoray, which persistently beamed the vision statement for the Millennium Festival into the makeshift conference room. 'I *know* Mads agrees with me.'

Boundless Tai crossed his arms, clearly miffed. As their expert on live performance, he and Curiosity Ariam had been at constant loggerheads—regarding each other as a crowd-pleasing hack and an outdated fossil, respectively.

Optimism Mahd'vi sighed, annoyed. 'I'm going with Ariam's recommendation; broadcasts are their domain. And stop sulking, Tai. I'm happy to go with your expertise for our *in-person* live events. The Legends of the Future special concert, the Millennium Season of the sinfonia, *all* our entertainment at the Millennium Feast...'

She glared at Boundless Tai, whose downcast gaze was dampening the spirit of all their planning. 'Not good enough for you?' she snapped. 'Maybe *you're* not good enough to rise to the occasion. Walk it off and think about that. Get a kaapi. Come back only once you've got your priorities straight.'

Boundless Tai shook his head and stalked away, the sound-bubble rippling as he left the meeting. As Optimism Mahd'vi watched him depart, registered Curiosity Ariam's barely-restrained smirk of triumph, and continued to turn the mystery of the Kaveri girl over in her mind, the skeins of an idea began to knit together.

'Ariam, run me through the current list of special broadcasts again?'

Curiosity Ariam complied. 'We're taking all our highest rated programming over the years, and tweaking it to appeal to an extended audience—Primian and other, human and alt-being. We've conducted extensive research to arrive at the following special broadcasts...'

Optimism Mahd'vi leaned forwards as corresponding vision boards were holorayed in the air. There were the usual suspects—never before seen special episodes and outtakes, featuring *Stars Unrivalled* and *Uru: Origins*, a dozen smash hit holo-reels with exclusive, interactive footage, story-sims, live-action epic poetry adaptations, a new documentary on Legends of the Future (for which Chloriana and Enigma had been paid exorbitant sums to hide their creative differences and growing rivalry), a *Teen Trouble: Twenty Years Gone* reunion season…

But all Optimism Mahd'vi could see was one enormous gaping hole in their programming. A void that held the solution to multiple problems she was grappling with. And it was stupidly, ridiculously easy to fill.

'Fen, do you have a proposal for the Feast yet?' Optimism Mahd'vi spun in her chair to regard the woman she was addressing. Honour Fen dropped a stack of swatches.

Curiosity Ariam stopped their presentation abruptly, but Optimism Mahd'vi waved for them to carry on. Curiosity Ariam dropped their voice, but studied Optimism Mahd'vi with curiosity and consternation, while continuing to address the rest of the committee, most of whom wore a glazed look, evidently transacting critical business on the Loop, now that their serving of conflict and drama for the day was over.

Optimism Mahd'vi eyed Honour Fen, scrabbling around on the floor to gather the colourful stack of cards together, and experienced a twinge of regret at having included her on the committee. She was a savant, but as it turned out, she was also the highly disorganized variety who jumped at small noises.

'Fen?' Optimism Mahd'vi repeated, tapping her foot.

'Working on it, your Excellency. I'm a bit behind on some of the details—'

'Do we have the food and catering sorted out?'

'N-no.'

Curiosity Ariam had come to the end of their presentation. Optimism Mahd'vi quickly scanned their broadcast line-up, hovering in the air before her. A slow smile slid across her face.

'Good, isn't it?' Curiosity Ariam said, misreading the situation hopefully.

'You've missed something,' Optimism Mahd'vi said.

'Huh?'

'Honestly, do I have to spell everything out for you?'

Curiosity Ariam looked from Optimism Mahd'vi to Honour Fen, then back at their presentation. A slight frown crept between their brows, and they muttered inaudibly. Optimism Mahd'vi waited in silence for the producer to work things out, and beamed when Curiosity Ariam laughed out loud.

'I can't believe I missed it!' they said. 'I can't believe the whole team dropped the ball on it.'

'Good, isn't it?'

'It's beyond good.'

'It's going to be the most-watched broadcast of the lot.'

'I bet you have a name for it, already.'

'I do.' Optimism Mahd'vi rose from her seat. '*Interstellar MegaChef: The Millennium Feast Special*.'

'I love it.'

'Winner gets to cater the Millennium Feast at the close of our celebrations.' Optimism Mahd'vi waved her hand vaguely in Honour Fen's direction. 'Biggest culinary contract in the history of the galaxy. Solves Fen's problem with the catering, too.'

'We need a new angle, though, to distinguish it from the usual competition.'

Optimism Mahd'vi's brain raced, decompressing a few navas' worth of conversation in milliseconds, focusing on every cue and hint she'd been handed in conversation. It fixated on her argument with Courage Ilio, and the pieces fell into place immediately. 'I have just the thing...'

You know how you negotiate? Grab 'em by the throat
when they aren't looking, look 'em in the eye, and
make your terms known. I guarantee they'll give you
whatever you want. If they don't, a gentle squeeze will
do the trick...

—Rebel Leader Bannon Akari,
from *Empire Quest*, Season 8, Episode 3
2073 Anno Earth | 1998 Interstellar Era

TWENTY-TWO

EXPERIENCE YOUR BEST Life! flashed the lights along the tunnel, urging Serenity Ko to be highly motivated with all the subtlety of a meteor strike. She didn't need the reminder. The tunnel's moving walkway thrust her into XP Inc.'s offices, and she strode forwards as if propelled by an invisible magnetic force, driving her into the heart of its whorls.

Her two-nava exile was over; eighteen Suriyan days times twenty-eight hours, which was more arithmetic than she was willing to do but felt like a lot. Now, every step filled her with renewed purpose. It hadn't all been wasted—here she was, on the verge of launching a culinary revolution. Her grandmother had bullied her into signing up for a learning opportunity in an *actual restaurant kitchen,* and she'd decided that she needed to keep the family peace, since she was the one who'd made the unwise decision of soliciting her grandmother's help in the first place. She wished she'd taken to learning about food on *Outcooked 5* instead, and it was not for the first time, and nor would it be the last.

She was going to accost Grace Kube at the earliest, and find a way to do this on XP Inc. sanctioned time.

Perhaps I even owe it to Kube, she thought, as her comms buzzed nonstop, the bright red bubble of an unread notification popping up constantly on her visual, ticking its way up past five hundred as every AI, human and alt-being in the office was alerted to her return. *Perhaps I'll even let Kube work for me, once I replace him as Director of Design,* she thought with a grin. She beamed at everyone she passed, and even when she made eye contact with Curiosity Nenna, she couldn't wipe the smile off her face.

'Are you all right, Ko?' Curiosity Nenna frowned. 'You look ill.'

'Never been better, Nenna!' Serenity Ko said brightly as she passed her. 'Stay tuned for updates that will change your life and skyrocket your career into the stars!'

'I don't understand…'

'Later!'

Courage Praia peeled off a wall at the exit to the forty-first whorl, where their design team was housed. Their right arm hung limp at their side, wrapped up in healing tape. Their usually neatly-slicked-back blond hair was dishevelled, and a light stubble dotted their face.

'Inoculation day?' Serenity Ko asked.

Courage Praia grimaced. 'Yeah, I've got no way to use my right arm for the next fifty-six hours. Delightful.'

Serenity Ko gave her friend a hug, which was most unlike her, and Courage Praia winced, caught off-guard as she squeezed their arm a little tighter than was comfortable. 'It'll be good—before you know it, your arm will be brand new again.'

'Thanks,' Courage Praia said. 'It's always frustrating. Waiting for the nanobots to fix the muscle degeneration in this stupid arm. I wish I could just get a mod, but it's so invasive. And they always tell me they want to save the limb.'

Serenity Ko nodded sympathetically. 'Someday, maybe.'

'Someday.'

'Want a distracting thought?' Serenity Ko asked, partly because she was genuinely concerned for her friend, but also unable to contain her excitement.

'Sure.'

'Kube's in the middle of a meeting of the Triumvirate. We're barging in,' Serenity Ko beamed.

'Is that why we're still in the tunnel?' Courage Praia's eyes widened in panic. 'I thought we were going to get a snack!'

'Good idea! We'll get kaapi and cricket chips for everyone!'

'Ko, are you out of your mind? We have a meeting scheduled with Kube for later this afternoon!' Courage Praia sagged against the railing. 'It took me half the last nava to find a free three-hour slot with Stella.'

'That AI of his is a bitch,' Serenity Ko said scornfully. 'She'll reschedule, just wait and watch. Does it to me all the time.'

'Ko, this is a terrible idea.'

'Shock and awe. Take 'em by surprise, I say,' Serenity Ko said, matter-of-factly.

'No, listen to me. We need their approval.' Courage Praia dropped eye contact, the way they did whenever they found themselves on the losing side of an argument. 'We need them on our side.'

'Exactly.' Serenity Ko nodded. 'Kaapi and cricket chips.'

She stepped off the tunnel walkway and headed to the exit to the nearest pantry. A tangle of martinia creepers trailed over its entrance, and she stepped through and into bright sunlight for an entire second, before her optics preferences took over and dimmed the light to more reasonable levels. *Boy, do I love my nanopills*, she thought.

The pantry was housed in a transparent flowmetal dome, and included a hothouse of some kind. Orchids from across the galaxy blossomed from large planters, or crept over hanging pots to fill the space with their heady scents. Serenity Ko dismissed the inputs on her Loop identifying each one, and stalked past the brightly-coloured picnic tables that lined the space, making a beeline for the elaborately decorated stall at the far side, which was a kaapi bar and snack counter.

'Ano!' She smiled at the barista. 'Just the person I was looking for!'

'Serenity Ko, how are you?' Boundless Ano grinned. 'I heard you were on vacation. Did you off-world? Wanderers' Paths?'

Boundless Ano wore six Wanderers' rings himself, for six tours of the Arc—once for mandatory service, voluntarily five more times. He told anyone who would listen that his dream was to quit Uru for the Arc someday, where he'd live in the Chlorosapient Commune, spending his days in quiet meditation and working towards self-sustenance. Serenity Ko knew him from school, and the only thing keeping him in the city was his sick mother. 'How's your mum?' she asked.

Boundless Ano smiled thinly. 'Same as ever. Nonstop supplements to help her breathe better in our atmosphere.'

'I'm sorry,' Serenity Ko said.

'Me too,' Courage Praia added.

'Thanks. What can I do for you?'

'I need two kaapi frothballs, one kaapi filter, two more with nutromilk, hold the sugar on one and add extra cream to the other,' Serenity Ko said with confidence.

Boundless Ano laughed. 'Are you pulling an all-nighter already?'

'Nope, important meeting.'

'Do you actually know their orders?' Courage Praia asked in surprise.

Serenity Ko shrugged. 'If it sounds fancy enough, none of them will turn it down.'

'This is a bad idea, Ko.'

'Oh, and I'd also like ten packs of cricket chips? I expect

this will run long.' Serenity Ko hopped up to sit on the counter, ignoring the half-dozen neatly arranged barstools.

'No can do, sorry,' Boundless Ano said, while Courage Praia pointedly patted a barstool and muttered, 'Ko, that isn't allowed.'

Serenity Ko scowled at Courage Praia and slid off her perch with a dramatic sigh. 'What do you mean, Ano? Are we out of chips?'

'Not allowed to sell cricket chips here.' Boundless Ano fiddled with some kind of machine, frothing a large bowl of nutromilk.

Serenity Ko scowled. 'Says who?'

'The Secretariat. Lots of talk about how they're insulting to the K'artri-tva.' Boundless Ano grabbed some kind of shaker and proceeded to add ingredients to it, with a generous helping of ice.

'The Katy-what?' Serenity Ko asked.

'You're being stupid on purpose.' Courage Praia poked her in the arm.

'No really, I have no idea…'

Boundless Ano and Courage Praia exchanged a look. 'The alt-beings we just established a treaty with.'

'Oh, those guys.'

'Apparently there are anatomical similarities, so cricket chips are now banned on Primus.' Boundless Ano started to blend their drinks.

'That's the stupidest thing I've heard.' Serenity Ko snorted. 'Half our food looks like B'naar anatomy, colourful and amorphous…'

'Shhhh!' Courage Praia hissed.

'She's trying to get a reaction,' Boundless Ano said knowingly. 'It's what she does when she's bored. In school, she once proclaimed that the UHC was full of it, and that only Earth knew what it was doing.' He laughed. 'What was your punishment again?'

'Scrollwork,' Serenity Ko said grouchily. 'Twenty history essays proving why Primian culture led the way for the UHC.'

'You deserved it,' Boundless Ano and Courage Praia said in unison.

'Deserved what?'

Serenity Ko's insides cringed at the sound of the smooth, low voice. She spun slowly around on her barstool, and saw Honour Aki, his hair neatly brushed, his expression stricken. He immediately collapsed on one knee before her, bowing his head.

'Ko, I'm so sorry for everything. I never should have pushed you into a monogamous commitment. After you ran away from me at the Uru and Beyond Marketplace that day, I heard you were fired, then that you were ill on the verge of death... I stopped by your space each day, but you weren't home and I had no way to reach you, so I figured you were in a hospital, and I visited every single one in Uru looking for you, and I was so worried,' he said in a single breath, before looking up at her. 'You never answered my comms,' he whined.

All the attraction Serenity Ko had ever felt for his well-built physique, or the stray bangs framing his perfect square jaw and falling into his deep green eyes, rushed out of her in less than a breath. She did a quick Loop check and found over a hundred unread messages from him, and what pity lingered for him drained away too. 'Aki, what the fuck?' she said. 'You *went to my space?*'

'It was all my fault,' he said sanctimoniously.

Boundless Ano cleared his throat pointedly. 'Drinks are good to go.'

She looked down at Honour Aki, who was on the verge of tears, mumbling inaudibly to himself.

'You're right,' she said harshly. 'It *was* all your fault. All of it. And I never want to see you again.'

She hoped against hope that he'd finally crack under the hostility, that it would be enough justification for their *final* final breakup, even though they'd never officially been in a relationship, and that she'd be rid of him for good.

Honour Aki met her gaze. 'I'll remove myself from your presence,' he said softly. 'But I will never, *never* stop making it up to you. You'll see. And someday, you'll give me a second chance.'

Serenity Ko fought the shudder threatening to run its way up her spine. He rose swiftly, and without a backward glance, fled the pantry.

'So... that went well,' Courage Praia said drily.

'Fuck, it totally backfired.' Serenity Ko rubbed a hand over her face.

'He's going to be hovering in corridors and following you around, isn't he?' Boundless Ano giggled. 'My last boyfriend was... similar. In the end, I only shook him off when I went into the Arc.'

'Lucky you, you get to be a Wanderer and escape these weirdos,' Serenity Ko sighed. A thought suddenly struck her. 'Hey, *you* don't hate me, do you?'

'How do you want me to answer that?' Boundless Ano smirked.

'No, for real...' Serenity Ko insisted, grabbing all the takeaway cups and carefully balancing them in her hands. 'The other day, I was Arcside, and things got out of hand...'

'Oh yeah,' Boundless Ano said. 'I heard about the riot you started.'

'So do Arcsiders and Wanderers really hate us here in Uru?'

Boundless Ano looked away, furrowed his brow. '"Hate" is a strong word. But there is a lot of discontent,' he said slowly. 'It's a long story. We can get a drink if you want to hear it?'

'Done,' Serenity Ko said. 'I'll stream you. And thanks for the kaapi!'

'Any time,' Boundless Ano said.

Serenity Ko handed Courage Praia their frothball, which they gingerly cradled in their functional left arm. She carried the rest as they made their way back into the tunnel, heading for the Ideatheque. She cleared her head of the tangles of information that had interrupted her triumphant return to work this morning: Courage Praia's disability acting up, the lack of cricket chips, the real trouble seemingly brewing between the Arc and Uru, and the confrontation with Honour Aki that she'd been dreading since she'd gone cold on him—though if she were being really honest, that last had turned out better than she'd expected. They stepped off the walkway and Serenity Ko led them past bright lights and potted plants. The flowmetal entrance to the conference room pulled apart, and she plastered a big smile on her face, held out the takeaway cups in her hands, and entered. 'Surprise! I'm back!'

The expressions on the faces of the Triumvirate were exactly as she'd expected. Optimism Sah'r pushed her puffy yellow armchair back from the table and rose to her feet, her eyes lighting up in genuine delight. Courage Na'vil scowled and crossed his arms over his chest, glowering. Grace Kubes' face was expressionless but for the corner of his mouth, which twitched as if threatening to break into a grin.

'I heard you were unwell,' Optimism Sah'r said, rushing forwards and hugging Serenity Ko. 'It's so good to see you back on your feet.'

'For you,' Serenity Ko said thickly, proffering a kaapi cup. She'd always had the teeniest tiniest crush on their Director of Tech, and it was downright school-girl embarrassing.

'Ooh, there's cream in mine!' Optimism Sah'r took a sip. Courage Praia chuckled, and Serenity Ko stepped on their foot.

'I bring kaapi...' Serenity Ko proclaimed, passing out the kaapi cups and helping herself to a seat that was conveniently vacant and at the head of the table, 'and a universe-changing idea to you all.'

'I thought we were scheduled for later this afternoon,' Grace Kube said, sipping on his kaapi.

'I thought you might reschedule,' Serenity Ko tossed back. 'This idea can't wait on the whims of AI assistants.'

'Fair. It would've been nice if you'd streamed me before interrupting our meeting, though.'

'So you could send me into exile again?' Serenity Ko said archly. 'I think not.'

'Let's not bicker here,' Optimism Sah'r said placatingly. 'We were nearly done anyway.'

'Yes, and I have four other back-to-back meetings scheduled, so if you want my time, schedule it.' Courage Na'vil rose. 'Though for that to happen, you'd actually have to use your comms,' he added nastily. 'Where have you been? I've been trying to schedule a meeting with you ever since you stepped into the building an hour ago.'

Serenity Ko stared at the man with open disdain, and contemplated throwing her frothball at him so it would splatter satisfyingly all over his pristine white lab coat. She might have done it, too, if Courage Praia hadn't kicked her under the table.

We need their blessing, Courage Praia streamed privately. _Be nice._

Serenity Ko channelled all her fake enthusiasm into her voice. 'We're in a meeting right now, Na'vil. And I promise, once you've heard me out, I'll spend as much time as you want addressing the concerns of the neuropsych team!' She smiled her most charming smile for added effect.

'Fine.' He sat down.

Grace Kube snorted. 'Let's hear it, then. Praia hinted that this was huge.'

'And so it is.' Serenity Ko paused dramatically and sipped slowly on her frothball, looking around the room, holding each Triumvir's eye for several seconds, before broadcasting the pitch she and Praia had put together on to the far wall.

'What if I told you that food could be an Immersive Reality experience?' she began. A montage of food prep holovids began to play out, everything from a chef's hands carefully blending the perfect nanotini, topped with a sourfruit glaze, to an elaborate beest braise accompanied with marbled cubes of gayam, pomo and spice-cream. Serenity Ko let it play two thirds of the way in silence.

'What if you could smell it, feel it, and taste it, but also *live it*?' she suggested. A large, many-layered cake appeared, covered in dripping white cream, spotted with brightly coloured berry-flavoured spheres. Serenity Ko watched everyone's eyes widen; even Courage Na'vil leaned forwards. 'That looks delicious, doesn't it?'

'It's the perfect Primian Gateau, prepared for you in this video by none other than the legendary Grace Menmo. Rich vanilla cream, layers of rougeberry, fraiseberry and himanso-infused spheres, topped with candyfoam and sprinkled with maccanut dust...' She waited for them to nod.

'Every single child on Primus has had Primian Gateau at one of their birthdays, if not more. Am I right?' She waited for another round of nods, then started circling for the kill. 'Na'vil, do you remember Primian Gateau at your birthday?'

Courage Na'vil sat back, startled by the question. 'Of course I remember,' he snapped. 'My mother crafted one for my thirteenth. I'm a second-generation immigrant, as many of you know. I was always the kid with the funny food at lunch—we didn't know how to cook Primian, though my mother tried. It took her years to learn how to do it right. When we invited my class over to our space, they spent the first hour bullying me—*on my birthday*—until the cake appeared.' His voice softened. 'That was a turning point; somehow, they treated me like I was normal ever after. All thanks to my mother. And that cake.'

'I'm sorry they were nasty to you,' Serenity Ko said. She felt a slight twinge of guilt; she'd heard Courage Na'vil's stories about being treated like an outsider, and hadn't realised her food pitch, which she'd targeted at him first, since he was the most likely to raise questions and objections to it, would trigger such an unpleasant memory. What if she'd blown it, pushed too far?

'That was the first dessert I ever made with my grandfather,' Optimism Sah'r said, smiling at the memory. 'I was probably five years old, and all I did was harvest the ras for the fruit spheres, but I'll never forget looking into the oven every three minutes, waiting for the cake to rise...'

'That's lovely!' Courage Praia said.

'Kube?' Serenity Ko turned to her boss.

'I had a lot of nerve damage from my experiments with mods,' he said quietly. 'I was once in hospital for weeks; I'd lost much of my sense of touch. This is one of the first foods I remember *tasting*—flavours rushing back to me in one massive *moment*, bringing me to life again.'

Serenity Ko had taken a wild stab at picking the most generic childhood dessert from her own memories, and she was relieved that it was resonating with her audience. The most she could remember of it was stealing half the cake out the fridge and hiding behind the kitchen island, eating it straight off the tray. She'd had a terrible tummy ache, which her parents decided had been punishment enough.

'Every single human on Primus has a deep connection to this dessert,' Serenity Ko said. 'But it's also historically significant.'

The presentation she'd assembled switched to large vistas of Primus, in all its pristine beauty. From here things would become more abstract, so she kept it brief, going off her summarised notes from the reading her grandmother had set her. 'The layers represent the Ursridge Cliffs; the cream is vanilla, one of the first Earth flora to be transplanted here. Each of the spheres is a fruit endemic to our planet.

The entire dessert captures historic moments of discovery and cultural evolution… it's all the stuff they tell you when they serve you a slice at any fancy restaurant, or when you're learning to make it at home.'

'My grandfather explained it all to me,' Optimism Sah'r said, eyes shining.

Serenity Ko stifled her excitement. Whatever she said next, their Director of Tech seemed to be on board.

'I'll cut to the chase,' Serenity Ko said. 'I'm proposing a new Immersive Reality sim. Every food you eat sets off all your happiest memories of eating it—we'll have filters, identify triggers, the whole nine yards. Every food you eat also draws on our databases to recreate its history, transporting you across space and time to discover its true meaning. It's part personal, part cultural, all experience.'

'Restaurants do this already.' Grace Kube frowned.

'They *try*.' Serenity Ko said firmly. 'I haven't even gotten to the best part, yet.'

'Go on,' Grace Kube said.

'We remove the need for food itself, the way it's created and presented today. We flatten the hierarchies of culinary skill in the kitchen, erase the need for all its complexity and incredibly rigid rules and techniques. We create food experiences that don't rely on what's on the plate. What's on the plate is immaterial, it's what's in your mind that counts.' Serenity Ko grinned. She'd hidden this bit from her grandmother—there was no way Ammamma would have helped her if she'd known about it.

'You mean, like ready-to-eat packaged food?' Courage Na'vil gasped in horror. 'But that's manufacturing… we've never done manufacturing, all the licences involved, the setup; it's madness!'

'I mean exactly that, and yes it could be a nightmare,' Serenity Ko said quickly. This was the bit she'd thought through the least, if she were being honest. She was annoyed

Courage Na'vil had caught onto it so quickly. She hastened to cover up the gaping hole in her plan. 'But it could also be revolutionary, accessible, exportable to off-worlds with food shortages…'

'But—'

'I think it's fascinating.' Optimism Sah'r cut Courage Na'vil off. 'I need a proof of concept.'

'SoundSpace for the tech is our starting point,' Serenity Ko said.

'Makes sense.' Optimism Sah'r nodded. 'We can discuss specifics after this.'

'*After* my meeting with Ko,' Courage Na'vil huffed. 'Which now has an extended agenda.'

Serenity Ko dipped her head, waiting to hear from the one person who could make or break the project. She glanced sideways at Grace Kube and found he was looking straight at her, his deep green eyes unreadable. 'It'll make everyone so angry,' he said.

She held his gaze and refused to drop it, waiting for him to crack. He cracked.

'I like it.' He grinned.

'Right?' It was time to send the message home. 'It'll upset the culinary world. It'll gain notoriety. It'll be so accessible that people will never want for food or food experiences. *Everyone* will need to try it. *Everyone* will buy our subscriptions.'

She caught Courage Praia's eye—they'd watched the proceedings in stunned silence—and beamed.

Mission accomplished, she streamed.

Wow. You… you evil genius!

'We can soft launch it at the Millennium Feast,' Grace Kube said, his eyes sparkling.

'At the what?'

'Seriously, Ko, don't you ever catch the news?' Optimism Sah'r laughed.

'There's going to be a *MegaChef* special episode,' Grace Kube explained patiently. 'Announced last night by the Chief Chef, herself. Winner gets to cater the Millennium Feast.'

'Oh, sure,' Serenity Ko said, annoyed at herself for dropping the ball.

'Relax, Ko.' Grace Kube winked. 'This is why we work in teams, after all.'

'It'll be an enormous platform,' Courage Na'vil said, wrinkling his nose. 'So many things can go wrong.'

'Or things could go very, *very* right,' Optimism Sah'r said gently.

'I'll Loop you all the contest details,' Grace Kube said. 'I'm approving the concept at a high level, but I need to see a roadmap for development. We'll check in every nava to see how it's going.'

'One step ahead of you, Kube,' Serenity Ko practically sang, regaining her buoyancy. She pulled up a roadmap. 'It all begins with a little internship to intimately understand flavour and its associations, arranged by none other than Grace Menmo herself, at this up-and-coming restaurant that's taking our world by storm…'

The perfect Primian plate is a curation of ingredients
and flavours, each chosen to represent an ideal and
evoke an emotion, always with restraint.

−(NOT) Everyone Can Cook,
Optimism Wight, the Wight School of Culinary Tradition
1845 Anno Earth | 1771 Interstellar Era

TWENTY-THREE

IN THE LAST twenty-eight hours, I'd had all my educated
guesses about Primian cuisine confirmed by Grace Menmo
in her sim-avatar. It was similar to avant-garde cooking back
on Earth, except without the use of natural raw ingredients.
Back home, avant-garde cooking had struggled to retain
popularity as celebrating natural ingredients captured
the public imagination in the post-scarcity era. With the
human population spread out across the galaxy, and One
Nation Earth *trying* to be more conscious of its gruesome
past—and of how very close humanity had come to its own
annihilation and that of the planet of our origins—food
sources had been less scarce, even if they weren't entirely
abundant. That was before Earth was One Nation in title
alone; now the Protectorates were constantly at war, and
resources were likely to dwindle again.

It struck me once again how absurd it was to live on a
planet of plenty, and wind up so frugal in the celebration of
all its riches. Maybe that was just the Earthling in me, hung
up on my old ways. Maybe I was primitive, like everyone
seemed to believe. But maybe, somehow, humanity had
finally reached a place in its long history where it could
exist in multitudes without each fragment needing to
judge the other-ness of its many facets, regardless of their

historic crimes. Well, fuck me, I was no philosopher, I was just a cook on a steep learning curve, as sim-Grace Menmo frequently reminded me.

I'd taken a ton of notes, and I had to admit the Loop made it easy to document my learnings. I'd known most of what she'd said, at least in principle, and I'd really taken care to study the specifics. In overview, all flavours here on Primus were harvested in the form of ras. Ras extracts were blended with specific types of "concentrators," depending on what flavour profiles you were seeking to highlight. These were infused into macro-rich substrates, and each gel, gelée, terrine, or sheet was an aesthetic decision that represented a core Nakshatran philosophy. Ras could also be infused directly into vat-grown meat, and there, the slicing of the meat was another aesthetic and philosophical choice. The infusions had rules: what flavours could blend and what couldn't, suitable ratios for each blend, techniques to determine their aesthetic effect on the plate, all governed by—you guessed it—some kind of symbolic meanings representing Primian culture. And then there were spice blends, marbling laws, infusion grips, extraction thresholds...

Don't even get me started on cooking techniques. Fire was a "violent transformation," so everything that needed heat to cook went into some kind of heat-generating machine— reinvented contraptions included everything from ovens to pans, all Suriyan-powered. No stovetops or fryers on this planet, because as sim-Grace Menmo said pompously, 'fire is the favoured recourse of barbarians.' I'd begun to experience a mild dislike towards her, and it had been hard to pay attention afterward, but I'd forced myself to listen. I needed to prove a point to Amol and all the chefs at Nonpareil.

Especially Good Cheer Chaangte, a voice kept whispering in my head.

It seemed like an awful lot of effort to make for straightforward, flavourful nutrition. And honestly, it smacked of propaganda. If every single food eaten here had to aspire towards reflecting their planetary philosophy, then Primians were pretty much consuming ideals by the dozen, unable to function without them.

I'd learned that the culture had spread outward, too. It was dominant on the neighbouring planet Harid. It existed on the planet Unity, in the B'naar-dominated Kepler System, which explained the number of B'naar chefs proficient in Primian cooking I'd encountered in every kitchen I'd been in here. Chomo and Sagaricus, all the way out in the Copernican System, had similar culinary traditions—with the former being a frost planet, and the latter known for its underwater habitats, a minimalist, flavour-infused cuisine made sense, and I wondered if the culture had arisen there independently. The Primians claimed they were the point of origin, however, shaping interstellar cuisine from their world.

Only the Fringe planets and moons—most located in the Solar System, and the occasional space station, which survived predominantly on nutritional supplements—seemed to have escaped Primian cuisine. The Primians had built a culinary empire, whether the initial settlers intended it or not.

You don't have to do this, Kili said, while I muttered over extractions in the kitchen, syringes tucked into the pocket of my jacket.

I do. I can. And I will. I did my best not to mutilate a fennelo-leaf vein.

I was glad I'd practised working on the fennelo-leaf last night; it was one of the main ingredients in the recipe I'd chosen for the day.

At Elé Oota, one of my signature dishes had been a shroom-keema foie gras, made from mushrooms foraged in the jungles of the Daxina Protectorate. I'd learnt the foaming technique working with avant-garde vegan cuisine during my apprenticeship at Exuberant back on Earth, and since sim-Grace Menmo had walked me through the additional steps required for the Primian version, it seemed like the easiest thing to make.

Hubris, I thought, wiping my hands on a cloth towel.

I couldn't use whole shrooms if this was to be Primian. And so, I spent a lot of time on my ras extraction, perfectly balancing the ratios of all the components using the Mela-Cortes Proportion Guide—probably the most mathematical thing I'd ever done in a kitchen. While the extractions steeped in their concentrators, I picked the perfect compound for the infusion, tasting my way through multiple textures and consistencies before settling on a soft, yet slightly chewy one called frofaux. I finished infusing the frofaux with ras, only for the self-heating pan to refuse to cooperate, offering uneven heating and taking far longer than I'd anticipated. My shroom-keema foie gras now less than perfect, I popped it into the oven to melt down, with added hydrocolloids to keep the air in—the Primian version was presented as a foam.

I washed my hands, and was about to create a solution of agar and konjac, when the flowmetal door slid open.

'I hear you have a quest,' Good Cheer Chaangte said from behind me. I ignored her.

'Hmm, let me see...' Entirely uninvited, she sidled up to my counter and began examining everything on it. 'Frofaux,' she simpered. 'Beginner's mistake.'

I continued to ignore her. She wasn't going to get to me; I trusted my palate. As insurance, I'd also done a spot of research on the Loop.

'It's a *convenient* dish to make,' she tried again. 'It's usually taught in week one of culinary school here, so you probably can't fuck it up. The marbling is very basic. And there's no knife-work involved at all.'

Luckily, I'd had enough practice with Ahana Shah at Nizami, whose breathless abuse, while I plated one perfect dish after another at the pass, would never leave my memory. *You're worthless, look at how slow you're going, your hands are shaking, are you sure you can place those micro-herbs on that shikampuri kebab without skewering it right through? If I were you I'd take those forceps and shove them in my eye, you're practically blind already, the way your proportions look on this plate. Why don't you put them down and walk away? You're the kind who'll quit, aren't you? Never had to work a day in your life, have you? You'll never make it in this industry, little fucks like you never do…*

She'd carry on nonstop, right through every service, as if willing me to burst into tears, which I often did, but only ever after I got home. So Good Cheer Chaangte could do her worst, and good luck to her. She hovered, watching me work. Out of the corner of my eye, I saw her lips twitch every now and again, as if she was thinking of something to say to throw me off my game.

Should I scare her off? Kili asked. Good Cheer Chaangte was always startled when Kili moved, burbled, or changed colours on his display, even if he was just resting on my shoulder.

Leave her be. She's grasping, I said.

'It would be a shame to fuck up such a *simple* dish. But it's probably in your genes,' Good Cheer Chaangte said archly. 'Being a fuck up, I mean.'

'Mmm. Is that the best you've got?' I said coolly. 'But you're Primian, after all, so I guess sharp wit *isn't* in your genes.'

'That's xenophobic!' she protested.

'Really?' I raised an eyebrow. 'Going to tell on me?'

She exhaled, clearly frustrated that I had her in a bind as far as telling tales went. I heard the flowmetal whoosh shut as she left.

Obnoxious, that one, Kili said.

Aren't they all?

I don't like that you're stooping to her level, though. It isn't your style.

I need her to understand that she can't get to me. And she'll only get it if I say it on *her* terms.

Oh, I think she's getting to you, all right. And it isn't nice to witness.

Kili, it's just the effect this planet's having on me! I said, defensively. _Cut me some slack._

You can't blame everyone from Primus, Kili said sagely.

I scowled at his sanctimonious tone. The nicest Primians I'd encountered were either the offspring of immigrants, like Boundless Baz, or people who'd settled here, like XX-29 or Moonage Daydream. All right, that wasn't entirely true; Courage Oslo at The New Palette, the pop-up restaurant where I'd shot to infamy (again), traced his roots to first-settler Primians, while Curiosity Zia's family had been on the planet for generations. They'd each done apprenticeships off-world, and were committed to incorporating techniques and flavours from other cultures into their food. They'd been incredibly encouraging since the incident, occasionally streaming me on the Loop to check in, and making it clear that their doors were always open in case I wanted to return. Maybe I had friends on this planet; Primians at that, too.

Point taken, I grumbled.

I knew you'd see reason.

I pulled the melted foie gras out the oven and re-emulsified it before placing it in an aerovalvulator, where the foaming would take place. I quickly prepped my garnish; sourfruit ras with beansalt spice infused in thin pop-spheres that mimicked the skins of berries, and some pickled pietrut, a sugary vegetable endemic to the planet, infused in an all-crunch sheet. The sourfruit spheres took on a deep purple hue, and the pietrut sheet turned a fresh green, a nice contrast to the more earthy colours of the foam.

I plated my dish carefully. The foie gras froth had taken on a lovely aerated appearance. I tasted a smidge, and it dissolved on my tongue like mousse, the earthy flavours rich and dense. I closed my eyes, and broke into a grin.

That good? Kili asked.

Couldn't be better.

I tested the other flavours I was about to present, then arranged them with care at the centre of the long rectangular plate I'd chosen for the meal. I ran over my mental notes on this dish, and its presentation, and then streamed Amol.

Bring it into the service kitchen, Amol streamed back. _I want all the chefs to taste it._

What the fuck?

I was outraged, and overcome with a surge of panic. I wasn't ready to have this plate, the first Primian food I'd ever cooked, tasted by an entire kitchen of professionals.

What a star-fucker, Kili said angrily, raining fireballs across my visual. _Say no._

What if it's some kind of test?

So what?

I don't want to show fear. I wiped my sweaty palms on the towel, then picked up the plate.

Kili whirred over and sat on my shoulder. _You got this._

My head spun, remembering the last time a dish I'd plated had been tasted on this sur-fucked planet. The flowmetal whooshed open, and as if in a trance, I walked the familiar hallway down to the service kitchen door. I stepped inside, and barely registered the team of chefs, all of whom were busy prepping for the night's service.

'Saraswati! That looks good,' Boundless Baz called from where he was slicing meat for the beest carpaccio.

'Excellent, you're here,' Amol said pleasantly, his expression unreadable. 'Pavi's in a meeting; she'll join us shortly.'

"I was hoping we could do it in private." Say it! Kili prompted.

I didn't say it.

'I'm presenting my first take on Primian cuisine,' I said calmly, forcing my voice to stay even.

'Put it down on the pass,' Amol said. 'Tell us what it is.'

I placed my dish on the pass and proceeded to explain its significance. The foie gras foam represented the waves of the great ocean, Sagarra. The sourfruit spheres were salty and tart, like the long journey that had led the Nakshatrans here. The pietrut sheet symbolised the unspoiled vibrance of Primus. I hated all this symbology; to me, it *reduced* food, and its meaning. But I did it anyway. If this was a test, I wasn't going to fail.

'As for the element that represents me,' I said, feeling like a pretentious suck-up trying to impress an examiner at culinary school, 'the foie gras is made from shroom-keema, and not vat-grown meat. It was one of my signature dishes at my award-winning restaurant on Earth.' Just to make sure they knew I came from a culinary background. Of course, Good Cheer Chaangte smirked at that and made a rude gesture from where she stood behind Amol.

Amol scooped up a small portion of each of the components individually and tasted them. Then, he combined them all and popped them into his mouth, as they were intended to be eaten. 'Anyone else want to try?' he asked.

Good Cheer Chaangte swaggered forwards. She grimaced dramatically after she took a mouthful. 'Completely imbalanced,' she pronounced, swallowing it with exaggerated disgust. 'Frofaux is the wrong substrate.'

She's lying, Kili said.

I know.

'Are you kidding?' Boundless Baz cried enthusiastically around a mouthful. 'This is some of the best foam foie gras I've ever tried.'

'Leave some for me,' XX-29 said through xir vox-box. Some kind of soft substance at the end of xir mechanical limb absorbed a section of food off the plate, and then xir globular being turned a cheery pink, humming and whistling in xir musical language. 'That's sublime.'

'What's sublime?' Pavi asked, entering the kitchen.

'Where's our guest?' Amol asked in turn. He smiled, looking a little strained.

'Washroom.'

'Good, you can try this before we get down to business.' Amol nodded at the plate.

'You made this?' Pavi asked coldly.

'I did.' I jutted my chin out defiantly.

She tasted. 'Foie gras mousse is a bit too creamy, too dense,' she said bluntly. 'Sourfruit checks out okay. I'd lose the pietrut altogether and replace it with some fennelo shavings.'

'I liked it.' Amol shrugged. 'Not bad for a first attempt at Primian cooking—'

'Yes, she can perform our ras extractions now,' Good Cheer Chaangte interrupted. 'Wouldn't let her near the concentrators yet, but—'

'The last time I checked, *Amol and I* were in charge, Chaangte,' Pavi snapped, glaring at her sous chef.

'Yes, Chef,' Good Cheer Chaangte mumbled, retreating against the nearest counter and seething in silence.

Interesting dynamic, Kili said.

Yes, too bad they *both* hate me, I replied.

Amol finished off the remains of the plate. 'There's definite promise here,' he said. 'How do you feel about shadowing Optimism Jordan on our garnish station?'

I beamed, cracking the first genuine smile I had in ages. 'I'd love to—' I began.

'Actually, Amol, hold that thought. There's something I need to talk to you about,' Pavi said loudly, cutting me off. She ushered her brother away, through the flowmetal doors, and into the hallway beyond.

'She hates you,' Good Cheer Chaangte said in a sing-song voice.

'You'd know,' Boundless Baz said. 'She *definitely* hates *you*.'

Good Cheer Chaangte opened her mouth to reply, then closed it again, settling for a scowl. My insides warmed up just a little at Boundless Baz having rushed to my defence. Or maybe he didn't get along with Good Cheer Chaangte; from the looks of things, none of them did.

'What're you all looking at?' Good Cheer Chaangte snapped. 'Back to work.'

XX-29 and Optimism Jordan scrambled to their stations immediately, along with a handful of the other chefs, but Boundless Baz stood his ground. 'I'll wait until the bosses tell me my break is over,' he said snidely.

A notification popped up on my visual.

Saraswati, can we see you in the office? Amol asked.

Coming, I replied, heart racing.

Sorry for the public demonstration, by the way, Amol popped up again. _Wanted you to prove your skills to the other chefs. And you did a very good job. Room for improvement, but a solid first go._

'She's going to get fired,' Good Cheer Chaangte proclaimed as I headed for the door.

'Maybe she's going to get *your* job,' Boundless Baz shot back at her.

They kept bickering as the flowmetal whooshed shut behind me. I was in the silence of the corridor behind the kitchen, Kili on my shoulder sending me holovids of fireworks on the Loop.

Thanks, Kili, I said, and meant it.

Let's go see what new bullshit is in store for us, Kili said.

I knocked twice on the office door instead of letting myself in. The door pulled apart and I stepped through it. My stomach did a succession of somersaults, not all of them unpleasant, but all of them violent.

'Saraswati,' Amol began. 'We have a slightly different project for you, very short term. Since you're learning about Primian cuisine, we thought you'd do well to guide our guest through your research while you're doing it. She'll be here for an entire nava. She really wants to grasp the fundamentals, and you've got a good handle on them already.'

I half-nodded, unable to tear my eyes away from the woman's face. She was seated in a chair across from the Khurshid siblings. Her lips curled upward in a lopsided grin; her long braid was neat and tucked back, highlighting her high forehead and rounded cheeks. Her fingers twitched nonstop, and I had no doubt she was firing off streams at the speed of thought, despite being in a meeting room with two of the best chefs on all this sur-fucked planet.

This is bad news, Kili said.

I barely heard him. She drew all my attention to her, a jumble of anticipation and dread subsuming me when she caught sight of me and her smile grew larger, apparently unthreatening but entirely unknowable, impossible to escape for better or for worse, like a supermassive black hole.

'Hello Earth girl,' Serenity Ko said. 'Fancy running into you here.'

The celebrations marking the first millennium of Primian civilisation included a breathtaking performance of the Nakshatranāma, spanning a nava. A carnival-like atmosphere swept the streets of Uru, from Collective One to the outer reaches in Collective Thirteen; people thronged the pavements, impromptu sinfonia performances broke out on street corners. An alternative form of music popped up in Heart Square, drawing huge crowds. Performers and listeners alike referred to it as many things, the most popular label being "smash."

And on the final eve of the celebratory nava, one thousand bio-degradable solar-powered lanterns were released into the sky against the backdrop of the Milky Way, a symbolic relinquishment of the murky Earth-waters of the past, a silent hope for the era of Nakshatran peace to continue...'

—Reporter, *The Primian Daily*
1075 Anno Earth | 1000 Interstellar Era

TWENTY-FOUR

'WHAT DO YOU make of the Millennium Feast?' Amol Khurshid asked, accepting a waffle cone filled with lemon-fraiseberry ice cream, topped with rougeberry sauce and covered in maccanut spheres from a server at a pop-up stall near the Nakshatran Museum. He handed it to his sister. 'It's intended to be the culmination of the Millennium Festival. Though I don't know how a single banquet can reflect two millennia of Primian culture.'

'It can't.' Pavi turned away, taking a bite of her dessert-for-breakfast.

Amol frowned. His twin was clearly very upset with him, and if he knew her well, she was about to explode. He waited for his order—smoothfruit gelato with mint-cilantrina chips, and a second cone with scoops of thenganut and mamba-zham ice cream—counting backward from twenty.

He got to five before Pavi snapped. 'You're really making a case for us. Hiring barbarians and handing internships to smooth-talking layabouts, while Ms. Primian Authenticity herself attempts to run our kitchen for us...'

'Thank you.' Amol smiled at the server as she handed him his cones. This was his favourite dessert-for-breakfast spot in all of the Heartland Park. They encountered it from time to time on their morning run—the stall was old-fashioned, bright yellow and red stripes running up its sides, appearing out of the blue with no Loop notifications, and selling out within hours. He often wondered why its owners never attempted to set up an all-out dessert bar. Either way, it was always worth cutting short his morning workout for.

He strolled away cheerily, Pavi following in his wake.

'This ice cream is so good,' he said between bites.

'Don't talk with your mouth full,' his sister snapped.

'It's only you here.'

Pavi rolled her eyes. 'Says the person who's always on about my Ur-speak accent.'

'You're angry with me.'

'Of course I am.'

'I can tell from your sharp vowel sounds; it's very Earthling.'

'Aargh!' Pavi kicked at a pebble in frustration. '*Stop picking on my accent!* You're the one turning our kitchen into a parade of freaks.' She stopped abruptly, nursing her ice cream cone. 'Let's start with that Earthling...'

'Okay, *first of all*, Saraswati—'

'—the Earthling—'

'—*Saraswati* is a talented cook who just needs to master the right techniques. *Primian* techniques.'

'She isn't all that impressive,' Pavi muttered, swirling her cone around to lick the ice cream before it could run down onto her hands. 'Certainly not as impressive as I was at her age.'

Amol snorted. 'Not this again. When are you going to let that old baggage go?'

'Right, that inconsequential incident where *none* of the kitchens on this sur-fucked planet would let me stage with them because I didn't have the *right background*.'

'They didn't let me in the door, either,' Amol said quietly.

'*And hurrah, good for you*, you've moved on. Well done you for keeping your shit together.'

'I'm not judging you. Come on, Pavi.'

'No, but you're doing everything you can to destabilise what we've struggled to build. Do you remember the thankless years we spent running pop-ups, when *nobody* would buy our food? Not because it wasn't Primian enough, but because we were *Earthlings*? Remember that shady deal where we got Honour Ora to run front of house and put her name on the restaurant sign, just so we could get customers?

'Never mind that our skill level was assessed Expert— we'd probably have made Savant but for our Earth-origins, mind you. Never mind that we topped our class at the Wight School—for fuck's sake, we went to *boarding* school on this planet, and we're as Primian as the rest of them. But no, we're always working to prove we're the ultimate not-Primians who deserve to be Primians out there. And then—' Pavi bit a chunk out of her ice cream cone. 'And then you go and pull this shit.'

Amol regarded his sister through the outburst, sweat beading on her brow and trickling down her neck, and calmly worked his way through the first of his desserts. The mint-cilantrina chips had a kick of spice; he'd been wondering if he could turn them into a ganache for a while… Maybe if he added some lemon to bring a hint of freshness, it could work.

Pavi glowered at him. 'You're not paying attention.'

'I am. Look, I'm no saint, Pavi. You know that,' Amol said. 'But Saraswati deserves better treatment than we got.' He looked around cautiously, making sure there were no passers-by in hearing range, or cam-drones hovering about. He closed the gap between them and lowered his voice. 'Plus, we owed *them* a favour.'

Pavi laughed bitterly. She was half-tempted to smash the rest of her ice cream cone into her brother's chest, but it was such good ice cream. So she desisted, and hissed at him instead. 'I told you *so many times* not to accept seed funding for our restaurant from the likes of *them*.'

'Our parents' employers, and later friends, you mean.'

'The gangsters running the Daxina Protectorate,' Pavi said pointedly.

'We had no other resources!' Amol said despairingly. 'There was no choice! Plus, you were on board by the end.'

'Don't remind me.' Pavi passed a hand over her face. 'I wonder how many deaths went into funding Nonpareil.'

'Don't be dramatic,' Amol snapped at last. This conversation was really getting in the way of his time with his ice cream. He took a bite of mamba-zham, closed his eyes at the satisfying ribbon of fresh fruit spheres bursting with ras, and opened his eyes again to find Pavi had strutted away. He rushed to follow her.

'I'm sorry, Pavi,' he said, catching up to her. 'But I really think you're over-reacting.'

'Who is she, anyway?' Pavi hissed.

Amol shrugged. 'Some royal house. Why else would the Godavari family ask us to keep her safe?'

'Her last name's Kaveri, I thought.' Pavi wrinkled her nose.

'Maybe she's a hostage,' Amol said.

'So we're aiding a *crime*?' Pavi's voice rose. 'What if the Primian authorities are watching us already? We could be suspected of espionage.'

'Relax, Pavi. You're letting your Earth-paranoias get the better of you.' Amol patted her on the back as they strode past an elaborate installation of sculptures celebrating the virtue of curiosity. They were architecturally fascinating; they seemed to almost be levitating above the ground. 'Do you think we can achieve this kind of suspension tech with our food?'

'You're thinking about the restaurant. Now. In the middle of this conversation.'

'It's always on my mind,' Amol said, nibbling at his cone.

'Ugh.'

'I can't help it.'

'I know. See, *this* is why I'm so upset!' Pavi exclaimed. She made her way to the nearest bench beside their path and flopped onto it. 'I see how hard you work, I *know* how driven you are. But celebrity chefs like Grace Aurelle are always trying to exploit our flaws. Don't tell me you haven't seen how Harmony Rhea looks at us…'

'Like she can't decide which one of us she wants to sleep with less.' Amol winked.

'Idiot!' Pavi laughed, and that lightened the uncomfortable tension that had grown between them over the last few days. Amol exhaled in relief; his sister was mad, but not *so* angry that she wouldn't talk to him for an entire year, like the time he'd pipped her to a scholarship in school. He leaned against a nearby carina tree, savouring his rapidly disappearing dessert.

'Amol,' Pavi moped. 'It's not just the *MegaChef* crowd, or the elites. Even little shits like Chaangte are lurking round every corner, always trying to undermine our authority.'

'She knows nowhere else will take her.'

'Yeah, should have thought twice before sabotaging

that rival of hers at the Wight School. What was it again? Something about knives… Not a stabbing?'

'Wouldn't put it past her, but I gather she stuck all her competitor's knives in gelatine the morning of their exam.'

'Childish. And you can see she's doing her best to bully people…'

'She's extremely talented, though,' Amol said. 'I'm hoping she'll grow a conscience.'

'This is your problem!' Pavi drew her knees up and buried her head in them, her jacket hood falling over her eyes. She glanced up. 'You think running your own business means turning it into some kind of lonely hearts club. Or a rehab for lost souls to find their way…'

'Think of how much better the universe would be if people actually *lived* the Nakshatran ideals they're always on about.'

'Fine, Saint Amol. Or would you prefer His Holiness? The Serene and Beatific?'

Amol popped the last of his ice cream into his mouth, chewing it slowly, trying to draw out its flavours for as long as possible. 'All of the above.'

'After taking pity on a disgraced Primian chef, and being blackmailed into caring for a wayward Earthling, His Holiness the Serene and Beatific Saint Amol saw it fit to open the doors of the restaurant he ran with his grounded, practical sister—*without consulting her*—and bring in some kind of hotshot wunderkind from XP Inc. What. The. fuck. Were you thinking?' Pavi bent forwards, picked up a pebble, and flicked it at him.

'Do you know who she is?'

'Who?' Pavi asked irritated. She fidgeted with the sleeves of her hoodie.

'Grace Menmo's granddaughter.'

'Get out.'

'I did some digging. She's working on some kind of culinary project at XP Inc. A food-based sim of some sort,'

Amol said. 'We treat her well and we're one step closer to getting into Grace Menmo's good books.'

Pavi rolled her eyes. 'Are you really this naive? All these years on the planet, and you think some ancient crone is going to trade favours with us?'

'She'll find it harder to disparage us, and that's something.'

'I guess,' Pavi conceded reluctantly.

'Think about it: this is *the* Grace Menmo. The very personification of modern Primian culture. The singular authority on food on this planet.' Amol's eyes lit up in delight. 'Imagine having her play for our team, or at the very least, not trying to destroy us. Our fellow judges on *MegaChef* will have a harder time being passive aggressive if they know she's an ally. Also…' Amol paused dramatically again.

'Also what?'

'She's working on a food-based sim. Why not have her do it right under our very noses? I've heard from XP Inc. about giving us a stake in whatever she winds up creating, so we get a share of the profits, if any.' Amol paused at the look of surprise on Pavi's face. 'I was going to tell you, but you didn't want to talk to me until this morning. Someone named Grace Kube called. He says they're planning to enter the *MegaChef* special episode with it—if their prototype is ready in time. And if they win…'

Pavi's eyes widened. 'We *need* her to succeed.'

'If they win, this food sim, or whatever it is, will be served at the Millennium Feast. It will have been invented in *our* kitchens. *We* get the jump on all the pedants and pretenders in this industry.

'And that's why I wanted to ask: why'd you pair her with Saraswati?'

Pavi snorted. 'I thought you'd see it right away. Since you *insist* on taking on strays, we need to keep them busy without damaging our kitchen's efficiency. The Earthling's *at least* a few māsas away from holding her own at a station during service. We need to find something for her to do so the other chefs don't get suspicious,' Pavi explained. 'This project's high risk for *her,* but this way, it doesn't upset our kitchen's morale.'

'So best case, we end up having a share in some proprietary tech, and maybe it spawns a culinary revolution, we wind up in Grace Menmo's good books, *and* we keep Saraswati busy and the Godavaris happy in the bargain. That's clever!'

'It is, isn't it?' Pavi said smugly. 'And worst case, this goes away in a few māsas, and we've lost absolutely nothing to it. Menmo's grandkid will go back to XP Inc., the Earth-people will come pick up their stray...'

Amol frowned, but decided to let his sister's rudeness slide. They were working towards a reconciliation. It seemed to be going well, and that was really the most important thing for their relationship, and for the restaurant.

'So we're on the same page?' he asked.

'For now,' Pavi said. 'But no more broken toys until we find homes for the ones we have.'

'Deal.'

'You'd better mean that.' Pavi bent to pick up another pebble to flick at him. Amol jogged away. 'Race you to the ice cream stall? Loser buys.'

Look around, Enso! We're at the heart of the universe!
   Listen to its beat...
[a bass drum booms in the background]
Thousands of years of art and culture, calling to me,
   singing to my soul!
Is this the sound of belonging?
[backup dancers appear on stage, the drum ride begins,
   accompanied by the strumming of a chordophone,
   and Alinia begins to sing...]

—from *An Immigrant on Primus: The Musical*
2034 Anno Earth | 1959 Interstellar Era

TWENTY-FIVE

SERENITY KO WAS turning out to be a nightmare to work with, and my patience was starting to wear thin. They'd set us up in the experimental kitchen at the back of the restaurant, the only piece of good news being that Good Cheer Chaangte wasn't allowed to interrupt us for "proprietary tech reasons," or some similarly worded phrase from Serenity Ko's contract. On that count, I suppose I owed her one, but that's where my appreciation for her ended.

On day one, she sat me down and outlined her project for me. I was supposed to help her understand flavour and cooking techniques, break down the textures and sensations of the dishes I was making, and describe my emotional responses while eating my way through various dishes. We were supposed to swap notes—my intentions as a creator and chef, versus her experience as a consumer of my food. She was building what she called a "flavour-emotion matrix," and I was meant to be her guide through the culinary world.

It sounded mysterious and fascinating, and if I'm being really honest, a tiny part of me wondered if I was working on something revolutionary that would impact the face of the culinary world. I was part ecstatic to be involved in the project, part terrified that I'd fuck it up because, well… Elé Oota haunted my dreams, when *Interstellar MegaChef* didn't.

And then we got down to work. Or rather, I did.

Serenity Ko would show up each morning with a bright smile, bearing two cups of kaapi, refusing to remember that my order was black, no sugar (I'm no food snob, but the kaapi with nutromilk crystals nonsense on this planet is terrible). She'd plonk down the kaapi cups, and cheerily ask me what I was going to be experimenting with.

The first day, I'd fallen for it, and launched into an explanation of basic flavour profiles and how I was going to blend them in a Borrian Balance, a fundamental Primian cooking technique…

She'd yawned less than five minutes into my speech.

'Ah yeah, saw that on a sim once. Seems deathly dull. Good luck. Tell me when we can taste and chat about it.'

And then she'd disappeared into the Loop, her fingers twitching nonstop, no doubt coordinating with someone at the XPerience Inc. office. She'd only re-emerged once I'd incorporated the technique into making a traditional Primian breakfast dish. 'Ooh, that looks good,' she'd said, before wolfing it down. I'd struggled to explain the texture-flavour experience, and how it harkened back to the wilderness of the Arcs, and she'd held up her hand. 'Say that again, more slowly so I can send Nenna the vid?' she'd asked. 'Hang on, can I set up a threeway chat one of these days? We should swap comms.'

I'd sent her my Loop details.

'Awesome, thanks.' And then her eyes lost focus, back in the Loop again.

What's she even here for? Kili had streamed.

Beats me.

Seems utterly disinterested in food.

She likes *eating* it.

You know what I mean. What a waste of your time. Can't you just quit this job and go hang out with the nice people at The New Palette?

It had been a valid question then, and it remained valid now, the better part of a nava later.

We'd just finished chatting with two people named Courage Praia and Curiosity Nenna; the former had seemed enthusiastic, but easily walked all over by Serenity Ko. The latter was naively cheerful, and something told me she'd carefully noted down everything I'd said.

Serenity Ko was still in some version of Immersive Reality. I made it a point to disconnect from the Loop while I was in the kitchen, only using my visual tech to relay essential information about ingredients, or occasionally sliding in to look something up. This was downright insulting.

'Serenity Ko,' I said firmly. 'I need your attention.'

Silence.

'Serenity Ko. Earth to Primus. Serenity Ko.'

She didn't respond. I grimaced. I slid into the Loop.

*Serenity Ko!* I streamed.

*Whoa!* What? Stop yelling!

I need your attention.

Is the restaurant on fire?

_No._

Can it wait fifteen minutes?

_No._

Ugh.

She emerged from the Loop with a scowl. 'What is it?' she asked sullenly. 'I was speaking with the chlorosapients about their nutritional substrates—ever heard of edibites? It would be useful if we could work with them. Unless you've got a better idea?'

'I don't.'

'Right. So what couldn't wait for me to hang up on my future sister-in-law who probably holds the best way forwards with this fucking prototype?'

'I need to know what you're doing here.'

'What?'

'Why're you *here*? Why am I working with you? Why are we stuck in this kitchen?' I asked.

'Are you having an existential crisis?' She tilted her head to the side, and the light caught on the curve of her cheek.

'No. I'm just wondering if there's a point to your being here.'

'Ah, that.' She stood lazily and stretched. 'I'm studying you. The way you work. The meaning of food to its creator—though honestly, I don't know why they paired me with you. It's a bit of a waste of time.'

Rude, Kili said.

Extremely.

'Don't get me wrong, you're a good cook,' she added.

I rolled my eyes.

'It's just that I need to work fast, and you're kind of detail-obsessed. I have zero interest in actually learning how to make anything. I'm just here to experience the flavours. It helps to know what spectrum of emotions goes with each dish. I won't be creating our entire library of sim experiences myself, but I'll be the one directing it, and I need to know what I'm setting the bar at,' she said.

She lost me after "flavours." She must have registered the blank expression on my face, because she laughed and relented. 'Okay, look. I'll break it down for you. When we create personalised sims—like SoundSpace, have you checked it out yet? You should. It'll help you understand what we're trying to do here. But yeah.' She bit the corner of her bottom lip, evidently thinking through her explanation. 'We create sims that are specific to your experiences. They feel *personal*. So we build these massive libraries of audiovisual experiences, yeah? So, say you eat something really sweet, our library will have, I don't know, a vid of bright pink flowers blossoming to cheery music. Shit example, but you get my drift?'

I nodded. I could see where she was going, even if her example was way off.

'So what I'm trying to do is blend these experiences from *our* libraries with people's *personal* experiences. Their memories. But not everyone is going to have a memory associated with a Paco-poplar emulsion, so what's the next best thing? That's where everything you're helping me with comes in. I know what a Paco-poplar emulsion evokes, as a spectrum of emotion, and I can get the neuropsych code to trigger it.' She looked at my face again. 'The neuropsych code runs in the bio-circuits when you subscribe to our sims,' she added.

'I can't design this stuff unless I understand it. I really don't need to know anything about the *technique,* but I'm here for the next few days to immerse myself in food spaces.' She paused. 'It's kinda disappointing that we're stuck back here, instead of out in the kitchen, you know?'

Before I could begin to explain what a supermassive impediment someone who lived halfway between the virtual and the real could be in a professional kitchen, she carried on.

'We'll head back to the office right after, but it sucks being away so early on in the project.' A frown creased the smooth skin on her forehead. 'This is a crucial point in time, when I set the vision for the whole team.'

She trailed off, then absentmindedly wandered over to the counter and picked up a syringe filled with palakki ras. She fidgeted with it, before sticking it into a trio-tart layer and jamming the plunger down. I winced. I'd never seen anyone be so indelicate with an infusion.

Seems stressed, Kili observed.

Yeah.

'So yeah, that's why I'm always on the Loop.' She shrugged, impaling another trio-tart layer. 'It's just—'

The flowmetal doors whooshed open.

Serenity Ko whirled around, and Kili sped off my shoulder towards the intruder on impulse. Good Cheer Chaangte squealed and batted him away, and I was secretly delighted by her discomfort.

'You aren't allowed in here, sorry,' Serenity Ko said politely.

'Yeah, sorry,' Good Cheer Chaangte said dismissively. 'Emergency. Earthling, the bosses want to see you in the office.' She left the room as abruptly as she'd arrived.

'Oh.' I headed towards the door. 'I'll see you in a bit.'

'I'd better come with,' Serenity Ko said imperiously.

I walked towards the office space a few doors down from the kitchen, Serenity Ko hovering uncomfortably close. She smelled like bitter kaapi, a hint of jasmine, and the slight sweetness of perspiration. None of it was unpleasant.

Don't go there, Kili warned.

I won't.

She's only being occasionally nice because she needs something.

That's judgmental.

It's a personality type. Trust me, you keep falling for them.

Do not.

*You* do not. Fall for her, I mean.

I stepped into Pavi and Amol's office.

'Oh, good, Saraswati, you're here,' Amol said. The pair looked worried. Amol perched at the edge of his desk, while Pavi paced up and down. This could only be bad news. 'Ah, and Serenity Ko as well,' he smiled. 'Welcome to the back office of a kitchen. This is a backstage pass into how things *really* work in the food industry.'

'Here to help,' Serenity Ko said self-assuredly, and meaninglessly, because really, I'd never met anyone so pointedly useless in a kitchen space.

'Optimism Beena's had an accident,' Pavi said, getting straight to the point.

My heart skipped a beat. 'Are they okay?'

'They'll be out of action for a few days,' Amol said. 'It's not devastating.'

'But Courage Meri is on vacation until tomorrow,' Pavi continued. 'So we don't have a dessert section, and all our other chefs have their hands full.'

'And we've got a dinner with the Secretary of Culture and Heritage tonight,' Amol said. 'It would be unforgivably rude to cancel.'

'We were wondering…'

'I'll do it,' I said.

'Oh, thank you!' Amol said.

'I'll help her,' Serenity Ko chimed in ominously.

'That isn't required,' Pavi said curtly, after exchanging a worried glance with her brother.

'No, no, it'll give me a chance to flex my fingers, try everything Saraswati's been teaching me…' Serenity Ko grinned.

'Okay, so we'll pick the simplest stuff on our dessert menu and walk you through it,' Pavi explained. 'Chaangte will be in charge in our absence.' She looked me up and down. 'Don't fuck this up.'

I MOANED, AND pressed myself into the comfortable shag armchair, slouching as low as I could go. I sipped on a jumpgate kick: all the alcohols you can imagine in the same drink, at one go, and way less disgusting than it sounds. The low, soothing tones of conversation surrounded me; the slow, sensual glissando of a mellosax played over a speaker system.

'I'm sorry that happened to you,' Curiosity Zia said. 'Panic attacks are awful.'

'Thanks,' I mumbled. I opened my eyes and saw six faces staring expectantly at me from around our table at The Wallflower. Courage Oslo's messy brown curls spilled across his shoulders, held in place by an elaborate set of pins. Curiosity Zia's neon face tats shimmered in the dimly-lit pub.

'It was completely engineered,' Boundless Baz said. 'Good Cheer Chaangte was unbelievably rude. I'm going to report her to Pavi and Amol.'

'So am I,' XX-29 added. 'She's been bullying me since I got here, but her hostility towards you was through the roof.'

'It was utter sur-fucking bullshit.' Boundless Baz scowled. 'She's had it in for you since your first day in the kitchen, by the way.' He then waved his arm out in a sweeping gesture. 'And then there was the other one.'

I sometimes believe that when someone expressly warns you not to be a screw-up, they harbour the secret desire that you will—well and truly, spectacularly, *colossally*—fuck something up. They send their secret hopes out into the universe, and it delivers.

'*Don't fuck this up,*' Pavi had said. And things had gone as well as possible under the hostile supervision of Good Cheer Chaangte. Until they hadn't.

Serenity Ko was an agent of destruction. If I hadn't seen it before, there was no unseeing it now.

Sometimes fuck ups happen because someone who's in the room really shouldn't be there.

'The other one,' XX-29 murmured, xir being pulsing with shades of red and orange.

'What other one?' Courage Oslo looked between the two of them and me in utter confusion.

'Saraswati's been paired with some designer at XP Inc. to

build a food-based sim,' Boundless Baz began. 'Her name's Serenity Ko. She seems nice enough, but she isn't much use in the kitchen…'

At that mild pronouncement, a spike of rage shot through me. I took a big swig of my jumpgate kick. 'That's putting it mildly,' I said. 'Trust me, you have no *idea* how frustrating she's been to work with.'

Boundless Baz's face fell, and he dipped his head, clearly hurt.

'I'm sorry,' I rushed to say. 'It's just… I've had the most painful nava.'

'Why don't you tell us about it?' Courage Oslo said, elbowing Boundless Baz in the ribs. They exchanged a look, and Boundless Baz seemed to cheer up immediately. 'Yeah, tell us,' he egged me on.

I pretended to not notice when they both unsubtly clinked their bira bottles together. They'd only just met and they seemed to be getting on like a house on fire. I filled them in on the XP Inc. project, saying as much as I could say without violating the contract they'd made me sign, swearing me to secrecy as an independent consultant.

'I'm sure Serenity Ko is an extremely competent designer,' I said honestly, 'but she has no place in the kitchen. None at all. And that would be *fine*, would have been *perfectly acceptable* if she hadn't decided to *help me* right through tonight's fucking service.'

I felt the anger building again as I explained how Pavi and Amol had redone their dessert offerings to accommodate my limited experience in the Primian kitchen. 'Simple food for simple people,' Good Cheer Chaangte had said, enunciating her words insultingly slowly. 'Try not to mess this up? Earthlings often struggle to understand refinement.' And Serenity Ko had stifled a giggle. She thought I hadn't noticed, but I had.

Curiosity Zia wrinkled her nose. 'Ugh, she sounds awful.'

Kili radiated a comforting warmth through the sleeve of my tunic, burbling softly on my shoulder.

'I don't know if she's a horrible person,' I said. 'Or just so self-assured, so sure she can do anything she wants to, that she can't see her own limitations.'

Good Cheer Chaangte had taken every opportunity to bully me from the start of the night's service, but I'd worked with enough abusive chefs before. The trick lay in delivering immaculate food. I was well on my way to doing so, until Serenity Ko had made that time-tested strategy impossible.

'This... this dessert they asked me to do,' I said. 'They call it the Hope Brook. It's carefully assembled out of multiple kinds of berry ras, and it's plated to represent the glacier that gives rise to the Unity River. It's got a molten blueberry centre, encased in a carefully marbled mousse—six different concentrations of nilaberry infusion, held within a xocolat sphere, plated on chocolate popping candy rocks. You're supposed to break into it and the blueberry and nilaberry spill out like the waters of a stream...' I took a deep breath, drained my jumpgate kick, and ordered another one on the Loop menu.

'Yeah it's got to be assembled carefully,' Boundless Baz said, giving me a moment to recover, and I shot him a grateful look. 'You do all the different layers individually, and place them all in moulds, freeze them separately and then assemble them. In case anyone hasn't seen it made before.'

'Serenity Ko decided that the marbled mousse wasn't looking "blue enough" to be believable,' I said. 'She kept hovering around arguing that it didn't look like the pics on the restaurant's recipe scrolls. But that's *chemistry*.'

I explained how the cold in the freezer was supposed to react with the infusions and render them in different shades of blue. *Accurate* shades of blue for a seven-nila marbling.

301

'The whole time, Serenity Ko was either at Saraswati's side bickering with her, or following the rest of us around making vids,' Boundless Baz grumbled.

'Yeah, and I have no idea why,' I said. 'She told me she had no interest in learning how to *make* anything.'

'What's she even at Nonpareil for?' Moonage Daydream asked, and that was the most uncharitable thing I'd ever heard them say.

'No fucking idea.' I slumped forwards on the table, recoiled from the sticky remains of alcohol past, but stayed there nonetheless. 'So once my moulds were in the freezer, I moved on to tempering my xocolat to make the domes, yeah? Serenity Ko disappeared for a bit. I thought she was bored, or annoying someone else, and fuck me, I was glad for the breathing room.' I grimaced. 'But no.'

'Oh, no,' Courage Oslo said.

'I didn't realise what she'd done until after they set, when I started plating. She triumphantly told me she'd helped, that she'd quadrupled the proportions of all the nilaberry infusions.'

'Fuck,' Curiosity Zia said.

'Fuck,' Courage Oslo echoed.

'Yeah.'

I saw a look of confusion cross Starlight Fantastic's eyes, their tentacles an uncertain pink-grey.

'She hyper-concentrated my infusions,' I explained, and my voice shook. '0.55 µg of nilaberry sets in pale turquoise, 0.61 µg of blueberry transforms into a beautiful aqua. She pulled my moulds out—behind my back, added something like *four times the required proportions* for the infusions, and then quietly put them back in the freezer. Glorious turquoise and aqua before, deep purple and inky black after. The molten blueberry centre turned the colour of charcoal.' I shuddered, then pressed on. 'Chaangte couldn't have been more delighted. She made me assemble *all* the desserts, told me we'd go ahead and serve them. But then, she gathered everyone around the pass. Sliced into one mousse mould after another and let the little molten rivers run out black.'

'She was horrible,' XX-29 said. 'The language she used.'

'"Is this the best you can do, Earthling? This is what your home world looks like, isn't it? Disgusting sludge, like the whole lot of you,"' I quoted her in a low, raspy voice.

Expressions of horror crossed every single face at the table. 'That's unacceptable!' Starlight Fantastic cried.

'Chaangte called me a savage, yelled at me in front of everyone, threw a couple of my mousse spheres at me, before dumping the rest into the trash, and kicked me out of the kitchen,' I mumbled. 'I went and hid in the vat-meat freezer, heart racing, hands clammy, didn't know what to do.'

'What did Serenity Ko do?' Curiosity Zia asked.

'No idea,' I said. 'I was too busy dying.' My hands shook in my lap, and I clenched my fists.

As it turned out, Kili had sent an SOS to Starlight Fantastic as my panic attack set in, while I huddled in the vat-meat freezer refusing to leave. Luckily, Starlight Fantastic had been planet-side. XX-29 and Boundless Baz had coaxed me out after cleaning their stations, and they'd hopped into their craft with us. I wasn't sure who'd summoned Curiosity Zia and Courage Oslo, but it was good to be with them.

'I'll bet she's fully aware of what she's doing,' Courage Oslo said grimly.

'You don't mean sabotage?' Starlight Fantastic's tentacles quivered where they rested on the table, turning a shade of green for deep disgust.

'I absolutely do mean sabotage.'

'There's no way it was intentional,' Curiosity Zia dismissed him. 'She and Saraswati are supposed to be working on the same team.'

'Never stopped a chef before,' Courage Oslo intoned darkly.

'No, that's true,' I conceded. 'But I don't think it was intentionally hurtful.'

Or so you hope, Kili streamed indignantly.

'I really think she was doing her best to help,' I said slowly, but then the memory of my beautifully crafted mousse—now splattered across my chef's jacket, and oozing into a dustbin—bubbled up, and I squeezed my eyes shut, willing myself not to cry.

'I am so sorry,' Curiosity Zia said. 'Can I give you a hug?'

'Yeah,' I said quietly.

She hopped off her chair and came round to me, and wrapped me up in a tight squeeze.

'I'm sorry, can we all give you a hug?' Courage Oslo asked.

'Yeah.'

I was enveloped. XX-29 couldn't get xir mechanical body to fold over and squeeze in, so xe extended an arm, and warmth flowed its way into me from the end of xir fingertips.

'I can't believe they'd treat you this way,' Starlight Fantastic said.

I burst into tears.

Primus has two dominant and distinct religious orders—the Faith of the Light and the Vyāsr Monkhood.

Believers in the Faith of the Light hold that it is humanity's purpose to strive towards complete self-reliance and self-sustenance, to be one with the greater universe. Material comfort is excess.

The Vyāsr Monkhood, on the other hand, believe that every being is a reincarnation of a dead star, living one final life before reunion with the coldness of the void. They hold that this life must be celebrated to the fullest.

—Courage Medi,
A Beginner's Guide to Primus, Seventh Edition
2068 Anno Earth | 1993 Interstellar Era

TWENTY-SIX

OPTIMISM RIHAN WAS on the verge of losing his appetite. It was partly due to his sister's attempts to create something in the kitchen—a sodden mess of greenish-blue spheres and layers sat on his plate in front of him. It was mostly because he was aghast at the story she was telling.

'You should have seen the look on her face!' Serenity Ko laughed loudly.

He glanced across the table at his fiancée. Good Cheer Eria's expression was grim.

'Seriously, she couldn't believe it. Those silly mousse spheres looked like tar,' Serenity Ko giggled. 'Priceless.'

Good Cheer Eria's herbal edibite terrine sat on her plate untouched. She sipped a glass of water in silence.

Serenity Ko seemed to realise that neither of her dinner guests was joining in her laughter. She looked at the utter lack of amusement on their faces and scowled. The sense of unease that had been crawling around in the pit of her stomach ever since Saraswati Kaveri had rushed out of the kitchen at Nonpareil grew. 'What's wrong?' she asked

'Ko. Has the thought struck you that you might have ruined someone's career?' her brother replied.

The discomfort grew, threatening to take the shape of a stomach ache, though that could have also been the food. Serenity Ko fought the feeling. 'No. Look, she's a good cook. *Really* good. And it was all in jest.' Serenity Ko grabbed a handful of her batata-cilantrina bake and crammed it in her mouth. She tried not to gag; she'd definitely done something wrong with that recipe.

Optimism Rihan regarded her in silence.

'In jest. Really?' Good Cheer Eria raised an eyebrow.

'Yeah, it's the done thing in professional kitchens, apparently,' Serenity Ko said. 'Good Cheer Chaangte told me so. It's a Nonpareil tradition to prank all their chefs at their first service.'

Serenity Ko caught her brother and his fiancée exchanging a look. 'You're behaving like I killed someone.'

'Ko,' Optimism Rihan said. 'This—Good Cheer Chaangte, her name is? Do you know her at all?'

'No.'

'Ever had a conversation with her? Is she the sort of nice person who'd play practical jokes in the spirit of fun?'

'No idea.'

'So you took her word for it, and decided to prank your *teammate*, who's helping you develop your food sim, because…'

'Because it was no big deal!' Ko wiped her hands on her napkin. 'Chaangte told me so.'

'And did you check with any of the other chefs? Were they in on it?' Good Cheer Eria asked pointedly.

'I… Er, no, why would I? I just assumed…'

'You "assumed" everyone would be okay with you being

cruel to someone who's a guest on our planet?' Optimism Rihan leaned forwards. 'Will you listen to yourself?'

'It's far less annoying than listening to *you*,' Serenity Ko snapped. She was hot around the ears, like when she'd been three years old and Ammamma had ticked her off for eating the popping candy base when her back was turned on her Nakshatran Gelato.

'You've got to see that this wasn't right.'

'How did this Chaangte react, if this was all a joke?' Good Cheer Eria interjected.

Serenity Ko glowered at the table, unwilling to make eye contact. The creeping unease pounced, and she broke out in a sweat. If this had been a prank, why had Good Cheer Chaangte flown off the handle so badly?

'Well?' Optimism Rihan pressed.

'She was awful to Saraswati,' Serenity Ko mumbled. She suspected she'd been used, and had screwed her teammate over in the bargain, and she didn't like the pairing in the least.

Good Cheer Eria sat up straighter. Her green makeup shimmered in the low light of Serenity Ko's space, and she steepled her hands, resting her chin on them. 'Ko, I'm a chlorosapient. We're treated like outsiders all the time,' she began.

Serenity Ko stifled a groan. 'Isn't it enough that my inner voice is telling me that I'm probably in the wrong?'

'There are times when the folks in Uru whisper loudly as I pass them by,' Good Cheer Eria carried on, ignoring her. 'In my second year at uni, when I discovered the Faith, I was made fun of to my face. People went out of their way to avoid me. I was all the things that made them uncomfortable, and I was made to feel as if I was the one who needed to apologise for it.'

'Eria, I'm sorry you had to go through that. I'll apologise to her and we can forget this ever happened. Can we just move on?' Serenity Ko asked politely.

'We cannot,' Good Cheer Eria said firmly. 'What you've done is a small thing for you, but I'm sure this Earth woman's had a raw deal from *everyone*, and you need to realise how you've impacted her life. And this isn't about me; I'm trying to show you how it feels to be treated the way she has.'

Serenity Ko's mouth set in a mutinous line. Optimism Rihan shot her a warning glare, so she swallowed her arguments and listened.

'In university, I believed not just in the Nakshatran principles, but in their natural evolution. Complete self-sustenance. The first time I got my chloro-mods, I was on top of the world.' She rolled her sleeves up and revealed the photovoltaic panels flashing silver and blue on her shoulders, like a tattoo in glossy ink. 'But I was bullied for them, made to feel ashamed of them. The Faith of the Light tells us that we will need to survive many trials on our path to complete independence from consumption.

'Do you know what it feels like to hear constant sniggering behind your back? To be followed by constant whispering, labelling you a "mutant" or a "species"? No, you don't, and I'm glad. I tell you, I lost faith—not because I was physically attacked, or openly discriminated against by people in power. But because of the *little* acts of cruelty: the snide comments, the subtle bullying.

'It saddens me that you've just done that to someone else who's being treated like an outsider,' Good Cheer Eria said softly. 'And while I believe that you're truly sorry about it, I feel like I don't know who you are any more.'

Shame—tinged with annoyance—bubbled up in Serenity Ko's gut, and she squashed it. 'I just pulled a harmless joke on someone!'

'Without thinking twice,' her brother said drily. 'Without asking if you were participating in some kind of micro-aggression. Without weighing the consequences for the target of this attack, and with zero empathy for that poor woman—and a refugee, too.'

Guilt flooded Serenity Ko's insides, and her walls went up even further. 'I *said* I'm sorry,' she spluttered. 'Let it drop? You're both taking this way too seriously!'

'You're taking it far too lightly,' Good Cheer Eria said sadly. 'I don't think I have anything to say to you right now. I'm saddened to see you turn into a bully.'

Serenity Ko flinched. She'd worked so hard to be friends with Good Cheer Eria, to build a relationship with her even though they had nothing in common, because her brother loved her.

'Excuse me,' Good Cheer Eria said, rising from the table. 'I need to use the washroom.'

Optimism Rihan's eyes followed her with concern as she left the living room. Serenity Ko watched him watch her, a mix of envy for their relationship and frustration that her brother was such a sap welling up inside her. Optimism Rihan caught her staring and exhaled slowly.

'What is it?' Serenity Ko asked dully.

'Well, you've really upset her, so congratulations. She was looking forward to seeing you, especially after you streamed her and said you'd cooked,' Optimism Rihan said, ticking her list of offences off on his fingers. 'And you know what? You've really upset me, too.'

'I didn't know you were so uptight,' Serenity Ko said harshly. 'I said I was wrong, and I'll apologise to her tomorrow. And to Eria, too, once she's back.'

'Listen. I'm only going to say this the one time, and I want you to hear it. I say this with love, and with concern for you.'

Serenity Ko rolled her eyes.

'Fine, be that way. We'll just leave, then.' Her brother made to rise from the table.

'No, Rihan! I'm sorry, I'm listening.'

'Switch off your Loop notifs first,' Optimism Rihan said. 'I can see your pupils flicking to them nonstop.'

'Ugh, fine.'

'Ko. I don't know what you're going through, but it's looking terrible on you,' her brother said flatly. 'You're kind of not a nice person any more. It isn't just about ignoring the family nonstop to chase success at XP Inc. It's gone beyond that. You take pride in your job, yes. You're fucking good at it. But you're hurting yourself, don't you see? We haven't said anything yet, but we're all very worried about you.'

Serenity Ko started to interrupt him, but he held up a hand.

'I'm not done, yet.'

'Go on,' she sighed.

'You were taking MellO shots while recovering from serious dehydration. You've been stringing that nice, considerate Honour Aki along for fuck knows how long—'

'He's been stringing himself along,' Serenity Ko interjected.

'Fair enough, but you keep hooking up with these random weirdos who never, ever, *not once* fulfil any part of your life other than a halfway good shag.'

'I'm happy alone,' Serenity Ko said.

'I'm not saying you need to find a romantic partner. I'm just saying... I don't know, make some nice friends, for fuck's sake? A handful of people who'll have your back, no matter what? Use the support system you have in the family. Be nicer to Courage Praia, who—bless their soul— is always by your side but so scared of you they're almost never honest with you. Find connections—Nine Virtues, the galaxy is limitless!—so you can reconnect with what makes you a good person. I *know* you're a good person.'

'Do you know how many times you use the word *nice* in a conversation, Rihan?' Serenity Ko asked icily.

Courage Rihan carried on without pausing for a breath. 'This kind of bullying is beneath you. It's not how our parents raised us. It's not the nice person I know is my sister. It's someone you're trying desperately hard to be, and it's awful. It isn't human. At least, it isn't Primian-human. And it isn't you.'

Serenity Ko rose, her eyes flashing with anger. 'You want to tell me what I'll get treats for and what I'll be sent to the corner for? Fuck you, Rihan! Stop taking your nice guy energy so seriously.'

'Sometimes, there's no reasoning with you.'

'Is that the worst you've got, Mr Nice Guy?' Serenity Ko stuck her hands in her pockets, slouching over, her brown eyes blazing defiantly.

'You want the worst? Here it is. I think you're desperate to prove yourself. Our family is a bunch of overachievers: Ammamma, the parents. Then there's me, I'm just a regular guy, but everyone's always said I'm—wait for it—*nice*.'

Serenity Ko snorted.

'Yes, I'm *nice*. Nice, nice, *nice!* And that's a reputation that's stuck. I've got no talents, but I've got a good heart. You think that gives me a free pass, and maybe it does because at least I can live with myself and my actions.'

'Must be *nice*,' Serenity Ko goaded.

'You, on the other hand…' Optimism Rihan continued, undaunted. 'You think you need to live up to everyone's expectations—outperform every benchmark that's ever been set—because for some reason, just being *nice* isn't enough for you.'

'Works at the bar, every single time,' Serenity Ko snickered.

'Not the point,' Optimism Rihan said, his voice now rising. Serenity Ko was satisfied that she seemed to be getting to him, at last.

'Why are you so obsessed with proving yourself, Ko?' Optimism Rihan asked. 'Everyone's loved you for who you are since the day you were born. You weren't always like this. You were…'

'Nice?' Serenity Ko suggested.

Optimism Rihan exhaled in frustration. 'You went off to university and graduated top of your class, and then got straight into XP Inc. after your assessment. Skipped your Wanderers' service and everything. It *changed* you. For the worse.'

'So, not nice, then?' Serenity Ko asked innocently.

'Ko, could you please take this seriously?'

'Fine, Rihan,' Serenity Ko snapped. 'You want to hear what that was like for me? You want to listen to all the things that made your little sister the un-nicest person on this sur-fucked planet?'

'I want to tell you—'

'No, stop. My turn. I've heard you out, and I've been lectured by Eria, and now it's time for me to say my piece. Do you know how much pressure that was, going straight to XP Inc. after uni?' Serenity Ko seethed. 'Youngest in the company, "Oh, here comes the Techno-Aesthete Savant; my, we haven't had one of these in decades! Wonder what genius she's going to bring to the table—oh, wait, there's no genius there, after all." I had to reinvent myself, prove why I owned that tag. It's fucking *hard* to be a prodigy.'

'It is, and I'm sorry you had to go through that,' Optimism Rihan said. 'But you've lost yourself entirely, and you're blaming the past for it. It's been eight years, Ko. Eight *years* since you were that prodigy kid. There's no excuse for being a terrible person, not anymore.'

'Are you kidding me? The pressure's just *grown*; each time I deliver, the expectations get worse…'

'I'm not saying it isn't hard!' Optimism Rihan snapped. 'But you've done *absolutely nothing* to address it! You can talk to any of us—you choose not to. You have a therapist—and Dad told me you haven't seen *her* for māsas now. You could confide in Praia, and… I don't know who else your friends even are!'

'Answer's easy: nobody,' Serenity Ko mumbled. She was suddenly very tired, and running out of steam.

'You keep pushing people away,' Optimism Rihan said softly. 'Take me; you don't reply to my comms. Eria's invited you to go spend time at the Faith of the Light's garden a billion times, and I know you're busy, but really, a new environment—a slow one—will do you so much good. That kid, Ano: you went to school with him, he even works in the same org, and you *never* hang out. You guys were thick as thieves in school.

'But instead of any of these people who care about you, you chase acceptance from random strangers, the more the better. You bought an entire Arcside bar drinks so they'd celebrate you—Yeah, I found out about that; it was all over the Wanderers' Paths by the Faith of the Light gardens. You followed this Good Cheer Chaangte's lead because you thought she'd accept you, and she seems like she has some kind of power in that kitchen. That Earthling? She sounds so nice, and you went and pulled this meaningless fucking prank on her. You could be *friends!* Why won't you see this?'

'So the takeaway is be more nice?' Serenity Ko laughed weakly.

A long silence stretched out between them. Tears prickled at her eyes, hot and wet, and she fought them back. She'd never felt so stripped bare before. It was as if her insides had been ripped out of her and were laid out on display, and it was all hideous. She was ugly and deformed, a broken thing patched together from bits and pieces of stuff she ought to be but could never live up to. And she hated that her brother could see right through her, had *seen* through her all this while.

'Ko, are you okay?' Courage Rihan said gently.

'Yeah.' Her voice felt very far away.

'I'm—I'm sorry. I think I went too far...'

'Yeah. You did.'

'I'm really so sorry.' Courage Rihan pushed his chair back and rushed to her side, attempting to pull her into a hug.

'Back off, Rihan.' Serenity Ko held her arms stiff at her sides and leaned away. 'Back off, and leave.'

'I'm sorry.'

'Get the fuck out,' Serenity Ko said softly. 'I don't want you here.'

Good Cheer Eria returned right at that moment, and frowned at the pair, standing awkwardly off to the side of the dinner table. 'Why do I feel like I missed something?' she asked.

'Ask your future husband,' Serenity Ko choked out. 'Everyone's favourite *nice* guy.'

'Rihan?' Good Cheer Eria tilted her head to the side.

'I don't want to relive this,' Serenity Ko said tonelessly. 'Please leave.'

'Ko, I'm really sorry, whatever it is I'm sure he didn't mean it—' Good Cheer Eria began.

'No, he most definitely did,' Serenity Ko said. 'I know because it's all true. Please leave.'

'Let's go,' Courage Rihan said, stepping out of the living room and heading to the door.

'We should do this again soon!' Serenity Ko called after him with brittle brightness. 'It's been so... *nice*.'

'We can't leave her like this,' she heard Good Cheer Eria murmur.

'We can, and we will,' Optimism Rihan said grouchily, handing his fiancée her jacket.

'You can leave, I'll be fine,' Serenity Ko announced. 'Have a *nice* evening!'

Optimism Rihan stomped out, evidently very frustrated, and Serenity Ko felt a rush of petty joy at having irritated her brother so successfully. And then she deflated, curling up on the couch, staring at the wall in silence as the seconds ticked by. They seemed interminable, and her brain was drawing a blank. Her brother had pushed *all* her buttons, listed *all* her insecurities. He'd forced her to reckon with thoughts she hadn't had in years, the kind that were always niggling at the back of her mind, the sort she never gave voice to. *How could I? And risk failing, and lose everything I've worked so hard for. What will I be worth then?*

She was too sober for this train of thought, but somehow, she didn't want to get up off the soft cushions and make herself a drink. The bar was right around the corner from her, her fridge was stocked with biras, but there was no point. There was drinking because you were low, and then there was being so low that not even a drink could help, and she was very much the latter.

What am I worth?

The thought popped up unexpectedly, and suddenly, the tears she'd held back all along began to stream down her face. She knew she was missing the point, somewhere. She was pretty sure she was still loved, even if Rihan and Eria were upset with her.

Are you sure *you're sure?*

Another ugly thought crawling into her brain. She didn't deserve love, she didn't deserve acceptance or forgiveness. Fucking Suriya, how did her family—or anyone, really—even put up with her?

Because I'm good at what I do, a voice inside her said. *I prove to them that I'm worthy, all the time.*

But you're an asshole, another voice replied. *You're not worthy of anything.*

She curled up into a ball and bawled.

This was unfair. All she'd done was pull a stupid prank. Why was it *her* fault when it hadn't even been *her* idea in the first place?

She should never have told that story; she knew her brother, the self-righteous, holier-than-thou, *nice*-as-all-the-Nine-Virtues-combined little fuck that he was, always setting impossible standards for her to live up to. Never threw tantrums as a kid. Never demanded more dessert. Never complained when the good roles in school-dramas went to some other kid. Never did anything not-nice, not once, not ever.

And what did they say about her? She couldn't remember. She slid into the Loop and scrolled through her comms with her parents. It struck her that half the time she'd left them unanswered.

Her stomach lurched.

Don't work too hard, kiddo. We love you as you are, you've got nothing to prove. That was Amma.

If you ever want to talk, just head home. I'll make the hot xocolat, said Appa.

Are you stressed out again? Remember, there's nothing worth working yourself up over. Winning is only temporary, it's the journey that counts. That was from Dad.

They were so kind. So fucking *nice*. Despite the fuck-up Rihan had said she was, that she *knew* she'd been turning out to be but had no idea how to stop, they were supportive and filled with goodness. She had to *do* something about herself. Things couldn't carry on this way.

After I'm done with Feast Inc., she thought, expecting her resolution to lighten the weight on her shoulders. It didn't. No, there was something more immediate. Something she could do right now.

The image of Saraswati being cornered by Good Cheer Chaangte popped into her brain; Saraswati's face expressionless as the sous chef splattered her jacket with the disastrous mousse. Serenity Ko had been frozen in place, held firmly by an invisible force when Saraswati rushed out of the kitchen and disappeared. She'd slunk away without saying a word to anyone, without bothering to check on Saraswati...

She dragged herself off the couch. She went into the washroom and splashed cold water across her face, then reapplied her lipstick. She went back outside and laced up her boots.

It wouldn't fix everything about her, but it would be a start. It was the middle of the night, but she owed her an apology. Serenity Ko set off to find Saraswati Kaveri.

Only to realise she had no idea where she lived.

The Daxina Protectorate appears to incorporate some form of democratic process into its governance; however, anecdotal evidence varies drastically depending on one's sources within the subcontinent. The Godavari family appears to hold dynastic power in the region, and seems to harbour an expansionist policy towards neighbouring areas, a philosophy shared by its close allies, the powerful Tunga clan…

—Anita Umar,
One Nation Earth: The Myth of Unity
2053 Anno Earth | 1978 Interstellar Era

TWENTY-SEVEN

I AWOKE TO sur-light streaming upon my face, rolled over, and groaned. My head was foggy, my limbs ached, and my sinuses were stuffy. There was the unmistakable sound of something sizzling, the smell of fat and grease wafting my way. I sat bolt upright. Those were Earth scents and sounds.

'Zee, our guest's awake!' Courage Oslo's voice came from behind me.

I blinked stupidly and surveyed my surroundings. Geometric decals covered the wall to my right. Across from me was a large circular window. I was tucked up on a plush sofa, my legs tangled in a duvet covered in swirling embroidery. A low, intricately-carved coffee table to my left was littered with paraphernalia—a pair of spectacles, a stack of papyro-scroll comics, and two succulents in shades of hot pink. I swung my legs over the side of the sofa, and immediately felt dizzy. My bare feet landed on a fuzzy carpet, and I scrunched up my toes. Across from me were a pair of curved armchairs with deep seats, a floral-patterned

318

throw carelessly draped over the back of one.

My mouth was dry and sour.

Welcome back! You've had quite a night, Kili said.

Oh no. Where are you?

Kitchen with Oslo. You owe these folks.

'Are you feeling okay?' Curiosity Zia stepped out of a room off to one side. 'You had quite a night.'

'So I figured,' my voice came out raspy.

'Washroom,' she said, jabbing a thumb over her shoulder the way she came. 'And then we'll feed you. We've got a surprise for you.'

I staggered over to the bathroom and splashed cold water on my face. I tried to freshen up my breath as best I could, but it tasted like one jumpgate kick too many. I found a dental cleanse kit and popped it into my mouth, letting the nanotech do its thing while wondering how I'd wound up in their space.

A twinge of panic kicked its way up my spine. I hadn't slept with either or both of them, had I? They were turning out to be really good friends, and I didn't want casual sex to ruin that, or destroy what seemed like a happy long-term relationship. I rushed out the bathroom, ignoring the pounding in my head, and followed my nose to the kitchen. Kili whizzed off the fridge—which was covered in magnets and print photographs—and landed on my shoulder.

'Good to see you alive.' Courage Oslo grinned at me from where he crouched on the ground. I glanced over his shoulder and an unnameable warmth spread through me, from the inside out. On some kind of makeshift burner, over what was very much an open flame, sat a frying pan. Sizzling in it were eggs and vat-grown bacon.

'Earth-style breakfast,' Courage Oslo said. 'We figure you deserve it.'

I was tongue-tied, entirely speechless at this act of kindness.

'Oslo, hang on. She probably has a hangover,' Curiosity Zia said from where she stood fussing over a Primian kaapi pot. She slid something across the kitchen counter to me. 'Cleanse compound. Instant hangover cure.'

I popped a bright pink pill into my mouth.

'Chew,' she ordered.

It was really sticky, but I felt it release its chemicals and nanotech, and the throbbing in my head receded. 'Fuck, that's magic. Thank you.'

'Figured you'd need it after last night.'

'What happened last night?' I asked, not really wanting the answer, heat rushing to my cheeks.

Courage Oslo laughed, and Curiosity Zia joined him. 'Sit. We'll tell you over breakfast.'

I took my place at their small, round dinner table, and Courage Oslo brought over a plate. 'I don't know if I've done this right; it's been a while.'

My mouth watered at the sight of the basic Earth breakfast I hadn't had in so long. 'Where'd you learn to make this? Why do you cook with fire? How haven't you been evicted yet?' The questions spilled out of me.

'We once vacationed on Luna for a month,' Curiosity Zia said, drawing up a chair. 'We've been cooking with fire for ages—we had to hunt through the smugglers' den on Allegro to find this burner, stripped it down to get it past the authorities as spare parts, and reassembled it here. It's illegal as fuck on Primus.'

'And we haven't been evicted because we disable our fire alarms, thanks to more smuggled tech,' Courage Oslo added, joining us with a plate of his own.

I dug in, cramming eggs and bacon into my mouth all at one go. The eggs were slightly runny, and the bacon wasn't as salty as the kind I was used to. Courage Oslo watched me nervously, and I tossed him a thumbs up and smiled wide around my food, still chewing. I didn't want to hurt his feelings, and it really was delicious, in a home-cooked sort of way.

'So. There were… *many* jumpgate kicks,' Courage Oslo began.

'Then shots,' Curiosity Zia said.

I had the haziest memory of a bright purple shot glass.

I've got footage, Kili said helpfully.

No, thanks.

'Then Starlight Fantastic pulled some killer dance moves, and you joined them.' Courage Oslo clumsily sliced into his eggs with a knife and fork. I was touched by the gesture— Primians only ever ate with their hands.

'You're not too bad,' Curiosity Zia said.

She's lying, added Kili helpfully. _I've got footage._

Nope.

A vague image of a neon-chequered dance floor popped into my mind; Starlight Fantastic's tentacles artfully creating beautiful shapes in a strobe light, my arms flailing at my sides.

'And then you disappeared, and I found you hugging the toilet.' Curiosity Zia smirked.

'We decided to bring you here before you did any more damage,' Courage Oslo said. 'And you passed out the minute we put you in our flowcab. Had to carry you in.'

'Oh, no, I'm so sorry,' I groaned. I was, however, secretly glad that I hadn't tried to come onto them, or make out with them.

Yeah, that didn't happen, Kili reassured me.

Courage Oslo and Curiosity Zia exchanged a look. Curiosity Zia then cleared her throat.

'You know, Saraswati…' she began.

'Call me Saras,' I said. 'All my friends do.'

'Saras, you seemed really upset last night,' she continued. 'And we've had this conversation before, but I'm not sure you know just how much we mean it when we say we'd love for you to come back and work with us.'

'We can't pay you much, but we'll never mistreat you like those monsters you were telling us about,' Courage Oslo added.

A surge of warmth rushed through me. 'I—I don't know what to say. That's so kind...'

'And it isn't pity,' Curiosity Zia said firmly. 'You're extremely talented, and you deserve a place where you can shine, not somewhere that will beat you down.'

'And then...' Courage Oslo and Curiosity Zia exchanged another look before he continued. 'There's the other thing.'

'What other thing?' I asked.

'We're not sure if you've given this food sim project enough thought,' Curiosity Zia said in a rush, her cheeks turning red where they weren't covered by her face tats.

'Apart from Ko sounding dreadful to work with, what she's building, well—doesn't it seem like a conflict of interest to you? Simulated food experiences, and all that. As a chef, a cook, someone who loves what they do in the kitchen?' Courage Oslo sounded uncertain as he said this, pushing his food around his plate without meeting my eye.

I looked from one face to the other, and neither of them seemed very happy to be having this conversation with me. I didn't know how to articulate the tangle of thoughts and feelings running through me. If I was being completely honest, I wasn't sure exactly what Serenity Ko intended to *do* with Feast Inc., but it seemed ambitious, and that held an unquantifiable kind of appeal. After being thrown around kitchens here on Primus like a dirty dishcloth, after fleeing my dubious credibility back on Earth, this project felt like a fresh start, with limitless potential. I settled for a version of this truth.

'I don't quite understand what she wants to do with the tech,' I said. 'I'm not sure how she's planning to build it, either. I just like the idea of being able to share my food experiences without any baggage—to talk about flavour while not simultaneously being judged for my origins all the time.'

'We understand that,' Curiosity Zia said immediately.

'Of course we do,' Courage Oslo added, then sighed. 'We just wanted to say, if ever you feel like you aren't *convinced* by it... you know you have a home here, at The New Palette.'

'No pressure, yeah? We don't need an answer right away,' Curiosity Zia said. 'Take your time and think about it, but *please* consider it. We'd love to have you.'

'Thanks, I will,' I mumbled, wondering how much I meant it. I didn't know how to tell them that I felt destined to bigger things—it was an unkind thought, but it resonated strongly within me. And yet, they were some of the loveliest people I'd met on this planet. Working with them would be satisfying for my soul, if not for my career path. I thanked them for their kindness, let Pavi and Amol know I'd be out sick for the day, and took my leave, guilt worming its way through me and feeling heavier than ever before.

Are you going to do it? Kili asked on the flowtram ride back to my space.

I don't know. I sulked. _I feel like I'm meant for more._

They're such good people.

They are.

Doing well for yourself doesn't always mean climbing to the top of an arbitrary ladder determined by a wholly imagined set of values that you probably don't even believe in. Like all the symbology in Primian food—you hate that stuff, but you're trying to do it because you're so desperate to fit in. And it comes with a massive side of criticism. I don't understand why you put up with it.

It's just how things are done in professional kitchens, I said. _It was the same back on Earth._

Not at Elé Oota, it wasn't.

I meant when I was starting out, like I am here on Primus.

323

And you'd cry yourself to sleep after every service, Kili argued.

I need this.

Need what? Kili shot back. _Being treated badly? You *always* have the choice to walk away, to start something of your own again—to work with these lovely people at The New Palette, even!_

But they're not why I'm here.

Then why *are* you here, Saras? Kili asked quietly. _Think about that, please? And promise me you'll consider Zia and Oslo's offer?_

I didn't respond. We hopped off the flowtram at my stop, and I strode towards my space, Kili buzzing by my side.

Promise me, Saras? he asked.

I shoved my way through the doorway of my hex, forcing the flowmetal to pull apart faster, and headed for my space.

Why won't you just accept that you're brilliant and meant for more wholesome things? Kili persisted.

I passed my palm over the lock to my door and it slid open. I stepped inside and recoiled.

All the lights were on. The furniture had been rearranged. A hideously opulent silken Earth-style carpet adorned the floor, adding the only cultural touch to my otherwise bare living room. And seated in my basic, grey, Collective-sanctioned armchair, leaning back against its basic, grey cushions, and sipping on an iced bira from my fridge, was one of the last people I wanted to see anywhere in the fucking universe.

'Do you like the present?' he asked, pointing to the horrid rug.

Kili dove straight into my tunic pocket, and shuddered violently against my thigh.

'How did you find me?' I asked hoarsely, stunned.

He crossed his long legs at the knee, fiddled with his ridiculous golden head-dress, and grinned at me. It was not a friendly smile.

'Heard you were in the neighbourhood,' he said.

My heart hammered erratically. I had to escape. I had to find a way out.

'You moved halfway across the galaxy for this… *squalor?*' my future brother-in law asked, wrinkling his nose in disgust and waving his arm in an arc to indicate my surroundings. 'Narmada will be so amused.'

'Why are you here?' I asked, rudely—and more courageously than I felt.

'It's barely been a few months since you ran away, and you've already lost your court manners, I see,' Jog Tunga said. 'They'll need to fix that.'

'Nobody will be "fixing" anything,' I said flatly. 'Get out of my house.'

Jog Tunga threw his head back and laughed. I stared at him, heir to the Tunga clan, husband-to-be to my odious sister the Priestess Immaculate Narmada, principle ally of the Godavari clan, and one of the most powerful people in the Daxina Protectorate. My insides were a mixture of disbelief that he was here, and loathing that he'd managed to find me.

'I have a message for you from your loving parents,' he said, wiping a tear from a kohl-streaked eye.

'No need to hear it.'

'Oh, there is every need to hear it,' he said snidely. 'Unless you want to be branded a traitor, with a price on your head.'

'Right,' I said, crossing my arms over my chest and leaning against the wall. 'For all my "crimes," is it?'

'Listen, Saraswati Godavari—oh, wait, *Kaveri* is the name you travelled under, isn't it? False claims of persecution to get a refugee passport, and all that.' He rose to his feet slowly and stretched languorously. 'Your grandparents had every last Kaveri killed for insurgency thirty years ago. Your existence is a crime as far as all of us are concerned.'

I shuddered involuntarily. I'd long suspected my grandparents had been mass murderers, but I hadn't expected this information to be thrown in my face like an indisputable truth.

'Want more?' he added. 'How do we know you aren't giving away state secrets here?'

I laughed at that. 'They were never discussed in front of me.' I pointed to myself. 'Too much of a loose cannon.'

'Your word against mine, and your sister's, and your parents if we can convince them.'

I scowled. 'Fuck off.'

'Your manners really are shocking. Insulting a prince of the Protectorate to his face, refusing to bow before him... These are all punishable,' Jog Tunga said. 'Or have you forgotten already? Has this fucking planet bent your brain so quick that you think you're untouchable?'

'I—'

'You know how easy it was to track you?' he continued. 'Despite your nanobleached skin and your awful perm? We knew where you were right from the start.'

'How?'

'That would be telling,' he said in a sing-song voice. 'Can't have you disappear again.' He smiled nastily. 'When they dismissed you from *MegaChef*—spectacular fuck up, by the way, I really enjoyed it—I got the Khurshids to give you a job. We have a long history.'

My heart stuttered. Had my parents worked their influence on this planet, too?

'Are you really surprised?' His lips curled superciliously. Something in my expression must have given me away. He hissed delightedly. 'There's no escaping us, not here, not anywhere in this fucking galaxy.'

'I'm calling the authorities,' I lied.

'Go ahead. I'll tell them about your false identity. Lying on your scrollwork's worth an interstellar travel ban, if I recall.'

He had me trapped and he knew it.

'You're better off just listening to my message.'

I mustered what little courage I had left, even as my knees knocked together. 'Couldn't they just send a stream? Or a scroll?'

'And have it scanned by spies here?' Jog Tunga spat. 'You really are an idiot. Don't know why they want you back, but they do.'

My mouth went dry. 'What do you mean, "want me back"?'

'Your parents say—Hang on, let me get this right.' His pupils flicked as he read from his Loop feed. '"Playtime is over, Saraswati. As a scion of the Godavari clan, it is time for you to report back to Earth and perform your sacred duty, the one we've trained you for all your life."'

He glanced at me. 'Whatever could that sacred duty be?'

'I'm sure you're dying to know,' I said, with every intention of annoying him.

'You have no idea,' he said dismissively.

Unfortunately for him, and for me, I knew exactly what they were referring to, and I was about to lose my breakfast. I shoved the feeling down, determined not to give anything away to this embodiment of Earth toxicity polluting my living room.

'You can tell them I'm not coming home,' I said flatly.

'I was hoping you'd say that,' he said.

That took me by surprise. 'What do you mean?'

'You want to stay here and play with your little cooking tools, right?' he asked, waiting for a response.

I glared at him in mutinous silence.

'You don't have to say it. I've seen everything you've done since you got here,' he said. 'I know you're building some kind of food tech; a sim-based thing.'

'How?'

'Like I said, the Khurshids owe our families for their relevance. They don't know who you are, though. I'd prefer to keep it that way.'

'I don't give a fuck about your preferences.'

'Tough.'

'What do you want?'

'Just stick with the food sim gig. I'll tell your parents you've asked for time. I'll make it *convincing*.' Jog Tunga grinned, and it was like looking into the jaws of a terrible, inescapable void.

'Why would you do that?'

'You'll find out. I'll be in touch.'

'Fuck you, I'll tell them myself,' I said savagely. 'I don't want to owe you fucking anything.'

'Too bad, you already owe me your entire life on this fucking planet so far.'

He strode towards me and I fought the urge to press myself into the wall and squeeze my eyes shut. At the last moment, he veered to his right, and slipped through my flowmetal doors just as they whooshed open, leaving the overpowering scent of sandalwood and musk in his wake.

My legs finally gave way under me and I collapsed onto the couch.

This is not good at all, Kili streamed softly from my pocket.

I pulled him out and stroked him, my hands trembling, my thoughts a blur. 'This is terrible.'

I wanted to curl up into a ball and disappear into the ground beneath my space, to hide and never be discovered, to forget who I was and my past and everything that seemed to lie ahead of me in the future, none of which felt good. I knew exactly what my fucking "sacred duty" was. My parents had been secretly building an alliance with the Bhadra clan, and they'd intended to marry me off into their family to destabilise the Tungas, to make sure little fucks like Jog never rose to complete power. A daughter in every house meant it was less likely to come to all-out war, even if the clans had a power struggle. I'd been sworn to secrecy;

forbidden to tell even my sister Narmada, which wasn't a problem because we hadn't spoken since I was thirteen.

I'd refused to be a pawn in this game, and had got away with it aided by sheer dumb luck. The eldest Bhadra son had died in a solar flare race; the middle one had married for love and been disowned. The youngest, about a decade younger than I, had probably just turned twenty-one, and everyone was perfectly happy with us getting married despite being strangers. I drew my knees up to my chest, sickened at the thought.

Of course, it didn't matter to them one bit that I only liked women.

"Keep a woman," my mother had said dismissively. "Keep a whole harem. Everyone's got one. So long as you produce the occasional heir, you'll be all right."

My insides had crawled back then, and they were threatening to expunge themselves even now.

And then there came a knock on the door.

Startled, adrenaline coursing through my back, I leapt from my seat and swiped my palm across the lock.

'*Fuck off! You can fuck right off!*' I yelled as the door pulled open.

The shocked, bemused face of Serenity Ko stared back at me, her jaw hanging open.

'Oh, it's you.' I deflated.

'Hey, Earth girl, do you know how hard it is to find you?' She recovered gamely, I had to give her that. 'I've spent half the night hunting for you, and you didn't respond to any of my comms.'

It all came rushing back to me; her stupidity in the kitchen, and how it had wrecked what should have been a perfect service. 'What do you want?'

'Um, yeah, listen,' she said, looking down at her feet, her cheeks flushed. She took a deep breath, then blew it out. 'Can I come in?'

I stepped back and she entered, pausing momentarily to look around. She spotted the hideously overwrought Earth-rug on the floor, winced at its tastelessness, caught me looking at her looking at it, and hurriedly covered it up. 'Nice touch of home,' she said with a false smile.

'Sit,' I said equally falsely, hoping she'd make it quick and leave.

She sat on the couch, leaned back, bit the corner of her lower lip, leaned forwards again. 'I'm terrible at these things,' she said, picking at her fingernails. She finally met my eye. 'I wanted to say I'm sorry. For last night. It was a terrible thing to do, and I didn't mean to cause you distress.'

'It was thoughtless,' I said frankly. 'I didn't ask for your help, and I didn't need it. Especially since you're absolutely no good in the kitchen.'

It was harsh, but it had to be said.

'I know.' She hung her head. 'I shouldn't have screwed you over. I mean, you're my teammate. I should never have taken Chaangte's word for it.'

'Wait, what about Chaangte?' I asked, my frayed nerves immediately paranoid.

'I—it was her idea.' Serenity Ko slumped back against the cushions, fidgeting with a stray tassel. 'She said it was a harmless prank. A tradition at Nonpareil to mess up every new chef's first service. I thought it would be hilarious. I took her word for it. I didn't think it was a setup, that she would lose her shit the way she did, and throw you out, and—'

My ears went hot and none of the words tumbling out of her mouth as an apology registered in my brain. 'A prank?' I asked. 'That was *a prank*? You fucking with my dinner service and my entire reputation was a *fucking prank*?'

'Yeah, I—'

'And you thought it would be *funny*?'

I was consumed by my anger; it flooded me in an

explosion. All the stress of the last two days rushed into me like a raging torrent.

'It wasn't, I know. And I'm sorry—'

'*Fuck you, and fuck your sorries!*' I yelled.

Serenity Ko started upright. Her deep brown eyes flashed dangerously, her cheeks crimson. 'Hey, there's no need to be rude.'

'Oh, right, I'm the Earthling, I've got to mind my manners. You—the "civilised" Primian—get to mess with me nonstop, say what you want, do what you want at the risk of *my career*, and I'm supposed to laugh it off and be grateful to be included in any way you permit.'

Sweat trickled down my nose.

'I'm sorry if I've been rude before, but you don't get to take all your frustrations about this planet out on me!' she retorted.

'Yeah, that one half-arsed apology is supposed to make up for your dismissiveness, your manipulativeness, your *fucking little prank*, just because you say it earnestly?'

'You know, you don't have to be so difficult.' She rolled her eyes.

'I'm difficult? *Me?* You know what's fucking difficult? Your entire planet, and its smug superiority. You're all so self-righteous and do-gooder and peace, love and harmony on the outside—fucking *bullshit*, I'll have you know—but you're filled with self-interest, self-promotion and naked ambition at the cost of everyone else around you. Was it *fun?*' I ranted. 'Did you and Chaangte get together for a bira afterward and have a good laugh? Did you celebrate me, the fucking failure, the loser from *MegaChef* who can't even put a basic mousse together?'

'Actually, I had dinner with my brother and his fiancée, and they told me I was being a shithead,' Serenity Ko said tonelessly. 'But no, you're right, go on. We're all savages just like you, aren't we?'

'*What* did you say?'

'I'm sorry,' she said hastily. 'I didn't mean that. It just slipped out.'

'Get out.'

'Really, I didn't mean that at all.'

'Cool, thanks for the apology. I'd like you to leave now.'

Serenity Ko rose to her feet, her expression strained. 'I didn't... That was...'

'Out of line and unacceptable,' I said.

'Let me take you out for dinner?' she wheedled. 'Things got out of hand, and it's my fault. I want to have a good working relationship with you. I really believe in what we're building, and I know you're the right person on my team.'

'Thanks for your approval,' I said sarcastically. 'But I quit. You're going to have to find a new chef. Pair up with Chaangte, she's a real charmer.'

'You can't quit!'

'Just did. Goodbye, Serenity Ko.'

> The Kaveri family was annihilated by the ruling
> Godavari family in a power struggle not uncommon to
> the Daxina Protectorate. There were no survivors.
>
> —Anita Umar,
> *One Nation Earth: The Myth of Unity*
> 2053 Anno Earth | 1978 Interstellar Era

TWENTY-EIGHT

SHE DIDN'T REMEMBER being a refugee; she'd barely been two years old when she and her brother had been put in an escape shuttle with their governess, headed straight for the planet Primus. Akkamma had dropped them off at the first orphanage she'd got to and disappeared into the mist— Optimism Mahd'vi had often wondered if she'd been hunted down by pursuers from Earth, shipped off-world, or integrated into Primian society. Her Primian parents had adopted her and Courage Kiva, who now worked on a mining station in the Osmos Girdle. They'd never really hidden her Earth origins from her, or shamed her for being from the primitive planet, but they hadn't ever explained her personal history beyond the fact that she'd been from a place called Daxina, and had held the last name Kaveri on her refugee scrollwork.

When she was a teenager, she'd discovered the name in an encyclopaedia dedicated to the history of Daxina, and checked the holoscroll out of the library immediately. Much to her horror, her family's history had been reduced to a single sentence, which had stayed with her for the better part of forty years:

The Kaveri family was annihilated by the ruling Godavari family in a power struggle not uncommon to the Daxina Protectorate. There were no survivors.

That was it.

There were no other records, and Optimism Mahd'vi had explored every possible avenue to discover more about her past. It didn't exist. It was as if someone had wiped her family off the curvature of spacetime, erased them entirely. She didn't even know her mother's name.

She remembered sobbing to her brother about it, who'd shrugged and told her that the past didn't matter. It was a philosophy he still held to. She'd been alone in her search ever since.

And now, Curiosity Ariam had said *the most fascinating thing*.

'Repeat that, will you?' Optimism Mahd'vi said, suddenly paying attention.

'The whole thing?' Curiosity Ariam tilted their head.

'Every word,' Optimism Mahd'vi said. She'd drifted somewhat as Curiosity Ariam had launched into one of their gossip-fuelled rants about their job. This meeting was supposed to be about programming for the Millennium Festival, but as usual, Curiosity Ariam had spent the first forty minutes prattling on about the sordid details of celebrity living. And then *the Earthlings* had popped up. Both of them.

Curiosity Ariam blew a smoke ring. 'You really are a *Stars Unrivalled* fan, huh?'

'Who isn't?' Optimism Mahd'vi lied.

Curiosity Ariam sipped on their starfruit wine. 'Boundless Nnika, yeah? She's been a world of trouble. You remember how she abandoned her polycule here for one on Allegro, and disappeared entirely? We had to send a ship after her, bring them all back—ghastly logistical nightmare getting all their scrollwork done, I tell you...'

'You can skip forwards. You told me this a while ago.'

'Yeah, so she went missing again, abandoning her newfound united 'cule, no word of where she was to *any of us*, and we're behind schedule on Season 5 already...'

Curiosity Ariam supplied. 'The other cast members had a fit, and I can't blame them! We've had Serenity Lea in a full-body flowmetal mould because she's playing a Mexamon.'

'I'm sorry, what?'

'Fictional alt-being,' Curiosity Ariam waved their hand carelessly. 'It's uncomfortable as fuck, and Lea's one of those method nutters who'll stay in it all through to stay in character, so the tantrums she threw when we told her the schedule was disrupted again... And don't even get me started on Honour Vee.'

'Yes, don't. Tell me about Nnika.' Optimism Mahd'vi smiled tersely, willing herself to stay patient.

'So yeah, Nnika walks out on everyone, there's a whole missing persons report, this goes on for an entire nava—a whole *nava!* And then suddenly, she's back on set two days ago, weeping her eyes out, because her new boyfriend is having an affair.'

This was the bit Optimism Mahd'vi had been waiting for. She leaned forwards, sipping her starfruit wine.

'Turns out, she'd been solar flare cruising with some Earth princeling named Jog Tunga. He disappeared without a word, and was photographed by cam-drones leaving the space of some Earthling immigrant on Primus. Boundless Nnika is inconsolable; we had to sedate her, and she's been knocking back the MellO since.'

Optimism Mahd'vi feigned horror. She didn't really care about the emotional specifics of Boundless Nnika's crisis. She just wanted to get to the only detail that mattered.

'Go on,' she said casually.

'Turns out it's the *same* Sara-something Kaveri from the *MegaChef* debacle,' Curiosity Ariam said, their eyes lighting up with the glee of spilling the grisly details of someone else's private life.

'What are the odds?' Optimism Mahd'vi suggested conspiratorially. *What are the odds, indeed?*

'I know, right? Imagine leaving your Drammy-winning, *Intergalactic Fame Magazine*'s sexiest person of the year— four years running, now—absolute hot mess of a partner, even if it is just a fling, for a hideous nobody,' Curiosity Ariam sniggered. 'All because they're from the same home world, I'm guessing. "Barbarians of a mind flock to their kind," after all.'

'Primitives,' Optimism Mahd'vi sniffed, but her heart stuttered with a familiar twinge of anxiety. She took a prolonged sip of her starfruit wine to gather her thoughts. Jog Tunga *and* the Kaveri girl—the two Earthlings who'd been popping up on her radar *nonstop*—meeting in a private location on *her* planet smacked of conspiracy. She couldn't sound the alarm—*not just yet*. But she had to draw at least one of them out of hiding.

'Let's focus on our plans for the Millennium Festival,' she said smoothly, working out the best way forwards.

'You mean your bid to remind the entire universe that they owe us, here on Primus, for the continued survival of human civilization?' Curiosity Ariam laughed loudly.

'Yes, that, but lower your voice,' Optimism Mahd'vi snapped. 'There's a reason this meeting isn't happening in the Courtyard. I want a no-filters update on everything.'

Right then, a server brought some food up to their chef's table at Leaf and Bone. It consisted of a pearlescent caviar, layered over a delicate petalescence resembling pipalia flowers.

'That's beautiful,' Curiosity Ariam gasped.

'Oh, the food here is an art form,' Optimism Mahd'vi said, nodding appreciatively at the server. 'Exactly what everything Primian stands for. Let's start with your proposal for the special episode of *MegaChef*?'

Curiosity Ariam flicked their thumb and forefinger together and transmitted a presentation to Optimism Mahd'vi. It popped up on her visual, and she focused on it, bringing it to the forefront of her field of view.

'I'm thinking of an extensive application process. This isn't just about finding a good chef,' Curiosity Ariam said. 'This is about finding somebody who can take our history— the Nakshatran philosophies about food—and honour it, while marrying it to the future...'

Curiosity Ariam walked Optimism Mahd'vi through the finer details of the programme, and while she made notes, Optimism Mahd'vi also mulled over the probability of this episode drawing the Kaveri girl out of hiding. She had to keep an eye on her, make contact without scaring her off, somehow. Was she really a relative? Another survivor? Or was she a masquerader, stealing the identity of a line long-dead on Earth, and using it for illicit purposes in collusion with Jog Tunga?

It was a shame surveillance was forbidden on Primus. Cam-drones occasionally latched on to celebrities, like the one that had spotted Jog Tunga leaving the Kaveri girl's residence, but *intentionally* tracking anyone, whether they were an immigrant or a citizen, was illegal. Even Curiosity Ariam—who Optimism Mahd'vi trusted, as far as trust could exist in circles of power and influence—would likely be repulsed by the suggestion. They were good for scheming up a visual spectacle and chasing interstellar ratings, but asking them to spy on someone, even under the guise of gaining celebrity gossip, would likely sever the slim threads of the alliance they were weaving together.

No, the special episode was her best bet at finding the Kaveri girl.

Optimism Mahd'vi ran another search on the Earthlings, while silently cursing because she didn't have security clearance to access immigrant files. The Kaveri girl had no social streaming presence. It was as if she didn't exist.

She turned to Jog Tunga's whereabouts. He was at a K'artri-pop concert on Sagaricus, three jumpgates away. She sighed in relief; at least he was out of the Suriyan

System for now, though he wasn't quite far enough.

Why had he visited the Kaveri girl before leaving, though? *What if she's a spy? Or some kind of informant?*

'This Saraswati Kaveri,' she said out loud, interrupting Curiosity Ariam midway through their update on the Legends of the Future documentary they were planning to broadcast. 'Where does she work?'

'Who knows?' Curiosity Ariam shrugged. 'There was some kind of kerfuffle at the Uru and Beyond Marketplace a few navas ago. Cam-drones spotted her at one of the food stalls there. The New Plate?'

'So one of the experimental places?'

'I guess. Can you imagine the *Primian* culinary elite hiring trash like that?' Curiosity Ariam shuddered.

'Spread the word far and wide, will you? About the *MegaChef* special?'

'Why, do you have a soft spot for the barbarian, Maddie?' Curiosity Ariam asked ingratiatingly.

'Of course not,' Optimism Mahd'vi snapped. 'I'm doing *your* job and thinking of *your* ratings. Imagine seeding a failure or two in the midst of the ones with actual talent, hmm? When has that ever failed?'

Curiosity Ariam smiled sheepishly. 'I'll take this note to Davi and the producers.'

'See that you do,' Optimism Mahd'vi said archly.

Curiosity Ariam's presentation now at an end, Optimism Mahd'vi returned her attention to the food on her plate. She scooped it up and popped it into her mouth.

'Any questions?' Curiosity Ariam asked.

'Nope. None at all.' Or none that she could ask out loud.

Fool me once, shame on you.
Fool me twice, shame on me.

—Ancient Earth Proverb

TWENTY-NINE

Don't panic.

I'm not panicking. Does this look like panic?

Kili didn't respond.

I surveyed my space. I'd accumulated far too many 3D-printed Primian clothes since I got here, and they were all heaped upon my Collective-issued sofa. The long sleeve of a tunic trailed into an unfinished mug of kaapi. A pair of boots I'd splurged on had been tossed carelessly in a packing cube, amidst a stash of socks and leggings. Bras and underwear festooned my newly-acquired, laughably hideous Earthling rug. All my skincare compounds dripped water onto my coffee table, where I'd hurriedly plonked them down after raiding my bathroom.

It looked like someone had broken in and made off with my non-existent valuables.

Right. So I'm panicking, I said, picking up a belt and fidgeting with its buckle.

Don't.

A strangled sob escaped me. _What am I going to do?_

Breathe.

I'm breathing, I snapped.

Easy, Kili said, landing gently on my shoulder. _Follow my lead._

He helped me through a deep-breathing exercise, vibrating to indicate when to inhale and exhale, probably from some mental health programme off the Loop. As oxygen flooded my brain, my fog of panic dulled to an ominous cloud, hovering on the horizon, and my thoughts sharpened to paint a very grim picture of my prospects.

Jog Tunga's found me. They *know where I am.*

A shiver ran down my spine as a far quieter thought struck me. Wasn't this exactly what I'd wanted? Why else would I have gone on a reality contest that was broadcast across the galaxy? I cringed, reminded of my hubris, and then laughed at the foolishness of my big idea.

I'd pictured a grand denouement to the narrative I'd built in my head. After a season's worth of sailing through episode after episode, while the judges heaped their praises upon my glorious cooking and audiences across the galaxy fell in love with my spirit, I'd seize the title of Interstellar MegaChef (or, at the very least, come a close second). I'd then use my moment of triumph to reveal my identity— *not* Saraswati Kaveri, but Saraswati *Godavari*, chased off my home world by my totalitarian parents, who refused to let me pursue my dreams. My fame would elicit sympathy, cause my family a great deal of embarrassment, and then finally—*finally*—they would leave me be, twenty-one jumpgates away. And if they *didn't* leave me alone, out of spite or any of the other usual power-tripping reasons, I'd threaten to spill all their grisly secrets before my newfound interstellar audience.

I hadn't factored being disgraced and eliminated on day one into the equation.

I hadn't accounted for being spied on while I fled Daxina in the middle of an uprising.

I hadn't imagined that my family's influence could extend beyond the Solar System.

Foolish egomaniac. And now they *know where I am.*

They'd always known. And now that they'd made it a point to find me, to let me know that they'd known my whereabouts all along, thereby reminding me of their persistent power over me, *Jog Tunga*—of all the slippery slimefish in the sea—was offering me a way out.

Jog Tunga embodied the very best of every beta-grade villain in every Ur-drama ever, from the petty headmistress in *Teen Trouble,* who denied her wards their tuckboxes from home, to the duplicitous double agent, Captain Courage Stryx, who sold UHC secrets to the warmongering (and wholly fictional) Reptars in *Intergalactic Invaders.*

I'd grown up with him lurking in the shadows of my childhood home. When he wasn't shooting rubber pellets at me from a slingshot or an airgun, or trapping moths by tempting them with tealights in bell-jars, or laying traps for the help, he was hanging onto Narmada's every word, especially since most of what she said was directed at encouraging him. He'd been sent away when he was fifteen, after Mani's second in command, Somu, was found riddled with holes, floating face-down in a pond—the result of an experiment with a tripwire and a platoon of robo-soldiers armed with real weapons.

If *Jog Tunga* wanted me on his team, I was in a whole new dimension of trouble. Even if he was going to give me what I wanted—a way to keep twenty-one jumpgates between me and my parents—I couldn't accept his offer without thinking it through.

'I need to get out of here,' I said out loud.

Where to, Saras? Kili asked, concerned. _Remember, we aren't panicking._

'I can't possibly *stay!*'

You can't leave. Not yet. We have no idea where to fake new scrollwork on this planet. We don't know how to file an application to move spaces. You still have a job at Nonpareil.

'A job *he* got me.' I snapped.

A job you deserve, but don't need, except it lets you accumulate funds for future escape plans—which I'm wholly in favour of, by the way—but let's stop and think this through. One step at a time, Kili said.

His calm demeanour was soothing, but also annoying because he was absolutely right. I flung the belt I'd been twisting in on itself to the floor, shaking my hands out, striding up and down.

'Right. Think, Saras. *Think.*'

My brain drew a blank.

According to the Loop, you can request a new space if yours is damaged, Kili said. _Just looked it up. If essential systems, like grav-management or climate control aren't working, say._

_Great. Where are the wires? Let's get some bolt-cutters. _

It's centralised. If you take yours out, the whole hex goes down. Also, no wires. Only code.

Oh, fuck me.

You can get a new space if your neighbours harass you...

I had no idea who my neighbours were, let alone how to pick a fight with them.

... or if your security is compromised.

I laughed bitterly at that. There was no way I could prove Jog Tunga was a security threat without revealing my false scrollwork, and he'd been right—that was worth a hefty fine and an interstellar travel ban. Plus, I'd be deported, sent straight back to my parents.

Religious reasons, Kili said. _I'm scanning the fine print._

'What do you mean?'

You can leave if you experience a spiritual epiphany and want to join a commune.

'Look up *everything* on the Faith of the Light.' As a Chloriana fan, it was the only Primian religious order I was vaguely familiar with.

Saras, Kili said uncertainly. _The lies are piling up._

'I know,' I said miserably.

I'd have to come out ahead of them, somehow. But first, I had to go into hiding. And I knew where to begin.

BOUNDLESS BAZ WAS surprised when I stepped through the kitchen door. He punched my shoulder gently. 'I'm glad you're back. Don't let the miserable insect bring you down.'

I smiled wanly. I didn't want everyone at Nonpareil thinking I was a talentless hack, and that Good Cheer Chaangte had called me out on being a fraud. I was here to rage-quit, but I was going to do so on my terms.

XX-29 wrapped me up in a big, wordless hug—it turned out xe loved physical contact, which let xir bypass the constraints of the voxbox. As xe'd explained to me once, backed enthusiastically by Starlight Fantastic, human languages, especially Vox and Ur-speak, were severely limited when it came to conveying true emotion.

The other chefs gave me a wide berth. I didn't want to, but I found myself surveying the kitchen, looking for her. Good Cheer Chaangte hadn't arrived yet.

I picked up a dishcloth and proceeded to wipe down the nearest flowmetal counter, for no other reason than to evade the awkward game people play when everyone is trying desperately hard to avoid eye contact. I felt everyone's gaze boring into the back of my skull while I worked. The kitchen was eerily silent. I whistled my favourite Legends of the Future song out loud.

Smooth, Kili said.

Someone's got to carve the carcass, I said, smiling wryly. This had been one of Juno's favourite lines, saved for when someone stuffed up and she called it out mid-service—a kind of folksy saying I'd never heard until I met her.

The sounds of kitchen busywork peppered the air; a knife snicking away, a freezer door being opened and shut again, muted conversations, the soft sucking sound—barely louder than a whisper—that I'd come to associate with industrial kitchen syringes, a zipper as someone did up their chef's jacket, all coming together in song.

You think they know you were set up by Chaangte? Kili asked.

I wouldn't be surprised if they don't. They're all so terrified of her, so bought into the Primian idea that Earthlings are capable of nothing, I said acidly.

I rode the wave of the crescendo, whistling loudly, timing the snick-snick of the knife to the beat, when I realised the kitchen had gone silent. The ambient sound dropped around me like a collapsing soufflé.

'Go on, *savage,*' came the grating ring of her voice. 'Please, disgrace a complex piece of music with your *Earthling* spin on it.'

I whistled—even louder—until I sounded positively shrill, like a pressure cooker out of key. I calmly continued scrubbing the already spotless counter.

'I didn't think you'd have it in you to come back,' Good Cheer Chaangte said, drawing into my line of vision. 'Not after you degraded yourself at dinner service.'

I focused even harder on the gleaming silver surface. I wasn't going to react. Not yet.

'You know what we served for dessert, after your *pathetic* inability to follow *basic* instructions? Fresh fruit. Worse than a street-side stall, except of course, *our fresh fruit is worth more than your entire planet.*' She cackled. I heard a guffaw behind me. It was probably Optimism Jordan, who it turned out, was Good Cheer Chaangte's acolyte of choice.

'Lost for words, are we?' she said softly, smugly. 'Can't even bring yourself to look me in the eye?'

'Leave her alone, Chaangte,' Boundless Baz said. I willed him not to interfere.

She stepped right up to me, standing on the other side of

the counter. 'Of course, I told Pavi and Amol all about it. They weren't pleased at all.'

My hands shook with rage, and I kept them concealed in the folds of the dishcloth. I held myself silent, counting down the seconds…

Kili buzzed on my shoulder. That was my cue.

'Told them *everything?*' I asked innocently, keeping my tone even, meeting her gaze at last. All those diplomacy and power establishment lessons with Chicko—the ones I'd attended, at least—hadn't been for nothing.

'Down to the last detail.' Good Cheer Chaangte leaned forwards menacingly. 'Kiss your career goodbye.'

'Did you mention the bit where it was a prank?'

Good Cheer Chaangte chuckled. 'I don't know what you're talking about.'

'No?' I asked innocently. 'You didn't just *happen* to tell Serenity Ko to double my infusions for the mousse spheres, *after* I'd prepped them and left them to set? You didn't just *happen* to mislead her into believing it was all a prank, par for the course, a *tradition* in the Nonpareil kitchen? Some workplace policy you've got here.'

Her face paled, and her mouth formed a grim line.

'I had a visit from Serenity Ko,' I said cheerfully. 'She told me that *you* put her up to sabotaging my dinner service. Told her *exactly* how to do it, too.'

'So what if I did?' Good Cheer Chaangte sneered.

'I wonder what Pavi and Amol will think about that. I wonder if I should tell them,' I said, watching her cheeks flush scarlet. 'After all, *they* own the restaurant, *they* ought to know who fucked *their* service. Maybe there was a food critic at a table that night, perhaps people left us a shitty rating for the no-show dessert… Oh wait, you served *fresh fruit* instead. Clever, ten on ten for improv.'

Good Cheer Chaangte appeared to swell like an overripe papaya.

'But you know, maybe the trade-off is worth it,' I continued, relentless. 'After all, you only fucked the restaurant as a team-building exercise, a spot of camaraderie with someone who isn't an employee—nice to make Ko feel like one of us, hmm? Demonstrating your leadership skills; you should be promoted.

'So what if it was xenophobic? Targeting a minority is a *hate crime*, last I checked, but what do I know? I'm just an Earthling.'

'Earthling *rat!*' Good Cheer Chaangte hissed.

'I know! I should tell *everyone* about it. Chaangte, who leads from the front, who never turns down an opportunity to make *the right sort* feel included. *It'll be so good for your career!*' I raised my voice to drown out Good Cheer Chaangte's screech of rage. She dove over the flowmetal counter at me and grabbed the lapel of my jacket. Kili bobbed off my shoulder and threw himself at her, but she ignored him, glaring at me, her spectacle frames all that separated us.

'Scum like *you* have no place in the kitchen, not on Earth, not anywhere in the galaxy, but *especially not on Primus*. I just hastened your inevitable failure. *You destroy things.* You have *no respect* for our culture,' she raged. Spittle flew at me, punctuating her ragged breathing. 'For two millennia, *we* have been humanity's hope and salvation. We have delivered civilization into a new era. *We. Primians. Not. You.*'

My ears rang with her shouting. It took every ounce of my restraint not to shove her in the chest.

'Everywhere I look, I see upstarts and pretenders *trying to be like us. None of you belong!*' Her eyes scanned the kitchen beyond my shoulder. '*Not you,* you fucking B'naar freak. *Not you,* you second-generation mongrel. *Not you,* you sorry excuse for a Primian—oh, grow a spine, defend what we stand for, stop following me around and making me do it for you. *Not you,* you fucking immigrant barbarians, straight off a spaceship, trying to profit from *our culture…*'

And then her eyes widened, and her hands began to shake against the collar of my jacket. Her eyes locked on mine, and they glowed with hatred. 'You fucking bitch,' she hissed. 'You set me up.'

I didn't see it coming. I only felt it when it smashed into the side of my face. I fell over backwards, bringing my hands up to shield my eyes, my ears ringing from the blow. Through a blur of tears, I made out the shape of a fist as she drew it back before throwing it again. I winced in anticipation, but it never landed. Someone hauled me to the floor, a confused babble of voices ringing out around me.

Good Cheer Chaangte disappeared from my field of view, and I became hyperaware of my hammering heart, the tears streaming down my cheeks, and a dull throb on the left side of my face.

Are you okay? Saras! Kanno! Anbe!

I'm not, I said weakly. _Not yet. Please tell me they were there._

This wasn't in the script, was it? Kili asked desperately.

I didn't know she'd pack such a strong punch, I joked.

Har. Fucking. Har. Not funny.

Please tell me they saw it all.

Kili sighed in exasperation. _That last bit about immigrant barbarians? She was looking right at Pavi and Amol._

Oh, good.

My head swum with a heady mix of emotions, relief and vindication intermingling with adrenaline and pain. Perhaps, somewhere, beneath it all, was a pop of dopamine.

'Make way for us, you morons,' Boundless Baz said off to my right.

I felt XX-29's mechatronic limbs beneath my armpits. Xe lifted me up effortlessly, laying me down on the flowmetal counter I'd been cleaning.

'Can you sit up?' I heard Amol ask.

I tried, and my head spun. 'Need a minute.'

I finally emerged from the thoughts swirling inside my head, and managed to sit up. Boundless Baz handed me a glass of water. I sipped from it gratefully.

'That was horrifying,' Amol said. 'That entire display—shocking. I'm so sorry, on behalf of *all of us* at Nonpareil. Xenophobia like that... physical assault... these are unforgivable crimes. I owe you all an apology, too,' Amol continued, visibly shaken as he surveyed the rest of the chefs in the kitchen. 'Good Cheer Chaangte is in the back office. We're going to deal with her.'

Pavi nodded sternly, taking her place beside him. 'I know we've had our differences,' she said, looking at me helplessly, 'but this is...' She shook her head, seemingly lost for words.

'Thanks.' I nodded, then winced as a new wave of wooziness kicked in.

'Would you like to come have a chat with us and Chaangte?' Pavi asked.

'Nope,' I said.

'We'd hate to tear the kitchen apart over this,' Pavi said quietly.

'I'm sorry, but you should have thought of that before you let Chaangte abuse half the chefs on your team for fuck knows how long.' I looked pointedly at the twins, but in the corner of my eye, I saw Boundless Baz put his arm around XX-29. 'None of the people in this kitchen deserve what she's been dishing, and you've let it carry on for reasons I can't fathom. I hope you'll reconsider them,' I finished politely.

'We'll deal with Chaangte,' Amol said firmly. 'But we'd also like a word with you.'

'Too bad. I'm out. I quit.'

I tore my chef's jacket off and dropped to my feet, ignoring the persistent ringing in my left ear. Boundless Baz walked up to me and offered me his arm in support, and I leaned into him while he led me to the door.

'You'd better hope I stay quiet,' I called, as the flowmetal whooshed shut behind me.

Dramatic exit. Everyone will be talking about the Earthling chef who got punched in the face and quit, Kili streamed.

Escape plan, check, I said woozily. _If we're lucky, they'll fire Chaangte, too._

Boundless Baz hailed a flowcab and helped me in. 'I'll tell you what happens,' he said. 'Please get some rest, Saras.'

'I will,' I lied.

By the time we pulled away, I was filling out an application to move into the Faith of the Light commune.

Every act of transformation, from a harvest to a finished plate, represents an ideology. Do you look to seize plants from the soil, or snatch a life to put it on your plate? Do you transform through fire?

If you're Primian, the answer is probably a resounding "no." Without our culinary traditions, we would be savages.

—Grace Menmo, from the sim *At Home in the Kitchen*,
4435 Anno Earth | 1990 Interstellar Era

THIRTY

It was Ammamma's fault in so many different ways. Serenity Ko had wanted a basic tutorial, not complete immersion in the deep end of Primian food culture. And yet, the more she'd studied, the more she'd been fascinated by it, although she'd never admit it out loud. She'd made her brother a meal the other night that had verged on the inedible, and while the dinner party had been disastrous, the process of *cooking* had been fulfilling, at least. She was paying more attention to the food her neighbours at the hex cooked together, and to what was on her plate—not just in her glass—at restaurants.

And something about how Saraswati Kaveri had talked about food, worked with it, savoured it, had felt like watching an artist at work. The memory of the Berry-anna tasting from a few navas before rushed back to her, and Serenity Ko's cheeks turned a deep shade of pink while she scowled at the flavour-emotion matrix she was compiling with the design team.

It was *almost* all Ammamma's fault. Saraswati quitting

was entirely on *her*, and she knew it. It was embarrassing and aggravating. She didn't know what to do about it.

Should have just stuck to OutCooked 5, *and hooked up with the adreno-bros*, she thought, not for the first or for the last time.

Why was I so stupid and mean? She didn't have an answer. Not true, she knew the answer; her brother had spelled it out for her. She was so wrapped up in her self-importance and her challenges that she'd lost empathy for other people's struggles. She was so desperate to fit in that she'd side with whomever had power. The thought was unbearable. She was a beastly person, and she needed to find a way to fix it—except she needed to design her food sim first.

So she'd thrown herself into the project wholeheartedly, and in the nava that had passed since Saraswati Kaveri had thrown her out of her space, she'd managed to do a lot of heavy lifting. Her to-do list, once seemingly endless, was still very long, but at least she'd got started.

Optimism Sah'r and her tech team had taken on the challenge of upgrading XP Inc.'s bio-circuits for additional capacity; plugging them into food experiences would need extensive new smell and taste circuitry. Serenity Ko trusted implicitly that they'd find the right hardware. She was less certain about Courage Na'vil and his neuropsych team— she had extensive meetings with him every day, and his obsession with the ethics of simulating sensory experiences was wearing her down.

'This is a complete disconnect from reality, Komala. We feed them a tasteless slab and their *brains* convince them it's edible, delicious, associated with positive feelings and memories. It's sensory manipulation,' he'd said.

'It's a *choice*. Nobody's compelled to try it,' Serenity Ko had shot back.

'But for those who *do* try it,' he'd carried on. 'Aren't we messing with their perception of reality?'

'Doesn't every sim? Even our basic visio-filters mess with reality.'

'Those are as intrusive as wearing sunglasses; all they do is prompt the optic nerve to process light differently. We aren't triggering *emotions* with any of our other offerings,' he'd said. 'This is deep-brain work.'

'SoundSpace does the same thing,' Serenity Ko had said promptly.

'Food is necessary for survival. Music is not.'

'That's what makes this revolutionary.'

Courage Na'vil had smiled sadly. 'Who controls the feelings and associations being triggered?'

'We do. I do.'

'For now,' he'd said, and it had sounded ominous.

'If you're so uncomfortable, then talk to Sah'r and Kube,' Serenity Ko had snapped.

'I tried. It didn't work.' He'd sounded bitter.

That bitterness was a great addition to his already sunny personality, Serenity Ko thought. At least she'd already finished their meeting for the day.

Meanwhile, Grace Kube, who usually insisted on esoteric creativity enhancement techniques and blue-sky artistic processes—the more abstruse the philosophy, the more appealing, all gathered from new-age cultural creators at parties—was nothing short of obsessed with their timelines. He'd mentioned something about an application cut-off date for a *MegaChef* special episode several times. Serenity Ko had agreed to it brightly at first, just to shut him up. Now, she had nothing but regrets, as the deadline drew upon them like a gathering storm.

She studied the large three-dimensional matrix holorayed across the wall. Intersecting spheres mapped a wheel of flavours to a wheel of emotions, and each emotion was linked to a cluster of associated auditory and visual cues.

'I can't help but think we're doing this all wrong, Ko,'

Courage Praia said hesitantly. 'Does sweetness always evoke joy? I mean, doesn't sweetness sometimes bring on a headache if it's overpowering?'

'I get migraines when I eat too much cream,' Curiosity Nenna piped up.

Serenity Ko's nostrils flared. They were asking too many questions. And they were right. Flavours weren't straightforward at all; every single one of the fucking things was a black hole of nuance. Her thoughts spiralled as she regarded her ever-growing list of open questions. It was bad enough attempting to map individual flavours to emotions, but what happened when they were combined? Would the whole be greater than the sum of its parts? Would each component flavour trigger a contradictory feeling or memory in a person's experience of it? Would a person want to experience only one strong memory associated with a specific taste, or a whole spectrum of them combined?

Her head spun. This was a mess. She needed Saraswati Kaveri to untangle it for her. She'd thoughtstreamed her every single day and received no response. She'd considered showing up at her space, and decided against it—it was a very Honour Aki thing to do. She'd shown up at Nonpareil instead, only to be informed that Saraswati had quit and disappeared into the wind, by none other than Good Cheer Chaangte, who'd also cheerfully mentioned that she was serving her notice period and free to collaborate, in case Serenity Ko needed a new partner. She hastily demurred; she definitely needed a new partner, but Good Cheer Chaangte was *not* at the top of her list.

She was seriously considering asking Ammamma for help, but the thought of proving her grandmother right—in every regard—was aggravating enough to cause ulcers. She watched helplessly as Courage Praia added more words to the wretched flavour-emotion matrix, and barely registered the sounds that kept tumbling out unasked-for from Curiosity Nenna's mouth.

This was overwhelming, and she was alone. She couldn't even go rant about things to Kube; he'd just throw it in her face with more criticism about her methods, point at the looming deadline, and label the project a failure.

San*AI, who monitored things on the design floor, popped up on her comms.

Good Cheer Eria to meet you, Serenity Ko.
I've shown her to Conference Chamber 11.

Well, that was a minor relief. At least Good Cheer Eria hadn't shut her out completely after their disastrous dinner.

'Back in a bit,' she announced, and made her way towards the tunnel, turning right instead of riding the walkway and heading into a maze of conference rooms. She steeled herself for the inevitable dressing down she was about to receive.

'Eria, glad you could make it,' she said haltingly.

'Ko!' Good Cheer Eria spun around in her chair, and smiled genuinely. She was dressed in a flowing luminoweave tunic, and between its iridescence and her chlorosapient mods, she looked like an ethereal being. 'How are you?'

'Good. I think,' Serenity Ko lied.

'I saw your apology, and I accept it,' Good Cheer Eria said. 'I'm also relieved you apologised to the woman from Earth for being such a bully. That really isn't who you are.'

'I was a shithead,' Serenity Ko agreed.

'You were,' Good Cheer Eria said cheerfully. 'But that's all in the past, now.'

'I'm so glad you came, Eria,' Serenity Ko said quickly. 'I really wasn't expecting you to be so kind after...' She trailed off.

'Everyone makes mistakes. The important thing is to do better. Tell me, how can I help you?'

'I was hoping—wondering—if you might know Harmony Li.'

'The edibites guy?'

'That's the one.'

'Of course. We share a community garden plot at the Faith of the Light commune.'

'Could you introduce me to him?' Serenity Ko asked in a rush. 'I was hoping we could use edibites for the food sim project. And I think our goals might align—he invented edibites to be a nutrition-packed substitute for food, right? If I simulate taste, and link that to his edibite substitutes, then we're both working towards the same kind of self-sustenance—the kind that doesn't rely on consuming the natural world around us.'

Good Cheer Eria frowned slightly. 'Edibites aren't really a commercial product,' she said slowly. 'In fact, outside the chlorosapient community, they're primarily donated off-world, to space stations and planets with resource shortages.'

'I'm not planning to steal from them,' Serenity Ko said. 'I want to license edibites. With the funds and publicity they get from XP Inc., they can increase production and donate more.'

'I don't doubt your intentions, Ko,' Good Cheer Eria said. 'But you know how close the Faith of the Light is to the Wanderers, and we—I mean, folks in the community—can be a bit suspicious of folks from Uru, especially when they have commerce in mind. You know the original Nakshatrans envisioned a money-free society?'

Serenity Ko stifled her impatience. 'Yes, but over here on Uru, at least, money is only recreational. The Secretariat provides us all with housing, clothes and food, and everything else we need to survive. Our money is only spent on enhancements and experiences.'

'Even so,' Good Cheer Eria said. 'There are those who dislike this focus on material things, even if they are only upscale, non-essential experiences.'

'Is Harmony Li one of them?'

'I don't know. I suppose I could ask.'

'Could you, please, Eria? Pretty please?'

Good Cheer Eria regarded her in silence, then sighed. 'You know I'm your friend, right?'

Serenity Ko's heart sank in anticipation of disappointment. 'Of course,' she said briskly. 'What's that got to do with anything?'

'You know I wouldn't criticise you, or your work, unduly?'

'Yes,' Serenity Ko lied, her eyes flicking to her dash as the minutes ticked past. 'Just tell me what it is, Eria. Please.'

'This project of yours, Feast Inc.,' Good Cheer Eria began. 'I have some concerns I'd like to bring to you.'

'Go on, then.'

'I say this as your friend, representative of only my views. I'm not channelling the general skepticism of the Wanderers when it comes to sims.' She smiled, though her eyes seemed to take on a faraway look, somewhat sad. 'I know how hard it is to be food-independent. Most chlorosapients do. Our mods aren't fully equipped to harvest and convert the light of the stars, certainly not enough to sustain a human being. We still need edibites to provide us with nutrition. Maybe we won't in the future, but I might not be around to see that.'

'Uh-huh,' Serenity Ko said, not quite following her train of thought.

'Edibites are recent—you know that, right? Barely fifty years old, constantly evolving. They made my transformation easier, paired with my mods, but that doesn't mean it was easy. Being unwilling to eat culturally acceptable food is a choice, and it's come with its limitations. A lot of people don't invite me to parties; "Oh no, a chlorosapient, what do we even put on their plate?" I don't know if you recall this;

there was a *MegaChef* episode a few years ago—fans call it the "Chlorosapient Conundrum"—where all the chefs had to make food our people would be willing to eat. Nobody takes that show seriously, of course, but it's a reflection of how isolating our food experiences are, of how we are always set apart from most people, and treated that way.'

'I'm sorry,' Serenity Ko said sincerely, still unable to see where Good Cheer Eria was going.

'Thank you,' Good Cheer Eria replied, then carried on. 'With Feast, I fear you might be creating something that will encourage isolation, while dressing it up as glamorous and revolutionary. "Here's an edibite that tastes like ice cream, eat it alone and lose yourself in unreality."

'As someone who's constantly lonely—outside my relationships with Rihan and your family, and the Faith of the Light—I don't want other people to lose themselves in your tech, only to discover, after dozens of family dinners and date nights have passed eating in solitude, that they've lost out on connecting with each other through a unifying human experience—food.'

Serenity Ko was taken aback. 'Wow, Eria. I didn't know you felt so strongly about this.'

Good Cheer Eria raised a shoulder in a half-shrug. 'I might be paranoid. I don't know exactly what you're doing, or how you plan to build it, but I had to be honest.'

'I—I appreciate it.' She didn't know quite what to make of Good Cheer Eria's words, so she filed them away for future reference. 'Give me some time to think it through?'

'Thank you for considering my thoughts.'

This could be a side-quest for Curiosity Nenna. It wasn't a big enough consideration to hold back the development of Feast Inc., at least not in Serenity Ko's estimation—after all, she was only seeking to build a new food experience. She couldn't control how people used the tech she was creating, and had never been able to. It would be something to address once they had a prototype ready, maybe even after the product went out into the market, based on user feedback. And that brought her back to the need of the hour.

'Will you introduce me to Harmony Li, now that I've heard you out?'

'Is this the only way forwards for your project?' Good Cheer Eria said softly.

'Yes.'

'Does your chef friend, Saraswati, think so, too?'

'Sarsawati, um… She quit.'

'What?' Good Cheer Eria's eyes widened.

'Yeah, didn't accept my apology.'

'Well, that won't do at all,' Good Cheer Eria said. 'I thought you were working together again.'

'No, sadly…'

'Then you really haven't made amends,' Good Cheer Eria said, shaking her head. 'Ko. I need you to do better before I help you out on this project.'

'That makes no sense at all,' Serenity Ko said tersely, catching herself before she snapped.

'It's all about intention,' Good Cheer Eria said serenely. 'You need to put positivity out into the universe if you want to do any good, and this is where you start.'

Serenity Ko balled her hands into fists on her lap, exhaled slowly, and tried to keep her temper in check. She stared at her future sister-in-law in stony silence.

'I'm sorry, but I won't help you until you help the Earth woman first.'

'She has a job, she's happy there,' Serenity Ko whined.

'In that den full of xenophobes?'

'She quit that restaurant,' Serenity Ko mumbled. 'I'm sure she has a new job… *somewhere?*'

Good Cheer Eria smiled. 'I trust you'll do the right thing.'

'What right—'

'Find her. Convince her you mean your apology. Get her a job here.'

'How in all of sur-fucking Uru...' Serenity Ko bit down the rest of her words at the expression on Good Cheer Eria's face, lacing the rest of her silent thoughts on the matter with expletives. She tapped her foot restlessly on the floor. 'Fine,' she said. 'I'll try and get her back on the team. But if I do, you'll introduce me to Harmony Li?'

'We have a deal.' Good Cheer Eria smiled brightly.

Serenity Ko took her to the pantry for kaapi, then showed her out before returning and ordering a long black filter-foam with a double espresso shot. She slumped over her stool at the counter.

Trust Good Cheer Eria to go all fucking Saint of the Light on her. No wonder Optimism Rihan loved her. Dream team, really, each nicer than the other in their do-gooder anti-grav shoes, floating miles above the rest of this sur-fucked planet.

'Bad day?' Boundless Ano asked.

'You're still here?'

'Filling in for Mona; she's running late. Aren't you glad to see me?'

Serenity Ko snorted, then lapsed into a moody silence. 'Do you really think humans are capable of transformation?' she finally asked.

'Yeah, why not?' Boundless Ano said. 'If the Earth-humans could give rise to the Nakshatrans...'

Serenity Ko's shoulders slumped. She sagged forwards, hunching over her tall coffee mug and stirring it listlessly— and pointlessly, since she never took her kaapi with sucre. 'So everyone's capable of transforming except me, huh?'

'Whoa! I didn't say that.'

'Didn't have to.'

'Things are that bad?'

'Don't ask.'

Serenity Ko studied the six glittering rings on her friend's long, tan fingers. Each stone was from a different asteroid mine in the Osmos Girdle, orbiting Suriya between Primus's neighbouring planet, Harid, and the outer planets in the Suriyan system. Each stone represented a different voluntary journey across the Arc, and every Primian had earned at least one ring for their mandatory service to the observation and protection of their home planet. Not Serenity Ko, and maybe that's why she was so broken, unable to see beyond the giant flowmetal network that was Uru.

No, I'm blaming other things for what I am, again. She sighed, utterly despondent.

'Okay, I'm sorry, but I'm going to ask,' Boundless Ano said. 'What's going on?'

The words cascaded out of her: the ridiculous ambition of her Immersive Reality food idea; the agony of wanting to prove herself worthy of belonging—not only to her peers, now, but to her family, and on this planet; her shoddy treatment of Saraswati Kaveri; Good Cheer Eria's remonstrations; and really, how her project was going to be an utter disaster.

'I don't even know why I'm telling you this,' she moaned. 'We aren't even friends.'

'Well, we used to be.'

'I'm sure I fucked that up, too.'

'You did. Remember when you got into XP Inc.?'

'Yeah.'

'I said I was going to be a Wanderer. And you yelled at me and told me I was abandoning my sick mother.'

'Fuck. I'm sorry.'

'You weren't entirely wrong—I always feel guilty when I take to the Arc. But you were kinda cruel about it.'

'It wasn't my place to judge.'

'No, it really wasn't. It's all right, though. It's never too late to make amends,' Boundless Ano said kindly. He picked up Serenity Ko's empty kaapi mug, and started blending another long black filter-foam for her.

'Thank you,' she said softly.

'You can try again with that Earth-chef, too.'

'She clearly wants nothing to do with me. It's the same story with you Wanderers.'

Boundless Ano frowned. 'You know, what happened to you—that riot you started—it wasn't personal. I mean, yes, you can be obnoxious and you probably triggered them, but tensions have been escalating for a while.'

'Why?' Serenity Ko drummed her fingers on the table. 'There's nothing wrong with sims! Or with people from Uru—heck, everyone starts their life off in Uru.'

'The Wanderers are observers and record-keepers,' Boundless Ano said. 'And over the years, we've noticed the folks in Uru straying from Nakshatran philosophy. The number of volunteer Wanderers keeps diminishing because life is more comfortable in the city. Awareness of what lies beyond—from the beauty of the Sagarra Sea to the trill-birds in the Urswood, the skit-insects and their marvellous dances around fresh morn-blossoms, and the way they all tie together to keep the balance of our world—that's *all* that keeps us from devolving into the monsters from which the Nakshatrans fled. And the *only* way to experience it, to gain that Nakshatran perspective, is to go wandering. What if wandering ceases to exist? What will stop us from devolving?'

'Um, history tells us it's bad?' Serenity Ko suggested, sipping on her fresh kaapi.

'History is easy to ignore, because it lies in our past. There have, and will always be, enough justifications for the exploitation of the natural world. Most times, it's called "progress." The more comfortable and cocooned life gets on Uru, the more human-centric our outlooks become, and the less we care about beings that aren't us.'

'But the Wanderers have comfort, too! I've read about it,' Serenity Ko said. 'Spaces every klick, communal kitchens and caravans...'

'I'm not suggesting suffering as a way of life,' Boundless Ano interjected. 'Though there are many Wanderers who might disagree. I think everything we do here—in the city, that is—is about sheltering our lives from the world beyond, from bigger questions and experiences. Even the sims designed in this building conjure custom-made dreams that make humans more insular, self-absorbed. *That's* why that riot went so badly for you.'

'Because I peddle dreams?'

'Because you peddle disconnection from reality, from all that is alive and natural. And the Wanderers don't like it.'

'But I also *enhance* reality. People get to experience things they never could because of me.'

'And so they never step out of the confines of their lives to seek it.'

'This conversation would be way more fun if we had shots and MellO,' Serenity Ko said lightly, but her mind raced with the perspective. This was a curious echo to everything Courage Na'vil had been saying about her food sim, and it was altogether discouraging.

'I'm open to that plan any time.' Boundless Ano winked. 'Though given your schedule right now, maybe next year at the Millennium High Spirits Pop Up.'

'What the fuck is that?'

'Come on, your grandmother must have told you about it already.'

Serenity Ko experienced a twinge of guilt. She hadn't returned Ammamma's thoughtstreams all nava.

'It's part of the Millennium Festival? A whole alcohol-fuelled nava, pop-up style in Heart Square, to celebrate two thousand years of Primian drinking culture. It'll probably be more popular than all those live re-enactments of the Nakshatran landing and epic poetry performances, *definitely* more popular than the entire sinfonia season dedicated to Primian music history—first performance is in two navas, and it's the *Galactic Heroes Concerto*.' Boundless Ano rolled his eyes, then added cheerfully, '*Maybe* it'll face stiff competition from the special episode of *Interstellar MegaChef*—winner gets to cater the Millennium Feast, and all.'

'Don't remind me of that,' Serenity Ko moaned. 'It's *all* Kube can talk about. Application's due soon, we need to finalise the design philosophy yesterday, and if we get on the show, it's our deadline for the prototype.'

Boundless Ano whistled. 'Nine Virtues! That's the big leagues. You'll be up against the best chefs from the galaxy!'

'Wait, what was that last one?' Serenity Ko snapped into alertness.

'The bit about the best chefs in the galaxy?' Boundless Ano laughed. 'I mean, no pressure, but—'

'The best chefs from the galaxy...' Serenity Ko repeated, her mind racing.

'Look, you're not going to have a meltdown, are you?'

'Gotta go, Ano. Thanks!' Serenity Ko hopped off her barstool. 'I owe you a drink, and before the Festival, even. I'll stream you.'

'What did I say?' Boundless Ano called after her.

'Everything that counts.'

She half-rushed, half-skipped out the pantry. Good Cheer Eria wanted Saraswati back on the team. Serenity Ko *needed* Saraswati back on the team. Saraswati might want absolutely nothing to do with her, and that was regrettable, but maybe, just maybe, she'd jump at the chance to get even on *Interstellar MegaChef*. It was less than half a chance, but Serenity Ko was going to take it.

Flavour. Texture. Visual.
That's all you need to make a meal an experience.
Food is easy.

2045 Anno Earth, Year 1970 Interstellar Era

THIRTY-ONE

Don't do it, Kili streamed.

'It's called *Interstellar MegaChef: The Millennium Feast Special*.'

Don't. Do not. *Do not do it*. Kili pummelled my thoughtstream with time-lapsed vids of exploding stars.

'It's part of the Millennium Festival. The entire known universe will be watching. We have the most exciting thing to happen to food since the origins of cooking. We can win this.' Serenity Ko's hair had come loose from its braid, and was fluttering into her eyes in the breeze. 'But I can't do it alone. I need you.'

I turned my gaze away. Suriya kissed the sky an incandescent pink, Ibnis a great luminous globe sinking into it, resembling a scoop of thenganut ice cream. Kili's many-hued frame was resplendent, shimmering chrome-green-and-red where he hovered above me. The suriana trees lining the strip of Arc around my hex cast shadows across the ground. The buildings rippled and transformed slowly, their flowmetal tech seamlessly integrating with the dawn, always readjusting, ever flexible. I wondered what it would be like to flow with such ease.

'Think of it as revenge,' Serenity Ko said, her voice rising over the trill of bluebuls and the burbling of silverwings.

Do not, Kili said.

'You can face down those stupid, elitist judges with an undeniable food revolution.'

No need to, Kili said.

'You can win and show them you should have won right from the start.'

She's manipulating you.

I shuffled my feet. I'd avoided Serenity Ko since her nonsensical apology. It had been far easier to do when she wasn't standing right outside my door, interrupting what would have been an otherwise pleasant morning walk. I crossed my arms over my chest and looked her straight in the eyes.

'It's going terribly, isn't it?' I asked.

'You have no idea.'

'Oh, I think I can imagine.'

'I have no idea how it all works. Flavours, blends, feelings: fuck me, it's rocket science,' she moaned, then kicked at the ground.

'You're only here because you need someone to fill the flavour void,' I said.

'I need *you*.' Serenity Ko pouted. 'You're really good at what you do, plus you've never *once* treated me like an idiot for not knowing a single thing about food. Everyone else does.'

'So you want someone who's going to tolerate your bullshit, but never call you out for being incompetent, or rude, or downright insufferable.'

'I, er...'

'This has nothing to do with whether I want revenge or not.'

'But do you?'

You do not.

Serenity Ko's deep brown eyes glimmered with light. She jutted her chin forwards, and the expression on her face was a curious mixture of desperation and hope. 'Don't you want to show them that they were wrong?'

I did, and I knew it, and she and Kili knew it, too. I didn't want to say it out loud.

'I see it in you. The desperate need to prove yourself, *to win*, to let the world know they can't push you around or take you for granted. Because you're fucking good at what you do, and all you're looking for is your moment to shine,' Serenity Ko pressed on. 'I'm sorry for being such a horrible person to work with. I'm working on not being a complete star-fucker. I can't promise I've changed overnight, but I can promise that this will change your life.'

A restless wind brought about a cascade of suriana flowers, purple and yellow petals streaming down from the trees around us.

I was working with Curiosity Zia and Courage Oslo again, under the firm condition that I would only be in the back of the house, preferably wearing a hoodie or a masquerade disguise from the wretched sim prototype Serenity Ko had sent me. They'd happily acquiesced.

I'd turned in my application to live at the Faith of the Light commune. I wanted to move spaces as soon as possible, but there was a waiting list, so I'd been using my time to brush up on their philosophy, and to concoct an appropriate story about religious epiphany, if asked.

I figured this was a good enough way to lie low until I could get off this planet and find a new home. I'd have to falsify my identity again, and I didn't know where to begin—Primian systems didn't seem as straightforwardly bribable as those I'd left behind on Earth. And I was cringing on the inside at the thought of leaving; I'd have to let go of my dreams as a chef for the billionth time, on the run to who-knows-where, for who-knows-how-long. I needed time and space to regroup.

And yet, a yawning hunger opened up in me at Serenity Ko's offer.

I could do something bigger than any other living chef ever had. I could change the meaning of food; not just on Primus, but across the galaxy. I could do it in style, in front of a public audience, before a panel of judges that had humiliated me in the past.

Revenge isn't worth it, Kili cautioned. He burbled disapprovingly, then gently descended to eye level. His emote-screen displayed a pair of big green eyes. _This is an unnecessary adventure into a world of pain._

I know, I said miserably. _But I want it._

Why?

Because if it works, I'll finally know I'm worth it.

Kili sighed.

At the back of my mind, a griping paranoia grasped my wild imaginings of success. Jog Tunga had also specifically instructed me to stay on the food sim project. That *did not* bode well, but if it succeeded, if I changed the universe with it, then I could finally shake off the hold that all of them— my family, my home world, my disgraced past—had on me. My old dreams that had pushed me to go on *MegaChef* in the first place returned. If I was too big to bully, then *surely* my parents wouldn't be able to force me to leave?

I made a snap decision. I exhaled slowly. 'I'll need to talk to Zia and Oslo first.'

'Great, whoever they are. Thank you.' Serenity Ko's shoulders sagged, and the frown lines creasing her forehead relaxed.

'Doesn't mean I forgive you. Or that we're friends,' I said.

'Understood.'

'Any obnoxious behaviour—from you *or* any of your teammates—and I walk.'

'Yes.'

'Tell me, then. How badly is it going?'

* * *

SERENITY KO REALLY hadn't been kidding about Feast Inc. being in a shambles. It was all over the place; the kind of thing that was bound to happen when a bunch of enthusiasts reduced food and food experiences to algorithms. I had to make them take several steps back to understand the basics of flavour.

'Flavour includes taste, but that's just one component,' I said, while a team of designers took copious notes, as if I were lecturing them in a university, and not in a swanky office with flashing lights and sim equipment everywhere. I'd sent them recommended reading and watching by the armload; they'd all consumed Grace Menmo's *At Home in the Kitchen*, studying all the food science without internalising any of the softer principles she'd talked about. I made them build me an experimental kitchen, introducing them to the basic principles of taste, like why a bira went so well with salted maccanuts.

'The salt tamps down the bitterness of the bira,' I said. 'It opens up other flavours in each brew.'

And then I'd revealed the complexity of "flavour" to them. I made them do a blind taste test of the same set of ingredients—the first time round, pinching their noses to cut off their sense of smell; the second time round, with their sense of smell accessible. 'So much of flavour, of the experience of food, is also visual and olfactory,' I revealed, as I watched their reactions. It was like the sun rising after a long winter in the Arctic Circle back on Earth. 'Of course,' I added, 'taste receptors on the tongue are the primary participants. And contrary to popular belief, there are way more than just the basic salty, sweet, sour and bitter ones.'

Optimism Sah'r had rapidly made changes to the code she and her team had been writing, to include triggering the olfactory nerve alongside the taste receptors. I worked to help them understand how to trigger multiple receptors at once, depending on the food being consumed, and to what degree each receptor would need to be stimulated. I was playing with food science like I'd never done before—building a mathematical model through trial and error, informed guesswork, and years of experience as a professional chef. And I couldn't wait to go back into a kitchen and fit everything I was learning into my process.

Courage Na'vil's team had developed their neuropsych 'mesh'—the tech that linked physical stimulation to feelings and memories—and I'd helped the design team on their flavour-emotion matrix, which had, up until that point, been beyond rudimentary, and filled with assumptions.

'Everyone reacts to flavours differently,' I said, and it was like I was addressing a primary school classroom. 'No two people consume the same flavour pairings the same way.'

I'd spelled out the role personal history and culture played in responses to flavours. I'd broken down how, even though a complete dish was an amalgamation, a sum of its individual parts, the people consuming it could still zero in on a single taste, or a single sensory experience that evoked memory. 'The theatre of food isn't just about pretentious, fancy experiences,' I said. 'From fine dining restaurants to home cooking, even the visual of steam rising from a broth, or bubbles frothing in a drink, evokes flavour.'

'We can't do that with edibites,' Serenity Ko objected.

'I'd drop the edibites if I were you,' I said.

'But then food isn't an Immersive Reality experience.' She scowled. 'Feast Inc. becomes just an enhancement to all the existing visual and olfactory cues from the real world.'

'So?'

'So? *So?* This tech is about going back to basics, removing the need for skill in the kitchen, delivering flavour with soulful thoughts and memories and all, without any fancy food needing to exist on the plate in front of you!' Serenity Ko exclaimed.

'You're pretty much telling me you want to make my job redundant,' I said.

'Yes! No. I want to help people connect with their memories without having to make an effort. Besides, people will always want real food; this will just give them another way to eat.'

'Most memories of food are evoked by the effort, by the process of *making it,* either alone or with a loved one. Or by the shared experience of eating it, together with a loved one.'

'You sound like my grandmother,' Serenity Ko sulked.

'I think what Serenity Ko is trying to say is that food, as it exists today, relies on access to natural resources,' Courage Praia ventured. 'It can be resource-constrained and culturally elitist. We want to level that experience.'

I raised an eyebrow skeptically.

'It isn't about replacing cooking,' Courage Praia carried on politely. 'It's about offering a substitute for those who can't. Or for those who want to try something new.'

'Is that really the intention?'

'Yes,' Serenity Ko said. 'Think about it this way. You're from Earth, and you never really had access to Primian food until you got here. Eating it, at least. But what if that could change? What if you could experience Primian flavours and textures—a Berry-anna entirely simulated by your brain? Imagine being in the Uru and Beyond Marketplace, halfway across the galaxy, and experiencing life on Primus while you savour a sim version on Earth. It could open up our universe to cultural experiences, without ever requiring you to travel.'

'It could build empathy.' Courage Praia smiled. 'I'd love to see what life is like on Earth.'

I hesitantly conceded the point. I still had other reservations, though. Everything about this project seemed focused on changing the meaning of food from every single way I'd ever understood it, regardless of culture. On Earth we used whole ingredients, while Primians infused ras into nutrition-rich layers, spheres and terrines of all kinds, but ultimately, all cooking came down to combining flavours in different proportions, to creating visually rich, stimulating, texturally complex edible experiences. But Feast wanted to present some kind of macro-nutrient-rich compound, and induce the *idea* of flavour, while delivering none of it on the plate. It made me uneasy, but its glorious, positively insane ambition filled me with a feverish excitement.

Serenity Ko then dragged me into a meeting with Harmony Li, the chlorosapient who'd invented edibites— the macro-nutrient-packed superfood designed to help humanity work towards self-reliance.

'Do you know why the chlorosapient transformation to edibites isn't mandatory, or immediate, or ever total, despite the Faith's belief in self-reliance?' He regarded us from under his bushy eyebrows, his long grey hair framing his face in an immaculate bob that seemed like it had been ironed into place. His cheeks glowed green, and his mods glittered on his arms like sleeves. 'Years ago, around the time I first developed edibites, they were licensed by a now-defunct fitness org—Galactic Glutes—as the ultimate diet food. They took a compound I designed to gradually *liberate* humanity from its parasitic reliance on plants and vat-meats for food, and turned it into a way to *shame* people into conforming to some arbitrary fitness and beauty standard. This is the early days; probably before either of you were born.' He sipped on water, the veins in his hands standing out beneath his paper-thin skin.

'Everyone tried it—celebrities and influencers, regular folks in Uru. And they wound up with eating disorders by the dozen. Ever heard of organic food processing disorder? That's when the human digestive system can't process non-formulaic nutrition—thousands of people obsessed with the diet struggled to eat normal, natural food while coming off it. What about flavour dysphoria?' He seemed to regard our blank expressions with amusement. 'That's when the natural food you're eating doesn't trigger the right taste receptors, because your tastebuds have been addled by supplements. It sounds silly, unserious, but it created a wave of food aversion, a proper health crisis.'

His shoulders slumped. 'I was young, back then. Foolish. They told me they wanted to license it to *augment* their meal plans, not replace food altogether. Naïve of me to believe them. I didn't take it lying down. Like I said, they're now defunct.'

He leaned forwards, looking from Serenity Ko to me, as the silence spun out heavily, like pasta made from dough that was far too dense. 'Don't make me do the same thing to you,' he said at last.

XP Inc. licensed the product shortly afterward. As soon as the deal was inked, we sent out our application for the *MegaChef* special episode, sneaking it in just under the deadline.

'It's all thanks to you,' Serenity Ko said generously.

'Liar,' I shot back.

Liar, Kili echoed. _She's buttering you up._

'It's true. Good Cheer Eria refused to introduce me to him unless I brought you back on board.'

'Nice to know how strategic that decision was.'

'That's not what I meant,' Serenity Ko said, pouting, and wandered off to review Curiosity Nenna's sim-library for a Primian Gateau. They'd compiled a list of two hundred Primian staples, from snacks to elaborate entrees and delicate desserts. Thanks to Optimism Sah'r's nanotech, each dish would trigger a different set of olfactory and taste cues, simulating the sensory experiences associated with eating it by directly pushing the right buttons on the relevant nerve endings. Courage Na'vil's mesh would link this physical sensation to an individual's emotional associations with each dish, spawning their memories. And Serenity Ko's sim-library would slide into that field of memory, supplying everything from visual experiences to music to accompany the sensation of eating each dish.

It seemed terribly complicated to me, but I had to admit, I was having the best time since I'd arrived in Uru, putting it all together. And then I invited them to explore texture and mouthfeel with me. Optimism Sah'r was thrilled at the prospect of refining her code.

I'm glad it's working for you, Kili said. _Even if it directly contradicts every single one of your beliefs about food,_ he added darkly.

It was end-nava, and I was crouched over the little gas burner in Courage Oslo and Curiosity Zia's space, batter-frying plantains, a simple snack I'd loved back on my home world. The pair had discovered the Earth-vegetable at Uru and Beyond, and streamed me in excitement. I was going to make them the best damned bajjis a la Daxina they'd ever tasted. Possibly the *only* bajjis they'd ever tasted, for that matter.

It was pouring rain outside, and the smell of damp mud and fresh foliage had prompted me to shamelessly ask if they'd be willing to host an impromptu Earth-style chai and bajjis party. They'd gleefully agreed, so the whole crew was gathered around their space, and delightful murmurs of conversation filled the air behind me, punctuated by the steady thrumming of raindrops upon the window.

Hearing the hot oil sizzle, watching the batter turn golden brown, and even physically gathering the bajjis up in a small strainer felt like release, after the constraints of Primian cuisine at Nonpareil, and the technobabble of my work on Feast Inc.

'That is the best smell that has ever filled this damned kitchen,' Curiosity Zia said, hovering in the arched doorway.

'Agreed.' Courage Oslo sipped on a cup of Earth-chai. I'd made it the traditional way, which didn't involve micro-frothed nutromilk and tea-leaf ras. Dry tea-leaves steeped and combined—way better than the Primian alternative, at least in my estimation, even without the natural milk.

'So you're back working with that horror story?' Boundless Baz asked.

What he said, Kili echoed.

'She's not too bad, this time round,' I replied, and I meant it. Something had changed within her, and while I didn't know what it was, I was glad of it.

Boundless Baz snorted. 'I'll believe it when I see it.'

'Better than Chaangte, though,' XX-29 murmured, and I shot xir a grateful look. My friends from Nonpareil had taken a few hours off before service, and it was good to see them—it felt like it'd been an age.

'I'm not trying to be critical, Saraswati, but—'

'Uh oh,' Courage Oslo laughed, cutting off his partner.

'But. You could have just stuck with us. We're nice people, we respect you and your culture, and sure, we're a small establishment, but at least we aren't trying to replace food with... *not-food,*' Curiosity Zia said.

I gathered up the bajjis in a small bowl, lined with tissue to soak up the excess oil, and took them out to where nearly everyone was seated around the coffee table, using the activity to buy time while I tried to cobble together an appropriate answer, the kind that would be genuine without revealing the truth—the unkind belief that I was intended for bigger things.

'We've had such a great time with you in the kitchen over the past nava or so,' she continued. 'And really, how do you know how this tech is going to turn out?'

'What Zia's trying to say,' Courage Oslo interjected, earning him an angry look from his partner, 'is that you aren't in charge of this project. You can't control the direction it goes in. What if it skews the very idea of food towards something only people with lots of money can afford, because it's a paid service on XP Inc.? That way, only people with access to the tech, and the means to afford a subscription, will be able to access an entire range of flavour experiences.

'Or worse, what if it cheapens them to such an extent that the sim becomes preferable to the real thing? The way I see it—as one chef to another—we'd stop making Berry-annas in our kitchen at The New Palette if our food was more expensive than a popular sim. There'd be no point, because we'd be wasting money on ingredients, for dishes nobody will want to buy.'

'I—'

'What if our hex gardens become irrelevant, and people lose touch with the natural world? I don't mean it in the Wanderers sense, not entirely, but for growing fruits and vegetables. Imagine a world that can't appreciate how a tiny seed, or a bit of root or stem, covered in dirt, watered every day, and exposed to sur-light, can transform into a source of nutrition, translated into love on a plate. It's part of an eternal cycle. People might lose sight of that, and then lose sight of their part in it.' Boundless Baz looked solemn.

'Ooh, these are delicious!' XX-29 chimed in, consuming the spiced snack in xir ever-mysterious way through xir mechanical appendage. 'Sorry,' xe continued. 'Didn't mean to interrupt.'

'I was going to say none of those things,' Curiosity Zia snapped, her eyes flashing dangerously at Courage Oslo. He quickly stuffed his mouth with a bajji, and pressed a finger to his lips, sinking into the couch. She grinned at him, then turned back to me, her brow furrowed. 'I mean, I'm worried about all those things, of course; but it gets worse, as far as I'm concerned. Have you ever been to Enceladus?' she asked.

'No.'

'Okay, history lesson. I'll try and keep it brief. I trace my ancestry back to Enceladus. There used to be a dominant religion there, very popular a few centuries ago, called Kan'suism, a kind of dream-reading that involved worshipping the unknown. Kan'su practitioners used natural hallucinogens to go on their dreamwalks—the coming of age ritual involved consuming a kannishroom, trippy stuff…' She trailed off, then shook her head. 'Turned out kannishrooms were smarter than humans; they began to take over human beings and use them as hosts to spread their spores. All kinds of nasty stuff happened—people died in the thousands, kannishroom spores were everywhere, highly infectious. There were quarantines, containment zones, mass culling, name your dystopian nightmare.'

My jaw dropped in shock. My insides shrivelled up, and the horror I was experiencing was reflected on the faces of everyone in the room, except for Courage Oslo, who seemed to have heard about this before, and just looked terribly sad.

'That was a biological evolution strategy for the kannishroom.' Curiosity Zia's voice shook. 'I don't blame the nightmare fungus, because I don't understand it. And it was hundreds of years ago. It was destroyed into extinction, and hasn't returned since. But Saras—humans, I understand.' She lowered her voice. 'You're designing a way to get inside human brains through something every human needs to survive: food.'

'Goodness, Zia. I'm so sorry, I had no idea…' I managed to choke out.

'So I can't see why you'd choose to go work on tech that could wreak such horrid destruction, when you could just come and work with us, instead,' Curiosity Zia said, angry again.

'I know, and you're right, and I wanted to, I mean, I'd really love to…' I fumbled, trying to find the right words to express why I still wanted to work on Feast, to explain why I thought the scenario she was outlining sounded completely impossible.

'I'm sorry about what happened on your planet, but I think we should cut Saras some slack, Zia,' Starlight Fantastic said. 'You know you aren't profitable yet, at the pop-up, and the poor thing has lost everything she had. Her savings, her home world... She needs to rebuild her life from nothing. Sure, money isn't *necessary* on this planet, but you don't know if she wants to live here forever or go off-world—and that *will* mean money for survival, depending on what planet she decides to live on.'

'Well, I hope they're paying you well.' Curiosity Zia glared at me, then suddenly deflated, and gave me a sudden hug. 'I'm sorry. I don't mean to put pressure on you. I understand your position; it just sucks to see you working with people who haven't respected you in the past, even if that's changed now. And on tech that could be so badly misused in the wrong hands...'

'Thanks,' I said, hugging her back.

Good time to tell them the truth about the whole refugee thing, Saras, Kili nudged.

I can't.

Your family already knows where you are. You've got nothing to lose.

I'm scared.

Of what?

Losing their respect and friendship.

The fact that they're standing up to you makes me believe they'll forgive you.

You really think so?

Yes.

I closed my eyes, scrunching them up and trying to work through my fears. 'I have a confession to make,' I said quickly.

'Oh no, you've slept with her, haven't you?' Boundless Baz groaned, passing a hand over his face.

'Huh, who?'

'The nightmare. Serenity Ko.'

'What? *No!*' I burst out laughing at the absurdity of the thought. And then a tiny part of me wondered if it was *entirely* out of the question under different circumstances. I pushed the intense rush of emotion bubbling up within me away.

'Thank goodness!' Boundless Baz exclaimed. 'Sorry, had to lighten the mood after Zia's visions of doom. Your vibe was killing the bajjis.' He raised one in her direction before stuffing his face with it.

'Wait until your home world is attacked by a malevolent fungus,' Curiosity Zia shot back, rounding on him.

I cleared my throat, but Boundless Baz and Curiosity Zia seemed to take no notice of me.

'Whatever it is, it's okay,' XX-29 said to me quietly. 'We're on your team.'

I struggled to find the right words. 'It's just...'

'Don't *need* killer shrooms on Earth,' Boundlass Baz said through a full mouth, rolling his eyes. 'We've got dictators and monarchs by the dozen. The Fleurre Dynasty in Paradiso, the Zherians in the United Federation, the fucking Godavaris in my own backyard, Daxina...'

My blood ran cold.

'You're both being incredibly rude,' Starlight Fantastic said loudly, their array turning bright red in annoyance. 'Saraswati was about to tell us something important, and you've just left her standing in the middle of the room while you bicker. After you've *all* picked on her. Look at her face; she looks like she's about to cry.'

My palms were sweaty.

'We're sorry, Saras,' Boundless Baz said, disengaging with Curiosity Zia's eyeroll. 'Tell us. We're good with anything, so long as you're not a Godavari.' He chuckled, then looked around at the other confused faces. 'Inside joke, one Earthling to another, am I right, Saras?'

My thoughts were blurry. I felt on the verge of passing out.

'Saras?' Boundless Baz said, his voice sounding very faraway and tinged with concern. 'I was just joking. Even if you are—'

'I'm going back to *MegaChef*,' I announced hurriedly, holding on to the back of a chair to steady myself. 'Serenity Ko and I just heard back from them. Our application's been accepted for the Millennium Feast Special.'

'*No!*' XX-29 moaned, directly contradicting the last thing xe'd said to me.

'Don't do it.' Courage Oslo shook his head. 'It's not worth it.'

'You don't *know* that,' Starlight Fantastic said. 'It could be different this time.'

Everyone was talking at and over each other while they argued over what was the best course of action for my career.

I can't believe you chickened out, Kili said.

It's not the right time. You heard what Baz said.

I never took you for a coward.

That's harsh.

Someone has to say it.

My closest friend whirred off my shoulder and settled as far away from me as he possibly could, tucking his wings up close to his person and seeming to shrink in size. I couldn't blame him for his disgust. The guilt uncoiled within me, squeezing my gut like a bad stomach cramp, overpowering the joyous smell of bajjis and hot tea, the pounding rain fading to the periphery of my senses.

*If we didn't dream, we'd never learn what lies out
there...*

—from "Daydreaming" by Legends of the Future

THIRTY-TWO

THE NAVAS SPED past so fast that Serenity Ko lost all track of
time. She spent most of her days with Saraswati in the XP
Inc. office, buried in holorays approximating what the Feast
experience might be once all the tech was in place, tweaking
it, nitpicking at it, stripping it down and rebuilding it. She
was designing an experience curve; everyone eating Feast
would start off with images and sounds from XP Inc.'s
databases, including homages to Nakshatran philosophy if
they were consuming Primian food, which would gradually
blend into their own personal memories while the mesh
unlocked them.

They'd chosen to introduce an intentional delay in the
meshing process. On the ethical side, it gave the mesh
sufficient time to coax personal memories without forcing
them, and feeling intrusive. On the entirely questionable
side, it also created opportunities for introducing specific
kinds of messaging in their databases, the kind that
generated revenue through advertising. It was being
experimented with in the SoundSpace design, and early
readouts were positive, so while Serenity Ko had been
unhappy to cede the argument to the suits, she really had
no defence to fall back on.

Optimism Sah'r and her tech team had delivered their
first edible prototype: an upgrade to the XP nanopill
subscription that would enable olfactory and taste receptor
stimulation. They'd embedded microscopic lines of code in

a batch of sample edibites to trigger different senses, and it had *almost* worked. Except it had been dead boring to eat—every bite of the Nakshatran Gelato they were trying to develop tasted like the same amalgam of flavours, and by the fourth handful, it was insufferable.

'Flavour has to exist in continuum,' Saraswati had said after the uninspiring tasting. 'It needs to be dynamic, retaining elements of the previous flavour experience, but constantly evolving, shifting. That's where excitement exists on any plate of food you consume today—its smooth unpredictability, like a great mellosax solo.'

Saraswati had caught her eye and smiled, and Serenity Ko had suddenly realised she was staring open-mouthed at the Earthling as if Saraswati were some kind of newly discovered genius. She'd turned a shade of deep pink, muttered about seeing to the neuropsych mesh, and disappeared from the meeting in a hurry. Dealing with Courage Na'vil was vastly preferable to processing the thoughts that followed spending too much time in the same room with Saraswati.

The longer she spent with her, the more awestruck she was by the depth of her expertise, and this was prompting unasked-for feelings in the pit of her stomach, fluttering and somersaulting like flutterwings gone rogue. And for once, it had nothing to do with how striking a figure Saraswati cut in her basic 3D-printed Primian outfits—though there was nothing wrong with her, in fact, there was more than everything right in her unruly curls and generous curves. But this was something more. Serenity Ko was beginning to suspect that she was the smartest, most passionate and opinionated human she'd ever met, and that was intriguing.

It was also unwanted. They were colleagues. She was never making that mistake again. Every once in a while, she'd find a buttercake or a jaggery tartlet at her workspace, and spot Honour Aki lurking conspicuously behind a topiary not too long after. It was hideously embarrassing. The only way to deal with him was to not make eye contact. And that wasn't what she wanted for herself and Saraswati.

'Stop it. There *is* no Saraswati and you,' she muttered to herself.

'Eh, sorry?' Boundless Ano asked from behind the kaapi counter.

'Not everything I say is meant for you to hear,' Serenity Ko snapped.

'Oh, I'm sorry, I didn't realise there were new rules for polite conversation,' Boundless Ano retorted.

'Sorry, big prototype review coming up,' Serenity Ko said, earnestly. 'Lots of pressure. Thanks for the kaapi.'

She grabbed the tray of brews—for everyone on the design team, and their partners in tech and neuropsych—and stepped into the tunnel, taking the walkway to Conference Room 4. She'd had the maintenance bots set it up like a banquet hall; circular tables surrounded by chairs, each with a holorayed tasting menu.

Everything had fallen into place in the last nava. Saraswati had worked with the tech team to specify the degree to which each flavour, in every single dish, would need to stimulate one's taste receptors and olfactory senses. It had come as quite the shock to Serenity Ko—and to the entire team—that every ingredient stimulated multiple receptors in different ways, and that taste changed in an emergent and recursive way when ingredients were mixed, depending upon the manner and proportions of their combination. As they'd standardised the recipes of each of the first fifty Primian dishes that Feast Inc. would introduce into the market, Saraswati had created mathematical matrices that evolved with every single bite, until Optimism Sah'r's team could create a flavour continuum that was satisfactory to her, for every single one of them. They called it the "flavour curve."

Serenity Ko and Courage Na'vil had paired up to make sure the mesh was optimised, syncing with the right blend of personal memories and sim-databases, and with minimal lag (apart from the intentional delay, which caused Serenity Ko and Courage Na'vil to *finally* unite on something, and wind up on the same losing side of the argument). Grace Kube had signed off on the entire database that would form the basis for all of Feast's experiences. Triumph was imminent. So were glitches, but if the proof of concept worked, then there was nothing that couldn't be ironed out. Sure, they might have to work double time if they wanted to debut Feast at *MegaChef* in a few days, but it would be worth it. They were so close to pulling it off, to changing the face of the culinary world.

Courage Praia flashed Serenity Ko a grin as she ushered the rest of their design team in. The important thing about sim-tests was to include as many people as possible—some with context, most with none. Curiosity Nenna had convinced the suits to join, and Optimism Sah'r had intentionally chosen a mix of people who were both deeply involved in and completely ignorant of the project.

As everyone took their seats, Serenity Ko knocked back a shot of MellO to calm her nerves. This was it. If this prototype worked, then it was all systems go, straight to the incredible publicity of launching on *MegaChef*—regardless of whether they won or not—and on to full production mode. She caught Saraswati's eye and smiled nervously, and Saraswati smiled back at her. Her heart raced; she felt like she was about to be sick. She grabbed a stack of plates and began to pass them around.

'Let's feast,' Serenity Ko said.

She wasn't just pleased with the prototype; she was positively ecstatic.

Curiosity Nenna sobbed into her plate of edibite while she consumed a simulated shroom-broth. 'My grandfather was a forager,' she wept. 'He'd pick fresh shrooms out in the Arc and we'd eat shroom-broth each nine-day.'

Courage Praia burst into fits of giggles through the Urswood pâté. 'We had this sweep of Arc right behind our space, and I once convinced my sister to lick a wild bitterbark tree,' they explained. 'I could see it clear as day while I was eating this… *goop*.'

Even Grace Kube had gone all misty-eyed during the dessert tasting, eating an edibite coded to taste like the perfect Primian Gateau. 'This was one of my first tasting experiences after life-saving surgery. I'm reliving the miracle of second chances right now.'

Serenity Ko knew the push to full-scale production would be a long one—as packaged food, it would need to get a ton of different approvals from the Uru Food Safety & Compliance Council, among countless other requirements. But the tech worked. She'd pulled it off.

No, that's not entirely true, she thought, lying in bed alone later that night. *I did nothing other than dream of the idea, and bring the right people together to work on it. Everyone else—especially Saraswati, they're the reason it's working at all.*

It was an odd kind of thought, a comforting one in many ways, to realise that while she might have been at the centre of it all—pulling all the different moving pieces together and fitting them in place—each of the components had been built and delivered by someone else, often with a skillset she couldn't even dream of possessing.

Curiosity Nenna had been relentless in her research while compiling the sim's experience database. Courage Praia's calm, ever-polite demeanour—something she'd written off in the past—had de-escalated conflict nearly every single day. Courage Na'vil had pushed his team to deliver a seamless mesh experience, despite his ethical concerns, which of course, he'd expressed for the billionth time even during the prototype tasting session. Optimism Sah'r had pulled off a code miracle, stimulating hundreds of taste receptors, across the spectrum of complex taste, despite edibites being a mostly flavourless substrate. Grace Kube had offered unwavering support and had been succinct and apposite in his criticisms.

And Saraswati… this would have been impossible without her. Ammamma had been right all along. Serenity Ko hadn't been equipped—not in the least—to build Feast Inc. She'd needed someone else to step in and help her create food from thin air, someone who matched her drive and ambition, and who far outclassed her on kindness and grace.

She'd never felt this way before; empowered by her own ignorance, appreciative of those who knew what she couldn't comprehend. It was oddly liberating to not know it all, to relinquish control and marvel at someone else's abilities. The burning need that had pushed her to start this project—to prove Grace Kube wrong and stick it to him, be promoted to Evocateur Extraordinaire with an unsurpassable, universe-altering sim—was fading into the back of her mind, and she rather liked the empty space it was leaving behind.

If it weren't for Saraswati, Feast Inc. would be the shittiest thing I've ever designed, Serenity Ko thought as she drifted.

She was jolted out of the best sleep she'd had in several navas by the persistent ringing of her comms.

You've got a visitor! You've got a visitor! flashed across her dash the moment she opened her eyes. She groaned, rolled out of bed, and shuffled down the stairs to open the door, running her hand through her wavy hair to try and achieve an approximation of presentability.

The flowmetal whooshed open, and she balked as her grandmother strode in in a huff.

'Is it true?' Ammamma asked roughly.

Brain still addled with sleep, and chasing an uncomfortable dream in which she and Saraswati had been seated somewhat too close upon a park bench, huddling under an umbrella in the pouring rain, Serenity Ko blinked stupidly, processing the words one at a time. 'Huh?'

'Is it true, Ko?' Ammamma repeated.

'What? No, whatever you heard, I'm not marrying Aki,' Serenity Ko mumbled stupidly.

'Who said anything about Aki? Who's Aki?' Ammamma stopped mid-stride.

'Oh, good, the rumour hasn't spread.' Serenity Ko sagged with relief. She'd returned to her workspace after the prototype test the previous day, only to find a brittlewood nose-pin placed at the centre of a love-heart made of deep purple rosinia petals. A note beside it said, *Give me another chance, and I'll give you the real thing.*

Serenity Ko had made a very dramatic show of sweeping the petals off of her desk and into the bin, and had then shredded the note laughing loudly.

'Are you okay, Ko?' Courage Praia had asked in a hushed voice.

'Laugh with me,' she'd growled, indicating the nose-pin, still at her workspace.

Courage Praia had caught the hint, and they'd both doubled over, pretending at hysteria, until Serenity Ko spotted a distinct auburn topknot rushing off in the direction of the restrooms.

'You'd think he'd understand that I'm not interested by now,' Serenity Ko had grumbled.

'Ex-boyfriend stalker?' Saraswati had smirked. 'On Earth, we have this trope in all our dramas. Girl says no, boy persists, girl eventually gives in, always a happy ending.'

'Shut up!' Serenity Ko had laughed.

'Always a happy ending.' Saraswati's lips had curled into a terribly inviting smile…

'Where are you, Ko?' Ammamma snapped her fingers in front of her face.

'Sorry, sleepy,' Serenity Ko mumbled, pushing her thoughts of Saraswati from her head.

'It's eight in the morning! How can you be sleepy? At a time like this, too!'

'Why don't you sit down, I'll make you some kaapi,' Serenity Ko suggested. Ammamma was making her dizzy, now that she'd resumed her pacing.

'Is it instant?' Ammamma asked suspiciously.

'Yes. But it's good—'

'Just water, please,' Ammamma said, though she took a seat on a tall narrow armchair. Serenity Ko, now somewhat more awake, regarded her with concern. It was an unspoken rule that nobody visited without notice unless someone had died...

'Has someone died?' she gasped, fear striking her like a thunderbolt.

'What? No, silly girl.'

'Why are you here, Ammamma?'

'Can't a grandmother visit her favourite granddaughter?'

Serenity Ko poured her a glass of water from a large jug, and took it over to her. Ammamma took a sip.

'Ammamma, we never visit without prior warning.'

'Yes, I know. I thought I'd take my chances of discovering you in a state of undress with your flavour of the week—Aki, is it?' the old lady said slyly. 'I've heard that name before.'

'*Nothing* happening there,' Serenity Ko said hurriedly.

'All right, I'll drop the civility. I'm here because I heard something, and I had to speak with you immediately.'

'Okay...'

'Your food sim project.'

'Feast?'

'Whatever you call it. I heard a rumour—nasty, silly things, those, usually entirely unfounded—about how you were planning to *replace food entirely* with edibles that spawn sims.' Ammamma laughed as if this was the funniest thing in the history of the known universe. '"Of course not," I said. I shut that down right away. "She's my grand-daughter," I said. "Even if she can't cook to save her life, she knows how central food is to Primian culture, to the culture of the universe. She'd never do something like this," I insisted.' She fixed her gaze upon Serenity Ko, who felt a tremor slide down her spine like something wet and disgusting that belonged in a cave. 'Would she? Look me in the eye and tell me that this isn't what you're doing.'

'Ammamma.'

'Say it, please.'

'Ammamma, it's not personal.'

'What?'

'It's got nothing to do with you, and it isn't intended as any disrespect to you, or to food culture anywhere in the universe. But the rumours are true.' Serenity Ko was glad her voice had held steady; her insides clenched like they were being squeezed through a jumpgate.

'You're trying to replace food?' Her grandmother's voice was dangerously low.

'Not "replace," of course not. I'm creating a new *form* of food.'

'Be serious, Ko.'

'I *am* being serious.'

Ammamma's stooped posture straightened in the chair, her eyes turning hard as stones from the Osmos Girdle. Grace Menmo regarded Serenity Ko coldly. 'Do you want me to remind you that food is a celebration, not just of our culture, but of our Nakshatran origins and the very values we stand for, that have guided us—all of humanity—for thousands of years?'

'Every single dish we're creating a sim for harkens back to our Nakshatran origins,' Serenity Ko protested. 'Visuals of Primus, music from the sinfonia, epic poetry accompany them all, until people's personal memories take over.'

'At least you aren't entirely witless,' Grace Menmo muttered. 'Have you considered that sim-food experiences will render skill in the kitchen meaningless? Everything I've worked hard to teach people over an entire lifetime will be irrelevant.'

'People always have the choice to make their own food. This is just an *option*.'

'So you say, but human history teaches us that humans pick convenience over commitment *every single time*. You're devaluing the worth of our natural produce, cheapening our culture by mass-producing it, destroying the livelihoods of hundreds of chefs across the galaxy... There are going to be chefs on strike, a positive *revolution*. It'll put a target on your back, and since I'm your grandmother, on mine. It'll discredit everything I've built my career on. But more importantly, it'll make life horribly difficult for *you*.'

'I'm doing none of those things, nobody could ever discredit you—*the* Grace Menmo—and if they want to come after me for building new ways to experience food, then let them,' Serenity Ko snapped. 'I'm creating an alternative to traditional food. It's a *choice*. It's a *fun* experience. I don't control humanity; it's up to them to decide how they want to engage with it.'

Grace Menmo laughed. 'No, you don't control humanity, dear child. That's my point, exactly. You have no idea where this could go.'

'I thought you'd be happy that I'd created an easy way to access Primian food and culture!'

'This isn't Primian food and culture,' Grace Menmo said. 'This is something else altogether; something monstrous that can be used to propagate all kinds of value systems, depending on how the sims accompanying it are designed.'

'We're going Primian first. We own the proprietary tech. Nobody can take it from us.'

'Anyone can take it from you if they've got the money to license it, foolish girl.'

'Kube would never—'

'Really, Ko?' Grace Menmo snapped. 'I thought you were smarter than this, but perhaps this is a deep-rooted flaw in our system here on Primus. Nobody needs money to survive here, so nobody knows just how valuable it can be. "Everyone can be bought for the right price." Isn't that the tagline of that Earth drama you've taken to watching? *Empire Battle?*'

'*Empire Quest*. And it's a drama, real life is nothing like it.'

'We should have sent you to university on Luna, or Mars, so you could see what life is like beyond our atmosphere.' Grace Menmo shook her head sadly. 'You know why we didn't? They charge insanely exorbitant fees for tuition and boarding. Money we don't *have*, because we *don't need it* to live well here.'

'Ammamma—'

'And I hear you're working with an Earthling chef? That planet has a history of violence inseparable from its people. Could you find *nobody* else on this planet, after all the contacts I sent your way?'

'She's got integrity,' Serenity Ko said hotly. 'And she's nothing like the Earth stereotypes we always hear about.'

'Do you know anything about her other than the fact that she *might* be a passable chef?'

'I know she believes in me. Unlike you.'

Grace Menmo deflated. 'I never said that.'

'You didn't have to,' Serenity Ko said bitterly.

Ammamma stared at her, hunched over once more, her glass of water trembling slightly in her hand. 'I believe in you, Ko,' she said softly. 'Tirelessly. Never had a moment of doubt in your ability, your intentions, your honesty. It's *other* humans I'm worried about.'

She put the glass of water down on the coffee table, then rose from her chair abruptly. 'I'm sorry I intruded. I guess I could have just streamed you.'

'Let's go get breakfast?' Serenity Ko suggested weakly.

'Not now, kiddo. I've rather lost my appetite.'

She swept from the room and was gone, and Serenity Ko was filled with a sense of foreboding.

Interviewer: What does it take to survive—No, I
  rephrase, to *thrive* as a celebrity chef here on
  Primus?
Grace Aurelle (laughing): Savagery.
Interviewer: Any words of advice for aspiring chefs who
  want to follow in your footsteps?
Grace Aurelle: Sharpen your knives, dearies. And don't
  forget to smile.

—*The Long Interview* feat. Grace Aurelle,
The Consummate Cuisinologist

THIRTY-THREE

THE MORNING OF the *MegaChef* special episode was the
rainy kind; Serenity Ko's ideal weather streamed down in
sheets outside while she prepped for what promised to be
an epic victory. Or so she hoped, despite trying her very
best not to be foolishly optimistic.

Her grandmother had been ominously cheerful at family
dinner the previous evening, even whistling as she brought
out the five-layered maccanut crumble she'd made for dessert.

'You've done something horrible, haven't you?' Serenity
Ko had asked uncertainly.

'I'd never sabotage you, Ko. Nine Virtues, how little you
think of me!' Ammamma had sulked. 'Just because I show
you some tough love every now and again.'

'You're far too cheerful, given our last conversation.'

'Your parents insisted I play nice. Don't want to
demotivate you before your big day tomorrow.'

'So you still hate what I'm doing?'

'"Hate" is a strong word, kiddo. Never use it lightly. I
disagree with you, and think nothing good can come of what

392

you're doing, but that doesn't mean I don't love you. I'm still rooting for you.' Ammamma had hugged her. 'I'm sure you'll win, in fact. I just hope you don't come to regret it.'

Serenity Ko knew regrets as well as the back of her hand, and she knew she wanted none as far as their showing at the *Interstellar MegaChef: Millennium Feast Special* went. She'd been through the rules a dozen times with Saraswati and they'd brainstormed the perfect presentation.

Participants had to create an interpretation of the traditional Nakshatran Banquet. It would need to simultaneously celebrate Primian history and look to the Primian future. Serenity Ko surmised that they had the "future" angle covered, so long as they could replicate the flavours and trigger the right blend of personal memories and sim-experiences.

Participants were allowed to take part as teams, but only one contestant was permitted to be in the actual kitchen, doing all the cooking. That had been a no-brainer; Serenity Ko was content to lurk backstage, or side stage, or wherever, far away from kitchen appliances. They'd have three hours to cook, and that presented a bit of a problem because there was really nothing *to* cook.

After going in circles for hours on end, and letting the wider team in on the discussion, Curiosity Nenna had suggested a dramatic solution. It was *ideal*. The prototype was tweaked to integrate it into their plan, and Saraswati had spent the rest of the intervening days preparing to pull it off.

And finally, there was the matter of giving the judges access to the prototype. They'd invited all peripheral equipment to be submitted prior to the episode, and Serenity Ko had duly shipped them a small envelope filled with Feast Inc.-enhanced nanopills. She was also carrying a small, neatly packaged cooler filled with their secret—and only—ingredient.

She looked in the mirror to make sure she was suitably attired: a long, high-necked tunic was cinched at the waist with a beaded belt, her leggings were her least ripped pair, tucked into her boots. She'd enhanced her high, curved cheeks with a touch of makeup, and accented her deep brown eyes with some green shimmer-gel in honour of the chlorosapient tech they were licensing. Her long, straight hair was swept back in a high braid, woven through with luminescent rocks from the uninhabited moon Ibnis. She supposed she looked presentable enough to be Grace Menmo's granddaughter. The only thing making her nervous was that her grandmother would be in the live audience, along with her family.

Good-luck streams flooded her comms from everyone she knew. The family comms group pinged nonstop.

We're so proud of you, Dad said.

No matter how this goes, you're a winner, Appa said.

Amma sent her a string of hearts exploding, then promptly shared a baby pic of Serenity Ko grinning with her two front teeth missing.

Ah, how they grow up to be monsters... Ammamma said.

Good Cheer Eria called to wish her luck, and told her to celebrate her eventual win by taking a nava-end off at the Faith of the Light gardens. On impulse, and much to her surprise, Serenity Ko actually agreed.

Grace Kube told her he'd see her on set. Honour Aki sent her a terse, tentative message wishing her well. She ignored him without a shred of guilt.

Where are you? she pinged Saraswati.

They were going to meet at her space, then take the flowtram together to the studio at Collective Two.

Grabbing us some kaapi. See you outside in five.

Serenity Ko couldn't wait. She was far too excited to sit still until there was a knock on the door. She grabbed an umbrella and stepped outside, peering through the rain and humming distractedly to herself. Her notifications on the Loop were chiming nonstop, so she disabled them, surprised at how good it felt to engage with reality instead.

A tall, curvy figure cut through the rain, drawing the entirety of Serenity Ko's attention to her. She brimmed with confidence, like a blazing star striking a path through a cold and indifferent universe. Even awkwardly balancing two cups of kaapi in one hand and an umbrella in the other, she was striking. She wore a stiff, architectural, flat-collared black top, buttons running down one side in embossed bronze. The long sleeves ended just below the elbow, and Serenity Ko noticed just how muscled her forearms were for the first time. Long, flared gold pants and a pair of black boots completed the outfit. She was trailed by a little chrome and red blur bobbing in the air beside her. Serenity Ko took care to shut her mouth and look away so she wouldn't be caught staring.

'Thanks,' she mumbled as Saraswati handed her a kaapi.

Hey, Kili.

Hello.

'You look good,' Saraswati said. 'It should be you on camera.'

Serenity Ko's insides soared at the compliment, and she smacked them down. 'Me? So I can set the kitchen on fire, sure.'

'I've already done that,' Saraswati laughed. It sounded like an otherworldly chime. How had she never noticed that?

Because that's the kind of shit that gets you in trouble. Stop it. It's just the adrenaline.

'You look perfect,' she said, and meant it. 'You're going to kill it.'

'I hope so,' Saraswati said, smoothing down the front of her shirt. 'I want to get this day over with.'

'Be careful what you wish for,' Serenity Ko said with a chuckle. 'When you win, you'll never want this day to end.'

'If.'

'When.'

They strolled down to the flowtram station in an easy silence, or so Serenity Ko supposed. What she really wanted to do was make Saraswati laugh in that tinkling way again, but that was a stupid idea, and she had nothing clever or witty to say, so she shut her mouth. They rode the train to the studio, and as it drew near, Saraswati took a deep breath, her face drawn and pale. On impulse, Serenity Ko grabbed her hand and gave it a squeeze. 'Don't worry. This is our day. *Your day.*'

Saraswati squeezed back, and it was like being electrocuted. Serenity Ko stifled a gasp, hyperaware of how sweaty her palm was, and counted to three in her head before removing her hand from Saraswati's, hoping it had all been one cool, smooth, casual gesture.

The studio resembled every other building on the street until Serenity Ko stepped inside. The ceilings were ridiculously high, and the foyer resembled the pics of the Faith of the Light cathedral that Good Cheer Eria kept sharing on their family comms channel. Dozens of people rushed about, some alone, some in small groups doing the typical Ur-drama thing of striding through corridors, holding intense conversations. The energy was intense; it was as if everyone was firing on all cylinders nonstop, and Serenity Ko suspected there might be a healthy proportion of performance-enhancing drugs involved. She stopped dead in her tracks, suddenly and inexplicably intimidated.

'Yeah, it was like this the last time I was here, too,' Saraswati whispered. 'Don't worry, it's all noise.'

She touched her elbow, and Serenity Ko nearly jumped out of her skin.

'Sorry, didn't mean to startle you.' Saraswati withdrew her hand.

'Yeah, um. You lead the way?' Serenity Ko said meekly.

This was the realm of celebrity, and as much as she loved the spotlight, it felt like she'd crossed some kind of invisible barrier that had always separated her life, and its behind-the-sims ambitions, from public view. Worse still, she felt hideous, as all the beautiful people disappeared into secret rooms behind exclusive access doorways. Shabby and underdressed, with bad posture.

Saraswati took the walkway into the heart of the building, flashing their *MegaChef* authorisation before half a dozen security scanners along the way. Somehow, she seemed to *belong*. She moved with complete ownership of the space around her, while Serenity Ko did her best to blend into all the walls.

They stopped at an unremarkable door. Saraswati passed her palm over a scanner and the flowmetal pulled apart. She stepped inside, and Serenity Ko followed.

The breath rushed out of her all at once. A pair of tall flowmetal doors trailing vines stood at the far end of the room. Small groups of people milled about, some sipping on kaapi, all of them making conversation. A man rushed to their side to verify their credentials. Serenity Ko let Saraswati handle all the registration and paperwork.

'Who'll be the primary participant?' the man asked. His nametag read *Harmony Davi, He/Him*.

'Me. Saraswati Kaveri.'

'And your tech will stay with your teammate?'

'That's correct.'

'It'll need to be disabled.'

'He.'

'I'm sorry?'

'*His* name's Kili, and my comms with him will be disabled.'

'Right, good, so the live audience is on the other side of those doors. There's a timer; when it hits two minutes, get ready to go on, yeah?'

'I know, I've been here before. We've met before.'

'Oh! I know you! You're the Earthling. *Firestarter.*' He grinned.

'One and the same.'

'Do you need me to switch to Vox?'

Saraswati shot the man a funny look. 'Ur-speak is just fine, thank you.'

'Sure. Nice to have you back,' Harmony Davi said, switching to Vox, anyway. Serenity Ko noticed that his expression seemed somewhat strained, and scowled at him.

'You'll enter together, then you take your place at Cook Station Seven. Got it?' Harmony Davi said to Saraswati. He turned his attention to Serenity Ko and Kili, switching back to Ur-speak. 'And you two will take your place at Team-Mate Station Seven. It's all marked, can't miss it.'

Serenity Ko nodded coldly. She didn't like the guy. In fact, she didn't like this environment one bit.

'Do you need anything to be added to your cook station?' Harmony Davi asked Sarswati, in Vox again. 'Any non-standard tech, ingredients or equipment?'

'Just this,' Serenity Ko cut in, handing over the cooler she'd been lugging around.

'Thanks. The intern will come round with the jackets,' the producer said, and stalked away.

Serenity Ko looked over at Saraswati. 'That was obnoxious. You okay?'

Saraswati shrugged in response.

'Sorry I dragged you back to this place. It's got dodgy vibes all over. I had no idea.'

Saraswati laughed bitterly at that. 'Primian culture, I guess.'

'Ouch.'

Saraswati's eyes widened as she caught sight of something behind Serenity Ko's shoulder. 'What—?'

'Oh, look, the dregs of the universe are here,' a voice

said. Serenity Ko whirled around and was confronted by the sight of Good Cheer Chaangte, impeccably dressed in a black, minimalist Primian jumpsuit, gemstones from the Osmos Girdle glittering at its collar.

'Nice to see you again,' Saraswati said icily.

'I wish I could say the same,' Good Cheer Chaangte sneered. For the first time, Serenity Ko saw the chef for who she was. Her fine blonde hair fell across her forehead in bangs. She wasn't wearing her spectacles, and her eyes were lined with purple shadows, pale beneath all the makeup. Her tall, willowy frame stooped slightly, and her mouth was an unhappy line. She radiated an insatiable hunger.

Saraswati set her jaw and looked Good Cheer Chaangte up and down with open hostility. The tension between them was so thick, Serenity Ko could swear the air was solid.

'I'm going to enjoy crushing you,' Good Cheer Chaangte said. She turned to Serenity Ko. 'And I see you've picked a side; congratulations. It's nothing personal, but I'll crush you, too.'

'Did Pavi and Amol give you permission to say that?' Saraswati asked innocently.

'I quit,' Good Cheer Chaangte said dismissively.

'Ah, so they fired you. Good on them.'

'When I win, I'll destroy their precious careers,' Good Cheer Chaangte hissed. 'And your non-existent one.'

'Nice to see you haven't changed, Chaangte,' Saraswati replied. 'Hold onto that positive spirit.'

'At least I have talent,' Good Cheer Chaangte shot back.

'Long way between talent and success.'

'And you count your last appearance on this show as a "success"?' Good Cheer Chaangte rolled her eyes.

'It takes more than the opinions of a handful of people to determine success. Or to throw off a *real* chef,' Saraswati said curtly, much to Serenity Ko's surprise. Her friend— were they friends, yet?—seemed to have an entirely different side to her in this environment, and Serenity Ko hated to admit it, but it was incredibly attractive.

'Ah, typical primitive Earthling. Don't know when to quit and go back home.'

'And here I'd heard Primians were *civilised*.'

'Can't wait to watch you lose. Again.' Good Cheer Chaangte grinned nastily. 'And this time, to me.'

'The feeling's mutual. Good luck.'

Saraswati turned around and stalked away, and Serenity Ko followed her as if drawn into her orbit, pausing only to shoot Good Cheer Chaangte her filthiest glower of contempt.

'You see those twins over there? They were there the last time. And I think I recognise the blonde guy.' Saraswati started rambling about all the chefs in the room, and Serenity Ko realised that she was nervous. Running into Good Cheer Chaangte had been an ominous start to the competition. She let her teammate prattle on. 'Everyone seems to be human...'

Serenity Ko hadn't even noticed that about the other contestants, and she felt a twinge of shame. She'd always taken being at the centre of the universe—the human universe, at least—for granted. For the first time in her life, she was completely out of her depth, like an outsider on her own planet. Was this what Saraswati felt like *all the time*?

An intern walked around handing out chef's jackets and bottles of water. Serenity Ko smiled at her, and she dropped a stack of jackets, muttered an apology, hurriedly picked them up and did her best to disappear as quickly as possible.

'Is everyone always so jittery in these places?' she asked, bewildered.

'I guess it depends on the vibe that the producers and judges foster,' Saraswati replied. 'I've worked in restaurants where I was afraid to *breathe* too loud.'

'Sur-fucking hell.'

A chime rang out. Serenity Ko looked towards the source of the sound: the timer was ticking down from two minutes.

'Here goes nothing,' Saraswati muttered beside her.

Serenity Ko took her hand and squeezed it, and this time, she left her fingers entwined with Saraswati's until the doors swung open and the world outside was lost in a haze of light, sound and colour.

> The present is a moment of imperfection; when we
> awaken to it, we are free.
>
> —Ancient Vyāsr Proverb

THIRTY-FOUR

I WAS A nervous wreck. My palms were sticky, my vision blurred in the haze of incandescence, my head pounded with the roar of cheering and applause, and my heart raced as the cam-drones tracked my every move.

I couldn't believe I was going to be taking on Good Cheer Chaangte. I wasn't nervous about pitting my skill against hers; it was just horrible being in the same room with her again. She'd destroyed me, that night at *Nonpareil*. And sure, I'd forced her to publically confess to setting me up— maybe even got her fired—but she'd clocked me in the jaw, so I couldn't exactly claim that as a win. And now, I could either put her in her place, once and for all, or crumble. I didn't want to crumble.

Serenity Ko was holding my hand, and the feeling of being in freefall at the touch of her skin against mine made everything worse. My stomach performed violent somersaults. She'd been incredibly nice and supportive ever since I rejoined Feast Inc., but this was not the right time to be side-tracked by her.

I reached my cook station and Kili, whose comms with me were disabled, nuzzled my cheek before flitting off behind Serenity Ko. She left my side abruptly and walked away without a second glance at me, for which I was grateful. The headrush from holding her hand had been nice at first, but then it had turned far too intense, and I really didn't need to think about what that meant, not now, not until I nailed this cook and proved my worth to the universe.

I retreated from all thought and emotion, like I did every time I was in a professional kitchen, and focused on the physicality of the world around me. I placed my hands on the countertop, feeling the cool flowmetal, and pressed my feet into the floor. I was every bit as scared as the first time I was on the show, even though they couldn't destroy my credibility any more than they had already. Perhaps it was irrational. Maybe I was overthinking how much this place meant to me. All I know is that my head was spinning and my shoulders were cramped, as if I were about to be punched in the gut and I knew it.

Do you think any of your success would be possible without who you are? Without who we are?

My father's voice echoed in my head, drowning out the show's host, Boundless Eli, who was doing his customary introduction to the judges.

Who bought off all those reviewers? Ensured people were eating at your restaurant? Kept you in business while the economy collapsed around us?

Grace Aurelle was talking, and I was dimly aware that she was explaining the special rules for this episode. The tasting would be blind; none of the judges would know which contestant was making each presentation of dishes. It wouldn't be as satisfying as seeing the shock on their faces when I turned up at the judges' table, but at least they wouldn't be able to write me off immediately. Serenity Ko had read this rule out to me half a dozen times, reassuring me that Pavi and Amol wouldn't be able to repeat their "star-fucker behaviour," as she referred to it.

As the judges were led off-sct, I ignored my father's booming laughter, worming its way into my head alongside my mother's cackle and my sister Narmada's hiccuping giggle. They weren't here. Maybe they'd bought some of my success back on Earth, but they hadn't influenced my life since.

Not true. Pavi and Amol gave me my job because they owed my family, somehow. Jog Tunga said so.

I clenched the flowmetal counter, willing myself to not throw up. And then the lights dimmed as individual spots lit each contestant, while Boundless Eli introduced them. As my eyes adjusted to the sudden gloom, I caught sight of a quartet of E'nemon tentacles winding their way together into an intricate knot. I was suddenly grateful for all the diplomacy lessons I'd been forced to sit through on Earth.

That was Starlight Fantastic. And they were signalling me the E'nemon sign for courage.

Beside them were Moonage Daydream, Courage Oslo and Curiosity Zia, and I could see them shouting my name with every ounce of strength they had, even though I couldn't hear them. I caught sight of Grace Kube and Courage Praia, whooping and cheering. And then the faces blurred as light flooded my spot and I heard my name announced.

'...Saraswati Kaveri! You might remember her as our Earthling firestarter, and we hope this time, we're in for far more pleasant surprises!' Boundless Eli boomed.

I smiled my biggest, most people-friendly smile while my brain worked its way through a long list of curse words, all of which I was sure Kili was echoing in Serenity Ko's thoughtstream. The people on this show all thought they were so *clever*, so *above it all*. And sure, maybe they were good at what they did, but that didn't give them the licence to treat everyone around them like garbage. I gave vent to the white-hot anger coursing through me for a full three minutes, while the remaining contestants were introduced, and then I let it go.

Today, I was going to show them all. *We* were. It wasn't just me and my food on the plate here: it was the work of over a hundred people at XP Inc., supported by the love of all the people who'd stood by me ever since I arrived on this sur-fucked planet. All of that had to count for something. I was going to make sure it did.

I felt like I was watching a film replaying my life in slow motion.

Boundless Eli wrapped up his introductions, then said with an air of great ceremony. 'You have three hours to bring us your unique spin on the Nakshatran Banquet. Honour our ancestors, but take their vision into a new millennium. We want to see *the future of Primus* on a plate.' He paused dramatically. 'Your time... starts... *now!*'

On the bench beneath my counter were all the staples— an assortment of gels, spheres, gelées, terrines and other compounds that were standards in Primian cuisine. Since they were showcasing new food technologies, the *MegaChef* production team had let us bring in any enhancements we might need, which *weren't* standard in the current Primian culinary world. I was very relieved to spy a discreet, neatly packaged flowmetal cooler emblazoned with the XP Inc. logo. I left it where it was; I wouldn't need it until we plated.

I set to my busywork, first making a trip to the pantry to gather all the ingredients for a Nakshatran Banquet. I'd researched it extensively once the *MegaChef* requirements had been delivered, and practised making it more than a dozen times over countless late nights. There'd been far too many leftovers to eat, even by the entire design team, so XP Inc. had set up a Nakshatran Banquet Table in one of their pantries, and it had been emptied as fast as its contents were replenished, which I took to be a good sign.

Historically, the Nakshatran Banquet was the first celebratory feast thrown by the settlers on the planet, after the establishment of the Secretariat. When the founders of the city had first built Collective One, it had been their first symbolic victory, establishing a civilisation far from the one they'd fled on Earth. The Banquet hadn't been as excessive as the word hinted at, but it had been a celebration for a fledgling community of barely five hundred people.

This was as traditional as food got on Primus. All their

advancements in food tech and aesthetics had scarcely changed the recipes, and the Banquet was served only once every year, on the last day of the Nakshatran Festival. It was like cooking a medieval feast back on my home world.

I harvested ras from all the required ingredients with a large stack of syringes: helioshroom and caneshoot, half a dozen vegetables and over a dozen spices, including gayam, cilantrina, and peprino-corn, and for the dessert courses, everberry, fraiseberry, rougeberry, mamba-zham and several other kinds of fruit. I picked fourteen different spice blends to be combined in complex infusions. I grabbed my vat-grown proteins: riverrover fish, filleted beest, wildfowl breast. And then I proceeded to mise en place.

The air was filled with the swift, sharp staccato of chopping and slicing, ten different beats blending together to form a percussive polyrhythm. I glanced around at what the other chefs were doing; I thought I saw a new experimental type of infusion device being used—a multi-pronged syringe of some kind, marbling a slab of beest with almost no effort from the chef using it, who turned out to be one of the twins. I bent over my ingredients, returning my focus to my own work.

I prepped my meats with their infusions first, letting them rest in their various marinades. The riverrover needed a citria-beurre infusion, and so I prepped it accordingly, rubbing it down with two spice blends to evoke the freshness of the waters of the River Serenity. I let it sit, moving on to the beest, which needed a rainbow marbling, a technique in which multiple kinds of ras were infused in rapid succession, into its fattiest reserves, to evoke the many-hued stalactites the Nakshatrans had discovered in the Cornucopia Caves. The wildfowl breast was prepped with a sheaf-grass feathering technique. I then turned my counter into multiple cook stations—none of which involved an open flame—and started to prepare my garnishes.

Cilantrina caviar, mamba-zham terrine, rougeberry spheres, honeycomb sheets—one by one I ticked each of the complex garnishes and courses off my list. A shroom-broth bubbled in a self-heating pan. Liquid nitrogen flash-froze a batch of peprino-corn poppers.

The judges had retreated to another room so they wouldn't know who had prepared which dish when judging. So Boundless Eli did the rounds of the contestants, stopping at each table to question them about their techniques. I overheard him talking to Good Cheer Chaangte, two stations ahead of me.

'I'm preparing everything in the Nakshatran Banquet as a foam,' she said, flicking her pale blonde braid over her shoulder. 'We've become far too obsessed with the *solidity* of food, the rootedness of experiences. In order to embrace the new millennium, and to carve a path into the future, we must remember our Nakshatran heritage, and our principle to "tread lightly." Foam is ephemeral, effervescent, fleeting. It is mutable, flexible. We must drop the rigid lines of our identities and embrace transience.'

I rolled my eyes. This was typical Primian chef philosopho-babble. It accompanied every single plate of food they served; it underscored every single decision they made. And it was all surface level. From everything I'd experienced, none of them actually embodied anything they talked about so self-righteously.

Well, maybe some of them were nice. Curiosity Zia and Courage Oslo, Courage Praia, Boundless Baz, even Serenity Ko in her own awkward, tangled way—though I quickly expunged all thought of her. They were all decent people, not as given to parroting away their so-called virtues.

What really got to me was the way all these virtues and values and whatsits were reinforced in Primian kitchens; the obsession with the symbolic significance attached to every single ingredient that went into a plate of food. The māsas I'd spent on Primus had done nothing to change that impression. I could appreciate the rich history behind the tradition, but it detracted from the personal experience of eating. I piped the helioshroom- and caneshoot-infused cream into pastry sheets, thinking about how each of the ingredients had its own meaning, and then playfully threatened one of the cam-drones with a squirt of cream, just as Boundless Eli reached my side.

'Not bringing your culture into this?' he asked, in his deep announcer's voice.

'Not this time round, I'm afraid.'

'No quaint fire methods, or whole ingredients?' He raised an eyebrow, regarding my station and continuing to ask entirely redundant questions where the answers were visible before him, cooking merrily away in traditionally Primian ways.

'Nope.'

'And here I thought, after your last performance on this show, that you'd be using this platform to make another political statement!' He winked, laughing entirely falsely.

'I'm definitely here to make a political statement, but not the kind you might imagine,' I said.

'Give us a hint?'

'What you see isn't necessarily what you might get on the plate!' I tried to mimic his overly enthusiastic tone, and felt utterly foolish doing it.

'Ooh! A bold announcement from an off-worlder!' Boundless Eli concluded. 'But as we all know, folks, Earth is all about making tall claims. It remains to be seen if she'll deliver!' he boomed into his microphone as he all but danced his way to the next contestant.

As he left my side, I had a revelation.

All of this, the entire thing, every single moment of it, was entirely ridiculous.

From the day I'd arrived on this planet, I'd been obsessed with proving myself to complete strangers who were so fixed in their own ways that they'd spent the better part of two millennia preserving them. They truly believed themselves to have reinvented humanity.

The principles that guided their culture were admirable: no-one knew better than me how stained with thoughtlessness, violence, consumerism and anthropocentrism the history of the Earth was. And yet, every single one of their traditions was preserved in a bell jar, hallowed like the ancient relic of a saint, never questioned or re-examined. They believed themselves to be the natural heirs to the Nakshatrans, never mind that six other Nakshatran-led civilisations had arisen on other planets across the galaxy. But simply because they'd happened to have a head start on them, they genuinely believed themselves to be the leaders of human civilization. And the only way they could do that was to hold steadfast to what had differentiated them from their ancestors—the people on Earth from two millennia ago—who had given rise to them in the first place. This was an entire culture *obsessed* with its past, while struggling desperately to assert its relevance in a rapidly evolving future.

If presenting an entire menu in the form of foam—*foam, for fuck's sake, of all things*—was a culinary revolution, then what was I even *doing here?*

The memory of my first tryst on this set rushed back to me: Grace Aurelle trying to arm-twist me into ignoring her xenophobic slurs; Harmony Rhea critiquing my methods and presentation in her shrill voice, like a hideously insecure bird strutting around in bright plumage; Pavi and Amol discrediting my Earthling food because they were so *desperate* to belong.

My life on Primus flashed before my eyes. The sad press reporter with her army of cam-drones trying to harass me at Uru and Beyond, and all the other nobody citizens jumping on the bandwagon as they chased me around. Good Cheer Chaangte's petty thirst for power, Grace

Menmo's insistence that fire was the favoured recourse of barbarians on her stupid sim…

And as I thought about the prank Serenity Ko had played on me, messing with my dessert spheres and turning them black as tar, I burst into laughter. I finally *got it*. I *understood*.

None of this *mattered*.

Serenity Ko wanted to be my friend, if I looked past the offensive language that inevitably tumbled out of her mouth. Moonage Daydream had welcomed me to their popup, and offered me a job. Courage Oslo and Curiosity Zia had cared for me when I'd been too drunk to notice. Boundless Baz and XX-29 had been my allies in the Nonpareil kitchen. None of *them* had cared at all that I didn't know my way around Primian food; of course they appreciated the fact that I knew flavours, but they valued me because I was a mostly good person, and they'd gone out of their way to make me feel at home on this foreign planet.

Starlight Fantastic had always been a thoughtstream away. And Kili… Kili had been at my side through it all, his faith in me unwavering, and often undeserved.

I laughed until my ribs ached, tears streaming down my cheeks.

It didn't matter if I won or lost. It didn't matter what these people thought of me. I had nothing to prove to them, just like I had nothing to prove to my parents, or my family, who couldn't tell a rougeberry on Primus from a strawberry back on Earth.

I wiped my eyes on my towel, replacing it on my shoulder. I realised that all the other contestants were staring at me as if I'd lost my mind.

'Has the Earthling cracked at last?' Good Cheer Chaangte asked loudly.

I beamed, straightened my shoulders, and tossed off a flurry of air-kisses at the cam-drones and audience alike. I didn't need to win this thing, impress these people, *or* have their approval. I just needed to be me.

'Ten minutes left! Time to get those plates going!' Boundless Eli announced.

Here it was, at last. Time to turn up the drama and bring it to its zenith.

I grabbed the stack of plates I'd assembled at the start of my cook. I arranged them on the counter before me. I plated course after perfect course.

I popped open the XP Inc. cooler, and removed the neatly stacked and labelled boxes within. Using a pair of forceps, I carefully withdrew an assemblage of small cubes, then placed them in a bowl. Each was neatly labelled to correspond to one course of the Banquet.

I poured water over them. They began to swell. The rules said the new spin on Primian food needed to be "cooked" or "transformed," and we'd come up with a simple solution for our coded edibites: Just add water.

I grinned smugly at the ingenuity of it all.

And then, with a dramatic flourish, I grabbed a ladle, and brought it down on the right half of *every single perfectly plated dish*. Each of my beautiful courses was smashed, smudged, splattered and squidged, and I delighted in my precise destruction of them all. When I was done, the left side of each plate bore an impeccable, traditional Primian dish; the right side of every plate was a many-hued mess.

I grabbed a pair of tongs.

I plated the cubes, affecting great precision, as each one went on the plate corresponding to its course. On the right side of each plate, that is.

Boundless Eli began his countdown. I whistled cheerily, stepping back from my cook station, right as he boomed, 'Time's up!'

He strutted around, doing a cursory evaluation of each contestant's plate, making comments for the benefit of the live audience and those watching at home. He nearly fell over when he reached my station.

'Your plates! They're... they're a mess!' he spluttered.

'I know,' I said.

'But... but the contest!'

'Out with the old, in with the new,' I said, passing my palm over the cubes on each plate. 'This is the future of food.'

'It's goop!' he exclaimed, sweat beading upon his brow.

'You're wrong.' I smiled, and for the first time, it felt genuine. The cam-drones surged forwards to cocoon us. 'It's a feast.'

The consummate chef is courageous and ever curious.
Nothing that crosses their plate is inedible at first
sight.

—Grace Menmo,
from the sim *At Home in the Kitchen*,
2065 Anno Earth | 1990 Interstellar Era

THIRTY-FIVE

'YOUR PRODIGAL EARTHLING has returned,' Harmony Rhea
trilled, regarding Pavi over the rim of her glass of flat water.
Her tone conveyed a challenge, and Pavi refused to rise to
the bait.

'Yes, we can't wait to see what she does,' she said smoothly
instead.

'But of course, you know what she's doing already,'
Courage Ab'dal said in their low, gravelly voice. 'I heard
rumours that you *hired* her?'

'Out of pity,' Amol said quickly. 'She's a refugee from
Earth, you know.'

'Ah, how magnanimous of you.' Grace Aurelle dipped her
head sagely.

Their guest judge for the episode leaned forwards. Her
narrow-set eyes narrowed even further, exaggerating her
aquiline nose to razor sharp proportions. Pavi almost
flinched, then caught herself. Secretary Optimism Mahd'vi'
was known for her sharp tongue, and even sharper mind.

'Fascinating,' Optimism Mahd'vi continued. 'She's a
long way from home. What's her name again?'

'Saraswati Kaveri,' Amol responded.

'And she works for you?'

Amol shared a quick glance with his sister. He considered

lying, but it was one thing to fib to the other chefs in the room, and another to cover up the truth when a powerful government official was involved. 'Not any more. She was working on some kind of experimental project while she was with us, but she left a few navas ago.'

'Ah, what a shame,' Optimism Mahd'vi said. 'I was hoping we could arrange a meeting. Encourage her.'

Pavi swallowed. 'I'll see what we can do.'

'And I hear one of your *other* employees is competing. A Good Cheer Chianti?' Courage Ab'dal rumbled.

'Good Cheer Chaangte,' Pavi corrected him, smiling tersely. It was bad enough that they might lose whatever proprietary share they could have had in Saraswati's project with XP Inc. When Saraswati had goaded Good Cheer Chaangte into confessing that she'd been behind the service debacle, and the Primian chef had actually *assaulted* her... They were lucky Saraswati wasn't pressing charges. Heated, ugly words had been exchanged in their office after the incident. Good Cheer Chaangte had threatened to quit. Amol had fired her instead.

Pavi and Amol hadn't had a chance to talk about it yet, but for her own part, she was extremely concerned about what might happen if Good Cheer Chaangte actually won the competition.

'It seems to me you have many horses in this race,' Grace Aurelle said suspiciously.

'Either that, or there's a mutiny at Nonpareil, hmm?' Harmony Rhea winked coyly.

'To my understanding,' Optimism Mahd'vi interjected, 'every single person at this table knows all of the chefs participating, which is why we decided on a blind tasting.'

'Yes, but there's only one of each of us, and there's *two* of them,' Courage Ab'dal complained, nodding their head to indicate Pavi and Amol. 'If they're familiar with their chefs' projects, in any capacity, they'll gain an undue advantage.'

'They aren't *our* chefs,' Amol clarified. 'Not anymore.'

'Even so, for the sake of fairness, and in good faith, could we limit the pair of you to a single vote? Does that work for everyone?'

Pavi shared a quick glance with Amol, and they nodded in unison.

The producers were called in, and they hurriedly drafted an addendum to everyone's contracts. The scrollwork was quickly signed, and the mood at the judges' table relaxed slightly.

Their conversation wandered freely until the cam-drones and recording equipment were switched on again. The ceiling was dome-shaped, and large archways framed the octagonal space in which they were seated, bathed in the halo of dozens of bright lights.

The degustation began.

About half a dozen perfectly delectable spins on the Nakshatran Banquet yielded themselves to their discerning palates. The banquet table and the chairs they sat upon were covered in an inky blue handwoven fabric, and course after course was produced upon it for their pleasure—and, more often than not, disdain. All the flavours seemed to be in order, presentation was inevitably impressive, but innovation seemed entirely lacking.

Until suddenly, it wasn't.

They tasted an offering that had been cooked in half the time allocated to its chef, thanks to machine-aided simultaneous infusions.

'Lacks delicacy of flavour,' said Grace Aurelle, 'and presentation is wanting. See how rough the marbling technique is? The machine doesn't seem to have the light touch required to make Primian food.'

'Is the intent to increase efficiency in the future, though?' Optimism Mahd'vi asked. 'That's valuable.'

'Possibly, but it needs refinement,' Courage Ab'dal said.

They tasted an all-liquid banquet, which had proven extremely dissatisfying.

'The future of Primus lies in a straw,' Optimism Mahd'vi quipped.

'I feel the distinct emptiness of a liquid diet,' Pavi ventured.

'Hospital food.' Harmony Rhea made a face.

They all raved about the Nakshatran Banquet presented entirely as a foam.

'Such immaculate technique!' Grace Aurelle said, reaching for more mamba-zham foam-pâté.

'Exquisite flavour profiles; somehow made even purer in their ephemeral form,' Courage Ab'dal said approvingly, consuming a second portion of riverrover fish froth, served with pearlescent cilantrina caviar-bubbles.

'Texturally, a delight,' Amol said approvingly, eating a large scoop of an allberry ice cream balloon.

'I think we might have a winner,' Optimism Mahd'vi smiled. 'Unless something surprises us.'

Grace Aurelle's eyebrows twitched at this pronouncement, and Pavi and Amol shared a quick glance. Their Chief Chef didn't seem to like this apparent challenge to her authority. 'There's still one tasting to go,' she said authoritatively.

'One more to go,' Courage Ab'dal echoed, drumming their fingers on the table.

'Finally!' Harmony Rhea chirped.

One of the episode's producers stepped into the chamber. 'Are you ready?'

'Yes,' Grace Aurelle said.

'Great, we'll bring in the next course.'

The already bright lights flared in intensity. The cam-drones whirred awake from where they'd settled inertly on the walls, like large moths. Pavi plastered a smile onto her face, every bit as falsely as all the other judges in the room.

'One last Nakshatran Banquet!' Grace Aurelle said enthusiastically as the cloches were carried in.

'It's hard enough getting through *one* of these every Nakshatran Festival,' Optimism Mahd'vi said. 'Today we'll have tasted ten!'

Everyone at the table laughed as the serving trays were laid down.

The servers hovered before the cloches before them, their hands poised to reveal what lay beneath. At a silent cue, in one smooth, deft movement, they raised them.

'Saving the best for la—' Amol said cheerily, and the words died instantly on his lips.

'What the fuck is this?' Harmony Rhea ventured, scrunching up her nose.

'A joke?' Courage Ab'dal asked, looking around, their eyes wide in confusion.

The servers retreated, and none of the producers stepped forwards to respond from where they lurked in the shadows.

'I'm asking you, is this a joke?' Courage Ab'dal repeated, their voice rising as they peered into the darkness beyond the set.

'I refuse to eat this,' Grace Aurelle said flatly. 'It's an insult to my senses.'

'Is this the thing we had to swallow those nanopills for?' Amol asked meekly. Pavi caught Amol's eye, a sinking feeling forming in the pit of her stomach. Somehow, inexplicably, she *knew* where this had come from, and she *knew* that there were going to be ugly consequences, whether the chef who made it won or lost.

The plates resembled a culinary fever dream.

The left side of each plate was immaculate, a visual spectacle of delicate infusions, impeccably marbled protein, glistening gels and gelées, perfectly golden brown pastry, impressively rich compotes and jams—a Nakshatran Banquet straight out of Grace Menmo's *At Home in the Kitchen*.

The right side of each plate was the art project of a deeply disturbed individual—some kind of misanthrope, or species-cynic with a violent past. Each otherwise-perfect dish had been half smashed to bits with joyous abandon, or perhaps disdain.

And crowning each puddle of spatter, sat a nondescript assortment of cubes made from a translucent kind of jelly that seemed to glow slightly green at its edges.

'I'm staging a walkout,' Courage Ab'dal said, rising to their feet.

'You can't do that. It's in your contract,' Optimism Mahd'vi said coldly. Courage Ab'dal sat back down, clearly seething. 'This is provocative,' Optimism Mahd'vi said, and arched an eyebrow. 'It feels like a challenge. I don't know how I feel about it, personally, but that makes it interesting.'

'This is an affront to my senses,' Courage Ab'dal growled. 'I refuse to eat it.'

'Are none of you bold enough to try something new?' Optimism Mahd'vi asked, glancing from face to face, her eyes wide in disbelief. 'You're supposed to be at the forefront of the culinary world here. Where's the Nakshatran virtue of curiosity? And what about optimism? No wonder Primian culture has stagnated!' She glared at Grace Aurelle. 'If all of you are going to be cowards, then I'll lead the way.'

'How do we taste this?' Harmony Rhea asked, and her voice came out as a squeak.

'The usual way,' Grace Aurelle said, taking charge. 'We divide the good side of each course into six—one for each of us. As for the strange cubes... there seem to be one portion for each of us, on every plate.'

'I'll join you,' Amol said.

Pavi's jaw dropped in shock.

'Let's do it together,' he continued.

'I'll try it, too,' Grace Aurelle said, swallowing hard.

Courage Ab'dal sighed, a hoarse, scraping sound. 'Let's all do it together, then?'

Grace Aurelle divided the offering into portions. Sensing

high drama, the cam-drones were whipped into a frenzy, descending towards the plates and the judges like a cloud.

'Let's go,' Optimism Mahd'vi said. 'We'll taste one course at a time, real food first. Presentation across the plates is impeccable, except for the smashed half of each one.' She smiled in delight.

Pavi popped the first course into her mouth. 'Perfectly balanced flavours.'

'Top-notch freshness,' Harmony Rhea said.

'This chef can cook!' Courage Ab'dal approved.

'Shall we try the... *goop?*' Grace Aurelle said, eyeing her plate hesitantly.

'Let's go,' Amol said enthusiastically.

Pavi scooped it into her mouth.

A rush of fresh scents flooded her senses, caneshoot and citrina rolling across her tastebuds with the lightness of air, their acidity smearing a trail of longing across her palate.

'Ohmygoodness,' Harmony Rhea choked from across the table.

A sim burst its way across her visual feed.

A breeze kisses the leaves in a woodland, fresh elemin blossoms in yellow and orange stir, their scent mingling with the salt in the air. She turns and sees a warpcraft behind her, then walks on, all the way to the edge of the treeline, where she's greeted by the waves of the Sagarra Sea, crashing into the rocks hundreds of feet below her. The sound of seabirds squalling fills the air, and Suriya lights the world in splendour.

The world falls away beneath her and she is weaving her way through street-food stalls lining the avenues of Collective Four. She looks down, and in her hands, she's carrying four cups of a frothing caneshoot flip, wending her way back to the table where her friends await. She's only fourteen, and unlike most of their friends, she and Amol have chosen to stay on at their boarding school for the holidays. This is the first time their school has let them go to the Nakshatran Festival, a planet-wide holiday. She spots Amol, and he's chatting up Trieste—the wretched playboy, no wonder he sent her off to buy drinks for the table. She plonks the cups down, and kicks him under the table as she takes her seat. They raise their glasses...

Pavi swallowed the remains of the sphere, and gasped as she surfaced. 'What... what the fuck was that?' Her voice was hoarse.

'I don't know,' Harmony Rhea whimpered, sinking lower in her chair, her reaction almost as shocking as the eating experience. 'But it was better than the real thing... and that was *excellent!*'

'I saw Trieste.' Amol smiled, looking at Pavi.

'So did I.'

Amol's high school girlfriend had broken up with him three months into their dramatic relationship, to transfer back to her home world Sagaricus. He still joked that she was the "one who got away."

'This...' Grace Aurelle spluttered. 'This is insanity.'

'Let's carry on,' Optimism Mahd'vi said. Her lips twitched as if she were about to smile.

They started with each traditional offering, working their way through course after course, following each up with the indescribable edible cubes that appeared unimpressive and smelled of nothing, but delivered sensory experiences like a sucker punch.

'That interplay of sweet and sour is divine!' Harmony Rhea exclaimed over her traditional riverrover portion.

'Texture is delightful,' Grace Aurelle murmured.

'Riverrover marbling is exceptional; consistent with every bite,' Amol said.

Courage Ab'dal grunted in acknowledgment, looking none too pleased as they reached for the cubes on their plates.

Pavi zoomed through rippling sheaf-grass meadows, following the path of a dandyllion, smelling the fresh sharp taste of summer roll across her tongue as she chewed upon filleted beest, marinaded in helioshroom sauce, remembering the first time she went foraging in the Arc after school. She was a riverrover, underwater in a cascading stream, basking in the diffused light of Suriya, and then she was flipping fish out of a rock pool with her grandfather, suddenly back on Earth. She was a honeybuzzer flitting through the leaves of a mamba-zham tree, the scent of sweet fruit overpowering, urging her on in an Arcside orchard, and then she was plunged into that rainy night in the loft of her ex-lover's home, where they sat by the large bay windows, and he taught her how to eat it with her bare hands. There was an excess harvest of mamba-zham that year, and Primians had been encouraged to eat the fruit whole, for once.

'Make a little incision with your teeth, right at the top,' he says. 'Just nip some of the skin off.'

'Like this?' she asks, a little scrap of the coarse mamba-zham peel between her teeth.

'Exactly. Now you place your thumb over the opening, and pulp the fruit with your hands, like this, see?'

She follows his lead.

'And now, feast...'

And rich, sweet flavour floods her senses...

'I don't understand this one bit!' she said out loud, and shivered.

'Me neither,' said Harmony Rhea, and she sounded miserable. 'The thing is even simulating *texture*. Did anyone else feel the crunch of fresh cilantrino?'

'It's unbelievable,' Grace Aurelle said, her tone empty of everything but utter honesty. 'I'm lost for words. It's making me relive my entire life, not just in the kitchen but as a diner.'

'It's an abomination,' Courage Ab'dal groused. 'This entire thing is a sick practical joke. It renders everything we do in the kitchen *meaningless*. I can't believe none of you can see it.'

'It makes what you do in the kitchen more accessible, my dear,' Optimism Mahd'vi said, her eyes twinkling.

'It's glorified packaged food. Gourmet fucking cricket chips,' Courage Ab'dal threw their napkin on the table. 'I've had it with this joke. I'm out.'

'Ab'dal, your contract—' Grace Aurelle began.

'Tear it up, stuff it in a wild riverrover, and send it out to the sea where it belongs!'

They made a loud exit, making sure to scrape their chair back, stomp their feet on their way out through the arches, and slam the flat of their palm against the wall right before the darkness swallowed them.

'Dramatic,' Optimism Mahd'vi said mildly.

'It isn't untrue, what they said,' Harmony Rhea said softly.

'No, it isn't. But I think it's exactly where opportunity lies for everyone in this room,' Optimism Mahd'vi said mysteriously.

'What do you mean, Secretary?' Grace Aurelle asked politely. 'This delivers all the flavours we've spent a lifetime learning to master, but it's goop on a plate.'

'This takes food beyond flavour,' Harmony Rhea tittered. 'It's glorious! It opens pathways into the reason we make food, at all: to evoke human emotion.'

'I'm surprised *you're* so positive about this, Rhea. I don't understand it one bit, if I'm being honest. I don't know how to feel about it. It insults us—as chefs, as culinary minds. It sits self-satisfied and smug on the plate, unpretentious about its presentation, bold and declarative in the flavours and mouthfeel it delivers. It's an affront, and it's delicious. What does it mean for Primian food, for our culture, for our restaurants and our thousands of qualified chefs, for all those people for whom food is a passion and not just something you vulgarly pop into your mouth when your stomach rumbles...?' Grace Aurelle said, shaking with what appeared to be rage and fear.

Amol opened his mouth momentarily, then thought the better of it, and shut it.

Grace Aurelle carried on. 'It's gourmet cricket chips, just like Ab'dal said, but it's also... more? It can be anything you want it to be? It seems dangerous.'

'When the Nakshatrans set out to find Primus, they embraced danger, and look what their courage gave us. A home, a future, a people we could believe in,' Optimism Mahd'vi said sagely, looking straight at the cam-drones that were hanging on to every word. 'Fear is a prelude to the stars, a gateway to infinity.'

'Of course,' Grace Aurelle smiled. 'I'm... I'm not opposed to it. I just can't wrap my head around it!'

The traditionally prepared wildfowl breast three ways was pronounced "stellar" and "impressive," the beest braise was "divine" and "succulent," the nested noodleshrooms were "delightful"... and Pavi started to lose all sense of time and place, as she popped the ineffable cubes into her mouth, packed with flavour and texture, sim after sim evoking memories and transporting her to live experiences she'd never had before, her tangled feelings of shock and despair, joy and helplessness, echoed in the faces of the judges assembled around her.

'One last course.' Optimism Mahd'vi nodded at the slice of Primian Gateau on the plate before her. 'Shall we?'

Everyone dug into the historic dessert.

'This chef is exceptional,' Optimism Mahd'vi commented. 'The berry ratios are the best I've ever tasted.'

'I need to hire them, whoever they are,' Harmony Rhea said. 'How haven't they been discovered yet?'

'The traditional dishes are par excellence,' Grace Aurelle said, and a hint of dismay crept into her voice. 'And then the simulated ones—*the goop on our plates*—take Primian food to the next level. Whoever's cooked this Banquet—both traditionally, and with this weird sim tech—has an incredible knowledge of flavour. I can't believe what we're tasting.'

Pavi caught Amol's gaze momentarily and dropped it, shame flushing her cheeks.

'One last goop cube!' Amol announced.

Pavi picked it up and placed it in her mouth. A rich, vibrant creaminess coated her tongue. Little explosions of popping candy ricocheted off her upper palate, and a symphony of flavour played across her senses, from the bright sour notes of rougeberry and fraiseberry, to the rich bitterness of himanso and the sweet lightness of candyfoam.

'Ohmygoodness, Primian Gateau,' Harmony Rhea moaned. 'The popping candy!'

Right before the audiovisual sim began, Pavi had a moment to glance around the table. Amol had wrapped his arms around himself, and was giving himself a hug. Harmony Rhea was making small sounds to herself, like she was singing along to a song only she could hear. Optimism Mahd'vi had an enormous smile drawn across her face, her eyes closed, her head leaning back against the neck cushions of her chair.

And Grace Aurelle…

Grace Aurelle was doubled over her plate, sobbing.

Pavi gave into the rush of feeling that was overpowering her. Reality blurred, and she was swept away into the remains of the feast.

A plate of food brings the universe together in the suspension of spacetime.

Past and present collide in a sublime moment of taste; galaxies collide, a shared culture in the silence of eating, in echoes of flavour.

—Saraswati Godavari,
Opening Night, Elé Oota
4367 CE | Year 1993 Interstellar Era

THIRTY-SIX

IF KILI HADN'T been on her shoulder, thoughtstreaming irreverent live commentary her way, Serenity Ko might have died a wretched mix of nerves and boredom. The adrenaline pounding through the small of her back had waned once the contestants were about thirty minutes into their cook. The Team-Mate Station didn't offer the sharpest of views, even on its raised platform. Each time the holoscreens around the set cut to a close-up of Saraswati's hands working, or her face, frowning in concentration as she bent over some infusion or combination, Serenity Ko cheered her loudest, accompanied by Kili screaming into her thoughts, and a wave of sound erupted from behind her, somewhere, where she supposed the rest of their supporters must be seated. But that was about it as far as excitement went. She had no idea what Saraswati was actually *doing,* and found herself paying far too much attention to the definition of her forearms, or the moue of her lips, moving silently while she muttered away to herself, fussing over the food on her counter. She kept these thoughts carefully shielded from Kili, who was radiating the kind of love it was impossible for most humans to feel.

Funny little machine, she thought. *Ancient tech, but no wonder she can't let go of him.*

When Saraswati half-smashed the beautiful, complex dishes she'd meticulously prepared and plated, and started adding the Feast edibites to each plate, the cam-drones peeled away one by one from all the other contestants, until only her hands—with her neat fingernails, cut short—were splayed across all the holoscreens in the room. Murmurs broke out all round, a susurrus of voices rising, tumbling and blurring into each other. The mysterious jellies on the plate appeared nonsensical. Serenity Ko felt a bubble of excitement welling within her at all the chatter. Boundless Eli rushed over to Saraswati's cook station, his face cycling through innumerable expressions of shock.

'It's goop!' he exclaimed, sweat pouring down his forehead.

'You're wrong.' Saraswati smiled. 'It's a feast.'

Serenity Ko felt like her insides were lined with fireworks, and they were all going off all at once. She rose to her feet, stamping hard on the ground, and whooped, applauding in a frenzy and screaming her teammate's name. Off in one corner, she heard a chorus of echoes from their contingent.

You tell them, Saras! Kili yelled in her thoughts, and she grinned. He sent a cascade of blossoming flowers, songbird choruses, and confetti bombs streaming across her visual feed, and Serenity Ko was suddenly dizzy.

Whoa, stop.

Too much? Kili asked.

Yeah.

Too bad.

After that, exciting events receded into utter boredom again. The cooks were ushered off to some kind of waiting room, and interminable hours seemed to pass. As it turned out, it was only ten minutes later that everyone in the audience was permitted to socialise, while they waited for the judges to finish their tasting and deliberations.

Serenity Ko hopped to her feet and stretched, yawning loudly. Her back muscles were starting to cramp. She ran her fingers through her braid, which was threatening to come apart under her fussing.

'Not bad, Ko.'

She spun around, and Grace Kube stood behind her, all smiles. 'Not bad at all. I think you might just make it to Evocateur Extraordinaire for this.'

'We haven't won, yet,' Serenity Ko said.

'Don't need to. Did you hear the shock ripple through the crowd when Saraswati started wrecking those plates? And when the Feast cubes appeared?'

Serenity Ko laughed at that. 'Yeah, we took them by surprise.'

'You started a conversation that's going to carry on until every corner in the universe can access Feast.'

'*I* didn't,' Serenity Ko said. 'It was all Saraswati today. In fact, the entire idea for that presentation—cook everything old-fashioned-like, then shock everyone with the plating— that was Nenna's. And if it hadn't been for Sah'r and that insane code push...'

Grace Kube hugged her unexpectedly.

'The fuck, Kube?'

'That's what I've been waiting to hear from you all along.'

'I... I don't understand.'

'It'll dawn on you.' Grace Kube broke off the hug and winked, then glanced over her shoulder, eyes widening. 'I see trouble incoming,' he muttered. 'Good luck.'

'Hang on, what do you—?'

'Ah, my lovely granddaughter.'

Serenity Ko winced at Ammamma's voice. It was pitched soft and low, and in her experience, that only ever meant bad news. The forced cheer from last night's dinner was gone. She spun around, plastering a bright smile upon her face. 'Ammamma!' she chirped.

Her grandmother pulled her into a hug. 'My monster, you've created a monster, just like I warned you would.' She squeezed her arm extra tight, and it hurt.

'What do you mean?' Serenity Ko asked, dismayed. 'All we've done so far is plate and serve Feast.'

Her grandmother sighed slowly, with a sad smile.

'You know, you could give me a straight answer for once,' Serenity Ko hissed. 'Instead of treating me like a five-year-old all the time.'

'When you stop behaving like one...'

'When I stop superseding all your elite culinary achievements by building food that everyone can access, you mean,' Serenity Ko said heatedly.

Her grandmother's jaw dropped, and she took a step back.

'This whole project, you've dragged me through fire and ice to try and prove to me that I'm going to fail,' Serenity Ko said. 'You're just salty that I haven't.'

'That's not what I meant,' her grandmother said. 'It was never my intention to put you down. I'm still on your side.'

'Right.'

'Fine, you want to know what's happening?' Ammamma snapped. 'My professional streams are exploding; every single chef who's caught the episode live is online right now and they're—'

'They're losing their minds, aren't they?' Serenity Ko grinned savagely. 'Exactly what we were hoping for.'

Her grandmother opened her mouth to argue.

'Stop taking up all her time and attention!' Serenity Ko's parents crowded in round her, congratulating her, all smiles. Dad and Appa had brought her flowers from their garden, and Optimism Rihan and Good Cheer Eria wrapped her up in a hug between them, but it was all drowned out by the ominous ring of her grandmother's words, who still didn't seem to believe that what she'd built was a good thing. She looked up and caught Ammamma's eye, which seemed to be filled with sadness mingled with pride.

That was... unpleasant? Kili's voice popped into her head.

I'll talk to her later.

'You're Serenity Ko?' A tall, sandy-haired man asked, walking up to her. His Loop tag read *Courage Oslo, He/Him* and he didn't appear particularly friendly.

She drew herself up to her full height, grateful that she'd chosen to wear her boots with the slight heel, because his lanky frame towered above hers. 'I am.'

'I'm Saraswati's friend. I hope this works out for you, but you'd better not try any funny shit in the future,' he said.

'What the—?'

He turned and strode away before she could finish the thought.

I second that, Kili echoed in her head.

I apologised to her already.

Even so. He's a good friend of hers. There are more in the audience. They'll always have her back, so you'd better not stick a knife in.

I won't!

A bell chimed off in the distance, and an AI voice buzzed over the announcement system. '*Beings from across the universe, the broadcast of* Interstellar MegaChef: Millennium Feast Special *will resume in five minutes. Kindly return to your seats. We have five minutes to go.*'

Serenity Ko was disoriented by the mixed reactions she'd received from everyone in the crowd. Her grandmother had seemed entirely disapproving, while Grace Kube had been brimming with excitement. Her family was proud of her, Saraswati's friends seemed to hate her...

What am I doing wrong?

Another bell chimed, and the large, trellis-covered doors at the far end of the stage swung inward. The contestants walked back in, and Serenity Ko's heart leapt at the sight of Saraswati. *Stop that*.

She seemed to have grown several inches taller since the competition had begun. Her shoulders were squared, and her hips even swung with a slight—and very attractive— swagger. Her face appeared less careworn, and her skin glowed. She was beautiful. *Stop that now*.

Is it just me or—?

Kili burbled with excitement on her shoulder. _She's made some big discovery,_ he said knowledgeably. _This is not the Saras that started this competition._

Wow.

Yeah. Wow.

The cook stations had been cleared away, and now a line of spots had replaced them. Saraswati took her place at number seven, caught Serenity Ko's eye, and flashed her a big smile. Serenity Ko's heart performed a loop-the-loop.

Boundless Eli took centre-stage. 'Ten of the best chefs from across the galaxy here tonight,' he said. 'Ten of the best chefs ever, and they all were tasked with breathing new life into the perennial, eternal classic, the Nakshatran Banquet.' He paused, waiting for the audience to finish cheering, then carried on. 'In three hours, these chefs have harvested, infused, marbled, basted, baked and foamed their hearts out, pouring years of culinary experience and expertise into one single cook. One single night, one shot to win the *Millennium Feast Special* and the chance to host the Millennium Feast.'

He grinned stupidly. 'And none of this would have been possible without the extraordinary vision of our Secretary for Culture and Heritage, and our guest judge for the evening: Optimism Mahd'vi.'

He held his arm out to the side, and Optimism Mahd'vi

made a grand entrance from one of the archways, resplendent in an emerald green tunic flecked with luminous gemstones. She bowed and took her place in the judges' circle.

'Of course, we also supplied her with the able skills of some of the best palates in the universe, our redoubtable judges from *Interstellar MegaChef*. Please put your hands together as they join us.'

Serenity Ko stifled a yawn as he introduced each judge, along with their credentials, for what felt like the billionth time that day. She fidgeted with one long sleeve, trying to do so discreetly in case there were stray cam-drones hovering around.

Serenity Ko sank into a stupor, registering the world around her dimly. Courage Ab'dal had gone missing; that was strange. Pavi and Amol were huddled together looking excited. Harmony Rhea seemed flustered. Optimism Mahd'vi stood poised and elegant, her hands clasped in front of her.

Grace Aurelle began to speak, and her voice sounded hoarse. She praised the courage and innovation of the contestants. She traced the history of Primian cuisine. She spoke of the significance of the Nakshatran Banquet in their culture. It was deathly dull.

'Get to the good bit,' Serenity Ko muttered.

Seriously, Kili echoed.

'When it really came down to it, we had two competing banquets to choose from,' Grace Aurelle said at last, and Serenity Ko perked up. 'One was extraordinary in its use of technique, its philosophy, and vision.' She paused. 'And the other was remarkable for its use of the science of flavour.'

That sounds like you, Kili said, whirring unsteadily against her shoulder.

Serenity Ko was suddenly aware that her heart was pounding in her ears. Her palms were sweating, and she felt feverish. "Technology of flavour," surely there couldn't be two of those?

'Could the chef who crafted the foam banquet please step forwards?' Grace Aurelle asked.

Serenity Ko scowled when Good Cheer Chaangte stepped into a spotlight right at the centre of the stage. She was possessed with the sudden urge to throw sharp objects at her.

'And could the chef who created the *provocative plate* please step forwards?' She was greeted with silence. 'The impeccable traditional Banquet-turned-mess, served with the food simulation jellies?'

Serenity Ko's head spun. She felt faint. Kili thrummed against her shoulder, practically bouncing up and down. Saraswati stepped into the unforgiving light at the centre of the stage, smiling with confidence.

Serenity Ko was suddenly aware that her face now occupied a large swathe of holoscreen in the room, along with Saraswati's, and Good Cheer Chaangte's, who appeared to have no teammates. Her mind drew a blank. She smiled and waved weakly, then cursed herself for her awkwardness, and abruptly blew kisses at the cam-drones.

Smooth, Kili said.

We'll talk when you stop using my shoulder like a trampoline.

'Good Cheer Chaangte,' Grace Aurelle said. 'As a judging panel, we really appreciated your...'

Serenity Ko stifled an exasperated sigh. It really felt like the old woman was drawing this out for everything it was worth, the horrible sadist. The minutes ticked by, and she found herself tapping her foot impatiently, as the Chief Chef heaped praise upon the insufferable woman.

'Saraswati Kaveri,' Grace Aurelle said at last. 'You prepared the most immaculate traditionally cooked Nakshatran Banquet of the night—probably one of the best we've ever tasted. And then you *provoked* us by destroying it, which we might have regarded as deeply disrespectful. Except...

'You served us something even better. Unpretentious, unassuming, positively hideous on a plate, if I'm being honest, but fresh, new and exciting. A food sim experience!

'You took us back to the *meaning* of food, beyond the plate, and why it lies at the heart of not just our culture, but every culture in the universe. And more importantly, you let us relive our deepest, most intimate connections to the plate... even if there were no open flames involved.'

That elicited a laugh from everyone in the audience behind Serenity Ko, but all she wanted to do was grab the judge and shake her. *Who's winning, already?*

'It was a terribly difficult decision,' Grace Aurelle continued. 'But in the end, it was practically unanimous.'

'Come on, come on...' Serenity Ko mumbled.

'Optimism Mahd'vi holds a golden envelope in her hands,' Grace Aurelle said.

Serenity Ko stifled a scream of annoyance and frustration.

'I now hand over to her.'

Time slowed down. The seconds ticked by. Serenity Ko's insides writhed with excitement and loathing, knotted themselves into agony, twisted inside out and spilled all over the floor of her mind. She heard the crinkle of papyro-scroll, the ripping open of the envelope, witnessed it as if it were happening light-years away.

Optimism Mahd'vi beamed. 'And the winner is...'

The scroll unfurled right as the cam-drones focused on a face. Optimism Mahd'vi said a name out loud, but it was drowned out in the roar of the crowd. Serenity Ko ran into the haze of light and colour and confetti.

It's not about winning or losing; it never is. But winning? Winning is great.

—Harmony Islion,
Eight-time *Outcooked 5* World Champion

THIRTY-SEVEN

THE CANNONS WENT off with a boom. I jumped, then realised I wasn't on Earth and this wasn't a war zone.

Holographic confetti rained down all around me. I thought I heard my name, but I couldn't be sure. A blur of metal thwacked me in the stomach before spinning away with momentum. And before I knew it, her arms were around me, her face was close, far too close, brown eyes shining with light, nose glistening with perspiration… and then her mouth was on mine, and she was kissing me. Her lips tasted like cinnamon and chilli, sending shivers through me, and her lips were full and her mouth was very warm, and I was kissing her back, my arms wrapped around her waist, her hands tangled in my curls. I was running out of air, but this was the only breath I needed.

The roar of sound around us dimmed into a distant hum. My heart spread its wings and soared, beating against my ribs. I pressed myself into the warmth of her curves, all the frustration and exhaustion from the day I'd first arrived on this planet dissipating, transforming into the promise of being exactly where I belonged. I could have sworn Primus jolted on its orbit around Suriya and gravity failed, because I was floating, weightless, a comet blazing my way through a cold and indifferent world…

And then my head spun, and Primus tilted, and I was awakened by the terrifying realisation that Serenity Ko had kissed me. And I was *kissing her back*. My eyes fluttered open, and I saw the exact same blend of fear and excitement that I was feeling mirrored in her eyes, now widened in shock and surprise, her pupils large and swallowing me whole, her irises flecked with gold in the blinding light of the MegaChef studio.

We pulled apart at the same time.

She was beaming, bouncing up and down on the balls of her feet. 'You won! Saraswati, *you won!*'

Time rushed in to fill the suspended moment, physical reality overwhelming me, dragging me back to the world we belonged to, the sudden space between us both unbearable and reassuring, strange and indecipherable. I looked around and saw a blur of faces, registering a mixture of shock and joy, wondered how long we'd kissed, somewhat horrified that we'd kissed in front of an interstellar audience.

'*You won!*' Serenity Ko shouted again.

And that's when it hit me, the still-fluttering confetti, my face on all the holoscreens, the giant trophy in Grace Aurelle's hands as she walked towards me and all.

'Oh, my goodness, I won,' I mumbled. 'We won.'

'Yes. Idiot,' Serenity Ko said, grabbing my hand and squeezing it.

Kili had settled on my shoulder and was thrumming away, but also chittering. I reconnected with him on the Loop.

...won! You're a winner! I always knew it! he yelled. _And you kissed her! Yay! But oh, no! But yay?_

Hello, Kili. I grinned.

Saras! You won!

'Congratulations,' Grace Aurelle said, handing me the trophy. 'You're the winner of *Interstellar MegaChef: The Millennium Feast Special!*'

The other judges came up to me and shook my hand, one by one. Harmony Rhea seemed both disappointed and elated that I was the chef behind Feast. 'I didn't think it would be you,' she said softly. 'You really blew us away. I might have misjudged you the first time round.'

'I knew you had it in you.' Amol winked, then gave his sister some side-eye.

'I didn't,' Pavi said, and she didn't look happy about it.

And then the crowd rushed in, and Serenity Ko and I were pulled apart by all the people who'd got us here. Starlight Fantastic wrapped me up in a many-tentacled hug, sobbing their congratulations through their vox-box. 'I'm so proud of you,' they kept saying. 'So, *so* proud of you.'

Curiosity Zia gave me a quick peck on the cheek, and Courage Oslo thumped my back, grinning from ear-to-ear. My wrists began to hurt from shaking hands, and I was introduced to too many new faces to keep track of. And then I caught sight of Good Cheer Chaangte, hovering uncertainly off to one side, surrounded by my fellow competitors, none of whom seemed very thrilled by the result.

You don't need to do this, Kili said, as I made my way to her.

It's the decent thing to do, I replied.

Yes, but you don't owe her a shred of decency.

I smiled at Good Cheer Chaangte as the competition parted before me. She looked me up and down like I was a piece of rotting vegetation. Her eyes narrowed and her shoulders stiffened. I ignored the reaction and stuck my hand out.

'Congratulations,' I said. 'Well fought.'

'Hmph,' she sulked, ignoring my proffered hand. 'Don't let this convince you you're worth anything, Earthling.'

'It doesn't need to be this way,' I said. 'We can part with mutual respect and never see each other again.'

'Respect?' she near-screeched. 'It has to be *earned*, Earthling. And I'll be the one to decide if you ever get there.'

'Suit yourself.' I shrugged. I hadn't expected much more, but something in me had told me I needed to make the attempt. 'Good luck with whatever's next,' I added, turning away.

'What's next is washing chefdom clean of dirt like you,' she muttered uncharitably.

Enough was enough. I threw her a sidelong glance. 'If today's anything to go by, it's going to take you many lifetimes,' I said coldly, and walked away.

Like I said, didn't need to do that, Kili reprimanded.

I scanned the set for Serenity Ko—or any familiar, friendly face. The feeling of euphoria was beginning to wear off, replaced by a bone-tiredness. A man named Optimism Rihan walked up to me, his nose-pin glittering in the bright lights, accompanied by an ethereal-looking woman, her face all made up in green.

'Congratulations! It's nice to finally meet the woman my sister's been obsessed with all this while,' Optimism Rihan said.

'It's so good to meet you!' I was suddenly hideously embarrassed by the fact that Serenity Ko and I had kissed in front of all our family and friends, when neither of us knew exactly what we felt for each other.

'Likewise,' Optimism Rihan smiled, and it lit up his soft, open face. 'This is Good Cheer Eria, by the way.'

'You're the one who set up our meeting with Harmony Li! Thank you so much.'

'Really glad to meet you, Saraswati,' she said, and her voice sounded like wind chimes.

'Where's Ko?' I asked.

Optimism Rihan nodded in the direction of a large crowd. 'The XP folks have claimed her. They're probably looking for you, so we won't keep you, but we'll be at the party later this evening.'

'What party?' I asked.

Optimism Rihan grinned. 'Your victory party. Of course we're throwing you one! See you in a bit!'

He and his fiancée linked arms and walked away from me, and I was very relieved they hadn't mentioned the kiss. It was sure to pop up some time, and my insides ran cold at the thought. Serenity Ko and I would have to talk about it, too.

'Where have you been?' Curiosity Zia grabbed me by the arm. 'We're heading to The Wallflower, everyone's invited, but obviously we can't go there without our star!'

'I'm tired,' I said, as a sudden wave of exhaustion made my knees go weak. 'Can't we just do this some other day?'

'We most certainly *cannot*,' someone said. Serenity Ko's boss, Grace Kube, sat cross-legged on one of the flowmetal cook stations. His eyes twinkled, and he appeared to be studying me. 'I don't know if you know how these things work,' he continued. 'But come tomorrow, you'll be so busy managing Feast and your celebrity career that you won't have time for mere mortals like us.'

'That's not true,' I said, right as a little voice in my head said, *Sounds about right*.

He's got a good point, Kili echoed.

Grace Kube's lips twitched, evidently seeing my thoughts play out on my face.

Plus, they showed up for you. Every single one of them.

I relented with a grin. 'All right, I'm in. But no shots!'

'Did someone say shots?' Serenity Ko reappeared, arm in arm with Courage Praia and Curiosity Nenna. 'I'm here for shots.'

'Revolutionary, controversial, extraordinary! Coming soon: an exclusive interview with Saraswati Kaveri, the culinary mastermind behind Feast Inc.!'

—Banner on the streampage for *Epicureans Elite*

THIRTY-EIGHT

IT WASN'T CONSIDERED surveillance if one just *happened* to be in a private booth at a bar right across the road from the establishment where the person one *might* be interested in watching was throwing a raucous celebration. There was no tech involved, there were no third parties, human, alt-being, or drone, and one was simply enjoying an evening drink in the company of one's thoughts.

Optimism Mahd'vi turned the new developments over in her head. Primus first. The Millennium Festival was yielding promising results already, and the full gamut of festivities hadn't even been revealed yet. *Interstellar MegaChef* had been a more than promising kick-off.

They'd called it Feast Inc. It was genius. Its potential was extraordinary, and insidious. To think that an entire technology team had decided to replace food with *simulations;* that was something that had surprised her with its innovation. She hadn't seen it coming, was awestruck by the infinite possibilities it presented.

She drafted notes. Sim technology had come into its own on Primus, and with Feast, it was being harnessed to create the flavours of Primian food. There were few things designed in recent times that perfectly encapsulated all things Primian, and this was one of them. To think that those bite-sized packets could be exported across the universe, taking the Nakshatran values inherent to life on their planet to the furthest reaches of the galaxy—the very ideals she was charged with protecting and propagating...

She smiled. She was going to arrange a meeting with Courage Ilio. She'd bully him to lift the ban on cricket chips, and arrange for Feast to compete with Earth's biggest export directly, out in the starry by-lanes of the universe. She'd ensure they were priced lower than most food available anywhere in the galaxy; what better way to appeal to people, gently swaying them back to the centre of human culture, than by having them eat its belief systems?

The thought was absurd. It made her laugh. If anyone had pitched it to her in another forum, she'd have removed them from her presence. But she'd tasted the proof of the idea, and she knew it worked.

Of course, Feast relied on a database of visual and auditory cues to unlock personal memories of each kind of food, but that code could be tweaked. Primian culture could still be messaged through every single simulation, directly to the mind. The thought was delectable. There were alternate messaging streams that could open up— advert spaces on Feast to inspire bidding wars for Primian products, Ur-dramas, tourism campaigns... She didn't understand the tech completely, but she wondered if it could become a platform for entire Ur-dramas—what if every time she ate a Nakshatran Gelato, she unlocked a new episode of an Ur-drama exclusively available to consumers of that dish? Or a sinfonia album? Or even an epic poetry performance?

They wouldn't be able to keep it exclusive forever; they'd have to eventually license it to other cultures if they wanted to retain control of what kind of sims were put out there, rather than have copies of the tech running rogue all over the place. That would be a veritable conundrum for the best legal minds in the Secretariat to solve, and she was going to challenge them with it.

Optimism Mahd'vi took a sip of her starfruit wine. The brew and the torrent of ideas rushing through her mind made for a heady combination.

Here, right at home on Primus, Feast would be all the rage. Her assistants had been monitoring public streams ever since the episode aired; citizens couldn't wait to try it, chefs wanted to destroy it. She'd address the chefs and smooth things over. She didn't see it as *competing* with the culinary arts, but rather, augmenting their relevance in a vast and ever-evolving universe. Something that would inspire people to want to be able to *make* the very dishes they were consuming in this instant, packaged form, to step out of their homes and experience the same foods in person. And perhaps, she thought slyly, she could induce Feast to create exclusive sims for Uru's top restaurants. That would placate the chefs; the sims would link to their *real* food.

The Wanderers would be most unhappy, she assumed. That was a thorny knot she'd need to get the Secretariat to resolve. It was one thing to use edibites; it was another thing altogether to layer sims on them. She braced herself for the inevitable protests to come, and ran through her list of Secretariat members to see whom she could work with to pacify them.

The sound of commotion broke out in the restaurant behind her, and she turned, peering through the one-way flowmetal screen that shielded her from the view of the other patrons.

'I made a reservation, you fools!' A man bellowed, his overlarge gilded crown shimmering in the ambient lighting.

'Please calm down, sir. We're sure we can find you a table somewhere else.'

'I *specifically* asked for a table by the window overlooking Astriana Street. There are no tables by the window in sight,' Jog Tunga said aggressively.

Optimism Mahd'vi felt a shiver run down her spine. This was interesting, to say the least. And his unexpected arrival at the restaurant brought her back to the other development that had dropped into her lap at the *MegaChef* special episode. She'd been trying to avoid it all evening, so she could relish it at ease in her space, perhaps with a hot bubble-cleanse and a glass of wine…

But it was impossible to ignore. Her plan—her secret, unspoken agenda for the special episode—had worked. The Earthling hadn't been able to resist her shot at glory and redemption.

Saraswati Kaveri.

And now, in the very same restaurant, fighting over a seat with a view of the pub where the Kaveri girl was celebrating her victory, was the *other one.*

Coincidence? Unlikely.

She made a snap decision.

'Why don't you join me at my booth? I believe we've met before.' She smiled and stepped through the flowmetal screen and into the restaurant.

Jog Tunga regarded her in confusion. 'We have?'

She resisted the urge to stomp down very hard upon his foot. 'At the K'artri-tva banquet,' she said smoothly.

'Ah! Secretary!' he said, adopting an obsequious tone and smiling insincerely. 'Didn't expect to see you in such a… *humble* setting.'

'Nor I you,' she said politely. 'Come, do take a seat.'

He flopped over in the chair across from her and ordered a sherraquiri. Optimism Mahd'vi stopped herself from wrinkling up her nose in disgust when it arrived; the cocktail was lurid green, with pops of bright pink candied mellonfruit sprinkled through it. He even sipped it through a straw.

'Are you here on official business?' Optimism Mahd'vi asked, after sufficient silence had lapsed.

Jog Tunga waved theatrically. 'Oh, now and again. Cricket chips have turned into a real issue; I've been meeting with Courage Ilio to iron it out. The K'artri-tva really don't mind, lovely beings, I'll tell you. I'm mostly here for the sights, though.' He leered at her, and Optimism Mahd'vi tamped down a laugh, and the temptation to throw her drink at him. He was probably half her age, and it really was a rather fine wine.

He began to ramble about Suriyan flare surfing, and Optimism Mahd'vi wondered what he'd been doing meeting with the Kaveri girl a few navas ago. Were they still meeting? He kept flicking his eyes towards The Wallflower, even as he monologued his way through his senseless stories.

She was glad she hadn't confronted the Kaveri girl at first sight. She'd sought distinctive signs that she might be any kind of relation—not that she knew what to expect, of course, her entire family having been murdered before they could impart what the family nose was supposed to be. But no, the Kaveri girl didn't resemble either herself or her brother.

Part of her had been keen to set up a meeting right away, to ask the chef how she'd escaped the Earth, if her last name really was Kaveri, and if not, what exactly she was playing at. But as she'd watched her celebrate in the studio, the beginnings of a better plan had begun to unfold in her mind.

If she were kind to the Kaveri girl, then maybe she could use her. She'd met the bumpkin seated across the table from her before. She might meet him again.

Optimism Mahd'vi could turn her into a source right within enemy territory, regardless of whether she was a pretender or the real deal. She would figure out what her story was along the way, and deal with her as required, afterward.

'I heard an Earthling won a cooking show today,' Jog Tunga said airily, bringing her attention back to their table.

'What an embarrassment for all the homegrown talent.' He smirked.

He sipped on his drink. It was his second already, another candied concoction that was neon purple. Optimism Mahd'vi wondered if he was taunting her; if he knew that she knew that he'd met the Kaveri girl before. He fished around in his drink for the bright orange spheres garnishing it, then impaled one on a stick, chomping on it. *Perhaps not,* she thought.

'We welcome people from all across the galaxy, here,' Optimism Mahd'vi said instead, infusing her voice with gravitas. 'On Primus, there are equal rights and opportunities for all…'

Jog Tunga scoffed. 'Don't take the official line with me, Secretary. We're all here incognito, without our diplomatic hats on.'

'Are we?' she asked haughtily, her eyes flicking to the bejewelled crown on his head.

'Guilty,' he said falsely. '"Heavy hangs the head," and so on… There's no escaping the vestments of my office.'

'Indeed.'

They lapsed into silence again. Optimism Mahd'vi had nothing to say to him; she looked out the window, but it seemed as if nobody had left the Feast Inc. victory party yet. Jog Tunga followed her gaze. 'That bar across the way seems livelier.'

'It's cheaper.'

'Ah.'

'I'll leave you to it, then,' Optimism Mahd'vi said, draining the remains of her drink and rising from the table. 'I've got an early start tomorrow. Drinks on the Secretariat of Primus.'

'Your generosity will not be forgotten,' Jog Tunga grinned.

'Enjoy the view.'

After a brief conversation with the servers about the bill, Optimism Mahd'vi left the restaurant, making it a point to pass right beneath the window she'd been seated at. She then circled back around it, and re-entered using the rear stairway. She seated herself in an alcove in the depths of the room she'd just been in, concealed from all the other patrons by flowmetal privacy screens.

She no longer needed to wait by the window to keep tabs on the Kaveri girl at The Wallflower. She stared at Jog Tunga's hunched form. He sat with his heavy, dark tresses to her, his coal-black eyes no doubt fixed upon the street. All she had to do was wait *him* out, and see where he went next.

She sipped on a freshly ordered cup of starfruit wine. It really was fine wine. And he'd be impossible to lose, with that tasteless crown on his head.

—Ancient Earth Proverb

THIRTY-NINE

EVERYONE SHOWED UP at the victory party.

We kissed, I kept reminding myself, even as Serenity Ko sat beside me at our table at The Wallflower, her thigh pressing into mine. Each time she shifted and her skin brushed against mine, my heart juddered, fresh waves of anticipation running through me like a shock to my system.

It was only a kiss, a quiet, worried voice would say. Everything about the way I felt told me it was something more. She was part black hole, part cactus, an inescapable gravitational field filled with spines, but capable of flowering when the time was right. But how could I know how she felt about me? Maybe she'd only kissed me in the overwhelming emotions of the moment. Maybe all her nerves had come undone. What if she was just happy to win? She seemed the sort to be exuberant with victory. And what if this was some Primian cultural thing I'd never read about, casual kisses between strangers? Well, no, we were friends. *Are we friends?*

She took my hand and squeezed it, and my heart felt like it was about to jump right out my chest. 'You're lost, Earth girl. Come back,' she said.

'Sorry, so tired,' I lied.

'Maybe this will bring you back to life,' she whispered, then leaned over and kissed my cheek suggestively, her palm tracing circles on my thigh.

'Everyone's watching,' I gasped.

'Get a room!' Boundless Baz said loudly, echoing my sentiments.

446

'After-party.' Serenity Ko winked at him, her breath hot on my ear as she pulled away. This was too much to take.

I shot to my feet. 'I'm getting another drink. Anyone want one?' I said, my voice suddenly squeaky. A sea of faces, all my friends, watched me in amusement.

'I'm getting a drink, too,' Serenity Ko said, draining hers.

I'm just going to stay here, Kili streamed. _I think you two need to talk._

I hope I can keep my mouth shut, I said darkly.

Bad for kissing.

Monster.

Serenity Ko followed me to the bar, and I was hyperaware of the space between us crackling like lightning before a storm.

'What's wrong, Saraswati?' Serenity Ko asked, as I ordered two jumpgate kicks. I turned to regard her, my back to the bar, unable to tear my eyes away from her curves, her face…

'Wrong?' I asked, in my most cheerful tone. 'Nothing's wrong. Nope, no, nothing.'

She pressed me back into the bar, leaning into me with her hips. 'You seem very hot and bothered,' she whispered. She reached a hand towards my face, and tucked a stray curl behind my ear. 'I can fix that if you want me to.'

I swallowed. 'I do. I really do. But…'

'But what?' she asked flatly, suddenly stepping away from me.

'But what does this mean?' I asked.

'What does anything mean?' she shrugged.

'What does this mean to you? I—we work together, Ko. This could change things.'

'I know, don't remind me.' Serenity Ko made a face. 'We could change that. Be different. Not let a hook-up get in the way, you know?'

'A hook-up?'

'Two jumpgate kicks!' the bartender called, placing our drinks on the bar.

'Is this just a hook-up, then?' I crossed my arms over my chest.

'I—I don't know,' Serenity Ko said. Her face took on an expression I'd never seen her wear before. Was it concern? Uncertainty? 'I really don't know,' she repeated. 'It's all happening so fast...'

'Because if it's just hooking up, we definitely shouldn't do it,' I said firmly. 'It'll ruin our work relationship. Our friendship.'

'What if this is more?' she asked, her voice slightly whiny.

'Is it, for you? Because it is for me,' I said, unnerved by my sudden honesty. 'I'm not sure how it happened, but I haven't been able to get you out of my head since the first time I met you, even though you were horribly rude to me. *A walking train wreck,* I thought at first, but then a voice in my head said, *come crash into me.*' My feelings poured out of me in waves; I'd never even let myself think them before. 'I'm drawn to your starlight, I can't escape the idea of you. I want all of you, I want to know your heart and your mind.' I softened my voice. 'And if it's just sex to you, and if we're going to be working together, it's just... a recipe for disaster.'

Serenity Ko seemed completely taken aback. 'I don't *know* how to define it; I don't know if I want to label it. I feel everything you've said, maybe a hundred times more strongly. I'm *obsessed* with you. It's thrilling. It's terrifying. But—' Her voice broke. 'But Saraswati, like you said, I'm a train wreck. I barely know my mind one moment to the next. Does it matter if we just see where this can go? Can't we just be friends who are sleeping together until we know if we can be more?'

'We can,' I said. 'Of course we can. But not if we're working together. Not if we're supposed to run the show with Feast. Even if it's just one of us in charge, that's a terrible idea.'

Serenity Ko's face fell. 'I—I don't know what to say.'

'Neither do I,' I said sadly.

'What do we do next?'

'I don't know.'

'It was only a kiss,' Serenity Ko said softly.

'It was only a kiss,' I echoed.

'Can we take some time to think this through?' she asked, her face lighting up.

'We can, most definitely,' I said, relieved.

'Just friends until then?'

'Just friends.' I nodded, the relief giving way to hollowness.

'You're going to ruin things,' Serenity Ko said abruptly, gathering our drinks off the bar.

'Huh?'

'It's a crime to look so hot, and then demand to be just friends,' she said with a wink, leading the way back to our table.

My cheeks burned as I followed her. She respectfully sat much further away from me than before.

That didn't go well? Kili asked.

Actually, it wasn't too bad.

Are you together or not? he demanded.

We're thinking this through.

So, together eventually, then?

I grinned. I couldn't help it. I was hopeful.

Boundless Baz passed his palm across my eyes. 'Don't tell me you're lost in a sim somewhere, Saras. Not while we're right here.'

That made me laugh, and staunched my anxiety for the moment. He'd taken the night off at Nonpareil, and so had XX-29. I imagined Pavi and Amol were none too pleased by that, but they could have shared this joy with me, too, if only they'd been nicer. XX-29 pulled me into a hug at once, xir entire mechatronic frame enfolding me and radiating warmth.

'I'm glad you beat her,' XX-29 said in a whisper. 'Chaangte, I mean. She needs her sense of self-importance checked.'

'And more than anything else, *I'm so proud of you!*' Boundless Baz yelled. He kept his voice high, and let it carry. 'Where's the parade? Can we throw this woman a parade?'

Almost immediately, Curiosity Zia and Courage Oslo were at my side, with Optimism Sah'r and Courage Na'vil in tow. They'd turned up with their teams, and many unfamiliar faces I recognised whose names I didn't know— and I was grateful they were flashing across the Loop— hoisted me onto their shoulders. I screamed, at first worried that they'd drop me, then with delight. They chanted my name, and all the other patrons in the bar seemed in suspended animation, staring at our little group and its rowdy celebration.

Is this what it's like to be a smooth-smash star? Or a solar-flare racing champion. I'm just a multiple-award-winning chef. I'm just me.

'Put me down!' I called. 'This isn't my victory, it's *ours*. We did this together. None of us could have done this alone. Especially without Serenity Ko!'

I scanned the bar for her, but couldn't spot her. 'Serenity Ko!' I yelled.

I was gently lowered to the ground, and right then, Courage Praia, Curiosity Nenna and Grace Kube turned up, each bearing trays laden with neon purple shot glasses.

'No. No way,' I laughed.

'One for the team! Come on!'

I hesitantly picked up a shot and knocked it back. And then there was another. And another.

Before I knew it, I was drenched in perspiration, bouncing around the dance floor with Curiosity Zia and Courage Oslo, to shredding glass-guitar solos and pounding bol-drums, my favourite Legends of the Future album streaming through the speakers. And then I was mesmerised by Starlight Fantastic and Moonage Daydream, who had taken to the floor after requesting an E'nemon classic. Quavering, long-drawn-out notes of an instrument that sounded like a blend of violin and harp filled the air, and two sets of Enemon tentacles shimmered and spun, catching the light as they formed intricate weaves, knotting together and pulling apart.

'So, Ko's disappeared,' Courage Praia murmured, appearing at my side.

'She has, hasn't she? Do you know where she is?' I asked, trying to sound casual.

'No idea.' They winked at me. 'She kissed you, so it's to be expected.'

'We talked about it,' I confessed. 'We aren't sure where things stand.'

Courage Praia exhaled slowly and gave me a long, searching look. 'Ko is… *complicated*. And that's me being kind. I've been her friend for years. If I were you, I'd take things slow, and not get my hopes up.'

'Of course,' I nodded, my stomach plummeting. 'It was only a kiss.'

'Good,' Courage Praia said. 'I'm only saying this because I like you, Saraswati. And I don't want to see either of you get hurt. So just… give her time? And take your time with this, too.'

'I will,' I said. 'After all, it was only a kiss.'

Was it?

Are you sure? Kili asked.

_No,_ I said miserably. _I don't know where this is going to go._

It's okay to not know, he said gently.

I was suddenly unaccountably warm. I grabbed a drink of water, and when it made no difference, I flopped into a seat at our usual table, fanning myself ineffectively with my hand.

'Air?' Boundless Baz asked.

'Huh?'

'You look like you need some air.'

I laughed weakly. 'That would be nice.'

'Have you ever been topside at this place?'

'Nope.'

'Let me show you,' he said, and led me to a staircase right beside the bar. Right at that moment, a patron spun around with an overlarge mug of bira in their hands, and crashed right into him.

'Gosh, no, I'm so sorry!' the stranger said. Their name on the Loop read *Honour Yas, She/Her*, and she had a slight build, her face round, her expression aghast.

'Ah, it's no problem!' Boundless Baz said hurriedly. 'I'll just wash this off...' He turned to me apologetically.

Buy her another drink, I streamed at him.

What?

You should ask if you can buy her a drink.

_Oh._

I'll be fine, I reassured him.

If you're sure.

_I am._

He smiled sheepishly at me, and I disappeared up the stairway. 'Let me buy you another one?' I heard him say smoothly behind me. 'It's my fault, really, I was in the way.'

Well done, Kili said approvingly.

I laughed, suddenly feeling lighter than I had in days— navas, māsas even. _Everyone deserves a shot at love. Or at least, a fun one-night stand,_ I said, suddenly filled with regret that I hadn't pursued the latter with Serenity Ko.

No, I reminded myself. *There are bigger things to consider, as far as she goes.*

The stairway was steep and narrow, and felt unending as I trudged to the top of it. I finally spotted a flowmetal door, and it pulled apart for me. I stepped out onto the rooftop, and gasped.

Sprawling outward in every direction, the city of Uru flowed and retracted, its lights twinkling, its spirals uncoiling and unfurling, a vast, living, breathing entity, encompassing all of its flowmetal structures and the people within them, the wonderful and the incorrigible, the beautiful and the star-fucked, a world unto itself that was stuck in the past, rooted to the present, and desperate to grasp the future. The river of stars that was the Milky Way seemed to pour down from the heavens into each of its reservoirs, which shimmered and reflected the universe back into the void of space, a mirror of starlight.

I didn't know how I fit into the enormity of the cosmos. I didn't know if there was even a place for me on this planet. I didn't know what Serenity Ko was going to want, and I didn't know what I was going to do with my own feelings for her. I didn't know if I'd done enough to free myself from the shadowy gaze of my parents, and now that I knew that they knew exactly where in the galaxy to find me, I didn't know what tomorrow would bring. Would I be free? And if I was free, would I be hated or loved for what I'd just helped create? Would the galaxy use it for better or for worse? It was impossible, the business of knowing.

And so, I stood in silence, Kili nestled on my shoulder, a pleasant wind stirring up my curls, drinking in the vision of infinite possibility.

THE END

ACKNOWLEDGEMENTS

ACKNOWLEDGEMENTS

THE FLOOR WAS made of lava while I wrote this novel. I found myself in a really twitchy videogame, except it was real life, and I had to keep moving or be swallowed whole.

The pandemic and the endless rise of the far right around the world dented my headspace (still does, as it likely hurts yours), I had a string of health issues that hampered my ability to work, from carpal tunnel syndrome to pneumonia, and I was heartbroken from losing close family and friends—especially my incredible dog, Scamper—to the relentless march of time.

What kept me going was the story in these pages. A story built around the idea of the warmth and comfort of a bowl of rasam rice, but a story that also happened to be about the clash of cultures on a plate.

Food has always been political. It unites and divides us in different contexts. Culinary traditions can be a way to other a people, a tool through which social barriers can be reinforced, but they can also be a way to connect with each other, discover new worlds, and honour one's ancestors. Everything we put on a plate reflects a deeply personal journey, for better or for worse, transcending time and space, and often, even death.

As Saras and Ko's story unfolded on the page, it brought me joy through a very difficult time. I hope I've managed to share some of that joy with you. Thank you for picking up this book, dear reader. You make the years that went into writing this novel entirely worth it.

My heart is filled with gratitude to a number of people for making this book possible at all.

David Moore, my wonderful editor at Solaris Books, who immediately extended my deadline after my nasty brush with pneumonia, and who is simply tremendous to work with. Sam for designing the delightfully whimsical cover, Jess for being such an excellent publicist, and the entire team at Solaris Books for being straight-up incredible. My brilliant agent, Cameron McClure, for believing in me and backing me, every step of the way, and the whole team at Donald Maass Literary Agency for their nonstop support.

Samit Basu, SB Divya, Tashan Mehta, Indra Das, Lavie Tidhar, Francesco Verso, and all the wonderful writers, editors, reviewers, and readers, who cheered me on through the impossible years that were. Amma and Appa, who shared these years with me, and supplied me with on-demand coffee and pep talks. Bhamini and Ani, who held me accountable to living my best life. Ammamma, who kept me on my toes with her sharp wit (while being far gentler than her counterpart in this book!). All my friends—you know who you are—who never gave up the good fight to get me to step outside my world on the page. Scamper and Tugger, for suffusing my life with more hope and joy than any heart can hold. Birdie, for all the song you brought me in your all-too-brief life. The legion of cats for... well, being cats. Shiv, for being there through it all: I'm glad there is you.

ABOUT THE AUTHOR

Lavanya Lakshminarayan is a Locus Award finalist and the first science fiction writer to win the *Times of India* AutHer Award and the Valley of Words Award, both prestigious literary awards in India, and her work has been longlisted for a BSFA Award.

She's occasionally a game designer, and has built worlds for Zynga Inc.'s *FarmVille* franchise, *Mafia Wars*, and other games. She lives in India, and is currently working on her next novel.

 lavanya_ln
lavanya.ln

FIND US ONLINE!

www.rebellionpublishing.com

/solarisbooks   /solarisbks   /solarisbooks

SIGN UP TO OUR NEWSLETTER!

rebellionpublishing.com/newsletter

YOUR REVIEWS MATTER!

Enjoy this book? Got something to say?

Leave a review on Amazon, GoodReads or with your favourite bookseller and let the world know!

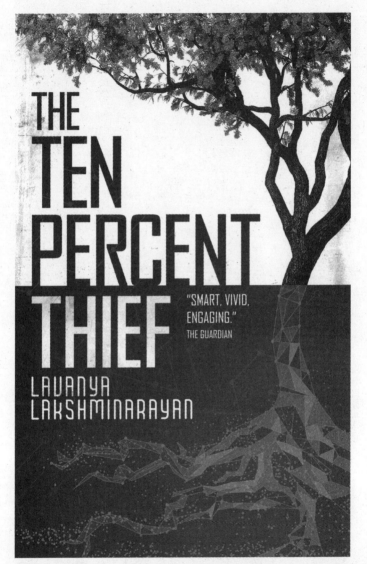

THE TEN PERCENT THIEF

"SMART, VIVID, ENGAGING."
THE GUARDIAN

LAVANYA LAKSHMINARAYAN

SOLARISBOOKS.COM

"DELICIOUS, PROPULSIVE FUN"
FREYA MARSKE, AUTHOR OF *THE LAST BINDING* SERIES

LADY
EVE'S
LAST
CON

REBECCA FRAIMOW

⌾ SOLARISBOOKS.COM